Morningwood

Ashes And Acorns Book One

Devon Veinot

Chapter One

They say it's not good to judge a book by its cover, and Sam was always of the mind that this were true. However, try as she might to adhere to her moral code, she just couldn't shake the rapey vibes radiating off the two men who joined her in the bus shelter. Sometimes the book cover was just too awful to want to peek inside.

Despite this inner turmoil, she offered a stiff nod and stretched her frozen cheeks into the warmest smile she could muster on this chilly winter evening, and said, "Hey."

The smiles exchanged by the men after her greeting did little to endear her to them, and to make it worse, they said nothing back.

She turned away and sighed, releasing a blast of frosty air into the glass wall of the shelter. The frost spread out, creating a fresh white canvas that tempted her to draw something, but fear of drawing attention stayed her hand.

This is stupid, she thought. There is nothing that says harmless, ordinary guys can't have creepy smiles. It's just unfortunate genetics. Nothing more. And many people in the city refuse to acknowledge those who greet them on the streets, for whatever rude and annoying reason they give themselves. That was always a peeve of hers.

No, clearly the labeling of these socially awkward men as sexual predators was an unfair judgment. One that was surely brought on by that stupid Ted Bundy documentary she was forced to watch earlier in the evening. She had been commissioned by an adorable elderly couple to paint their portrait as a gift to each other for their fiftieth wedding anniversary, but there was nothing adorable about their choice in background entertainment. Why they chose to watch a serial killer documentary during the painting was something she preferred to leave as a mystery.

She imagined the bride wearing widow black to the wedding, walking down the aisle to *Monster Mash,* while the flower girl chucked poison ivy leaves from her basket. Those thoughts were mildly amusing in the couple's well lit apartment, but the questionable anniversary flick lingered in her mind as she set out into the night. It colored every shadow just a shade darker on her way to the bus stop.

She shuddered, and shook the thoughts from her head. Bundy was a *real* monster. These guys were nothing. There must be *something* positive she could think of them. She chanced a quick glance. They were muttering to themselves.

So they *were* capable of speech. That's positive, and they looked cozy in their bulky winter coats and woolly hats. That showed a measure of intelligence, more so than her shivering, shaking form displayed in her thin fall jacket. And how much warmer would her cheeks be if she had a bushy black beard like the one sported by the taller man? She could rock one, sure, at least until Spring, or until she went on another date. Probably Spring. She'd shave it in the Spring.

Those thoughts were enough to instill some courage into her hand. She drew a bus on the frosted glass, as if doing so might instantly conjure one. It did not. She shoved her hand back into her pocket before it could freeze and fall off.

Her thoughts then wandered to elevators, and the comparable awkwardness of riding an elevator with a quiet stranger. She always felt as if she should say something in those situations, but never knew *what* to say. Clearly "Hey" wasn't a winner. If only she *was* in an elevator. Elevators were much warmer, and quicker. The radio of her mind began to play the song, *Love In An Elevator,* which was altogether inappropriate and completely unhelpful in the situation, so she moved from elevators to Christmas.

Christmas was still weeks away, but the first light snows had already fallen, planting the seeds that sprouted glittery fir trees and red ribbons in parks and stores and living rooms throughout Halifax. That, in turn, inspired the first droves of people to rush from their warm homes and out into the chilly city streets to chuck money around that they didn't seem to have any other time of year. The shopping centers and downtown area would only get busier and crazier from then on.

Sam was proud of the fact that she wouldn't be a part of it. She did her Christmas shopping with the tips of her paint brushes in the comforts of her spare bedroom, and her paint cabinet was always well stocked. Her latest gift was a squirrel, found and baited with almonds in Point Pleasant Park, and captured by cell phone. Later, she transferred the squirrel's image to canvas with oil paints. She named the squirrel Gary, after a sort-of ex-boyfriend who also chattered and squeaked obnoxiously whenever his mouth wasn't occupied by food. On

Christmas Day, Gary would be hanging somewhere in her parents' house. Squirrel Gary, that is. Her parents always hung her artwork right away. Their house was beginning to look like her personal art gallery.

Absently, her eyes met with one of the strangers. The beardless one. He was smiling at her. Not a friendly smile, but a disturbing one that chased her own smile into hiding. The bearded man wasn't looking at her face, not at all, and suddenly she regretted wearing her favorite leggings for reasons beyond the weather. She was proud of her legs, but at that moment she cursed them.

She pulled a curtain of long hair across the side of her face, hiding the men from her peripheral vision to make it harder for accidental glances.

Let them look, she thought. The bus would arrive soon and she would sit as close to the front as possible. She pulled out her phone to check the time.

Shit.

Twenty-five minutes to go. She thought for a moment to go for a walk, maybe back to the seniors' apartment building she had come from, but there was no one else around, and the driveway leading to it was too long and shadowed too dark by tall trees. She could walk to the next bus stop.

What if they follow me?

Perhaps abandoning her post would trigger the men in some way. Maybe it was best to just stay where she was. They were only looking, after all. The shelter was well lit, and perhaps she had a guardian angel watching over from the trailer court across the street, though she could only see the dim flickering lights of televisions in some of the windows. Probably more serial killer documentaries. There was a marathon on that day.

She wanted to stare at her phone and pretend to read or text to keep her eyes from meeting the strangers again, but the cold trapped her bare hands inside her pockets. She would make a point to go to the thrift store tomorrow. She'd find the warmest gloves, and the warmest, longest, bulkiest monstrosity of a winter coat to hide her figure. Probably some snow pants as well. And maybe she'd start eating dozens of cupcakes every morning for breakfast and before bed, and just to be safe, she'd take up smoking crack. *That* would avert the gaze of future Bus Stop Bundys. Maybe.

A terrible idea. Crack was far too expensive.

Flurries began to fall. Sam watched with exaggerated interest as the white flakes fell from the sky, dancing slowly downward until they kissed the asphalt and melted away to nothing. Dark clouds and city lights robbed the sky of its stars, but the moon was still fighting for its spot, shining full and bright whenever it broke through the clouds.

The street was too quiet. Nearby construction had pinched the road off to one lane, so most commuters were likely to skip this section of the Bay Road in favor of the highway. Hardly a vehicle seemed to pass during what felt like an eternity waiting for the bus to arrive, and it was getting colder. Her shivering grew worse, and she was painfully aware of the sound of the men's breathing.

A rough voice broke the silence. "You look cold."

It was the beardless one, still smiling that awful smile.

"A little," was all she could say. All she *wanted* to say.

She clutched her tote bag close to her chest and looked away from them again, anxiously watching the road in the direction from which the bus would be coming. She heard another voice, the bearded one mumbled something to the other one, and they both laughed.

A few long seconds passed and the beardless voice came again, louder.

"It's so hard to watch a pretty thing like you shiver and shake like that from the cold," continued Beardless. "I got some body heat here I wouldn't mind sharin' if you wanna cuddle up."

A chill ran down her spine.

Why did he have to say that?

They were closer now. Both of them. Their faces twisted into hideous grins.

"N-no, thank you. I'll be fine."

Her thumping heart disagreed.

Beardless looked offended. "Oh? But what about me? I'm cold too." He winked.

"Are you?" Sam frowned. "You just said you had body heat to spare. Why don't you share it with your friend?"

Blackbeard laughed.

Beardless did not. He scoffed, and looked her over like a cut of meat. "You're prettier than he is. I'd rather share it with you. Plenty of time before the bus comes. Don't gotta be shy. How 'bout a smash of rum? I bet that'd loosen you up."

Sam inched her way to the shelter exit. So did Beardless. Blackbeard produced a pint bottle of white rum from his coat and took a swig before offering it to her.

"No," she said, sharply. "I'm not interested."

Blackbeard shrugged, and tucked the bottle back into his coat.

Beardless was not so indifferent about the rejection. His smile flattened. His dark eyes turned hateful. He was blocking the shelter exit.

"Maybe you'd rather give me your bag then, huh? Since you're such a—"

Sam sent her foot up into the man's groin. It connected, but not as forcefully as she had hoped. He squeezed his thighs together, mid kick, ensnaring her foot. Before she could free herself, Blackbeard was on her from behind, forcing her arms behind her back.

She tried to scream for help, but her efforts were quickly muffled by Beardless's dirty palm. He removed her foot from between his legs, and kept it raised as he pressed in closer to sandwich her. She was trapped, as quick as that. She was surprised and disappointed with herself.

The beardless man's smile was huge now, inches from her face. His teeth were yellow, at least the ones not blackened by rot, and his breath was awful, a rank blend of onions and stale beer. He laughed while she squirmed.

"That wasn't very nice," he growled.

Blackbeard slipped the tote bag from her shoulder and tossed it to the concrete. A sickening feeling ran through her. Normally, the bag wouldn't be much of a loss, but the old couple had paid her in cash. Cash that would make her rent payment that month a lot more bearable. And these assholes were going to get every penny of it.

"Check her pockets," said Blackbeard, shifting himself so that he could hold both of her arms with only one of his own, freeing his other to take over the muffling of her mouth.

"With *pleasure*," Beardless replied.

He yanked the zipper down on Sam's coat, exposing her Red Hot Chili Peppers t-shirt to the cold. She squirmed some more, helplessly, as her shirt was raised and icy fingers fondled their way around her back to her bra catch.

Beardless was practically drooling over her while he fumbled with the catch. Her wiggling would never free her from the two men, but she wasn't about to make it easy for Beardless to remove her bra.

"Stop that, you idiot," shouted Blackbeard. "Her pockets! Hurry up. Somebody will see. Get her phone. Mike will pay good for it."

Beardless merely grunted his disgust for Blackbeard's command. Sam felt his hot, rancid breath on her neck as he leaned in closer to take a sickening whiff of her hair. His dry lips violated her neck for a horrible second, until she bit Blackbeard's hand. It tasted awful.

She instantly regretted using her fleeting freedom to tell Beardless to go to hell. She should have screamed for help, but before she could do anything else, her mouth was stuffed with Beardless's cap. Greasy blond hair spilled from the man's head.

Sam made a mental note of her assailant's features. If nothing else, she could at least report the incident to the police. If the men didn't decide to kidnap her, that is.

Blackbeard cursed. He tightened his hold on her arms so much they started to hurt. It felt as if he'd pull them right out of their sockets. Her squirming was completely useless against this new approach.

"Pockets!" he commanded. "Now!"

This time Beardless actually obeyed, but before his hands could find the slits in her coat, all three were startled by the angry roar of a truck engine.

Beardless stepped away and turned to face the sound.

Sam thought to run again as Blackbeard released her arms from behind her back, but over her shoulder he growled, "You keep your mouth shut. Or else..."

A sharp pressure against her lower back echoed the threat with sincerity.

An old red pickup truck pulled into the seniors' apartment driveway just enough to be off the road, close to the bus shelter. The headlights were turned off, but even so, it was a wonder that something so loud could sneak up on them like it had.

The two men waved cheerfully at the driver when he stepped out of his truck. He was a young man, perhaps close to Sam's own age, wearing a red flannel jacket and navy blue ball cap. He didn't seem to notice them. He was grumbling and cursing about salt and rust and shitty houses as he stalked around the front of the vehicle. Only when he made it around to the passenger side did he seem to realize he was not alone, and at once he stopped complaining. He paused to regard his audience, noticeably embarrassed.

Sam's attackers waved again and shouted greetings at him. Sam said nothing.

"Cold out tonight!" said Beardless.

The driver nodded, and scratched his neck. He looked from the bus shelter to his truck, and then again at the shelter. An awkward silence followed.

Then he threw his arms akimbo and called, "Wendy??? Is that really you?" His voice was thick with an accent she couldn't place. Some kind of British, maybe. Or maybe he was just from Lunenburg County, outside of the city. They talked funny down that way.

Sam glanced around. There were no other women about, and neither of her attackers looked like a Wendy. When she looked back to the driver, she saw that he was looking straight at *her*. Still, Sam said nothing.

"It *is* you!" he decided, walking towards them. "What a surprise. It's been a dog's age, Wendy. Do I get a hug, or what?"

Sam's mouth opened wide to warn him, but the words wouldn't come out. The driver looked sturdy enough, but he was outnumbered, and at least one of the men had a knife. She closed her eyes as the driver approached, as if doing so would make it all disappear.

Her eyes remained closed even after the pressure released from her back, and didn't open again until her feet were lifted off the ground. She found herself wrapped tightly in a bear hug.

The driver hugged her as if they were old friends, though she was certain she had never seen him before in her life. Even if he were some time-altered friend from her childhood, she would have remembered his eyes. They were a sky blue, and held a warmth that was as friendly as the smile he beamed at her.

He set her down gently and adjusted his ball cap. "Your friends are right. It's pretty cold out tonight. Wanna skip the bus shelter thing and get a coffee? We've got a lot of catching up to do, I'd say."

"S-sure," said Sam. She glanced nervously at the two men, and was relieved to see they had backed away several steps, without bothering to pick up her stolen tote bag. *Three cheers for cowardice.*

Her *old friend* tipped his hat to her attackers, "Sorry guys. I don't think I've got enough room in my truck for everyone. Meet us at Mary's Diner, maybe?"

The attackers waved their hands as if to dismiss any potential slight, and Blackbeard replied that he "wasn't much of a coffee drinker." They both continued to back further away.

Sam's old friend scooped her bag off the concrete and held it out questioningly to her. She nodded that it was hers, and thanked him when he handed it to her. He placed his hand on her back and guided her to the passenger side of his truck. It wasn't a red truck after all. Not all of it, anyway. Only the hood was red. The passenger door was blue, and the box was black with patches of yellow primer. The thing was like a rusty rainbow after a terrible shit storm.

He opened the door for her, and drew a gasp from her lips when he reached inside her unzipped coat. His hands already found her shirt by the time she defensively grabbed to push them away. He tugged on the shirt anyways, *downward,* and pulled it back into place over her chest and stomach.

My shirt! She had been too frightened to notice her shirt had stiffened in the cold and had not fallen back down, but the driver did. She flushed a little with embarrassment, but her old friend merely nodded as he released his wrists from her grip.

"A little cold for belly tops this time of year, isn't it?" He grinned with one side of his mouth. He cautiously touched her again to lift her up into his truck, and flicked the lock before he closed the door. For an instant the action startled her, but she quickly realized he hadn't locked her in. He had locked *them* out. The muffled sound of his voice continued through the glass. "I'll just be a sec."

Sam thought he might go after her attackers, but when she looked for them she just caught their backs as they disappeared behind an old telephone company building. Instead, her old friend crawled under the truck somewhere near the middle. He was under there for several minutes, grumbling through the floor boards amidst a cacophony of rattles and clanks. Finally, he emerged, clutching half of his exhaust system in blackened hands, his red and black flannel jacket now smudged with dirt and grease. He grinned at her again and tossed the broken pipe into the box of his truck and hopped in the driver's side.

The bus arrived as the truck roared to life.

There was a crack in the windshield that began directly in front of the driver and made its way towards the passenger side before curving up and disappearing into the roof line, just beyond the rear view mirror. Or it would have, had the rear view mirror not been laying on the floor, drowning in a sea of coffee cups. The headlights hadn't been turned off when the truck approached, they simply didn't work at all. The bench seat was torn in several places, exposing its yellow foam innards wherever the duct tape failed to conceal it, and a spring was jutting uncomfortably up into Sam's backside, but the heater, noisy at it was, worked its magic beautifully to thaw her cheeks and fingers.

It was the best truck in the world.

Sam regarded her savior curiously. She had pegged him as one of those easy conversation starter types she admired, based on how he handled the men at the bus stop, but now that they were alone he seemed to be quite shy. He adjusted his cap several times in the course of a minute, and hardly spoke since giving her the options of taking the bus or having him drive her home. She chose the second option.

I bet he feels uncomfortable in elevators too, she thought. That thought propelled her to repay his heroism with some bravery of her own. She spoke up.

"My name's not Wendy, you know," she said, loud enough for him to hear her over the drone of the broken exhaust. She suspected he *did* know, but she was determined to start a conversation and keep the drive from turning into an elevator ride.

"I do now." He grinned. Unlike Beardless, this man's teeth were no stranger to the toothbrush, at least in contrast to the smears of black grease across his nose and cheeks. Even the unkempt brown hair creeping out from under his cap shined black at the tips.

He offered nothing else for a long moment, long enough for her eyes to fall to the knife laying on the seat between them. It was a jagged, evil looking thing. She didn't believe he would threaten her with it, but she considered moving it out of his reach.

"Where are we going?" she asked, still looking at the knife. "You didn't ask me where I lived. Are you taking me somewhere to kill me with this thing?"

She looked up to see a wickedly serious expression on his face.

"You guessed it, Wendy. Out of the frying pan and into the fire, eh?"

Another Bundy.

She reached for the knife, but he was quicker, his stronger hand pinned hers easily to the seat.

"Hey hey!" he said. "I was only kidding. Don't stab me."

She slapped him across the face with her free hand. He took his hand back from hers.

"Right. I deserved that. Just... don't stab me, please. Bad time for jokes. I know. My bad..."

Sam hadn't meant to *actually* slap him, only to pretend.

A great conversation starter, she thought, feeling guilty. She decided to continue scolding him anyways. Scolding still counted as conversation.

"Who makes jokes like that? After what just happened back there?"

He stared ahead at the bus in front of them until it came to another stop, and waited for the passengers to get on.

"Well, I don't know what actually happened back there, but... *Luke,*" he said.

"What?"

"Luke Fletcher. That's the name of the guy with the shitty jokes. Me. I should've known better. Sorry."

Sam thought it was sweet of him to be completely oblivious of her role in starting the not-so-funny joke, until he said, "I should probably just keep my mouth shut."

NO NO! She wanted to scream. *I'm so bad at this.*

She looked down at her hands. The hand she slapped him with and the hand he grabbed were both streaked with black grease.

"Sorry for that too," he said, noticing. "I just undercoated this thing last week. I wasn't expecting to be rolling around under it so soon. I really thought the exhaust would wait until Spring, at least, before it broke off."

He held his arm out to her. "You can wipe your hands on my jacket if you want. And... all these coffee cups... If I had known you—"

She started laughing.

"What is it?" he asked.

"Your jacket." She rubbed the palm of her right hand against the fabric of his jacket. As suspected, her hand came away dirtier than before. She held it up to him, smiling.

"*This* is what you offer me for cleaning my hands?"

"Ahh shit. I'm—"

Sam cut him off before he could assert his Canadian citizenship again. "It's fine. There are worse things."

She wiped her hands on an empty sandwich wrapper.

"My name's Samantha Vale. But my friends call me Sam, and my *old friends,* I guess, call me Wendy. And since you and I are *old friends,* you can get away with the coffee cups, the grease, and the threatening to kill me. These are just the things I've come to expect from you after all this time we've known each other."

His smile returned. She thought herself quite clever.

"It's good to see you again, Wendy."

He stopped his truck again behind the bus as it spat out another passenger.

"It's a drywall saw," he said of the knife, "and I'm taking you home. In one piece."

"Well that's good to hear. I didn't mean to react like that. I knew it was a joke. You'll have to forgive me. I guess I'm just a little on edge. Things could have went much worse, though. But tell me, how do you know where I live? Have you been stalking me?"

His mouth curled into a larger smile and he opened it as if to say something, but hesitated, likely weighing the risk of spitting out another smart comment. She beat him to it.

"I'll take that as a yes. Next time, try and kidnap me just a little sooner, please."

He nodded. "I'll do my best. But uh, no, I don't really know where you live. I've just been following this bus you were waiting for, and assumed you would tell me when to turn or stop."

"I *was* waiting for a bus, but I don't think I told you it was *this* one. Maybe I was waiting for one going the other direction?"

He looked thoughtful for a second, and then said, "Well, in that case, our drive would just be a little longer, I guess. Eventually this bus will end its route and head back in the other direction."

"Nope. Not this one," she said, smiling triumphantly. "This one will go back to the station. It's the last bus of the night."

He went back to his thinking for a moment, then asked, "Are we going the right way?"

"Yes. Yes, we are. You did well, Luke. We're almost there actually. Just around the corner."

"Perfect."

Shortly after the bus rounded the corner, it pulled over to swing open its doors. "That's it. That's my stop. I live in that apartment building up the hill there."

Luke didn't pull over at the bus stop. Instead, he continued up the side street to the building she indicated and parked on the curb by the entrance. Before Sam could zip up her coat, he was out of the truck and dashing around to the passenger side to open her door, but he had locked it earlier, and left his keys in the ignition, so she had to unlock the door herself before he could be chivalrous.

"Safe and sound, miss. Enjoy the rest of your evening."

He tipped his hat to her and started back into his truck, until she stopped him. She was not at all surprised when he flinched away from an attempted hug, but she forced it on him anyway, wrapping her arms tightly around his neck.

"It's okay," she said. "I'm buying a new coat tomorrow anyways."

"If you say so, Wendy."

She smiled when she felt his hands squeeze her waist, imagining his greasy finger prints on her jacket.

"Can I get your number?" she asked, suddenly.

His eyebrows raised out of sight, hidden behind his grease tipped hair. "My phone number?"

"No. Your social insurance number. Yes. Your phone number. If you don't mind, that is. I want to call the police and tell them about those guys. Maybe their next victim won't be so lucky. And maybe the police will ask for a witness or something. So your number might come in handy."

"Ah, right. Yeah, sure. No problem."

Sam braved the cold air on her fingers a little longer to add Luke to the contacts list in her phone. They said their goodbyes, but before she turned to leave she added, "I'm sorry your muffler fell off tonight. But I'm kinda really glad it did."

He nodded. "So am I. Don't need it anyways."

Another grin.

"Goodnight Sam."

Sam hung her coat and untied her boots, paying little attention to the paper that had been slid under her door. Another late rent notice, she knew, without reading it.

The gas station she worked at part-time had cut her hours back to almost nothing, and despite her efforts, the resumes she had been passing around had yet to yield any results. Perhaps she should have stuck with the teaching degree. But it was no matter, not this month. The commission she earned from painting the old couple in Timberlea would be plenty to cover it, and buy her some winter clothes.

Bulkier clothing fell lower on her priority list, though, as she entered her bathroom to clean herself up for bed. She couldn't help but laugh out loud when she saw her reflection in the mirror, and spent the next twenty minutes scrubbing grease from her cheek, neck, hands and hair. By the time the last of the dark liquid was washed down into the shower drain, with it seemed to go the thoughts of those two creeps at the bus stop. She went to bed thinking of coffee cups rustling around her feet.

CHAPTER TWO

Dennis Stewart was an arrogant, know-it-all, know-nothing prick of a man, but everyone agreed that the sandwiches served at his funeral were amazing. Refreshments were distributed *during* the ceremony, to speed up the process and to give the speakers something to speak about. The peanut butter and jam sandwiches received the highest praise during the eulogies, with the ham and cheese coming in at a close second.

The procession was attended almost entirely by co-workers, who showed up only because it took place on a work day and they were given time off by upper management, who, more than likely had never met Dennis. If not for the "WE'LL MISS YOU, DENNIS" banner floating overhead, likely thought of, and hung, by the funeral director, one would have believed that all these people had gathered in the parlor specifically to mourn the empty snack trays. The fact that that was exactly what they were doing was just how it worked out.

Luke sided with the peanut butter and jam crowd. It wasn't that he didn't enjoy the ham and cheese sandwiches, because he did, there was just no beating a good peanut butter and jam sandwich. They always took him back to his childhood.

He found the entire funeral to be a pleasant affair. It would easily be his fondest memory of Dennis, because it was the only time he'd ever been in a room with the man without experiencing a creeping desire to kill him. A weak heart apparently took care of that for him, though Luke had his doubts. As far as he knew, Dennis had no heart at all.

Stephanie Stewart, who had been the departed man's wife, was always a miserable, sulky thing whenever Luke saw her at company get-togethers. At the funeral, however, she looked about ten years younger, was all smiles, and dressed to kill in a sparkling little black dress that would have been far more appropriate at a New Year's Eve party. It would not have been surprising or disappointing to find out that she had poisoned him.

Luke politely declined her invitation to go club hopping afterward, but was not against a few sips of wine from her Tim Hortons cup. While chatting with the increasingly frisky widow, he learned of her plans to sell all of Dennis's "shit", as she called it, and live as long as she could down in Mexico or Costa Rica on the money. She had already enrolled in Spanish lessons. A few more sips of wine somehow led to a gratuitous make-out session in the coat room, and Luke agreeing to purchase a property that Dennis planned on flipping but never "got off his ass" to actually flip.

They sealed the deal with a selfie of them pinky swearing, and an audio recording that, if it were to be used, would have to be edited to remove a highly inappropriate alternate payment plan. Then, before he could get himself into anymore trouble that evening, Luke carefully removed the widow's claws from his back, and strategically directed her toward Brian, his friend and co-worker.

Brian *did* go club hopping with her that night, and two months later, Luke received a text saying the two of them were moving to Mazunte, a beautiful beach-side village on the south-western coast of Mexico. A few days after the funeral, when the effects of Stephanie's celebration wore off, she actually honored the deal she made in the coat room without question.

Six months later, Luke was on a step ladder, thinking of that funeral and cursing profusely. Even in death, Dennis continued to haunt him. He shouldn't have been surprised.

Wiring the thing was the easy part. The real trick to installing the new light fixture was managing the overcomplicated mounting bracket while balancing precariously on an ancient step ladder his grandfather had once ran over with his truck. The ladder always made Luke nervous, especially at times when he needed to ascend the full twelve feet. He often vowed to replace the ladder, but just as often forgot entirely that it existed until he needed it again.

He squinted his eyes, struggling to line up the screw holes. Darkness was creeping up on him as the sun outside sank below the tree line. Luke had counted on the natural light to aid him while the power was shut off to the fixture, but it was looking more and more like he would have to finish the task by flashlight. He grumbled loudly to himself about the unexpected difficulty, the house in general, and more than anything, about his unshakable habit of procrastinating.

Yet again, a book had absorbed more daylight than he could afford, but he couldn't possibly set the book aside and leave poor Watson hanging while a murderous canine prowled the gloomy village of Dartmoor in the Sherlock Holmes mystery, *Hound of the Baskervilles*. The book was one of many that peaked Luke's interest while sorting through the items left behind by the home's previous occupant. The house had apparently been abandoned for many years before Dennis purchased it, and another two or three years after that.

It was a *Victorian* house. That was the word Stephanie used to describe it. *Derelict,* or *run down shithole* were the words that came quicker to Luke's mind, and often out of his mouth. For that reason, he would starve to death if his living ever depended on him selling the house himself.

He was a carpenter, and a carpenter was exactly what the house needed. It also needed a plumber, a mason, an electrician, an exterminator, and frequently, he included a demolition expert to this list as well, but he persevered. It had taken several months of sacrificing evenings, weekends and holidays, but the ramshackle bargain was now watertight. It now sat on a more seaworthy foundation and was less inclined to sink into the ground, as was the case when he purchased it. It screamed for a coat or two of fresh paint, but to that, Luke was deaf. Paint could wait.

The interior was much further from perfection than the exterior. Aside from the room he was currently putting the finishing touches on, the *Great Room*, as he liked to call it, the rest of the house remained in ruin. Stephanie had also boasted the house as fully furnished. That, too, proved largely disappointing, as the ruined rooms were unfortunately furnished with junk that only added to Luke's ample workload. A considerable amount had been sorted and found its way to the dump, though anyone who ventured beyond the Great Room would not assume so. As of yet, he found no treasures worthy of an antique dealer's money, or any furniture worth keeping.

Luke called it the Great Room because it was the largest room in the house, watched over by an enormous stone hearth with a wide chimney that extended up through a vaulted ceiling. Of course, the roof leaked around this chimney when he first arrived, making it something of a water feature for a time, but even then he was impressed by it. It was this chimney, the first thing anyone would see upon entering the house proper, that drove him to renovate that room first, over a more functional room like the bathroom, or kitchen, or even one of the two bedrooms upstairs.

For the time being, Luke was more than content to sleep on a couch near the fireplace. From there, he couldn't see the disastrous state the upstairs bedrooms were in. They and the hallway connecting them suffered the brunt of the leaky roof's wrath. Nearly everything on the upper floor was ruined, but he had taken the time to pretty up the stairs and railing leading up to it from the Great Room. A beautiful portal to a dismal abyss.

That evening, the Great Room would finally be finished. If he could just get the pesky light fixture mounted.

Almost there!

His cell phone rang. Of course it did.

He had left it below on his work bench, so that if the rickety ladder should throw him, it would be one of the few things that *wouldn't* break in the fall. He abandoned the fixture, trusting it to the questionable integrity of just one of the screws, partially turned in. He made it halfway down the ladder, further than he expected, before he felt the screw bounce off his head. Thankfully, the fixture only fell as far as the wires would allow it to dangle, so he suffered no head trauma on his way down to the phone, though he grumbled nearly as much as if he had.

Luke had been in the habit of ignoring most phone calls, especially numbers he didn't recognize. It seemed since purchasing the house, no day was complete without a call from this bank or that bank trying to bury him in more credit line debt, or hounding him to buy useless insurance. They were nearly deaf to the word *no*, so he dreaded speaking with them.

This was another number he didn't recognize, but he took a chance, and answered the call.

"Hello? Can I speak with Mr. Fletcher, please?"

Dammit. He heaved a disgusted sigh and replied, "I'd rather you didn't."

"Excuse me, sir?"

"Yeah. This is him."

"Excellent. I hope you are well today, sir."

"I was."

"Happy to hear it, Mr. Fletcher. Before we begin, I'd like to mention that this call will be monitored for quality control purposes."

"Of course."

The man on the other end of the phone droned out his purpose, and Luke occasionally muttered his bored, mechanical "uh huh" and "oh yeah?" responses. When the proposal finally came, he rejected it, and as expected, the caller did not hear him, and began wording his offer in a different way.

Luke groaned. The shadows were stretching further across the room. He frowned up at the fixture swaying gently above the ladder.

"I'm sorry. I'm really not interested. Goodbye." *Click.*

He felt bad for hanging up on the guy. He was just doing his job, after all, but Luke had a job of his own to finish. Before he could set the phone back down, it was ringing again.

"Enough!" he barked into the phone. "Don't call again. I told you I'm not interested."

"Hmm. I don't think that's true. If I remember correctly, you gave me your number pretty willingly. But maybe I was imagining things? It *was* a bit of a rough night."

His stomach knotted up. It was the voice he had hoped to hear, but not how he imagined answering it.

"I... not you. I didn't mean... Shit. Sorry..."

Sam laughed. "Telemarketers get to the best of us."

He was thankful, at least, that she couldn't see his face, which he was sure to be beet red at that moment. He swallowed his embarrassment and spit out another apology.

"It's completely fine," she said. "I understand. Really. But hey, if it really is a bad time, I can call back."

"No no! It's all good." He didn't even glance up. "Did you sleep okay last night?"

"I slept well actually. Thanks to you. I spoke with the police this morning."

"Oh good. I'm glad you called. Them, I mean." He shook his head. "So do you need a witness?"

"Nope. It won't be necessary. As it turns out, two men by my description were already under suspicion for a convenience store robbery in Fairview a couple weeks ago. There have even been posters up. I guess I missed them. But anyways, the funny part. Well, at least *I* found it funny, is that the police investigated reports of a drunken fist fight in a gas station parking lot early this morning. Guess who the two participants were? I've already been in to identify them."

"That's awesome!"

"It is. So the reason I called actually was to ask about that coffee we agreed on. What happened to that?"

Luke smiled. "Nothing happened to it. I'm sure it's still sitting in the percolator at Mary's. We can go anytime you want."

"We should probably go pretty soon then. Don't want it to get cold. How about in a half hour?"

"Yeah, sure. I'm not doing anything." He slipped out of his dirty jeans.

"Perfect. Would you mind picking me up? Same place you dropped me off last night."

"I think I can manage that," he said, digging a fresh pair of jeans out of his laundry basket.

"Great! See you in thirty minutes."

Luke pulled his truck up to the curb in front of Sam's apartment building twenty minutes later, and Sam came outside twenty minutes after that. This time, he made sure to unlock the passenger side door before he tried to open it for her.

She was wearing a warmer coat that evening. One of those classy looking wool ones with the big buttons in the front. It was olive green, and she had on a matching colored wool cap with a fluffy white bobble on top that jiggled when she moved her head. To the untrained eye, Luke was wearing the exact same clothes as the night before, but he was, in fact, wearing a different coat. It was just an identical copy of the red and black flannel from the night before, with a few less stains. This was complimented by an identical pair of cheap, but not quite as faded, blue jeans.

"What have you done??" she asked, in shock, when he hopped back into the driver's seat.

"What's wrong??"

"The coffee cups. They're all gone! Our toes will freeze now."

Luke grinned. "Eh, well they lose their R-value after awhile. It's good to make room for fresh ones every so often."

The first thing he had done after dropping Sam off the night before was pull his truck into his barn and empty out all of the junk, everything really, except the spare distributor cap and a ratchet set. He tucked those behind the seat, just in case. Then he spent some time patching more of the torn seat fabric with duct tape before it dawned on him to wrap the entire seat in a clean bed sheet. It was slightly more aesthetically pleasing that way. He didn't have any glue, but some two-sided tape worked well enough to hold the rear view mirror back in place.

"I'll just wear my thickest socks until the cups pile up again," he added, and lifted his pant leg to reveal the thick wool socks his grandmother had knitted for him. A very comfortable pair of red and green striped Christmas socks with an "L" stitched on the sides.

"Very clever, Mr. Fletcher," she said, taking off her mittens. "Thanks for picking me up."

"My pleasure, Miss Vale. You can fill the tank up later." He grinned again, and then frowned when he noticed the rear view mirror wasn't centered on the windshield. Sam didn't seem to notice.

After a short drive they arrived in the diner parking lot, and Luke slid out of the truck first to open Sam's door. However, the rear view mirror fell off again, and he stood staring glum faced at it, shaking his head. A laughing Sam opened her own door. She hooked her arm in his and drug him into the diner.

As a gentlemen, and for complete lack of preference, he conceded the choice of table to her and they settled into a cozy corner booth by the window. She wasn't hungry, so he simply ordered the agreed upon coffees. The service was quick as usual, but slightly more embarrassing, as his server winked approvingly at him when seeing him order *two* coffees. Thankfully, Sam had been on her way to the table at the time and didn't see it.

Luke sat down and blew on his coffee before taking a sip. He couldn't remember seeing a happier image than that of Sam sitting across from him with a steaming mug of coffee in her hands. She took a deep whiff, as if to sample the taste of the coveted liquid first with her nose. Her large brown eyes closed when she took her first sip, and opened again with a smile.

"This is good coffee," she said.

"It is," Luke agreed. "And the price is great. You can taste the money you're saving."

"Hmm." She took another sip and smacked her lips. "No. No I can't really taste the money. Have you tasted money before? I have. I choked on a penny once when I was little. It was quite frightening."

"Your parents had you on an interesting diet." He turned his palm up towards her. "But it seems to have worked out. I guess."

"You *guess?*" She raised her eyebrows at him, and then took off her hat, allowing her auburn hair to flow freely to her chest. She brushed it away from her face. Her eyes shown brightly with another sip of coffee.

No, I'm certain, he thought, but instead asked, "Is that your new coat? You look a lot warmer today."

"Yes, it is! Not what I planned to buy, of course. Nothing ever is. I splurged a bit more than I should have, *but* it was on sale, and it's much warmer than my old coat."

"And cleaner."

"Yes. That too."

She smiled, and cast a scrutinizing gaze upon his hands. He raised them to show her they weren't *always* filthy. Of course, *normally* they still would be. Whenever he was forced to work around the greasier parts of his truck, something that was beginning to happen far too frequently, his hands would stay black for days. Not that he didn't wash his hands, he just didn't like hard scrubbing.

"Very good, Luke."

They exchanged a few awkward seconds of silence before a trio of giggling women at a table behind and across the aisle from Sam caught Luke's attention. They seemed to be giggling at them, or more specifically, him. He recognized one of them, a short, raven haired woman, but he couldn't quite place her.

"Friends of yours?" Sam asked, turning a glance at the group.

He shrugged. "Apparently."

Another handful of awkward seconds trickled by, and all Luke was able to put together was, *Come on, you idiot,* to himself, inside of his head. His vocabulary always chose the best times to abandon him.

Sam rescued him.

"Okay. So I know maybe this is kind of weird, but I wanna tell you anyways."

"No worries," he said.

"Well, my sleep wasn't entirely great, actually. I think I was a little more affected by that incident than I thought. I mean, I know nothing *really* happened, but it was still pretty awful. I don't think I'll ever be able to eat onions again."

"Good. I've always hated onions, myself. Do they really have to get slopped into everything?"

Sam smiled.

"Sorry," he said. "Continue."

"I had a dream. We were driving in your truck, away from the bus stop, when suddenly one of those bus stop guys runs right out in front of us, like a deer. We screamed. You slammed on your brakes, but hit him anyways."

"Eh, well, he had it coming."

"He did. Screw that guy. But anyways. We get out to take a look. The truck is okay. Well, no less okay than it was…"

Luke grinned. "Fair enough."

"You kneel down to see if the guy is still alive, and his arm shoots up and grabs you by the throat!"

"Jesus…"

"You were digging at the man's fingers, and cursing, a lot. Even with his hands on your throat."

"Sounds about right."

"I tried to help you, but the second man arrived, swooping down from the tree tops. Yes, he had wings…"

Luke raised his eyebrows.

"I know… but he did, and he landed right on top of me, pinning me to the ground. The last thing I saw before I woke up, all sweaty, was the first man ripping your head off and smashing it through the truck windshield."

"That sounds… fun. I guess we're pretty lucky those guys are locked up then, huh?"

"Totally. I hope you're not too put off that I decided to share my dreams of your death. You can run now, if you'd like."

"Oh no. It's all good. I had the same dream."

"Seriously??"

"No."

Her eyes narrowed behind her coffee cup as she took another sip.

"Actually," he began, "I was out walking barefoot in a field beside a house my parents rented when I was young. The neighbors kept goats and cows. I'm not sure why I was out walking this field in the dark, but I was, and clearly it was a mistake."

"*Clearly*. How would you see all the cow patties? You must have stepped in so much shit. And barefoot, no less."

"Probably, yeah. But I didn't notice, because before long, I was running as fast as I could away from a witch on a broomstick. She was cackling away and blasting fireballs at me."

"Oh my. Let me guess. The witch was incredibly beautiful, and she was me."

He laughed. "I wish. I mean, no. No, she was definitely a lot greener and wartier than you. Thankfully, I did manage to wake up before any of those fireballs hit me. So yeah, not quite the same dream, but either way, it seems it was a pretty bad night for Dream Luke."

"Poor Dream Luke."

"I remember that field being a bit more pleasant," he continued. "Back when it didn't have witches in it. When I was a kid I liked to rake up big piles of leaves in the fall so I could watch the goats eat them."

"Adorable."

"It was. Except for this one asshole of a goat. He had those big, um, curl up and around horns, you know what I mean? And he'd head butt the others. He was a real dick. Ah, and sometimes he'd drink his own piss. Er, sorry that's a bit, much, eh?"

This time, Luke silently cursed his vocabulary for *not* abandoning him.

Somehow, Sam seemed unfazed by his inappropriate spillage.

She took another sip of coffee and said, "Not at all. Billy goats can be nasty creatures. I was pretty amazed the first time I saw that same thing. I even called my grandmother outside to point it out to her."

Oh this woman is great.

"Excuse me. Sorry," said the raven haired mystery woman as she plopped herself down in the booth beside Sam. "But I have to." She had been drinking something a little stronger than coffee.

"You have to what?" asked Luke. He still had no idea who the woman was, but assumed nothing good would come from this.

"Do you remember me?"

Luke shook his head.

"We used to work together! In Dartmouth."

"Ahh, *Jessica,*" he said, putting it together. He was quite sure they had never spoken before, but he remembered seeing her. She was a cashier while he worked out back in receiving, unloading trucks. He had only been there a few months. It was a shitty job.

"Good to see you again, Luke" she said. "I was just telling my friends about you."

"You were?"

Jessica looked back to her friends and laughed, then turned back to him. "Do you remember what you spent your Christmas coupons on?"

"Er... ah. Yes. I do." He felt his cheeks begin to flush.

She turned to Sam, grinning.

Sam smiled politely back.

"This guy..." Jessica began. "We were all given three Christmas coupons to buy anything we wanted in the store. Twenty percent off. This guy comes up to my cash register with his three items. Guess what he buys?"

Luke grunted.

"What did he buy?" asked Sam.

"Condoms! Three boxes of condoms. Three. He used all three of his coupons on condoms. The bulk value packs."

Her laughter was joined by her friends, listening intently from the other table.

Sam shot him a cheeky squint.

Luke sighed and took a long sip of his coffee to hide behind the mug. "Yep."

"It totally made my night. Most people were buying televisions or furniture or video games. But not this guy. *This guy* had other plans."

Luke remembered vividly the red faced cashier when he plopped the boxes down at her register. He remembered also that she called a manager about the purchase, because it was unclear whether someone could use their coupons to buy three of the same items. The manager appeared, raised his eyebrows, quickly said everything was fine, and walked away just as quickly as he appeared, with a bewildered look on his face.

"Yep," he said again.

Jessica threw her arm around Sam.

"Was this the lucky lady?" she asked.

"Er, no," said Luke. "That was what, six years ago? Seven? I'm surprised you remember that."

"How could I forget?" she laughed. "I've seen you a few times since then, and every time I see you it's all I can think about. Tonight I thought, enough is enough. I'm gonna go and say hello."

"Well you've done it, and what a perfect time to do it. Hello to you too, Jessica."

"Aw, I'm so glad you remember my name."

Her cell phone rang then, and she answered. "Hello? Yes. Sweet! Be right out!" She tucked her phone away. "I'd love to stay and chat, but our cab's here. We're going downtown."

She rose unsteadily from the booth and, with a wink, said to Sam, "Have fun tonight."

Sam laughed, "Thanks. You too. Nice to meet you!"

"Aw. You're too sweet." Without warning she leaned in and planted a big kiss on Sam's cheek, and before Luke could react, she landed one on him as well.

Her laughing friends pulled her away. As they drug her out through the diner doors, she turned her head back and cried, "Goodbye you crazy kids!"

He was fairly certain Jessica was a couple years younger than him.

"Er, sorry about that," said Luke, wiping his cheek with his coat sleeve.

"Don't be. She seems fun."

"Probably. Do you want to join them? I'm sure they'll make room for us in the cab."

"I'll pass on that for tonight, I think. Another time though, maybe. This coffee is too good to rush. So tell me. What is it you do now, Mr. Fletcher? Besides drive around in your truck offering damsel rescue services. Can't imagine that being a profitable business, with gas prices these days. Do you do vehicle upholstery on the side?"

He laughed. "I did a good job on that truck seat, didn't I?"

"Oh yes. A great job." She took another sip of her coffee and flashed a warm grin. "I hardly felt the spring in my ass this time."

"Ah then you noticed the couch cushion I stuffed down there. My finest work," he said with exaggerated pride. "Not bad for a carpenter, I'd say."

"So you're a carpenter? That's cool. It must be cold, building houses this time of year."

"Eh, it's not too bad if you dress for it. A little cold on the hands, but there are a lot of inside jobs to balance things out. Actually, I'm only working for a few more days. Then I'll be laid off."

"Oh no. I'm sorry to hear that. You'll have to rescue damsels full time."

"Maybe so. It'll just be until January. We usually slow down a bit in the winter, and some guys get cut. This year I volunteered."

"How come?"

"I bought an old house in Timberlea earlier this year. A bit of a dump, really. I thought the time off might speed up the renovations. Make it a bit more… livable."

"That sounds awesome actually. Old houses have so much character."

"More like a lot of rats."

Sam's smile flickered slightly at that, so Luke quickly continued, "And you? What do you do?"

"I'm an artist!" she said proudly. "I was also studying to become a teacher, and sometimes I work at a gas station, but yesterday I finished a commissioned painting for a lovely elderly couple. Questionable taste in television programs, but a lovely couple. They gave me a pretty generous bonus."

"That's great. I wish I could paint. If I were to paint someone's portrait, they'd probably take me to court."

"Perhaps you could start with cats, then."

"Cats?"

"Yes. Cats. To boost your skills while at the same time avoiding lawsuits. Cats won't sue you. And if you paint enough cats, and hang them strategically throughout your house, your rat friends may take notice."

Luke scratched his stubbly chin. "That's pretty clever actually.

"Of course. I *am* clever."

"Maybe you could show me sometime, you know, as part of your teacher studies."

For a brief moment he allowed himself the image of Sam as an art teacher to hijack his imagination. They were standing in front of a canvas. Sam was behind him, whispering instructions into his ear and reaching around him to guide his brush strokes.

Another scene flashed through his mind. A scene from the movie *Billie Madison*, in which Billy's teacher encourages his studying by removing an article of clothing each time he answered a question correctly.

"Hello?" came Sam's voice, drifting into his mind from what sounded like a great distance.

He smacked aside his reverie, realizing with embarrassment that it had drowned out her reply to his suggestion, leaving him with no idea how to respond to her response.

"Um, hello!" he tried, "Er, yeah. It would be good practice. For sharpening your teaching skills."

"You just said that."

"Did I? Right." He shook his head. *Idiot.* "Just uh, making sure you were listening is all. Yep. So you'll teach me?"

Sam narrowed her eyes. Curious. Or suspicious. Surely she couldn't have read his mind. Mind reading was impossible. Sherlock Holmes, however, didn't need to read minds. He could read faces. Body language. Tone of voice. Beads of sweat, like the ones forming on his forehead.

A sly grin spread across her face as she nodded. "Well. I told you I had given up on teaching, but I suppose if you enjoy my company, painting lessons are as good of an excuse as any to see me again."

She *was* Sherlock Holmes.

"I... um..." Luke stammered.

Sam winked, and said "Yes please!" when the waitress came by with the coffee pot.

CHAPTER THREE

The older fairy tales often spoke of beautiful, distressed maidens being rescued by handsome princes atop mighty steeds. As a child, Sam was fond of such tales. She liked to imagine herself in the role of one of those maidens. No matter what danger the princess had found herself in, the prince always showed up just in the nick of time to save the day. But that was when she was a child. Now that she was a young woman of twenty-eight years, she preferred the modern princesses, the ones who rescued themselves. Life had taught her that this was a far more likely scenario. Frogs didn't turn into princes. Princes turned into frogs.

She was quite disappointed in her handling of the bus stop situation. She was *supposed* to rescue herself. She had tried, at least, but failed miserably. However, she was grateful to discover some merit to the fairy tales of old. A prince *actually* showed up. He was a bit scruffier than the fairy tale princes, and technically he didn't really *do* anything, but he did show up.

Two weeks had gone by since the incident, and she was sitting on the passenger side of said prince's truck, pondering her dismissal of those childhood fantasies. Luke, of course, did not possess any royal blood. None that he confessed to, anyway, and none that she suspected. His face had yet to appear on the cover of any of those scandalous tabloid magazines that always littered grocery store checkout racks. Nor did he ride around on any mighty steeds, though his truck did produce a mighty racket. He never bothered to fix the exhaust.

Although it was now Sam's seventh time in Luke's passenger seat, it still tickled her how spotless he kept his truck since the first night she sat in it. She had yet to see another loose coffee cup floating about on the floor or bouncing in the cup holder. In fact, he switched to using a travel mug, like her, and today there had been a second travel mug, brand new, in the cup holder, already filled and waiting for her when she climbed in. She didn't have the heart to tell him that his instant coffee was terrible.

That was the second thing she had noticed, the first was that the bed sheet had been changed since the last time she was with him. During a drive downtown, Luke was forced to slam on his brakes to avoid a reckless pedestrian. The sudden stop sent his coffee, which happened to be between his legs and lidless at the time so it could cool down quicker, all over his lap and seat, and a few not so princely words escaped his lips. He apologized, to her, but not the pedestrian. The pedestrian was treated to a special hand gesture instead. The blue sheet was a green sheet now, and nearly matched the color of her coat. She wondered if that was intentional.

She also wondered what would happen if they kissed. How would he respond if she leaned over and planted one on him at that moment? Would he turn into a frog? That would be most inconvenient, as he was driving, and unless he turned into an *enormous* frog, he'd lose control of the truck and they'd crash into something or roll over into the ditch.

She smiled and pretended she wasn't staring when Luke noticed her looking at him. He smiled back, and nervously adjusted his cap. The greasy blue cap must have been his favorite. He wore it all the time. She tried to imagine the cap as a golden crown, and that led to an image of Sleeping Beauty waking up with oil stains all over her dress.

She *knew* he was interested in her for more than just coffee dates and for those painting lessons that hadn't happened yet. Luke was either shy, or simply taking things painfully slow. She didn't even consider the possibility that he wasn't interested.

A guy isn't going to clean his truck and roll out the green sheets just for some coffee buddy.

As slow as he was moving, she had no expectations of him quickening the pace too much that night, but the skin under her jeans was hairless when she stepped out of his truck and onto his gravel driveway for the first time.

Luke was embarrassed by the state of his property, even though he was continually working to restore it. It took a fair bit of convincing for him to allow Sam to see it in an unfinished state, as if he were afraid she'd run for the hills at the sight of faded paint or sixties wallpaper. Finally, she wore him down and emerged victorious. Tonight, he would cook for her at his house.

"It's fantastic!" she said, surveying the property with her hands on her hips.

"You should get your eyes checked."

Sam shook her head. "Nonsense."

The house was in need of a paint job, yes. Patches of gray peaked out through the flaking white paint just about everywhere, and maybe the staircase leading up to the front entrance looked like a good place to lose a foot, and it would probably be a terrible idea to lean on any part of the railing along the porch that wrapped around the right side of the house, but there were new shingles on the roof, and at least two of the windows appeared to be from this century. It was rough, but Sam could see the finished potential.

The porch had view of a patchy red barn, which also cried for paint. A small pasture lay between the two buildings, though most of the fencing had fallen into disrepair. She imagined how nice it must have been for the previous owner in the warmer seasons to sit on the porch swing, before it became a death trap, with a cup of coffee and look out at the cows or goats or whatever used to graze there.

After maneuvering carefully up the stairs, she found herself in the entryway of the house; a tiny, unheated room with firewood stacked from floor to ceiling against the left and right walls. Luke removed his boots there on an old welcome mat, so she did the same before following him into the house proper.

The words "Oh wow," fell out of her mouth when she saw the fireplace, a great stone sentinel rising up through the roof at the back of the room. An ornately railed switchback staircase to the right of it led up to a second floor balcony and an open door into another section. This was the room with the new windows she had seen from outside, looking out at the barn. It was clearly the main focus of Luke's efforts. The walls and ceiling around the rafters were freshly colored with beige paint, and a chandelier that looked like, or perhaps was, an old wagon wheel shown light down from the center of the ceiling. The room felt enormous with so little furniture to populate it, just a well worn couch in the middle of the room, and an equally used arm chair and end table near the fireplace.

She narrowed her eyes at him. "I don't know why you made such a fuss. This is phenomenal. I love it."

Luke shrugged. "This room is the only one that's finished, really. Well, this and the bathroom. I just finished the bathroom yesterday. The kitchen will be next, I think."

"You're doing great. I mean..." She switched to her best 'unimpressed' voice, "It's passable, anyways."

Luke grinned.

She turned her attention to several precariously high stacks of dusty books in the corner.

"And these?" she asked. "Do you read much?"

"Lately yeah, quite a bit."

She picked one off the top of the closest stack. *A Study In Scarlet.*

"Oh nice. I love the Sherlock Holmes mysteries. I've read them all."

"Awesome," said Luke. "I'm working on them. I have the whole set I think. The house was filled with books when I bought it, though a lot of them were ruined by leaks in the roof. I'll uh, get around to building a book shelf or two for them. Eventually."

"Yes you should," she smirked. "Shelves full of books are a great way to artificially inflate a homeowner's perceived intelligence level."

Luke narrowed his eyes in thought for a moment, than narrowed them further, "Hey, watch it lady."

He shook his head, and failed an attempt to suppress another grin. "I'll get supper started. Feel free to wander, pick through the books, sit, whatever you want. Just watch your step if you go upstairs. It's still pretty wrecked up there. And if you find any pornographic materials in your travels, I swear they aren't mine."

"I'll bet not."

Sam shuffled through a few more of the books before taking the staircase to the second floor. The second floor consisted of a narrow hallway with several barn facing windows and two large bedrooms, both of which were, indeed, *pretty wrecked*. The ceiling had collapsed in each of the rooms, splattering everything with dust and plaster and rat droppings. She found more stacks of books upstairs, though most of them were in rough shape. In the second bedroom, there was a creepy old rocking chair next to a rusty bed frame, facing towards the window. That would have been the first thing Sam threw out. She shivered at the thought of it starting to rock on its own.

The bedroom window offered a view of the forest behind the house, but it was something under a clump of plaster on the rocking chair that caught her eye.

Luke was measuring out the pasta when she entered the kitchen with her prize.

"Find something you like?" he asked.

"I think I found something for your coffee table. When you get a coffee table, that is. It was upstairs."

"Really? I thought everything up there was ruined."

"Not this."

She held the dark leather bound book for him to see. There was no title to suggest its content. It fit in the palm of her hand and looked a bit like one of those classic "Little Black Books" that she'd never actually seen anyone carry. At first she was worried that she might cross the line into snooping if she opened it, but he *did* give her freedom to roam. Luckily, her worries were groundless. There were no names or phone numbers for booty calls inside, just a collection of paintings. A tiny art book of sorts, with some notes on the first page written in a foreign language.

She flipped to the first page to show Luke, and again felt the same peculiar reaction to the paper that she felt upstairs. It tickled her fingertips, and sent a warm sensation down her spine. Old books were normally a joy to flip through, but this was something else.

"What language is that?" Luke asked of the notes scrawled on the page.

"Latin, I think. Not that I can read it, but that's what it looks like. This book is *old,* Luke. The paper feels funny when you touch it, and these paintings..."

She flipped through a few of the next pages.

"These are *actual* paintings. Not prints, but I can't tell what kind of paint that is. And the detail is phenomenal. I'm a bit jealous."

"Hey is that, um, that *Sound of Music* place? Where your grandmother lives? Salzburg?"

"No," she laughed. "My grandmother lives just outside of Salzburg, yes, but there's much more to Salzburg than the *Sound of Music.* It's a beautiful city. Anyway, that's definitely not Salzburg. I can see how you might think it, though. Green domed cathedrals. Castle on the hill. But this castle is different, and Salzburg isn't on the ocean either."

"Ah, right right. And I suppose the buildings in Salzburg aren't all covered in vines and sunflowers."

"Don't think so. Looks like nature took back the city, doesn't it? And there. Look. There are buildings coming up out of the water, like in Venice."

Luke nodded, and shrugged. "Maybe it's just somebody's imagination."

"Could be."

"Oh shit!" Luke cried. "The lid!"

He rushed to remove the cover from the pot on the stove. The water hissed as it boiled over onto the heating element.

"Sorry! I'm distracting you, aren't I?"

"You're a good distraction," he coughed. "No worries. I always forget about the lid."

Sam set the book on the counter.

"Let me help. I like to feel useful. I'll get the sauce ready. Or should I grate the cheese? I don't want you to cut yourself on that cheese grater, Chef Fletcher."

He shot her a spiteful glare, but a few threatening waves of her wooden spoon soon set him to his task without complaint.

The remainder of the cooking went without incident. Plates were heaped up with alfredo drenched penne noodles and chicken, and carried over to the table. It was here that Luke groaned.

There were no chairs at the dinner table.

"I could have planned this a little better, eh? Just a second. I have chairs. They've just been... re-purposed."

He pulled a dusty tarp from over a large lump of something in the corner of the room by the window. Two kitchen chairs sat a brooms length apart, facing away from each other. A wicker broom bridged the chairs together, fastened in place by duct tape.

Sam chuckled. This was where Luke kept his wardrobe. His clothes hung neatly on the broom handle between the chairs.

Luke ripped off the duct tape, tearing away strips of paint from the chairs as he did so, and carried the clothes somewhere in the living room.

Sam smiled and shook her head at the contrast between Luke's careless dismantling of the clothes rack and the courtly way he presented her with a chair.

"What?" he asked. "Is there something on the chair?"

He began swatting his hand back and forth over the seat cushion, brushing away specks of dust.

"No, no. It's fine. Everything is perfect."

She'd never say no to pasta, anyhow, even if it *was* a little mushy.

After the food was devoured and the dishes were drying on the rack, Sam placed her tote bag on the counter. From it, she drew a thin rectangular present, neatly wrapped in red and gold paper, and handed it to Luke.

"For me?" he asked, looking a bit awkward.

"No, it's for the rats," she teased, though the statement wasn't entirely inaccurate. "Yes, it's for you, dummy. But don't open it until Christmas."

"Of course. Thanks Sam. I... Your present is..."

"Not necessary. Really. It's nothing to go crazy over or anything. Just a little thank you for all the gas money you've been wasting on me."

He shook his head. "I haven't wasted anything."

"Are you sure? If you hadn't been wasting so much time with me, these kitchen cupboards might be mounted on the wall instead of sitting on the counter."

"Eh, maybe. Maybe not. I don't have to reach as high this way."

"Okay. If you say so. Who needs counter space anyways, right? What about a bedroom? A twenty-seven year old guy should have a bedroom, don't you think?"

He shrugged. "I don't have a bed to put in the bedroom. The couch does the job."

"Does it?" she asked, raising her eyebrows and smiling imp-ishly at him.

"Yeah it-" he started, but cocked his head when he noticed her expression.

Sure. Maybe she was reaching a little bit with that one, but someone had to make a move.

"It... does?" His confirmation turned into a question. He looked away, blushing. "Um..."

It seemed almost cruel to enjoy watching him squirm like he was, but he deserved a little torment for leaving her hanging the other night after the movies. When he opened the truck door for her in front of her apartment, she stood extra close, and thanked him as sweetly as she could for a "really great evening". She caught him looking at her lips while she spoke. When he leaned in, she puckered, just a little, and closed her eyes, but apparently she hadn't puckered enough because he chickened out and hugged her at the last second. It was a good hug. His hugs were great actually, but she decided she wasn't about to settle for a hug tonight.

He coughed. "It does. Well..." His eyes met hers. "At least I think it does."

"Are you fishing for my opinion?"

"What? No no—"

"Shush," she said, grabbing him by the shirt. "To the couch, Mr. Fletcher. We'll see if it really does *the job*..." To further torment Luke, she added, "of a bed."

It took little effort to drag him into the living room and to the couch. She turned again to face him, still clutching his shirt, and with the slightest tug, fell backwards into the cushions, bringing him down on top of her.

This close, their faces inches apart, made for a difficult hug-ging position. There was no excuse. Luke *had* to.

And he did.

His hands found her cheeks, and he kissed her, lightly on the lips.

Finally.

He pulled back, looking into her eyes, stupidly wondering if kissing her was okay.

She answered him with a smile, and he kissed her again, deeper that time. His fingers curled into her hair and her hands crept around him. She kissed him back, fiercely, eager to satisfy a hunger no pasta ever could. Except maybe that gnocchi she had in Rome. *That* was good. A sensation surged through her, curling her toes. She shivered. Their lips parted.

"We're adults, right?" she asked, tracing her fingers over the muscles of his back.

"Er, sometimes."

"Are we adults right now?"

"Do you wanna be?"

She smiled, and nodded.

He kissed her again, just once on the lips, then her cheek. His breath warmed her neck, before his lips landed beneath her ear. He kissed her there softly, several wonderful, tingly times. Her nails pressed into his back, just a little, but when his lips started on the trail down her neck, her fingers dug deeper with minds of their own. Suddenly the feeling of his back through his shirt wasn't good enough for her. Her hands fell to his waist and tugged up on his shirt, a silent command for him to remove it.

Luke leaned back to obey when a stack of books fell over, and a terrible squeal ripped them from the moment.

They both shouted, "What was that?" but even as the words left their lips, the answer was revealed to them in the form of a gray blur shooting desperately across the room away from a heap of literature. A rat.

They sat upright, like respectable couch sitting people, but with their feet tucked under them. Anxiously, they scanned the room for signs of the rodent. Luke got up and poked around.

"Where did it go?" Sam asked, hoping the answer was "Hell."

His answer was disappointing.

"I don't know. Maybe the kitchen."

She admired his bravery as he went into the kitchen in search of the rat, until the thought struck her that if the rat was still in the living room, she would be alone with it. She curled her knees up into her chest and darted her eyes about, expecting at any second to catch its beady little eyes staring back at her from some dark corner.

Luke offered a defeated shrug when he returned.

"I don't see it anywhere. It's probably gone for the night."

"How do you know that, if you couldn't find it?"

He sat down on the couch next to her. Again he shrugged, "It's more afraid of us than we are of it, Sam."

"Are you sure? That's what they say about everything."

"No-yes! Yes, of course it's scared of us. We're like a hundred times the size of it."

"Yeah I guess. But rats can chew through bones, you know. *I* can't chew through bones."

"Eh, you could probably chew through a rat's bones. They're small."

"That was *not* a small rat."

"I've seen bigger."

"Oh my god. Enough. Not another word. Just shut up and kiss me."

She grabbed him roughly by the back of his neck and practically forced herself on him, anything to prevent further mention of rats.

They were just getting back into the swing of things when an obnoxious tropical bird began squawking in the kitchen, followed by a screeching monkey and a rhythmic string of xylophone beats. As the rhythm increased tempo, so did the number of birds and monkeys.

Sam sighed. This was obviously the perfect time for Luke to hear her ring tone for the first time. She was pleased at least to see him bobbing his head along to it, and when she made him walk ahead of her into the kitchen, he danced the whole way.

She watched him from the doorway, shaking her head, until it seemed the coast was clear. She ran up and smacked his ass before digging her phone from the tote bag.

It was the rental office. That was odd. She had been a day late that month with the rent, but that shouldn't have been enough of a problem to warrant a phone call.

"Hello?" she answered.

"Hi. Samantha Vale?"

"Yes, that's me."

"Great. This is Judith calling from the rental office. Is this a bad time?"

Yeah, kinda!

"No, not at all," she said with little enthusiasm. "What's up?"

"Oh good. Look, I'm sorry for the late notice, but the boss's grandson, Kyle, has started working here."

Sam could almost hear Judith's eyes roll.

"Anyway, apparently he set up a viewing for your apartment tonight without telling anyone. The interested couple just called me. I had no idea."

"Oh really?"

"Yeah. I know. You *are* still looking to sublet, though, are you?"

"Yes, definitely."

"Okay. Good. That's good, at least. Um, the viewing was set up for seven-thirty tonight. A weird time, I know. The husband and wife work opposite schedules, but they were hoping to see it together. I knocked on your door and saw that you weren't home. Is the viewing going to be a problem? Of course I can cancel it if you'd like, or I can just show it to them myself. Whatever is okay with you, Samantha."

On one hand, the situation was a real pain in the ass. Such terrible timing. On the other hand, hope. A surprise viewing, but a viewing. *Finally* a viewing. Somebody to potentially rescue her from the financial ruin she was slipping toward by continuing to rent a much bigger apartment than she needed. She would have been fine with Judith showing the apartment for her, saving her evening with Luke, but there was one small problem.

"Um... Well I'd like to be there actually. I'll come home right away."

"Oh that's great. Again, sorry about this. Very sorry. See you shortly, Samantha."

Sam looked at the time. Shortly was right.

"Great..."

"Is something wrong?" Luke asked.

"No. Well. Sort of. Apparently I have twenty-seven minutes before someone is coming to look at my apartment. It'd be nice to do a quick tidy before they get there. The place is a... disaster. Um..."

He held his hand up dismissively. "No worries. Let's go."

"You're a doll."

Her apartment, of course, was immaculate. She always lived by the logic that it was much easier to keep a place clean with steady maintenance then to have to clean everything all at once in a panic. She was particularly religious with this practice since she began the process to sublet her apartment. The problem was that she had recently gave her vibrator a thorough cleaning, and couldn't remember for certain if she had put it away properly after leaving it out to dry.

CHAPTER FOUR

"Are you sure you wouldn't rather live with me?" Luke asked again.

Again he received no response.

He sighed. *Unbelievable.*

"You'd really rather live out here in the cold? It's freezing out here! You can trust me, really. I'm harmless. Ah, but you don't have any trouble eating the food I buy you, though, do you? Huh? Why not eat that food inside, where it's warm?"

He had been trying off and on for months to lure the creature into his home, with similar promises of food and warmth, but the cat was just not interested. It was a wild thing, with bushy gray fur and a set of eyes that could probably kill a rat with one look. How easily he could sleep with such a predator stalking the shadows of his house at night.

The rats had mostly kept to themselves, not since an incident that occurred on his second week in the house. He had awoke one night to a chihuahua dog crawling up onto his chest to cuddle. It was an adorable moment, *for a moment.* He still had one foot in dreamland, so he was slow to remember that he didn't *have* a chihuahua dog. In fact, he didn't live with any dogs at all.

He wiggled his torso a little, and the rat did the same, but was not discouraged. A few seconds went by, and Luke wiggled again, violently. The rat leaped from his chest and hit the floor running, its little claws scratched furiously for purchase on the slippery hardwood as it moved at a breakneck pace to wherever it disappeared to.

He had closed his eyes and went back to sleep.

Since then, he and the rats had lived in relative peace. He was still annoyed by the noises they made in the walls at night, but rarely did they make an appearance. Their decision to finally reappear during such a critical moment in Luke's love life was the last straw. The rats had to go.

He shook the box of treats one last time. Nothing.

"Well at the very least, don't let any *new* rats find their way to the house, alright? Good. I'll just leave this here."

He sprinkled a few treats into the cat's bowl in the corner of the barn, and went back to the house to set some live traps.

He preferred the catch and release method, as there was nothing pleasant about waking up to the sound of a crippled rat screaming and dragging a trap across the floor in the middle of the night. With Dennis no longer alive and living in his usual dumping spot, he wasn't sure where he would release the rats that he caught, but he would find a place. Perhaps the cemetery where Dennis was buried.

With the traps set, his mind jumped to one of the bedrooms, and his body soon followed.

He had not been upstairs in several months, not since confirming that the roof no longer leaked during the first rainfall after shingling it. The room was still as disastrous as he remembered, with the addition of a few more rat droppings and cob webs. The collapsed ceiling was still scattered about in clumps of plaster and jagged boards that bristled with rusty nails. He picked his steps carefully to avoid cutting himself as he moved about the room with a tape measure and notepad, taking measurements and compiling a list of materials necessary to make it fit to sleep in.

Satisfied with his quick estimate, he started out of the room, but couldn't resist yanking down a section of wallpaper. An easy task, as the hideous wall covering had already begun to separate from the wall, folding down over itself. He tore down another. Then another. Before he knew it, his work boots were on and he was lugging buckets of plaster and arm loads of scrap wood out to a large scrap heap beside the barn. The cat was nowhere to be seen, and neither were the treats.

It was three in the morning when Luke kicked his boots back off in the porch. At that time, all evidence of disarray was displaced from the bedroom. The walls and ceiling were completely stripped to the studs and rafters. Not a speck of dust nor a stray nail could be found. It was ready for reconstruction. If a building supply store had been open at the time, he would have started on that as well.

His feet were pleased that this wasn't the case, as instead Luke changed into his favorite Christmas socks. The alpaca wool was like stepping into a cloud. They seemed particularly appropriate that night, since the first thing he had done after dropping Sam off was pick up a Christmas tree. It was the biggest tree on the lot, though it looked like a table top tree now that it stood near his giant fireplace, by the stairs. He left it naked, thinking Sam might enjoy decorating it more than he would.

He picked up two gifts for her as well, though he cursed himself for forgetting the wrapping paper. Newspaper did the job, and with some pink flagging tape from the dash of his truck he made a crudely tied bow to complete the package.

Luke was happy with his accomplishments that night, but his stomach was not. The grumbling organ drove him to root through his cupboards. Why he never kept snacks on hand was beyond him. That was another thing he added to his mental list of things that might make Sam's visits more comfortable, if the rats hadn't already scared her off for good. He settled on spooning from a jar of peanut butter.

The nameless art book was still sitting on the counter. He brought it with him into the Great Room. When a proper fire was crackling in the fireplace, he plopped down, finally, into his arm chair. He loved sitting close to the fire, warming his feet. His toes wiggled happily inside the woolly clouds.

He shoveled peanut butter into his mouth as he flipped through the book, stopping for a moment on a page portraying a village nestled in the middle of a thick jungle. A monkey sat on one of the thatched roofs, and appeared to have been throwing handfuls of straw down at the homeowner, who had his fist raised in anger to the vandal. Whatever the place was called before didn't matter. Luke renamed it Monkey Village. There were monkeys everywhere in the picture, all engaged in similar mischievous disputes with the human residents.

He chuckled at an unfortunate man leading a lucky donkey through the middle of the village. The donkey was pulling a cart laden with bananas, and, of course, monkeys. Wherever the donkey was going, its load would surely be lighter by the time it arrived.

Lanterns and torches were fixed to poles throughout the village, suggesting a simpler level of technology than the ocean city Sam had shown him earlier. Like the ocean city, this place was peppered with enormous sunflowers growing along and up the sides of the buildings. Clearly the artist had a thing for sunflowers. Most of the villagers were dressed simply in colorful shorts and tank tops, though oddly, one guy was decked out in a three piece suit, slate gray in color, complete with a tie and trilby hat. A monkey hanging from one of the torch poles was reaching out to snatch that hat.

There was a stunning amount of detail in the painting. It looked as near to an actual photograph of a place as you could get.

An equally well crafted image awaited him on the next page. The picture was simply of a forest with a handful of picnic tables in front of it, but he could almost smell the fir trees it was so good. Of course, having an actual fir tree standing a few feet away from him probably had something to do with that. Ominous black clouds swirled above, casting perfectly rendered shadows over the forest and picnic tables. A small wooden sign was pegged into the grass at the edge of the forest. Luke had to squint to read it, but the words drew his lips into a smirk.

THIS WAY DANGER LAY

He sat and chewed away at several more gobs of peanut butter, and made to flip the page again, but paused.

He hadn't noticed the figure at the edge of the forest. A person, standing right beside the danger sign. In fact, the person was leaning right on it, looking into the forest. He rubbed his eyes.

How did I miss that?

The person appeared to be a man, and was wearing faded blue jeans and a brown t-shirt. Luke looked down at his own outfit. He was wearing a brown t-shirt himself, and his jeans, like all of the jeans he owned, were faded. But there was another thing. A far more peculiar thing. He set the peanut butter jar between his legs and leaned close to the fire with the book.

The figure at the edge of the forest was wearing faded blue jeans, a brown t-shirt, and *red and green striped socks.*

CHAPTER FIVE

eg Hunter was a spunky, middle aged blond woman born and raised in Halifax. She spent a year traveling when she was younger and met the "man of her dreams," as she called him, in Mexico. Fernando was that man. He approached her while she was sunbathing on a beach in Puerto Escondido, pushing a wheelbarrow full of questionable tacos. She took a chance on one of those tacos, and took a chance on Fernando. Now she was Meg Rodriguez, and their second child was in the oven, though she had yet to show.

Sam couldn't have been beaver dammed by a nicer family.

The viewing was a success. Sam would be free from the financial burden of a lonely three bedroom apartment at the end of the month. The other two bedrooms had emptied one after the other as her roommates ventured out with their boyfriends. Vanessa was the last to leave, three months ago. Sam had expressed to the office her desire to sublet the apartment immediately after Vanessa's departure, but until Meg and Fernando and their little boy David came along, there had been no biters.

Not only did they agree to take over the lease, they purchased a few of her paintings to boot.

To celebrate, it felt appropriate to share a few bottles of Corona with Fernando. For the preggo, however, she fixed some tea. They spent the night talking and laughing. Meg's travel adventures were particularly striking. Sam had done a little traveling herself throughout Europe, but never had she experienced anything like a midnight ride through a mountainous jungle on the back of a pickup truck, or ate a chicken quesadilla in a dirt floor restaurant with a live chicken sitting at the table across from her.

As she lay in bed that night, a nagging desire to experience her own such adventure kept her awake. Perhaps it was time. Her current employment was not exactly gainful, but that made it expendable. She could quit her job and go traveling for months, maybe even a year, and easily find a similar paying job when she returned. That was the plus side of having nothing. Having nothing to lose. Maybe she wouldn't return at all. Meg had worked on farms for room and board to support her travels. There was no reason Sam couldn't do the same.

Yes. A grand adventure would be great, but then there was Luke. What would he think of something like that? Would he want to come along? He was already a step ahead of her by being off work. She fell asleep imagining him doing the farm work for their accommodation while she watched him sweat from a shaded hammock.

Sam awoke bright and early the next morning, with a disposition as sunny as the day itself. It was one of those false spring days that showed up at random in Nova Scotia. These conditions could occur on any day at all between the first snowfall and the last.

She showered and made herself a coffee to go, and then thought to make another, for Luke. He had probably already had one by now, but Sam's coffee machine was far superior to his primitive instant coffee setup. She wanted him wide awake for a second, more definitive couch inspection. Rats were less active in the daylight. She hoped.

A short bus ride brought her close to Luke's house, and within ten minutes her feet were crunching up his gravel driveway. She knocked on his front door, and idly prodded at the spongy deck boards with her foot for several moments while waiting. He didn't answer, so she knocked again. Still nothing. His truck was in the driveway. He couldn't be too far.

She peeked through one of the porch windows into the living room. The lights were on, and a naked Christmas tree stood near the bottom of the staircase with her gift to Luke beneath it. She smiled. He couldn't have been too upset about her untimely departure last night, though she still couldn't spot him.

Maybe he's in the bathroom.

It was terribly awkward to be caught on the toilet when company arrived, but she tried the door anyways. It was unlocked. Luke's work boots, the only footwear he seemed to own, were in the wood room.

"Hello?" she called from the great room entrance.

Nothing.

He wasn't in the kitchen either, or dead on the toilet. Thankfully.

There was no trace of him upstairs, or of anything at all in one of the bedrooms. No mess on the floor, no creepy old rocking chairs, even the walls and ceiling were stripped of plaster. She stood for a moment, shaking her head in awe. Luke had a busy night. She knew he was content to sleep on the couch in the living room. The expedited bedroom renovation was clearly inspired by her chastising. But where was he now?

She found two presents marked for her on the end table by Luke's arm chair, crudely wrapped in newspaper, but prettied up with some pink ribbon.

A very busy night, she thought as she placed the presents under the tree. His cell phone was charging on the table behind the presents, so calling him was out of the question. Even his hat lay on the table. Rarely had she seen him take it off.

In a moment borne of silly temptation, she pulled off her poofball hat and stuffed it in her tote bag, and popped Luke's hat onto her own head, backwards. Then she took a pouty selfie with her phone to send Luke at a later date. If someone were to ask why, she'd have no answer.

Sam shook her head at her own foolishness. Unsure what else to do, she decided to make herself comfortable while Luke was out doing whatever he was doing. She attempted to make a fire, stacking a couple logs on some paper and kindling, but was unable to find matches or a lighter. She shrugged. The electric heat was on anyhow.

She saw the art book sitting in the arm chair, and decided to sit and peruse it. The page Luke had left open showed some picnic tables and a moonlit forest beneath a blanket of beautifully painted stars. She just couldn't get over the artist's skill level. The stars *really* glowed. Though for all the artist's skill, one of the trees looked a bit... off. A small tree on the edge of the forest, next to a sign that read THIS WAY DANGER LAY.

She studied the tree closer. It wasn't a tree at all. It was a woman in an olive green jacket and a navy blue ball cap, worn backwards, looking away and up at the trees.

Sam laughed.

"Luke," she said aloud.

He did this, and he left it here for me to see. But the hat...

While she didn't entirely agree with defiling someone's artwork, the book was technically his now. He could draw in it whatever he liked. Or maybe it actually was *his* collection of paintings. The painting of her was no stick figure, though. If he painted that, there would certainly be no need of her giving him painting lessons, unless, of course, the intention was as she said, an excuse to see her again.

She smiled.

And then her chair was *gone.*

CHAPTER SIX

The first thing Luke did when his chair slipped out from under him was the only thing he could do; brace his ass for collision with the hardwood floor. Oddly, the impact was a fair bit softer and a great deal *wetter* than he expected. He landed with a loud splash.

The mysterious water source retaliated immediately, soaking through the fabric of his jeans and launching a chilly assault on his boxer shorts. Luke responded with a fury of colorful language that lasted until a sudden sickness scrambled his expletives.

He was hurling out the contents of his stomach when the lights came back on.

The light did not come from his new light fixture, or from the lamp on his end table. It couldn't have, because his lamp and end table were gone, and his new light fixture had been replaced. Sunlight did the job, filtered dimly down through a threatening mass of black clouds above. His entire house had disappeared.

He was kneeling in a puddle, in front of a forest that only a moment ago was his fireplace.

Bewildered, Luke staggered up out of the puddle and to his feet. He stood there, wobbling in wonder for some time. Not only was his house nowhere to be seen, he didn't appear to be anywhere near where the house should be. For one thing, there was no sign of snow anywhere, and the air, while damp, was not at all cold. He found that he was as comfortable as a person with wet socks and underwear could be.

As he looked from the forest to the clouds in the sky, a thought occurred to him.

This looks exactly like the scene from that book. Rain clouds and all.

He relaxed then, realizing it was just a dream. A lucid dream, but certainly a dream. Many times he had nodded off in that same chair and entered into the realm of whatever novel he was reading at the time. One such time, he had dreamed himself into the gruel lineup just ahead of Oliver Twist, and, after tasting the stuff, had very nearly tossed his own bowl of gruel into the trash, had his ears not picked up on little Oliver pleading with the master for more. When the master growled for the boy to repeat his request, Luke waved the master away, took Oliver aside and happily placed his bowl of horrid slop into Oliver's more appreciative hands.

The peanut butter jar Luke had been snacking from, and the spoon, had followed him into the dream world. By luck, or just dream magic, it had landed favorably beside the puddle, and not in it. Its golden brown contents remained unsaturated. His stomach was far too queasy at the moment to think about eating, but he was never one to litter, a dream was no excuse. So he squeezed the jar and spoon into his back pocket.

He wished there had been a caption to go with the picture in the book. Something to give him some idea as to where he was supposed to be or what he could expect to happen to him while he was there. The forest near to the front of him stretched as far to the left and right as he could see, and behind him was a dirt road. Beyond the road was a rocky field playing buffer to yet another long stretch of trees. The road was marred with potholes and peculiarly narrow wheel ruts. From dirt bikes, perhaps. Why couldn't he have dreamed of the monkey village instead? That would have been far more interesting than a cluster of picnic tables in the middle of nowhere.

That was as far as Luke got with his investigation when a loud bang nearly caused him to wet the *front* of his boxer shorts. A second clap of thunder boomed, and the dark clouds overhead burst all at once into a sudden downpour. In an instant, he was entirely drenched and running madly for the shelter of the trees, *until he wasn't.*

His foot snagged something, and another furious rainbow of language exploded from his lips, but guttered out just as quickly as his face fell into a sloppy mud hole. The rain beat down on him, as if trying to suffocate him in the mud, and the mud itself was maliciously eager to keep him there. It made loud sucking noises in protest as he clawed his way out, spitting dirt and curses everywhere.

He won the battle, making it to the shelter of the trees, but he lost his socks. He frowned through the veil of rain, towards the red and green tops of his socks which were sticking up out of the mud. The mud could keep them for now. He wasn't going back out in that.

The forest canopy slowed the torrential bombardment to a mere pelting of tiny chilling missiles. Luke moved further in, from tree to tree, seeking to determine which one made the best umbrella.

What a lovely dream, he thought. Each time one of his feet found a sharp stick or rock at the wrong angle, he missed his thick socks just a little more. Long gone were the summers of his childhood where he'd happily run barefoot in the yard, the fields, and the streets. His feet complained more these days.

A particularly snappy pine cone startled a nearby rabbit, which in turn startled Luke, as it skittered and crashed recklessly through the underbrush to the safety of its den. This ruckus heralded his presence to the forest's avian residents, which was not an ear pleasing welcome, as the birds sounded nearly exclusively to be blue jays. A horrendous cacophony ensued. The blue jays flapped from branch to branch overhead, stopping each time to screech wildly, at each other, at him, and everything else. Hopefully the element of surprise would not be important in this dream.

It was easy to forgive the rabbit for triggering the noisy jays, however, after noticing a heavily weighted raspberry patch along its escape route. Queasy or not, Luke took it upon himself to ease the burden of those thorny branches. The berries worked wonders in dispelling the taste of vomit from his mouth.

Blue jays were nice enough looking birds, he thought as he gorged himself. A small consolation for being loud and obnoxious. He held a handful of berries out for the birds to see, and tossed them out into an opening. In answer, several jays began their downward swoop before the berries even landed. An easy meal outweighed any concerns they might have had as to whether or not he was a danger.

Luke smiled at this, and entertained himself this way for several minutes. A few berries for the birds, a fistful of berries for himself. The dream was improving.

A squirrel burst onto the scene to protest this feeding, quickly knocking the jays out of the top spot for noisiest creature in the forest. It chittered and chattered furiously as it darted amongst the birds, its tail snapping and vibrating. Luke tossed some berries to the squirrel as well, but the squirrel was adamant that the berries thrown to the birds were the better berries, and snatched as many from them as it could before the jays rallied and chased it back up into the trees.

Sometime during this dinner theater, the rain had stopped. For the sake of his toes, he made his way back to the forest edge for his socks, only to find there was no forest edge. The forest kept going and going. He hadn't ventured far into the forest, surely he couldn't have gotten turned around. After several minutes of walking, however, he came upon another berry patch. Curiously, it looked identical to the last one, complete with naked branches and blue jays hopping about nearby. Maybe he did get turned around somehow.

Impossible.

To be sure, he turned and headed away from the bush, making a conscious effort to travel perfectly straight, until he came across the berry bush again. He hung his head and sighed.

"Ah. It's one of *those* dreams, then," he said aloud, apparently to the blue jays. They looked at him with tilted heads.

No socks for him. An inconvenience, but there was nothing to be done about it. He'd just have to pick his way more carefully through the forest, and eventually he would wake up with his socks back on his feet. It was as simple as that.

He passed the bush several more times without waking up. On the fourth or fifth pass he began to feel as if the trees were growing closer around him. At about the tenth pass, he was sure of it.

Naturally, around that time, dense, knee-high snakes of fog began weaving through the trees, pulling another sigh from Luke. It added an element of creepiness to the whole thing, but even more so, it furthered the element of frustration, as it made it harder to avoid stepping on things he'd rather not step on, like sharp sticks and rocks, and animal droppings.

As he walked, the screeching of the jays faded into low squawks before eventually giving way entirely to the wind that whispered through the leaves, and Luke's occasional cursing when something stabbed his feet. His cursing grew more and more frequent as the gathering trees squeezed out the light, and soon the trees were squeezing him as well, their dark skeletal fingers scratched and grabbed. When an overly lusty tree branch drew a nasty red line across his tricep, he turned back in frustration.

Again he found what was behind him was not behind him any longer. When he turned, he saw the same villainous branch that attacked him, marked by his blood dripping from one of its fingers. He found the same image on his left. And his right. Every direction was the same now in this terrible forest.

He grabbed the bloody branch and snapped it off as far back as he could.

"Time to wake up now!" he yelled into the darkness. He snapped another branch, and another, stubbornly tearing his way onward. Hopefully toward his precious arm chair.

The trees sent a fir cone bouncing off his head in defense, but he barely acknowledged it. He continued his push forward until another cone hit his head, followed by an acorn. Then a dozen acorns.

"What the—"

Luke looked up just in time to avoid another hail of acorns and fir cones. A dark creature dropped more projectiles as it moved swiftly through the trees above. He squinted to see it better, but it was the spastic chittering which blasted from it next that marked it clearly as a squirrel.

"Ahh. Still upset about those jays, eh?" he called up to it, grinning.

The squirrel hammered back a few rapid retorts and disappeared, leaving him in peace as suddenly as it had appeared.

After a moment, Luke shook his head, and reached to break another branch when a loud snap drew his attention to his right. Dry leaves crackled and brush rustled violently. Something was coming toward him, and fast. He swallowed hard. There was nowhere to go, so he braced himself.

Being *his* dream, any manner of creature could be barreling through the forest towards him. Anything, from a bear, to a werewolf, to a raptor, or even a getaway car driven by the eleven year old boy that accompanied Indiana Jones to the Temple of Doom.

Oh please let it be Short Round!

Luke's surprise was complete when it was not an antique convertible that crashed through the brush in front of him, but the same angry gray squirrel from earlier. It immediately began peppering him with acorns.

Luke swatted as many aside as he could, laughing.

"You little shit! You had me worried for a moment."

Several acorns caught him in the forehead.

"Where are you even getting those things?? I don't see any oak trees."

The squirrel chattered and squeaked fiercely, standing defiant on its hind legs. In an instant, the creature passed between Luke's legs, and before he could turn around, it had already returned to where it was.

"What do you want? This can't still be about the jays."

The squirrel was again on its hind legs, looking up at Luke and chattering. It hopped on and off his foot several times before heading back a short distance ahead of him. Then it turned and squeaked loudly and bounded out of sight.

Luke eyed the squirrel curiously as it reappeared and disappeared several more times before stopping to verbally assault him some more.

"What are you doing?"

When he approached the squirrel, it stopped squeaking, hopped off the trail, and again back onto the trail. Luke stopped walking and scratched his head.

The squirrel immediately started chattering again.

"Okay! What? Do you want me to follow you or something? After all this-"

He dodged another acorn.

"After all this hostility?"

The furry creature *nodded* and gave a single sharp squeak.

This conjured up the memory of a drunk fisherman at a bar telling Luke a questionable story about how a chipmunk once led him and his cousin to a berry patch when they were lost and starving on a failed hunting trip in Newfoundland. Apparently, they had been starving for several days before this chipmunk got their attention and led them to the berries. Luke also recalled the man mentioning that his cousin shot and ate their unfortunate hero. Luckily, for the sake of said chipmunk, the legitimacy of this story was greatly diminished when the fisherman followed it up with some *braggadocio* about his involvement in a threesome with two A-list celebrities.

Regardless, Luke saw nothing to lose by taking a chance on the squirrel. Every way was the same way, after all. At least he'd have company.

After a few moments of the bushy tailed guide leading the way, the trees seemed less eager to swallow him up. It wasn't long before the path widened considerably, and even more surprising, the dirt and roots beneath his feet gave way to flat cobble stones. They were rough and cool, a joy to traverse compared to the poky forest floor.

The squirrel double squeaked.

"Yes," said Luke, "I agree. Very odd."

As they rounded a bend, the path further ahead was illuminated by a pulsing golden glow. The glow led them into a large clearing. There, the sunlight was blocked completely by a tightly woven web of branches above, like a football huddle where the players were enormous and each had a hundred arms, yet the area was bathed in golden light from an army of fist sized fireflies and clusters of glowing mushrooms.

In the center of the clearing was a wide trunked tree, thick enough that four Luke's could link arms around it. Its limbs fanned out above it in a perfect sphere without touching the ceiling or sides of the grove, as if it rested in a natural grand cathedral grown specifically for it. There were no leaves to be seen, but the rough bark was dotted with shiny blue gems, and dozens of golden apples dangled here and there from the branches. The apples glowed and pulsed, much like the fireflies.

Forbidden fruit, if he ever saw any.

The atmosphere seemed like a fitting place to eat one of those glowing mushrooms. The only thing missing was the pounding rave music.

Also scattered throughout the grove, almost as numerous as the mushrooms, were tiny houses with mossy peaked roofs, built with twigs. They had little doors and little windows, and some of them were even illuminated with a cozy amber glow, as if some tiny person were inside warming themselves by a fire.

Those persons turned out to be fireflies, casually floating in and out through the doors or windows.

"What kind of rabbit hole have you taken me down, squirrel?"

The squirrel offered no explanation.

While focused on the light show around him, he nearly took a tumble when he caught his foot on a dark object. It was a large, vintage looking backpack with button up compartments. A quick inspection revealed it to be stocked for camping. A bedroll was strapped to the bottom of it, and some cooking utensils and two rock hard sticks of bread wrapped in cloth occupied the main compartment.

No thanks, he thought, tossing the bread aside.

The left side compartment held an empty water canteen, and the right contained a little drawstring purse half filled with what looked like squished pennies. One side featured the head of a rabbit with upright ears, the other a bearded man with a crown who looked nothing like Queen Elisabeth II.

He looked around, half expecting the owner of the suspiciously convenient equipment to finish shitting behind the tree and throttle him for going through his things, but saw only the fireflies floating around and the squirrel perched on one of the tree branches, checking its reflection in one of the apples.

He shrugged and added his peanut butter jar to the pack's main compartment and slipped his arms through the straps. It was a nice backpack. No sense in leaving it behind.

What's this now?

Beneath the pack was a partially buried glass bottle. Luke pulled it free and went to work rubbing off the caked on dirt with his thumb. There was a roll of paper inside. He tried without success to remove the cork before simply smashing it open on a rock.

The paper contained a strange combination of letters that seemed like gibberish to him. He held the paper up for his furry guide to see. The squirrel was watching him with its head cocked to one side.

"Maybe *you* understand this, Mr. Squirrel."

He read the words aloud, if words were what they actually were, several times. Each time trying to work the pronunciation into something intelligible. In the end, he shook his head and stuffed the note into his pocket.

The squirrel made no efforts to translate the words. Instead, it hopped out of the tree, chirped at him, and bounced off toward another cobblestone pathway, visible on the opposite side of the clearing. It waited at the mouth of the trail until Luke began to follow.

"Right," he said. "I guess we're doing the 'follow me' thing again, are we?"

As before, the squirrel *nodded.*

Luke sighed and took one last look at the glowing apples before leaving the grove.

The sun melted into a range of mountains beyond the forest, painting the sky a fiery red. Gray wisps of clouds made it look as if the mountains were burning. Sunsets always seemed more beautiful after a good rainfall, and the grassy hilltop where Luke stood made a perfect view point. He was glad to be out of the strange forest in time to see it.

He was glad to be out of forest, *period*, though his concern was growing as to whether or not he was going to wake up from the dream.

While pondering that issue, he opened his new backpack to see what other goodies he might have missed earlier before the sunlight left him. He was pulling out the utensils when the mysterious squirrel came bounding up the hill toward him. It stopped just a few feet away and stood on its hind legs, its head cocked.

"Ah! You're back!" said Luke. "I have no idea what your game is, squirrel, but thanks for your help back there. And believe me when I say I have no intentions of eating you."

"Well, I'm certainly glad to hear *that,* my boy! I dare say it would not be a pleasant experience. For either of us. I'd imagine myself to be a bit gamy, wouldn't you think?"

Luke's mouth fell open. He took a step backward, and the rest of him fell as well, backwards over his backpack. A deep pain spread over the back of his head, and his vision began fading quickly to black. The last few seconds of his consciousness were spent questioning the reality of this encounter, before he succumbed to his undeniably real encounter with a chunk of rock.

Chapter Seven

When Sam's vision returned, she was staring at the partially digested remains of her egg and cheese breakfast bagel. Damp grass crept through the fabric of her jeans and chilled her knees.

"What..." she gasped, wiping a string of vomit from her chin. "What just happened?"

A thousand crickets chirped in response from hiding places throughout the tall grass around her, though the deafening chorus did nothing to shed light on what happened to make her lose her breakfast, or *why* she was suddenly surrounded by tall grass and crickets. Beyond the grass, an unexplained forest rose up toward a dark sky filled with twinkling stars, more stars than she had ever seen. Beautiful, sure, but not only was she outside and not in Luke's living room, she'd lost an entire day in the blink of an eye. That could never be a good thing.

She closed her eyes and took several deep breaths, hoping the war inside her stomach would sort itself out. Flipping back through the pages of her mind for an explanation, her thoughts landed on Luke. It was his house she was trespassing in after all. Did he come home and fly into a rage at the sight of her in his favorite chair, shoot a blow dart full of some crazy fast acting poison into her neck, and dump her body in the field behind his house?

She frowned. That was a bit far fetched. If he were to get upset about anything, it would be for desecrating his sacred hat. The hat, however, remained on her head. He'd probably have taken it if he was behind all of this.

Meg and Fernando, perhaps? She had split the four Corona that her last roommate left behind with Fernando, but the couple seemed far too sweet to want to drug her. Maybe that was their game. No. That's just those stupid serial killer documentaries creeping in again. Even if they had somehow managed to drug her, surely the effects would have worn off before she even reached Luke's. That was last night, and she had woken up safe and sound in her own bed. Super *slow* acting poison?

She shook her head. It wasn't them. Far more likely of a culprit was the well tanned blonde that served her coffee at Tim Hortons. Her eyebrows were just a little too perfect and her teeth far too white. She was clearly up to no good.

Sam sighed.

No, that was yesterday.

She made her own coffee and breakfast that morning.

Her eyes widened.

The trees. The impossibly real looking stars painted in the book Luke had left open on the chair. She looked around for the sign she had seen in the picture, when the twang of a guitar, followed by gentle applause, stole her attention. Someone said something in a language that sounded like Spanish, and the guitarist began plucking a tune.

Fernando?

She turned to see a light further along the forest face, featuring a flickering projection of a silhouette holding a guitar. Was Luke having a campfire? With Fernando and Megan? Did he know them? A building blocked her view of the answer. It wasn't Luke's house though, or his barn. Some sort of travel trailer was parked between her and the fire.

Another matter was how *warm* the night air was. It was much too warm for her wool coat. Soon she'd be sweating. The false spring morning had turned into a hot summer night. The snow that fell a few days ago was gone, melted away completely throughout the day.

While she was undoing the buttons on her coat, the shadow guitarist suddenly disappeared, swallowed by a larger shadow. The screen went black momentarily as a figure emerged from around the trailer, blocking the light. The figure stepped toward Sam.

"Luke?" she asked, but her throat was dry from vomiting. Her voice came out too low, and the figure appeared not to hear.

The figure continued its advance. It was about the right height to be Luke, but she couldn't immediately make out any features. By the time the moonlight revealed the figure as a shirtless man she had never seen before, she saw too that he was fiddling with his belt buckle.

Sam swallowed hard to clear her throat, and yelled, "Hey!!" as the man's pants fell to his ankles.

The guitar stopped.

Her mind flashed back to the bus stop. Her face twisted in anger.

Not this time, asshole.

Sam moved from her kneeling position to a seated one, and wound her leg back to strike.

"Any closer and that dick's going up inside you!" she promised.

She would have kept that promise, but the man didn't come closer. He went sideways, moaning and stumbling into the side of the trailer. He bent down to grab the top of his pants in what might have been an attempt to pull them back up. Instead, he tumbled forward, landing face first in the grass just inches from her.

Though he had *technically* come closer, all desire to geld the man faded when he raised his head from the grass to look at her. His dark eyes were wide and fearful. She relaxed her leg.

"Don't... kick. My... apologeesh" the man slurred. One whiff of his breath was enough to tell he was wasted.

"Where didjoo... I juss wanted to..." His face flopped back down. "Piss."

Sam frowned.

"Charming."

She racked her brain, but was certain she didn't know the man, nor the short, silver haired woman who came around the trailer next.

"What's going on here?" the woman demanded.

Perhaps it was another side affect of whatever happened to her, but the woman appeared to be wearing some sort of monk's robe, hooded and flowing down to her ankles. It was emerald green in color, matching her eyes and the football sized gem on top of her walking stick. The cherry on top of this witchy hallucination was the light by which Sam was able to see her so clearly. It was not from a flashlight, but from a *torch*. She held an actual flaming stick in her hand, and Sam could feel the heat from it when she came close.

And then she felt the butt of the walking stick pushing against her chest.

"Well, go on then. Explain yourself. Who are you and what do you want?"

Sam pushed the stick aside, rose to her feet and poked a demanding finger back at the old woman.

"How 'bout *you* tell me who *you* are, and what I'm doing here?"

The old woman glared at her. She glared back, her hands on her hips. After a few long seconds, the old woman laughed.

"Fine, fine. Have it your way, princess. I care not. I'm Sophie, and what you are doing here is standing over the body of my Gerald. Would you care to tell me why? Or is that also a secret?"

They both looked at the shirtless man, who was still face down in the grass with his pants around his ankles.

"I didn't do—" Sam started.

"Get up, Gerald!"

Sophie jabbed the man in the back several times with her stick, until she sparked a sign of life. He grunted, but did not move.

"I didn't do anything to him. I swear."

"Oh? So you expect me to believe he just walked back here and fell over all by himself? And you just happened to be here when he did so, I suppose?"

"Well. Yes, I do. Because that's exactly what happened."

Sophie raised an eyebrow.

"It's the truth!" Sam insisted. "A strange truth, I'll admit. But the truth, nonetheless."

The old woman looked her over, as if Sam's outfit might speak some hidden secret her mouth refused to tell, or perhaps she just liked her coat. The whole thing could easily be seen as suspicious, but was that a flicker of amusement in the old woman's eyes? Before Sam could say anything else, a crowd of people came around to investigate the situation.

The crowd stopped behind Sophie and addressed her in Spanish. Yes, it was definitely Spanish, yet none of them looked like Meg or Fernando. Sophie laughed and replied, also in Spanish, and waved her staff dismissively.

The newcomers walked straight off the pages of a National Geographic magazine. The women, around their thirties, wore beautifully patterned dresses of red, green, and yellow, and wrapped their shoulders or heads in equally colorful shawls. The men were more or less ordinary, though a couple of them sported ponchos and straw hats, and dark bushy mustaches.

Sam smiled sheepishly at them, and to Sophie, she said, "You have to believe me. He—"

Are those swords?

Resting casually on the hips of several of the men, and one of the women, were indeed swords.

No. They were machetes. Not as pointy. *Still sharp though.* The blades shimmered in the torch light.

Sophie followed Sam's wide eyes and laughed.

"Fear not, princess. Gaian's carry those things everywhere. They use them for everything. Francesca even uses the damn things to shave her legs."

The woman with the machete on her hip laughed and said in prettily accented English, "You really must learn to shout before barging into tents that don't belong to you, Sophie."

Sophie waved the comment aside, and said to Sam, "I used to change her diapers, you know. Please, relax, princess. Of course I believe you. Look how drunk he is. It's a wonder he made it back here at all. By the Gods, get up Gerald!"

This time she rolled Gerald over, pushing him with her stick. After a bout of incoherent mumbling, he rose to his feet, steady as a tall tree in a hurricane.

"Ah-hem," coughed Sophie.

Gerald looked at Sophie, confused, prompting Sophie to poke her stick at the pants puddled around his feet. The crowd laughed.

"Ahh!" he cried, bending to pull them up. He very nearly fell again, and would have, had Sam not grabbed and braced him upright.

"Thank you, miss."

Sam smiled and apologized for frightening him. "Really, I don't know how I got here."

"Then you must be even more pickled than he is," said Sophie, sniffing at Sam. "Please tell me you at least know your name."

"Of course. I'm not drunk. My name's Samantha. Or Sam if you like."

"Well, that's a start. And a relief. I was worried your name might have something to do with chili peppers."

Sam narrowed her eyes. "Chili— Oh." She was wearing her Red Hot Chili Peppers shirt under her coat, but it was still an odd thing to assume.

"People are naming their children crazier and crazier names every day," Sophie continued. "But enough of this lurking in the shadows. We have a perfectly good fire blazing on the other side of the wagon. Come sit. You're a little late for supper, but there's always plenty of wine. Good wine too, I might add. Nothing like that spittle they brew in Atlantis. Perhaps a few sips will jog your memory."

Before Sam could reply, a little girl with a large green bow tied in her blond hair pushed her way through the crowd.

She was shouting, "Yes! Yes! Oh *please* say you'll join us, princess! Please! You can sit next to me!"

Her arms jingled as she tugged on Sam's sleeve. It seemed as if the girl had recently discovered her mother's jewelry box and decided to wear *all* of it. She must have been wearing twenty necklaces, and at least a dozen bracelets on each arm.

"Young lady!" gasped Sophie, turning the girl around with her stick. "What did I tell you?"

"You told me to go into the wagon and stay there until you said it was safe."

"Oh good. You *did* hear me. I was worried you'd gone deaf. So, *why* are you not where I told you to be?"

"I *was* in the wagon, listening from the window. That one right there. And I heard you say she was a *princess.* So it's safe. A princess wouldn't hurt us." She turned back to Sam. "Right, princess?"

Sam laughed. "Right!"

The old woman groaned. "How foolish I am to forget that no creature alive has bigger ears than a child. At least when it comes to things they *want* to hear."

The little girl didn't hear her. She took Sam's sleeve again and led her through the crowd.

"I'll show you to your seat, princess."

Sam's seat was on the edge of one of four picnic table benches, placed around a crackling fire. The little girl introduced herself as Lia, and sat as close to Sam as she possibly could. Her blue eyes sparkled with reverence up at the visiting monarch.

The full light of the campfire revealed the travel trailer to be more of a tiny home on wheels than any typical travel trailer Sam had ever seen. It was fashioned in a style reminiscent of the old Romani wagons. The wheels themselves were wooden, rimmed with steel, and in place of a tongue for a truck, there were two long poles sticking out from under the balcony in front. Sam guessed these fastened to the powerful looking horses tethered nearby.

Behind her were several homemade looking tents, as well as another wagon, longer but with just a skeletal frame on top, the siding only skirted up the bottom few feet with rough planks. The front quarter was mounded up with sacks and other baggage.

When everyone had settled, Sophie, seated on the bench opposite Sam, shook her head at the sight of Lia cuddled up so quickly to a stranger, and said, "Right then, *princess...*"

Lia's entire body perked up at that.

"You've met Gerald and I, and little Lia. This smooth legged creature next to me is my old friend Francesca. Well, a younger version of an old friend, I should say. I used to chum with her mother. You heard me say I used to change her diapers, didn't you?"

Francesca rolled her brown eyes and sighed, but a smile spread across her face by the time she acknowledged Sam.

"Hola," she said, crossing one smooth leg over the other.

"Hola!" repeated Sam, excited to put her cartoon network language studies to use.

"Encantada de conocerte!" said Francesca, bowing her head.

Shit. Had she known better, she'd have gotten a quick Spanish lesson from Meg and Fernando when she had the chance. "Ummm..."

Sophie chuckled. "She said she likes to eat children. Enchanted by the very thought, she is."

Lia gasped.

Francesca slapped Sophie's shoulder. "Yo no dije eso! I didn't say that, Samantha. I said it's nice to meet you. Don't listen to this old *bruja.*"

Sophie shrugged. "I must be a bit rusty," she said, grinning. "Francesca and her band of wannabe sewage workers are also, like you, princess, surprise guests around our fire tonight.

That's what we get for stopping at one of these *traditional resting places*. Last one between here and Atlantis. *They*, however, had the courtesy to announce themselves when they arrived."

Sam offered her palms up helplessly.

Did she say Atlantis?

Francesca took over the introduction duties as it pertained to her party, and Sam listened and *hola*'d in the direction of the owner of each name as it rang out.

"The others don't speak a word of Arthurian." Sophie explained. "Though I'm sure they'll at least know the word *shit* well enough by the end of their adventure."

"Sophie!" cried Lia.

The Spanish crowd laughed. It seemed they already knew that one, actually.

Sophie mumbled an apology to the little girl for her profanity.

"The Tumblestone district is dealing with a major drainage problem in the sewers," said Francesca. "Things are backed up real bad. The citizens have resorted to the old ways."

When Francesca noticed Sam's questioning gaze, she added, "Chamber pots," with a chuckle. "Of course, they don't want to deal with it themselves. So the call was put out to outsource the job. We're answering the call. If you're looking for work, the more hands the better. Likely, it'll only be for a few weeks, but we'll be asking a handsome fee from the city for our services. They'll pay it too."

"Oh, no thank you," said Sam. "I already have a job." She couldn't imagine a woman as beautiful as Francesca crawling around in a sewer.

"No hay problema. Just an offer."

"It's a shame I can't speak your language. Really," Sam lamented. "There's a language book that's just been sitting on my bookshelf since I bought it. I only know a few words and phrases, and some questions I won't understand the answers to. But... You said something about Arthurian? I've never heard of any Arthurian language."

Sophie laughed. "Well, you speak it quite well for someone who's never heard of it. So let's see. You know your name, you know that you can't speak Gaian, but what else? Do you remember anything before Gerald's hairy legs addled your brain?"

"I remember... I remember going into Luke's house. The door was unlocked, but he wasn't there. I looked everywhere and still couldn't find him. Finally I gave up and sat down in his chair by the fireplace, thinking I'd just wait for him to come back from wherever he was. There was a book laying open on the chair. I had to pick it up before I could sit down."

"Hmm." Sophie scratched her chin. "What kind of book?"

"Well, it was more like somebody's personal art portfolio. A little book of paintings. Landscape portraits. They were done so well it was almost like looking at a photograph. Earlier, I was thinking that maybe that book had something to do with me being here. There was a picture of, well, *this*." She waved her arm to encompass her surroundings. The picnic tables. The forest.

"Ah. Interesting. Very interesting. Mystery solved then."

"I know, right? It doesn't make any sense to me either. Wait. You're serious. How? What do you mean?"

"Your Luke is a wizard, obviously."

Lia squealed happily and squeezed Sam's arm. Her eyes were as big as wagon wheels. The others, who had been chatting amongst themselves in their own language, seemed to understand at least one more of the last words Sophie said. All at once they stopped talking and fixed their eyes on Sam.

"A wizard?" she laughed. "That would be great! But I'm pretty sure he's just a carpenter."

'Wizards can be carpenters. A carpenter would benefit greatly from the use of magic. It would certainly help with the heavy lifting."

"He'd probably love that, yes. But I'm *sure* he's not a wizard."

"Then *you* are a witch?" asked Sophie. A particularly odd accusation coming from a robed woman with an enormous gem fixed to the top of her walking stick.

Lia's grip tightened on Sam's arm hard enough that she had to pat the girl on the wrist to calm her before she tore her arm off.

"I'm definitely not a witch."

"Well, unless there is someone else involved, you're a witch, or he's a wizard."

"I'm not a witch. Luke is not a wizard. Harry Potter is *not* real. That stuff doesn't exist."

"Harry Potter? Is this Harry person the one who sent you here?"

"No!"

"Relax, princess. Do I look like I have a problem with witches and wizards?"

Sophie plucked at the fabric of her robes.

"She's a bit of a fan," added Francesca.

"You don't have to tell me," said Sophie. "But if you don't, I'll just assume what I will. Either way, I have no trouble with keeping secrets."

This last statement was punctuated by Lia, who pinched her fingers together and pulled them across her lips in a zip-shut motion. She beamed at Sam.

Sam sighed. "I'm not worried about that. I just don't understand. I *must* be on drugs. I have to be. Maybe that old book had some intoxicating mold growing in the pages somewhere."

Sophie chuckled. "Well there's certainly a few screws loose up there, we can agree on that. Oh my, how could I forget? Hold on a second."

She reached into the crate beside her, and after some clinking of glass on glass, she produced a wine bottle.

"I promised you wine. We can't have a proper fireside discussion about drugs and teleportation without alcohol."

She popped the cork and passed Sam the bottle labeled *Summerfall Select* before digging out an identical bottle for herself.

The label promised strawberries, and her tongue begged to confirm the truth of it. Strawberry wine was lovely, but still...

"I don't know... Thank you for this. But I have no idea where I am, or how I got here. Drinking is probably not the best idea."

Sophie twisted the cap off her own bottle and shrugged. "Suit yourself. You're probably correct. But if you change your mind, try not to drink yourself into Gerald's state. I can't be held responsible for any hangovers or whatever acts of indecent exposure you may commit."

Gerald, who was curled up in the grass beside them, groaned in protest.

Sam chuckled, and pinched her lips in thought. Although she couldn't understand most of the people gathered around the fire, they seemed friendly enough. Everyone was sipping and chatting with bright smiles on their faces, and when Sam made eye contact with one of the Spanish men, his smile reached his eyes.

Screw it. Lia would never allow harm to come to her princess. She'd just drink a little, anyhow.

It had a slight kick, but the wine went down smooth. There were indeed strawberries. More remarkably, it settled her stomach.

Sophie nodded approvingly, and clinked her bottle to Sam's.

"Cheers," she said.

Sam sipped in silent thought for several moments, searching her mind for the lost memories of her day, until her eyes fell on the wooden sign posted at the edge of the forest. It was too far away to read.

"That's the sign," she mumbled. "The sign from the picture..."

"What was that?" asked Sophie. "You'll have to speak up."

"You jumped pretty quickly to the idea of me... appearing here. Let's say that were possible."

"It is."

"Right. Sure. I'll humor you in that, but isn't it a tad more likely that I blacked out from mold spores and wandered here in a drunken stupor? Maybe the picture I saw in the book awoke within me some subconscious memory of a place I didn't know I knew, or something like that."

"It might have been so, had you been here when we arrived earlier today. I might be old, but I'm not blind. You weren't here, and you didn't arrive with the Gaians." Sophie took a sip of wine. "A starry eyed stowaway in a nice coat like *that* could hardly go unnoticed. I should have the name of your tailor."

Sam smiled. "You like it? I got it from H&M actually."

"Who?"

"Never mind. Well, perhaps I snuck up on you after dark?"

"In my experience, people under the influence make for poor sneaks."

She cast an amused glance at Gerald, who seemed to be asleep already.

"A fair point, I guess." Sam took another long pull from the bottle. It was good wine. Too good. "The forest then. I came through the forest."

"Uh-uh!" Lia piped in. "Sophie says the forest is haunted!"

THIS WAY DANGER LAY. That's what the sign said.

"Haunted?" Sam laughed. "Right. Sure it is. Why would you decide to camp right next to a forest that you think is haunted? Shouldn't that bother you? Just a little? I'd be shitting myself."

"Please don't," said Sophie. "There's no danger to us, so long as we don't go *into* the forest. People have been stopping here for decades. Centuries, perhaps. Nothing has ever come out of the forest, and that's really the only issue. If you go in, you don't come out. Simple as that. So, we'll stay out."

Sam frowned. It looked like an ordinary forest. Maybe a *bit* creepy, but that was to be expected of any forest in the dark. "Um. *Why?* What's in there?"

"The trees eat people," said Lia, simply.

"Really?"

"Probably," said Sophie. "Nobody knows really, because nobody has ever returned after entering. To be honest, I'm not too keen on staying here myself, but I'm content just knowing that we won't be set upon by deathwings in the middle of the night. We spotted a flock of them flying around the Twins on the way here, you see. They wouldn't dare swoop near this forest. Things in the wild have a sense for such things. So this is the safest place for us. Only thing we have to worry about here is lost princesses, it seems."

Sam shook her head. "*Death wings??*"

"It's true. They're not just in Gaia anymore. Must have built a nest in the mountains. Some folks claim they've seen raptors too, but I have my doubts. Most don't see a raptor until it's too late."

"But raptors hate fire!" added Lia.

"Yes, that's right." Sophie agreed. "We'll keep a fire all night. Better to be safe than torn to shreds, wouldn't you say?"

"Er, yeah. Sure. Raptors..."

"Don't worry, princess. We'll keep you safe!" Lia promised.

Sam took another smash of wine. And then another. The bottle was already half empty. Her head was starting to swim.

"Thank you, Lia. Thank you."

Another sip.

"Raptors, witches and Mexicans. And *Death Wings*... What an *interesting* evening this is!"

"What's a Mexican?" asked Sophie.

"Oh dear."

She took several more deep sips, and sighed, "Okay. Let's just forget how I got here, and all that other stuff. Tell me, really. Where are we? Are we still near Timberlea?"

"Never heard of it," said Sophie. "So I would say no. We're probably not *near* Timberlea. The cursed forest there is called Morningwood. Not much else of note around here at all, really, but we're about a day's travel from the Tumblestone district of Atlantis."

Sam narrowed her eyes. Her lips tightened, suppressing a laugh. *Morning wood. Atlantis.* She looked the old woman over. She didn't look obviously related, but maybe she was Luke's grandmother or something. Or maybe she was just some old friend of his he'd got to play a joke on her. It's possible that Luke owned more land than she thought and his house was just on the other side of the trees. The forest being cursed would be a good way to keep her from passing through and spoiling the joke. But the blackout. She couldn't imagine him drugging her or knocking her out for any reason, let alone a silly prank.

She smirked. "Are you really talking about the Lost City of Atlantis? The one that supposedly sunk beneath the ocean? If it even existed at all."

Sophie and Francesca looked at her like she was crazy.

"Of course it exists," said Sophie. "I've been there many times. It's the capital city of the region."

"I've been there too!" chimed Lia. She tugged at one of her bracelets, a blue and gold beaded one. "I got this in the market."

"I've been there as well," said Francesca. "But I don't have any pretty souvenirs to prove it."

"You see, princess?" said Sophie. "It's far from lost, unlike you. Hmm. Part of it *did* sink. I'll give you some credit for that. But that was a long, long time ago. The city has been rebuilt for at least a thousand years."

Sam tipped her bottle back for several swallows, then wiped her lips, laughing. "I bet it has. You guys are great. Really. But seriously, this is ridiculous."

The old woman shrugged. "We're heading there in the morning. You're welcome to come with us if you want to see for yourself."

"Oh yes!" Lia tugged her sleeve. "Please come with us. You'll love Atlantis."

"I don't know about that," said Sophie. "There are nicer places."

A thought struck Sam then. Her phone could tell her exactly where she was, without the jokes. She patted her pockets. Finding nothing, she remembered her phone was still in her tote bag. Maybe it was back where Gerald found her. She also needed to pee. Two birds with one stone.

"If I'm still here in the morning, sure. Why not?" she said. "But if you'll excuse me. I need to use the ladies room."

"By all means," said Sophie. "Here, take a torch."

The old woman ignited a torch by dipping it in the campfire, and handed it to Sam. She accepted the flaming stick with some reluctance. It was hot. Much too hot for someone wearing a winter coat, even with it held at arm's length. She picked each step carefully from the campfire to the area between the forest and the wagon where she had awoken, scared of what might happen if she tripped and dropped the thing in the tall grass.

With the torch, however, she easily found her tote bag lying in the grass. She had more difficulty finding her phone amongst all the junk she kept in the bag. The bag was a little damp, but not yet soaked through. It couldn't have been there that long. Finally, she found her phone. Luke hadn't even responded to the message she sent that morning. That was odd. He was always quick to respond.

Had he not been home yet? None of this made any sense. She started to type a follow up message, questioning him about her current predicament when she noticed her phone had no signal. Her clock had also gone slow. It still showed 10:13 in the morning.

She heaved a heavy sigh, and planted the torch in the soft earth, well away from where she decided to do her *business*. When she finished, she returned to the campfire with her mind made up to begin walking in the direction of the city. Halifax, Atlantis, whatever they wanted to call it. Eventually she'd get signal, and make Luke come find her. It was the best plan she could think of after drinking a bottle of wine.

"Don't be foolish," Sophie scolded. "We can take you to the city in the morning. You won't make it anywhere worthwhile on foot at this hour. And didn't you hear me mention the deathwings?"

"And raptors!" cried Lia.

Francesca agreed with Sophie, but Sam remained adamant. Raptors only existed in museums, and deathwings weren't even a thing. There was no telling them that, but it didn't matter. Eventually, Sophie relented.

"You're free to do as you wish," she said. "At least try to stay out of the forest. I can't help you if you go in there, but we can pick you up in the morning if you stay on the road. If you're not picked off by then, that is."

Sam declined a torch. The moon was bright enough to see the rutted trail that would supposedly led her to the city. It was likely a poor choice, but she did, however, nod vigorously when a second bottle of wine was offered to her for the road. Apparently, Sophie owned a large winery in a place called Summerfall Valley. Wherever that was. She had an entire crate of the stuff, so Sam didn't doubt the truth of it. She *did* have doubts as to whether the forest was actually cursed. Being told not to go into the forest was almost enough to make her want to go in anyways, but cursed or not, she didn't want to stumble blindly through it in the dark.

She didn't make it beyond the flickering glow of the campfire. Before she could step into the darkness, little Lia caught up with her and pulled on her coat to turn her around, her face full of worry.

"You can't go, princess. You can't. I won't let you. It's not safe. You're just not thinking right because of Sophie's wine. It makes people dumb."

Lia's bracelets shook and jingled as she tugged pleadingly on Sam's wrist.

"Oh, Lia. It's sweet of you to worry about me, but I'll be fine. There's nothing to worry about." Sam crouched to wrap the little girl in a goodbye hug, and pried herself from her grasp. "You just enjoy your evening."

She turned again to leave. A strange tingling sensation rippled down Sam's spine, all the way to her toes, when Lia whimpered. She shivered. There was no wind, and the air was too warm for cold chills. Perhaps it was just the wine.

She made it two steps before bumping into *nothing,* though she bounced back as if she had hit a rubber wall.

"What the-" She reached out with her hand. There was nothing but air, to the eye, but she could feel a solid elasticity as she tried to push forward. The air pushed back.

At the same time, there was a gasp behind her, and the fire dimmed. Sam turned to see the fire nearly guttered out before flickering back to life, then guttered out again. Lia stood stiff with her hands squeezed into tight fists at her sides. Moonlight shimmered in her sad blue eyes, her lips pouted. She wasn't moving, but her jewelry was vibrating noisily in pulsing bursts. The bursts seemed to match the rise and fall of the campfire.

The Spanish group was gasping and chattering excitedly. Sophie said something that calmed them, and started in Sam's direction.

"It's alright, It's alright," she said. "Lia, enough."

Lia exhaled. Sam felt another tingle in her spine, and the girl's jewelry stopped jingling. The fire returned to normal. She suspected the invisible wall had disappeared as well.

Magic? Really?

"I'm sorry, princess," whispered Lia. She looked at her shoes. "You can leave if you really want to."

If the girl was able to do something like *that*, what else was she capable of? And maybe there really was something special about that book in Luke's house. She might very well be far beyond walking distance to anywhere familiar.

In light of this, Sam twisted the cap off of her wine bottle. If she wasn't in Kansas anymore, Lia might be her ticket home. "You know what, Lia. I think I'll stay." Best to stay on her good side.

Lia squealed and flung her arms around Sam's waist, and promptly collapsed.

"Lia!" Sam cried, spilling the neck of her wine in a desperate bid to catch the little girl before she hit the ground. Her tiny form was as limp as a rag doll.

"Is she..." Sam shot a horrified look at Sophie, before pressing her face closer to Lia's chest. "No. She's..."

Lia's chest rose. When it fell seconds later, her lips emitted a soft purring sound.

Sam smiled incredulously. "Snoring. She's asleep."

Sophie nodded. "Yes. Magic takes too much out of her. I suspect with better control, she wouldn't exhaust herself so much. Are you sure you aren't a witch, princess? The girl needs a teacher, and I'm willing to pay."

Sam laughed, quietly, as to not disturb the sleeping child. She shook her head. Perhaps she had given up on her teaching degree too early. She missed the parts on magic instruction.

CHAPTER EIGHT

The air was electric with chitter and chatter. A massive army, perhaps hundreds of thousands in number, of noisy gray squirrels marched on the hilltop from all sides. There was no direction Luke could take where he wouldn't have to wade through a sea of bushy tails. Every second brought hundreds more, pouring from the forest in an endless wave.

A curious blue jay glided overhead and stirred the mass into a frenzy. The bird was promptly brought down in a hail of acorns. It crashed, beak first, into the grass between Luke and the squirrels. Dead.

What the hell is going on here??

In response to Luke's thought, a single squirrel emerged from the horde and issued an earsplitting chirp. It looked identical to the others, but the silence that followed its command marked it clearly as the leader.

Perched proudly atop the luckless blue jay, the leader raised a paw to the sky and barked another command. This command produced thousands of ominous *click-clack* sounds as each squirrel armed itself with two acorns.

"Hey! Wait a minute!" Luke yelled, but the barrage came anyway.

The sky went black with acorns.

His arms shot forward in defense. To his surprise, he sent forth a barrage of his own.

Leaves?

In a blink, Luke was on his back with outstretched arms, reaching up at a clear blue sky. Oak leaves danced and fell around and on him. He blew one away from his mouth. All was silent.

Just a ridiculous dream.

He rolled onto his side and scraped some leaves together to make himself a pillow. His eyes pleaded to stay shut.

Five more minutes.

Fifteen minutes or so later, Luke's body informed his brain that he was not at home on his couch, nor in his arm chair. His eyes snapped open, and he sat up almost as quickly. Too quickly, cursing himself with a dash of vertigo.

He was just dizzy enough that from his seated position he saw two squirrels seated atop his new backpack. He tried rubbing his eyes back to normal, but only partially succeeded. One squirrel remained seated on his backpack, waving excitedly at him.

"At last! You're awake, my dear boy. How *are* you feeling?" came the words quite evidently from the squirrel's moving mouth.

Luke glanced around to be sure. There was no one else. When his own mouth proved unable to function, the squirrel continued in a sophisticated accent.

"Of course, of course. Take your time, lad. Let the brain warm up a bit. I must say you had me quite worried after you took that little tumble. Still breathing I noticed. No traces of blood, but it was not until the snores began that I felt truly assured of your survival."

Where am I? Why is a squirrel talking to me? How can I understand it? What the hell is going on?

These were the questions in his mind, but all he managed to spit out was a pained groan. Thinking paired poorly with the throbbing lump on the back of his head.

"Truly you're a most fortunate individual! Yes, very lucky indeed. Must be a horseshoe hidden somewhere up that bottom of yours!"

Luke stared incredulously at the impossible creature.

The squirrel's oil drop eyes sparkled right back at him. It chuckled. "I suppose you're not feeling very lucky then, are you? Everything is relative, my boy. The alternate scenario, and sadly the one I'd grown accustomed to, would have had me digging your grave right about now. I'm quite tickled that that's not the case. I was running out of places to put the bodies."

Luke's eyes narrowed. "Bodies?"

"He speaks! Fantastic! And oh yes. Bodies! *So many bodies!* Probably hundreds of them over the years. The forest is full of them. Do you have any idea how long it takes to bury a body such as yours *without* magic? With paws *this* size? Days, my boy. Days! Granted, I could always let nature take its course, but a pile of skeletons scattered about around the base of that novarius tree would have been a little foreboding for future guests, wouldn't you say? Not to mention the havoc they wreak on the feng shui of the place. Ah, and the worst part, because I've buried so many, for so many years, imagine my frustration when I'm digging for one of my acorn stashes and, 'Ohh what's *this* now? A pelvis? How lovely!' No! Not lovely at all. So as I've mentioned, relatively, this is a wonderful day for the both of us!"

"Right. Yes. Just wonderful. Where am I? How are you talking right now? And... wait a minute. What was that about burying me?"

"Ah! Questions, questions. The mind begins to stir. Excellent. To answer your first question, we are on a hill..."

The squirrel looked around until it found the sun. "Just east of Morningwood."

Luke grinned. "Morning wood? Really?" The squirrel was definitely a product of *his* imagination. Maybe there was still hope that it was all a dream.

"Indeed! Congratulations are in order. You're the first person ever to conquer the mysterious Morningwood."

"Ha! I doubt that. I imagine there's probably thousands of people who *conquer* it every day. This moment even."

The squirrel looked to the forest, and then cocked its head curiously at Luke, eyebrows raised. *Do squirrels even have eyebrows?* This one certainly did. Bushy ones, a few shades darker than the gray of its coat.

"No. No, I don't believe so," said the squirrel. "I'd certainly know about it."

Luke couldn't resist the urge to sing, "*He sees you when you're sleeping. He knows when you're awake...*" He laughed. "A dream within a dream within a dream?"

The squirrel's black eyes narrowed. If it had pupils, they blended seamlessly.

"Hmm. Ridiculous assertions. Hysteria. Are you feeling alright? Perhaps that tumble did more of a number on you than I thought. Do you have brain damage?"

"Probably had that for a long time. It's fine. Don't worry about it."

"As you wish, my boy, but please, lay back down and rest if you need to. There's no shame in it. I will happily watch over you."

It was a tempting offer, but Luke replied, "I'll keep that in mind if I start to question my sanity..."

"Excellent. Now, as to your second question, the one regarding my speaking abilities. I'm afraid my answer will be a poor one. I must admit to a lack of knowledge on the technical specifics of the function. Anatomy has never been a strong subject for me, though I can confidently say it has something to do with vocal cords and the opening and closing of the mouth. That's the best I can offer. Oh, and I suppose the tongue plays an important role in articulation as well."

Luke sighed. "Good enough."

The squirrel bowed his head. "Question number three, then. The burying you thing. You didn't die, so there was no need to bury you. Simple as that. Well, I did bury you in leaves, I suppose. But only to hide you from predators."

Luke had wondered where the leaves had come from, but it was a small wonder compared to the presence of a talking squirrel. There were no trees on the hill. The squirrel had been busy.

"Um, thank you," he said.

"Think nothing of it, my boy. It was the least I could do, really."

"Okay. So... I didn't die. That's... good, but... there was a *chance* that I could have?"

"Oh far more than a chance. *Everyone* who came before you is feeding the forest these days."

"Feeding the forest?"

"Dead and buried. Nutrients for the soil."

"Right. Of course. But how? Starvation? Suicide? Did *you* kill them?"

"None of that. Everyone goes straight for the apples. Foolish creatures. Gold and shiny has long been a bane of mankind. Gets them every time. Ah, but not this time, and not you!"

"Ah," Luke nodded. The apples had looked suspicious. "So the apples were like, poisonous or something?"

"Oh no. The apples themselves are perfectly safe. It's the faeries one has to watch out for. They've taken it upon themselves to protect the Novarius, and have proven to be quite adept at it. I have to commend them, really, for the tree is one of the last, if not *the* last of its kind. The last one to still produce apples, that is. Though sometimes I feel the faeries are a little too vigilant in their duty. Any action at all taken towards their beloved tree is viewed as an assault. Countless people have attempted to pick the apples, but I've seen one unfortunate lad swarmed simply because he happened into the grove just as the tree itself decided its branches were too heavy. An apple dropped and so did he. Another time, an elderly chap made the fatal mistake of resting his back against the trunk. There were many similar occurrences, but they are trivial now. Not your problem. I'll just say simply that all of your predecessors may as well have been swinging axes and torches in the eyes of the faeries."

"Faeries? What faeries?"

"Surely you saw them." The squirrel waved a paw back and forth. "How's your vision? There were hundreds of them floating about by the tree, and not exactly camouflaged."

"You mean the fireflies?"

"If fireflies are what you call the littlest of the Fae folk, then yes. The fireflies."

"But faeries..." He shook his head. They couldn't be *faeries*. "Fireflies are harmless. What could they possibly do to someone?"

The squirrel chuckled. "Harmless indeed. Everything is harmless until it wishes to harm you. Have you ever touched a hot stove, my boy?"

"I have, actually. Yes."

"It hurt, didn't it? And you pulled your hand back as quick as anything, yes?"

"Yes and yes."

"Well, now imagine touching a hot stove and *not* having the option of pulling your hand away. And then imagine the stove exploding into tiny pieces, and all those tiny pieces flew at you, and embedded themselves into every inch of your skin. Right through your clothes, even, with no hope of removing them."

The squirrel closed its eyes and placed a paw on its chest. "They always died screaming. Always. Poor souls."

After a few seconds of respectful silence on the squirrel's part, and a few seconds of mortified silence on Luke's part, the squirrel sighed, opened its eyes, and threw its paws akimbo.

"Ah, but some of them deserved it. Some really *did* bring axes and torches. It was quick, at least. Never more than five or ten seconds."

A frown soured Luke's face. "Hold on a second. So you figured that I would have went for one of those apples, or touched the tree just like everybody else?"

"Yes. I was certain of it. I was quite surprised when you didn't. *Pleasantly* surprised, I might add."

"*You,*" said Luke, pointing an accusing finger at the squirrel, "You led me to that tree! You led me there assuming I would be, what, burned alive?"

The squirrel scratched its chin. "When you put it so plainly, I do sound a bit monstrous, don't I?"

"A bit! A bit more than a bit, I'd say."

"A fair observation, boy, from your perspective, but really, in that forest *all* ways lead to the novarius. Inevitably, you would have stumbled into the grove on your own, possibly a far wearier version of yourself. The forest would have taken you there on its own. I merely expedited the process. At the very least, I certainly cannot be accused of goading you into picking the forbidden fruit. Your fate was entirely in your own hands, and you performed admirably!"

Luke sighed.

"Please," the squirrel continued. "Let's not dwell on this talk of death. Goodness me! All this prattling away, and we haven't even introduced ourselves yet! You must forgive me. It has been so very long since I've been able to chat with anyone. It's quite lovely, really. I'm enjoying it."

The squirrel gave an exaggerated, low sweeping bow, motioning as if removing an imaginary hat from his head and extended his little arm high towards Luke.

"My name is Henry. Surname, the Squirrel. Yes. Henry the Squirrel. That will serve. And whom do I have the great pleasure of not having to bury on this fine day?"

Henry the Squirrel awaited his reply with bright, eager eyes, but for a long moment Luke could do nothing more than blink in response to the furry creature. It had a name now. Suddenly, it, *he,* became more real. The squirrel was patient for a time, then grunted as if to clear his throat, and finally began to whistle. The *squirrel* was whistling. A nice melody, too. Finally, Luke shook out a response.

"I'm Luke. Luke Fletcher. Um. Yeah. Nice to meet you... Henry."

I've completely lost my mind.

With any luck, in a moment or two he would wake up in his arm chair, take a shower, and head to Tim Hortons or Mary's for breakfast. This would all be nothing more than a long and ridiculous dream within a dream within a dream. Something he and Sam could share a laugh over. His throbbing head argued that he would not likely be so lucky.

"A fine name," said Henry, hopping down from the backpack. "Luke Fletcher, Master of Morningwood. The bards will *sing.*"

Luke was too taken aback to properly respond to such a title, so he just smiled.

"Last evening, Master Fletcher, before you took your tumble, you honored me with praise for guiding you out of the forest, but truly I should be the grateful one, and of course I am. It was *you* who freed the pair of us from that woodland prison. You fetched the keys, so to speak."

"And how did I do that, exactly?"

"With magic, my dear boy! Could you not feel it? Back there in the grove, that wonderful, tingling sensation in the tip of your tail."

"I don't have a tail."

"Oh yes. My apologies. Your finger tips, perhaps?"

"No? Should I have felt something?"

"Hmm. Well, perhaps not. If you felt nothing, the magic must have been distributed remotely through the scroll itself, with no need of channeling through the orator. Ahh. Never too old to learn something new!"

"What are you talking about? What scroll?"

Then it came to him.

"That paper in the bottle?"

"Yes, that's it," Henry nodded. "Thank the Gods the scroll was not a picky one. That was the clumsiest rendition of a spell I've ever heard, but it worked."

"I didn't notice anything."

"Well, not every spell is accompanied by a light show. Most magic is quite subtle. Had you not tucked the scroll into your trousers so quickly, you might have watched the words fade away before your eyes. If you check the scroll again, I think you'll find the message rather boring."

Luke fished the crumpled paper from his pocket and inspected both sides.

"You're right. There's nothing on it."

Henry nodded. "This indicates its magic has been spent. And powerful magic it was, to dispel a curse such as the one over Morningwood. The enchanter of that scroll poured a lot of sweat and blood into it. Particularly the latter."

"If it was that simple, how come *you* didn't just read it and free yourself?"

"If it *was* that simple, my boy, I surely would have. For one, nobody ever told me there was a bottle with the means to my release inside the forest. Mind you, I did find the bottle shortly after I arrived, but try as I might, I could not break or open the thing to get at its contents. I never knew what was inside. Twice even, I carried the bottle to the tallest tree in the forest and dropped it onto a boulder, to no avail. Not even a crack! And even if I had succeeded, there is also the small matter of squirrels not being able to conduct magic of any kind. I can feel it, but I can't do anything with it."

The last statement seemed to dampen the squirrel's spirit. He sighed.

"So I guess I got lucky then, huh?" said Luke.

"Indeed, we both *got lucky*. Or perhaps it was fate that brought us together, my dear Luke. I think we get on quite naturally, wouldn't you say? As if it were meant to be."

Luke smiled, "Sure. About as naturally as a man and a talking squirrel can *get on*. Are there, um, are there more of you? You know, talking animals."

"Well, all animals talk, of course, in their own way. Some of them far too much, like those terrible screeching blue jays. They see a leaf fall and they have to squawk about it to each other for thirty minutes."

Luke figured the squirrel had more in common with those blue jays then he realized.

Henry continued, "Ah, but you are asking if there are others who speak Arthurian, like us. I've personally never met one, but it's been awhile since I've been free to roam. Anything is possible, I suppose."

"I see. I think. And you were imprisoned within the forest?"

The squirrel nodded sadly.

"What for? Were you caught raiding someone's pantry? Or am I now responsible for releasing a demon of some sort on the poor unsuspecting people of..."

Luke stood up, slowly, careful not to dizzy himself, and gazed beyond the squirrel, upon the entirely unfamiliar scenery around him.

"Of wherever the hell I am."

He shook his head in disbelief. There was no sign of civilization in sight.

From left to right, the landscape was dominated by varying shades of green, bright rolling hills of grass, smudged here and there with darker patches of forest. The only snow to be seen was far off on the peaks of mountains that chewed at the skyline.

"Mountains?" he wondered aloud. Looking around, he spied more of the same. To where he guessed was the south, based on the sunset from the day before, there were actually two towering twin mountains within walking distance. Suspiciously large birds circled their peaks.

There was nothing in Nova Scotia that Luke would consider a mountain. Nothing of any great size, anyway. None of it was familiar. Not even a little bit.

He was startled then, when Henry leaped onto his back and scampered up onto his shoulder to share the view.

The squirrel chuckled. "I like that bit with the pantry. That may have happened once or twice, but I assure you, Master Luke, I'm no demon."

"I'll take your word for it, Henry. But I have another question. This one is very important. Very."

"My boy, I'm entirely at your service. I owe you a tremendous debt. Questions are a pittance. Ask me anything."

"Thank you. Is there anywhere to get a coffee around here? A Tim Hortons, maybe? They're usually everywhere."

Surely the beautiful virgin landscape surrounding him could withstand a big red logo or two without significant sacrifice. Unfortunately, he could see nothing of the sort. Nothing but hills and trees and grass and mountains and rivers. Hideous, coffee-less nature.

This hill would be a perfect location for a coffee shop. What a view.

"I'm sure coffee can be procured, but might I ask who Tim Hortons is? A friend of yours?"

"No no. He was a hockey player. Been dead for awhile now. Started a coffee shop franchise."

"Amazing! I haven't the slightest idea what a hockey player is, but do you really trust the dead to handle your beverages?

All sorts of nasty afflictions have been known to fall upon those who poke around old corpses."

"Eh... I'm pretty sure he's not physically involved in the business anymore. Hey! Do you see that?"

"Oh my! Indeed I do."

Over the crest of one of the hills, in the direction of the twin mountains, appeared a white mass, speeding toward them, before disappearing again down the hill. Before long, the mass appeared again atop a nearer hill, easier to see but still difficult to identify. Luke's heart began to race, his stomach turned. It was not until he heard a loud "Baaaaa!" that his breaths came easier.

The rushing mass was a herd of fluffy white sheep, an odd but harmless sight. And then Henry deflated his sense of calm with logic.

"What's got them so spooked, I wonder?" The squirrel had to say.

What indeed.

The answer came swiftly in the form of a large dark object torpedoing up onto the scene from behind the first hill. It looked like a missile at first, hurtling upwards and then downwards on a direct collision course with the sheep. Just before impact, the missile exploded open into the shape of an enormous bird, its wings spread wide to slow itself before snatching an unfortunate sheep from the herd. The bleating grew pitifully frantic as the bird beat its wings, powerfully thrusting itself back up into the sky.

Luke's mouth hung open. He looked to the peaks of the mountains where he saw the birds circling earlier. He confirmed they were the same. More of them were swooping down toward the herd.

"Ah yes. Those. I forgot about those," said the squirrel. "Blue Jays don't seem quite so terrible now, do they, Luke?"

"What the hell are those things?" he asked.

"Deathwings," answered the squirrel in a manner far too casual for someone speaking of something called a *deathwing*.

"Of course they are…"

In no time at all, the skies were filled with deathwings, many clutching a bleating prize.

"Nasty creatures, to be sure, but the sheep should keep them busy."

Luke wasn't so sure. There were still plenty of the creatures flying around without a meal. He shooed the squirrel off his shoulder long enough to don the backpack.

He cursed under his breath. One of the airborne goats managed to squirm free from its predator, and would have surely plummeted to its death had it not been scooped up by another of the deathwings. Luke would have preferred the fall.

"I feel like I'm in a movie or something, and not the kind I'd want to be in. A talking squirrel? Sure, why not? Beautiful scenery and wild sheep? Right on. Giant killer birds snatching up those sheep? Not so much. No thanks."

"Deathwings are classified as reptiles, actually," said Henry.

"Oh well that changes every— Hey! What happened to '*the sheep should keep them busy*'?"

The deathwing that lost its meal had targeted a new one. *Him.* It was coming right for him.

"The key word there was 'should'," said the squirrel. "The key word now is *run*. Run, my boy! Run!"

Luke was already running down the hill towards Morningwood.

"Not that way! The other way!" barked the squirrel. "We don't want to get trapped in there again."

"Dammit. Fine."

He began in the opposite direction, towards a different forest, and glanced over his shoulder. His eyes bulged. At that moment he realized without any doubt that deathwings were *fast*. He was screwed.

"Get away from me, Henry. There's no sense in it catching both of us."

The squirrel, now on Luke's head, answered by curling all four of his paws into Luke's hair.

It was not long before his pace slackened, his heart threatening to beat itself right out of his chest. If only he could run as fast as his heart was beating. Why did he bother with the stupid backpack? Maybe he wouldn't have gotten winded so fast. The forest was just too far. He looked back again to see the deathwing lower its taloned feet to snatch him. It looked a lot like a pterodactyl.

"Dive!" cried Henry.

Luke dove. He flung himself to the ground and felt a rush of air as the creature passed over him. *Yes!* He scrambled to get back on his feet, but there was another deathwing on him in an instant. It dug its talons into his backpack and the earth began to move away from him.

Luke cursed and the deathwing shrieked, beating its leathery wings furiously. Luke was heavier than a sheep. The deathwing struggled to gain altitude. He tried desperately to free himself from the straps, but to no avail.

Henry abandoned his grip on Luke's hair then. At least the squirrel would be safe, he thought, but he didn't see the squirrel drop back to the earth.

Henry's shout sounded from above. "Unhand him you foul beast!"

The deathwing's shriek cut the air. It wobbled, then dipped slightly, sending Luke's stomach into a whirl.

Another shriek. Another wobble.

Luke closed his eyes.

A blue jay, perched on the end of an oak limb, heard the shrieking loud and clear, and knew the dangerous creature associated with it. The rest of his flock had already flown to a safer location, but he was a curious bird, and clever. He knew the predator was too big to fly amongst the dense web of branches in the forest. He would simply drop to a lower branch if it came too close.

The fearless jay watched the larger bird approach the forest. It was bobbing and swerving, flying sloppily and shrieking wildly. It sank lower and lower, but the jay was sure it would miss his oak, so he remained.

His surprise was absolute when he saw that the unfortunate earthbound creature clutched in its talons was not the source of the predator's malfunction. Not the main source, anyhow. As the predator flashed by overhead, the jay glimpsed a thick bushy tail.

His beak fell open.

The thick bushy tail was attached to a squirrel, and the squirrel was attached to the giant bird's face, clawing and scratching with intense violence.

The giant bird crashed heavily into a fir, impaling itself on a stubborn branch. It thrashed and screeched, and then fell silent.

The blue jay took a shit then. Not out of fear, but out of casual necessity. He knew the predator was dead. He would, however, think twice before engaging in anymore disputes with squirrels.

He flew off then, to spend the next half hour or so describing the scene to his family and comrades.

CHAPTER NINE

S am had never been in a desert before, but she imagined a
camel would feel right at home inside her dry and aching
head. It was pleasant to think of camels. She'd seen them on
television, with their handsome faces and noble humps. *They*
spat in the face of dehydration, while she, unfortunately, could
not spit at all, even if she wanted to. Could camels get hangovers? If the answer were no, she would want nothing more at
that particular moment than to be a camel.

Pleasant thoughts did little to dull the consequences of the
previous night's stupidity. She deeply regretted that second bottle of wine. *I'll just drink a little,* she remembered thinking. It
wasn't her fault that the wine went down as easily as juice. Now
it threatened to come back up as the rickety wagon bounced and
rolled along beneath her.

Her new companions were veterans of such actions, it
seemed. The sun itself had barely woke when Sophie and Gerald
hitched up the horses and set the wooden wheels, and Sam's
stomach, into motion. Sam rose long enough to shake her head

at the idea that the group was heading to *Atlantis* before crashing back into Sophie's bed. The old woman insisted on upgrading Sam from her previous nest of blankets on the floor when she and Gerald left the wagon's cabin to drive the horses. It felt like sinking into a cloud, and she said so, but Sophie claimed to have made the mattress herself from chicken and duck feathers.

"Clouds are harder to catch than chickens," she said.

Sam wasn't sure exactly how long she slept after that, but without opening her eyes she could feel the sun's warm rays shining bright through the little cabin windows. Too bright. Her eyes begged to stay hidden for just a few more hours, and she aimed to comply. With a groan, she rolled onto her opposite side, but the decision would not be hers to make.

Her groan signaled the end of her peaceful stay in bed.

A rustling and jingling began on the other side of the cabin, and grew louder until its source stopped, right beside her bed. There was no surprise when she opened her eyes to find Lia, the bedazzled seven year old, standing over her. With her, detectable by sight alone, was another child she didn't recognize. She guessed the child to be a boy by the cut of his shirt, but she could only guess, as the child's face was all but hidden under a high domed hat. Only his eyes were visible through a couple of holes crudely poked in the fabric above the brim.

Perhaps more curious, the child concealed its hands within a pair of red and green wool socks. His shirt sleeves were filthy with dried mud, as were his pants. She felt as if she had seen socks like that somewhere else recently, but had no time to contemplate it. Lia immediately began her nursing duties.

"Good morning, princess!" she said cheerily. "Here is some bread, and here is something to drink. Sophie told me to take care of you today, and I will! I'll take the best care of you. Promise."

Lia was beaming, her head held high. There was no denying the little girl her *honor*.

Sam pushed herself into a more upright position to accept the eager servant's refreshments. She motioned for the jug first, and without caring if it were piss or poison, she tipped it to her lips and gulped greedily, spilling some down her chin. The diligent Lia was right there with a cloth to mop it up.

"Thank you, Lia," she gasped.

She devoured the bread. It was dry and crunchy, but it hit the spot.

Lia was a smart girl. Next she opened one of the little windows to let in some fresh air, and instructed *"Oliver"* to open the other. Clearly, Lia had experience in the treatment of hangovers.

Warm air flowed through the cabin, smelling and feeling of spring, and nothing at all of the crisp cold of winter. This was not entirely out of the question for Nova Scotia weather. The province's winters were habitually flopping back and forth between freezing cold and balmy. Still, whether she was in Nova Scotia or not, she had somehow left Luke's house in the blink of an eye. The book had something to do with it, she knew, but did Luke have something to do with the book? Originally, she had entirely disregarded Sophie's insistence that Luke was a wizard, and that he had magically whisked her away. Now she wasn't so sure. Lia had conjured an invisible wall, after all.

Luke, a wizard!

She grinned, and closed her eyes, conjuring another image to battle the ache in her head.

She was back at the bus stop with the two would-be muggers. Luke had just arrived in his rusty old truck, grumbling and cursing as before, but instead of approaching them immediately, he waved, and crawled under the truck. When he reemerged, his trademark ball cap and red flannel jacket were gone, replaced by a tattered gray robe and a large pointy hat. He then approached Sam and the muggers, wielding the broken exhaust pipe like a wizard's staff.

"Get behind me, Wendy!" he commanded, and she did.

The bewildered muggers gaped as Luke raised the exhaust pipe above his head with both hands. He roared powerfully, "YOU SHALL NOT PASS!!" and slammed the exhaust pipe into the pavement with all his might.

Nothing special came of this, just a few sparks from the metal striking the asphalt.

He sighed loudly, muttered, "Shit," and looked back at her. He shrugged. The muggers stood, blinking. Sam chuckled to herself and opened her eyes. Lia was again at her bedside, awaiting her next command.

"You don't happen to have a magical remedy for hangovers, do you?"

Lia shook her head. "No," she giggled. "Sophie always asks me that. I'm not very good with magic. Just walls, sometimes. And sometimes I can knock things over, but that's not very useful."

"Hey, it could be. How do you do it?"

Lia turned up her palms and shrugged. "I don't know. Most of the time it happens when I don't mean for it to. That's why Sophie is trying to find me a teacher. Are you *sure* you aren't a witch? You could be my teacher!"

Sam smiled. "I'd love to be able to help with that, Lia, but unfortunately no. I'm just an ordinary girl."

Lia shook her head. "Not ordinary. Princesses aren't ordinary, even if they aren't witches."

"Right, of course. How silly of me. But you know, you're pretty special yourself, young lady."

Lia beamed at the compliment, then turned her head towards the front of the cabin, listening.

"Your bag has been making noises," she said.

My phone! Maybe Luke had messaged her. She started to get up, but Lia stopped her.

"Don't move. I'll get it for you."

She didn't have to go far. A few steps took her to a row of coat hooks by the door, where Sam's coat and bag were hanging.

The cabin was small and simply furnished. Clockwise from the door were the coat hooks, followed by a built in table and two bench seats, like in a diner. Next was a little wood stove with a chimney pipe poking up and out through the wall. A frying pan and a pot hung above the stove, bouncing and clanging softly against the wall whenever the horses swerved around a pothole. To the left of the door was another bench and some storage cabinets. The rest of the space was taken by two sets of bunk beds with a dresser between them. There was no toilet. A visiting princess would have to stop the wagon and do her business on the side of the road again if the need arose.

She thanked Lia for the bag, and began rummaging around for her phone. *Someday* she would clear out all the extra junk she kept in her bag. *Someday.*

Gotcha! She found it relatively quickly that time, but her excitement deflated when she heard the low battery beep, and saw that she still had no signal, and no messages from Luke. Her battery life was showing six percent.

Of course. She dug her charge cord out, and knew the answer even as she asked, "Is there an outlet in here?"

Lia tilted her head quizzically, "An outlet for what? The door is right there." She pointed. "What is the string for?"

Sam laughed. "It's a charge cord. For my phone."

Lia shook her head, confusion on her face.

"I guess this rig doesn't come equipped with electricity."
Another head shake.

"Electricity? You do know what that is, don't you? No? Really? Not ringing any bells? Are you Amish?"

"Bells! I have a tambourine! I'll go get it for—"

"No no! Please no. Maybe later. You're a walking tambourine as it is! Look at all that pretty jewelry you have!"

Lia grinned from ear to ear. She was obviously proud of her collection. "I buy something in every place we visit. Well, Sophie buys them, but I get them. This bracelet is my favorite. I know it's just an old rope, but it's all I could find in Glimmer. There were no jewelry people in Glimmer, but a really nice old man let me play with his dog for a *whole day!* This was the dog's collar from when it was just a puppy. His name was Martin. I wish Sophie would let us keep a dog. She says a dog would ruin her carpets."

"It's a lovely bracelet, Lia."

"Oh! And this one's from Danube. There's a really pretty river there, full of beavers!"

"Wow!" said Sam, with an exaggerated expression.

Lia carried on with the history of each of the million pieces of jewelry she wore, but Sam was only half listening. She was studying the silent Oliver's mysterious gloves again.

I've seen them before. I know it.

It came to her during Lia's narrative on a seashell necklace from some place called Laguna.

"Where did you get those socks?" she asked Oliver.

Luke had a pair just like them. Red and green stripes. Oliver's pair even had the large white L's stitched on the sides. No question. They belonged to Luke.

"The trees," said Oliver. He *could* speak.

"The trees? What trees?"

"*Your* trees." He pointed a woolly hand at her.

"*My* trees? I don't think I own any trees."

Lia took over. "Oliver found them in the mud this morning when we were getting the horses ready. Oliver made a mess of himself getting them out. Sophie was mad. Well, not really mad. Sophie just likes to grumble. She *loves* grumbling, actually. Don't you remember? Sophie asked if they were yours, and you said '*uuhhhh*' and shook your head no."

Sam blinked. "Er..." She vaguely remembered grunting an answer to *something* when she first woke up, but she thought it was a question about breakfast. "Well, it's true they aren't *my* socks.

"So I can keep them??" Oliver blurted.

Sam shrugged. "Fill your boots." She grinned at her own joke. *That's what a normal person would do with socks.* "But I'm sure those socks belong to my friend, Luke. That would mean..."

She had found the book already open in his arm chair. His phone was on the table next to it. His work boots were in the porch.

"He came through the book before me," she realized. "That's why it looked like he hadn't gone far. He was there! Lia! Did you see anyone else near the forest yesterday? A man. Kinda my height, kinda scruffy."

Lia shook her head. "No. Only Francesca and her friends."

"Those are Luke's socks. The guy that Sophie thinks is a wizard. If his socks were there, that means he must have been there as well."

He said he hadn't seen the book before, but what if he had? It was in *his* house, after all. She hadn't told him she was coming until that morning, and he hadn't replied. He could already have been gone by then. Maybe she wasn't supposed to know about this secret world of his. She frowned. But why wouldn't he have brought his boots?

"I hope he didn't go into the forest," said Lia. "That would be bad."

Sam groaned. "Of course. Of course he didn't bring his boots, because he *didn't* know about it. He stumbled here just like I did. And if you didn't see him, there might not have been anyone to warn him about the forest."

"There was a sign?" Lia offered.

Sam smirked. "Where I come from, that wouldn't stop anybody."

"Not good," said Lia. "Sophie says nobody ever comes out once they enter Morningwood. Even if they take just one step. Just one!"

"That's ridiculous," said Sam. "If he did go in, he's probably still back there. I'm so stupid. I should have been looking for him instead of drinking. I need to go back! What if he's hurt?"

Sam sprang out of bed, too quickly, and stumbled and fell into the adjacent bunk. Her head was spinning. Her stomach was sloshing.

"Princess!" cried Lia.

"The princess is fine, Lia. Just fine. I just need a... moment."

Sam closed her eyes. The new bed was just as comfy as the old one. In a moment, everything would stop spinning.

She heard Sophie's voice. "What's going on in here?"

Sam answered with a sleepy, "Hmmm. Hello."

She couldn't make out the next batch of words spoken in the room, or who was speaking them. They sounded too far away, but after a time, Lia's voice rang true.

"Sophie?"

"Yes dear?"

"Am I Amish?"

"Probably."

Chapter Ten

"Isn't this grand, lad?" asked the squirrel. "Two good ol' boys off on an old fashioned adventure. Just *feel* that sunshine!"

"Oh believe me, Henry. I feel it."

The sun had been relentless after they left the forest. A nagging itch told Luke he could add a sunburn to his list of injuries. Perhaps he should have stayed in the shade of the forest up on the ridge, but there were no quarrels between his bare feet and the sand bar along the creek. The warm sand felt pleasant between his toes, and he needed some pleasant feelings. The sun burn was nothing compared to the terrible ache that throbbed in his testicles, and the stomach sickness that accompanied such pain. He imagined with each awkward step that he walked like someone who had been riding a horse for far too long.

The deathwing pterodactyl creature had it worse, of course, being impaled and dead and all, but crashing from the top of a tree through dozens of branches before landing balls first onto an unbreakable branch near the bottom, severely tempered that consolation. His resulting howl likely reached the deathwing in the afterlife. He didn't want to think about what would have happened to his manhood had the upper branches not slowed his descent. He was alive, at least. He may never produce children, but he was alive.

The sun was finally sinking in the sky, though his mood had sank long before. He was *hangry*, but for the squirrel's sake he did his best to manage his frustration. The pair traveled by way of a shallow valley, cut between two low, tree lined ridges. The valley itself was populated mostly by smaller trees and shrubs, and a gently flowing creek that acted as their guide. Henry assured him the creek would lead them to coffee, not a Tim Hortons, but to an inn where he'd find food as well. This promise kept Luke's feet moving, one step at a time.

Nearly as constant as the sun, had been Henry's mouth. All day long, Henry was either bouncing along beside him or leisurely perched on one of his shoulders, but he was always chattering. The only reprieve came when Luke stopped to polish off the jar of peanut butter that traveled with him from home. Henry was elated to be offered a couple spoonfuls, and for just a few moments, the squirrel was nearly silent. Save for the smacking noises he made as his tongue fought with the sticky peanut butter in his mouth. However, these moments of silence were spent replenishing his arsenal of questions.

It was difficult to process, especially without coffee, but discussion with the squirrel brought the pair to the conclusion that Luke had entered another world. Belief in such a thing came fairly easy, given the presence of a magic forest, murderous dinosaur birds, and the squirrel who was verbally guiding him through it. Supposedly, when they reached the inn, they would have a clear view of the not-so-lost city of Atlantis. Given the rest, Luke did not suppose otherwise.

They spent most of the morning making comparisons between their respective worlds. This *new* world did not have things like cell phones, television, or Internet, though it did have powered lights and radio, and perhaps most importantly, indoor plumbing. Henry was particularly interested in hearing about airplanes. They didn't have those either. Unfortunately, Luke had never flown anywhere, so he was a poor one to ask.

According to the squirrel, there was a solid chance that the book Sam found in his house was responsible for transporting him to the forest. When Luke described the contents of the book and how the image of himself had appeared on the page, Henry labeled the thing as a *Travel Tome* with supreme confidence. Some people who practiced magic could capture an image of their location and place it within a book. Something like a travel photo album, except instead of looking at the pictures and simply remembering the places they'd been, they could teleport back to them instantly. Normally, the book would travel with the user, but without any idea how to control the magical object, it was likely left behind when Luke used it.

"That is most unfortunate, Luke," said the squirrel. "That book might have been your ticket home."

"Hmm, Probably. That would be my luck." He sighed. His last night with Sam had been ruined by rats, and here he was stuck in another world, possibly forever.

"Cheer up, lad. What I might have said was your *swift* ticket home. We'll find you another tome. There should be a spectacular library in Tumblestone, if it's still standing. That's the closest borough of Atlantis. They had all sorts of books there, and librarians are the most helpful creatures around. Since we're heading in that direction for coffee anyways, I vote that we continue onward to the city."

Luke shrugged. "Sure. Why not? But would a book that teleports people really just be sitting around in a library? Wouldn't a *wizard* want to keep something like that on them?"

"That is a fair point, Luke. But as I said, librarians are quite helpful. They might not have a tome, but they might be able to point us in the right direction. A local mage, perhaps. Although I suppose you could just ask people on the street."

"The library is fine. We can start with that."

"Excellent! It's been so long since I've been in a library. It would bring me great joy to return to one. I was once a librarian myself, you see."

"Were you now?" A squirrel librarian. Images of shredded books harvested for nesting material and scattered peanut shells everywhere came to mind, but he nodded and said, "Good enough. I hope it's not much further. Ugh. I wish I had my truck right now."

"Your truck?" Henry asked.

Luke smiled, "I guess you probably don't have trucks here, eh?"

"No, none that I've heard of. Tell me, my boy. What is your truck?"

"Well. *My* truck is a piece of shit, really. But it gets me where I need to go. It, uh, well it has four wheels. Do you have wheels here?"

The squirrel tilted his head. "Yes. We have wheels... but in your world, you travel around on... pieces of *shit?* How do you attach the wheels? Is the excrement baked somehow? Hardened in a kiln?"

"Er... No, no. Um... It's made of metal actually. Shit is just... Never mind that. It's made of metal. It has an engine. You put gas in it. You uh, sit inside of it and steer with a steering wheel, and it takes you where you want to go without having to walk. Like riding a horse or something, you know, but not quite."

"You mean an automobile?"

"Yes!" cried Luke. "You have automobiles??"

"Indeed," said the squirrel. "The wealthier folks have them, but they don't run on gasoline. You can't be serious, Luke. You're not still using gasoline engines, are you?"

"Uh... Yes?"

"Fascinating. It's a wonder you're not coughing and wheezing right now. The emissions from those things are terrible. Are there many people living in your world? Do they all have breathing problems? Or perhaps you're just a little behind, and it's all new for you. The problems might not have surfaced yet. Well. We had gasoline engines here for a time. Awful time, that was. Especially for small creatures like myself. Oil was needed to keep things running smoothly. Wars were fought over the stuff. Can you imagine, people fighting, killing each other and laying waste to vast amounts of land, all for the sake of a smelly black liquid that requires even further destruction of the land to acquire? I hope your people are better about it than ours were."

"Hmm. Yeah, I'm not so sure."

"I'm sure they'll figure it out. The shift from oil and gas to cleaner energy was a brutal one here. The oil giants fought the mages every step of the way."

"The mages? Wait, so everything runs on *magic* now?" Luke asked, genuinely intrigued.

"Not quite. It was the magical community that first discovered green energy, harnessing the power of the earth and sun. The ecological footprint of this energy is a far prettier one than that of oil or coal, infinitely sustainable and cheaper to boot. Good for the people and good for the coffers. It should have been an easy decision for the Atlantean King Demitel to make the switch, but he was in bed, figuratively and, if rumors are to be believed, *actually*, with the oil giants. They had him wrapped around their enormous fingers. This brought some dark times for the magical community. An absolute ban on all things magic. Novarius trees were destroyed. Mages were hunted and killed. Even my... dear friend, Aradia, was burnt at the stake." The squirrel sighed. "Simply because they stood in the way of oil profits."

"Wow," said Luke. "That seems like a very extreme way to reject an energy proposal."

"Indeed, but oil giants would have done anything to protect their treasure hordes, and they were spiteful. With their vast wealth, it was nothing for the giants to begin spreading false propaganda, labeling the mages as *dangerous monsters* who'd use the public dependency on their energy source to enslave all non-magical folk."

"I see. But I'm assuming mages had been around for awhile. They weren't like, living in secret before the energy thing, were they?"

"Oh no. They were always prominent members of their respective communities. They made the best doctors, but worked in all branches of society."

"Right. So why would people just suddenly turn on them because somebody said they should?"

The squirrel smiled. "I like you, Luke. But answer me this, good citizen!" His voice suddenly loud and official. "If a child were using a stick to play in the mud, you know, to dig little rivers and such, would you allow him to keep his stick?" He looked at Luke expectantly.

"Umm... Sure? Why not?"

"Now what if that child used that stick to direct a bolt of lightning down onto another child? Would you still allow him to dig his rivers with it?"

"Er... I guess not."

"Of course you wouldn't. And this was part of the oil giants' campaign. The one I remember best, anyway. They knew nobody would answer that question any differently, so they used it at all their rallies."

"Yeah, but what does that have to do with anything? Were children actually blowing each other up with lightning bolts?"

The squirrel gave another smile of approval. "Never, to my knowledge. In truth, even mages who have fought in wars over the years, wars over oil included, I might add, were more for spectacle than anything. Imagine standing in the middle of a raging battle, reading from a bulky magical tome or desperately trying to recall from memory a long winded incantation to produce a fireball. Most mages would fall asleep long before they could accomplish anything. A child with a slingshot and a clump of pitch would have been far more effective. But the propagandists never allowed for further questions. They always followed up immediately with what would happen to the property of captured or slain magical beings. Who wouldn't want to live in a wizard's house? They're usually quite fun and whimsical in their design. Those with lower paying jobs may benefit from a vacated position above them. Things like this."

"Ah, shitty people." Luke lamented.

The squirrel nodded. "Yes. But to humanity's credit, the propaganda really had little effect in the beginning. Unfortunately, it was around this time that the only truly dangerous magic user in centuries, Faron Oldjoy, created that massive snake pit north of Atlantis. Although, that incident was less malevolent and more... hmm, unlucky. Faron had a touch of sickness in him."

"Sickness? You mean crazy?"

Henry chuckled. "Crazy you could say. Mad. He was madly in love. Faron promised his dear lady the moon and stars, he did. And one evening he endeavored to make good on that promise. Well, he certainly did! As it turns out, stars are a little bigger up close than they appear while they're twinkling away up in the night sky. An unfortunate lesson he did not get the chance to learn from. A shame really. He would have made a great astronomer."

"So he crushed himself?"

"Indeed he did. Quite thoroughly. The local wildlife was terrorized for *months* by the snakes that slithered out of that crater, but it did turn out as an economic boon for Atlantis. The city's coffers overflowed from the mining of silver found after the snakes cleared out."

"That sounds like a point *for* magic to me."

"One would think. Had the incident occurred during a different time, it might not have been received so poorly by the public, but as it were, it added tremendous merit to the oil giants' campaign. How quickly everyone forgot that before the giants became rich off of oil, most of them were savage raiders, terrorizing villages in the countryside and eating livestock and children."

"Wait. What?? They were *actual giants*? Like the big ones?"

"Yes. Of course. *Big ones*. Were you not listening each time I mentioned 'giants'?"

Luke shook his head. He definitely didn't want to run into one of those.

"Anyhow," continued the squirrel when Luke didn't respond. "There are also individuals who believe Demitel's stance against the energy proposal was further swayed by a certain healer employed at the royal palace. The healer was tasked with finding a magical cure for the king's impotency, but, not only did the healer fail at this, he was also caught demonstrating his own, hmm, lack of impotency to the Princess Penelope."

Luke sucked air in through his teeth, "Ahh. Yeah…"

"The pot always boils over when you add hearts to the mix. So that's that. A series of unfortunate events muddled together to create a much larger travesty, but that's all in the past now. In the end, the mages prevailed. A settlement was reached. How are the mages doing in your world, Luke?"

"Um, magic doesn't exist in *my world.*" It felt strange to refer to Earth as a different place.

"I wouldn't be so sure of that. By your own account, you did arrive here magically, after all."

Luke bobbed his head thoughtfully, "Yeah I suppose so, eh. Huh."

"At any rate, I don't think you'll have too much trouble adjusting here. You're already off to a good start by speaking such fluent Arthurian. Your accent is a bit… hmm… noticeable, but you'll be understood. The bulk of what you'll hear in Atlantis should be Arthurian. It was fast becoming the closest thing to a universal language before I took my little vacation."

"Arthurian? You mentioned that once before, I think. What do you mean by that? I'm speaking English."

"Perhaps in *your* world you call it English, but here it's Arthurian. You might want to remember that. You don't want people to think you're crazy, do you? I don't think knowledge of your world is very common."

"Hmph. *English* sounds better. Arthurian…"

"I don't disagree, Luke. Less syllables, falls off the tongue quicker, like that young *Grimmish* language. King Arthur might disagree though. Well, he might if he were still alive.

Perhaps, he, like your Tim, has a coffee shop franchise now. We might be able to ask him."

Luke's eyebrows lifted. "King Arthur?" He felt foolish about it, but asked anyways. "Of Camelot?"

"Indeed. The one and only. Ah! So you do know something about this world. Splendid. Yes. The language bares Arthur's namesake, but it was his advisor, Merlin, who taught it to him. Merlin was a powerful magician. It's quite possible that he traveled to your world before and learned it there, or perhaps he went there and taught it. Who knows? They're both long dead now, but the language has spread far. Arthur had great influence."

"I guess he did," said Luke, scratching his chin. "Interesting. Are you sure King Arthur is dead? I heard some thing about him being like, the once and future King. Like he'd come back someday"

"Oh I'm positive he's dead. His mummified corpse is on display in one of Camelot's gambling dens. Merlin's too. I've seen them myself. Say, my boy. Do you see that? Smoke!"

Luke nodded. As they rounded a bend in the creek, it was plain to see a smoking campfire upon the ridge to the right. When they were close enough, the figure of a man with a long beard appeared to be tending it. Periodically the man turned the crank on a makeshift spit, roasting what looked like a large bird over the fire.

The bearded man spotted Luke and waved a fir branch in the air to signal him before tossing it into the flames, darkening the smoke.

Luke waved back at him, but the man didn't see the gesture, or much of anything for that matter. The wind shifted, sending him into a coughing, gagging fit as the black smoke rolled over him.

Henry urged that they continue onward. The inn was not much further. Luke's stomach had the loudest voice in the discussion, though. Whatever the man was roasting smelled delicious.

"Ah, it's just an old man, Henry. I'm starving. Maybe he'll share."

"Even dangerous men can grow old, Luke," said the squirrel.

Luke frowned. "That's a little dramatic, isn't it? He can't be any worse than those deathwings."

Henry chuckled. "Perhaps you're right. Very well. Let's go have a chat with the naked old man."

"Naked?"

When they were a little closer, and the smoke had cleared enough, the man was indeed naked.

Luke groaned. He began to regret his approach, but the old man shot him another friendly wave. It would be rude to turn away now.

"Is it normal for people to not wear clothes around here?" Luke asked.

Henry chuckled again, "It is not. We're either dealing with a lunatic or a free spirit."

"Great."

As they drew closer, Luke was relieved to find the old man not *entirely* naked. His private bits were covered in what one could only guess was a loin cloth. A long, scraggly gray beard acted as a natural tank top of sorts, covering much of his chest and ending in a point just above his navel.

When Luke crossed the stream and crawled up the bank, the stranger greeted him with a gap toothed grin and a beckoning wave of his long, sinewy arm.

There was music playing from a small radio nestled amongst a group of flowers. Though the genre of music was at first unfamiliar to him, within seconds there were several mentions of beer, and several more mentions of women. The old man was undoubtedly listening to the local brand of country music.

He was pleasantly surprised when the man offered him a civilized handshake, and even more so, when they were able to articulately exchange names during that handshake. By appearances, he fully expected the man to communicate through a series of grunts and hand gestures.

Free spirit it is, then.

And then the man saw Henry bounding along beside him. His blue eyes widened.

"You brought an appetizer!" shouted the man called Rufus, and made a dash for the squirrel, but came nowhere close to catching him. Henry shot away and up a tree, where he proceeded to fire a beech nut at the old man.

Rufus laughed as the nut bounced off his forehead, a hearty ho-ho-ho that cast him as a gangly Santa Clause. "I was only foolin'."

Beneath the squirrel's tree, Luke saw then the man's wet clothes, hanging and dripping on a lower branch, and smelled evidence on the man's breath that suggested that somewhere in this world was the technology to produce alcohol. Luke's confidence in the local civilization's ability to brew a cup of coffee soared.

"Come! Warm yourself by my fire, my friend," said Rufus. He gestured to a log bench. "As you can see, there's no need for an appetizer. I bagged a nice fat pheasant today and I can't possibly eat all of it by myself. I'd much rather share it with a fellow traveler than the crows. Won't you stay awhile and share some meat and words with an old man?"

The man's liquor sparkled eyes seemed friendly enough. That was as far as Luke's thoughts went before his stomach answered for him. It was a balmy day for sitting on a log next to a nearly naked old man, but the bird was cooked and he was starving.

Rufus cut a strip of meat from the bird and passed it to Luke on a piece of beech bark. Luke took the primitive plate and bit a large chunk off the strip in the same motion. The pheasant was deliciously flavored with spices he didn't recognize, not that he was too familiar with anything beyond salt and pepper and ketchup anyways. An embarrassingly sexual moan escaped his lips.

The old man Santa-laughed again. "Hungry, are you? That's good, that's good. We won't be wasteful. How 'bout a splash of something to wash that down with?"

Luke's mouth was too full of pheasant to answer with anything but a nod.

From his rucksack, Rufus produced a green bottle. A red label on the bottle marked it as an offering of wine from some-place called Dawn Valley. *Sunrise Wine.* Henry's perhaps not so dramatic words of warning rang in his ears when the bottle was extended to him, so Luke insisted that it would be rude for the guest to take the first drink. What a lovely progression of events it would be, if he were to follow up his ruined night on the couch with Sam by being sodomized by an old hermit in the woods the very next day.

The old man smiled knowingly. "A wise lad to be so cautious, but perhaps I already poisoned the meat you're eating? Hmm?" He winked.

Luke paused to think about that, shrugged, and swallowed another bite.

"Mm. Well. At least I'll die with something in my stomach." *So long as* he *doesn't end up in my stomach as well.* "Sorry. This is great, really. Thank you. Things have just been a little... *odd* for me lately. I meant no offense."

"Oh, none taken, lad. None taken," said Rufus, but he did take a deep swig from the bottle before again offering it to Luke.

That time Luke accepted. The wine tasted of blueberries. After starving and baking in the sun all day, the effect of the wine was instant. It felt as if the drink had taken the scenic route up to his brain before continuing on to his stomach. In his condition, it was best not to risk a hangover, so he passed the bottle back to Rufus.

"So what brings you out here, then?" Rufus asked. "You're lookin' mighty burnt, my friend. Are you lost? No, wait a moment. You don't have any shoes, either." He grinned. "Wild night, I bet?"

"Eh, you could say that, yes."

The old man nodded. "We've all been there. Yes, oh yes we have." A far away look twinkled in his eyes. "You're not from Atlantis are you? I've never heard your accent before, and it's not too often you see trousers like *that* anymore."

"Just visiting, actually." *I hope.* "Is it much further back to the city? I haven't uh, been out this way before." he asked, more to steer the conversation away from where he was from then anything. Henry had already told him it wasn't far, and there was no reason not to believe the squirrel.

"Sounds like a *very* good night," Rufus laughed. "You're almost there. You'll come to the Riverview Inn first if you continue along the river and get up over the crest of that hill there, see. From there you'll see the inn, a mile or two from the hill. Then just take the road by the bridge to the city. You'll see that too. Can't miss it. Big castle on a hill overlooking it all."

Was Atlantis the city with the castle on the hill in the travel tome? How much easier would his journey have been if he had just been admiring the picture of Atlantis instead of the forest in the middle of nowhere?

Luke wolfed down another chunk of pheasant. "Thanks."

"Oh, no problem at all. So where *are* you from?"

Luke looked away to hide his frown. What could it hurt to tell Rufus where he was from? Would this naked Santa Claus think he was crazy? He glanced up to where Henry had busied himself liberating the cones from a nearby pine tree. The squirrel, whose hearing must be extraordinary, stopped his foraging to wag a finger at him. Maybe it would be safer not to come right out and say he was an alien from another world. Such explanations would be better handled on a full stomach, and with a coffee charged brain.

"Um, oh. Just a small village. That way." He pointed back the way he had come. "A long ways that way. Really small village actually. Blink and you'll miss it. You probably never heard of it."

"Try me."

"Halifax?"

Rufus shook his head. "Nope. Can't say that I have. But that must mean it's really nice and quiet there. What brings you to the noisy city? You're not in to unclog the sewers are you?" He leaned in awkwardly close to take a whiff of Luke's hair. "Don't smell like it. You'd *need* a wild night out after a day down there."

"No no. Definitely not interested in anything like that. Just a short trip, hopefully. I'd like to return home as soon as possible."

Rufus tore a strip off the bird for himself and said, between chews, "Girlfriend waitin' for ye? Wife? Husband?" He nudged his elbow into Luke's ribs.

"Eh, girlfriend, sort of," Luke mumbled.

Several pine cones fell to the ground at once. Henry had stopped his foraging to watch him.

The old man grinned. He took a long swill from his bottle and smiled foolishly up at the squirrel for an awkward moment before suddenly cocking his head and asking, "Does she have a name?"

"Er, yeah. Sure. It's Sam."

Sorry Sam.

"Perrrfect," slurred Rufus. "To Sam, then!"

The bottle was tipped again, and passed to Luke. He sighed and toasted her as well. A second mouthful shouldn't hurt. It proved uncomfortable to tell someone, even this stranger, that Sam was his girlfriend when such a conversation had yet to take place between them. If he didn't make it home, it would *never* happen. He wondered if those mysterious itches people were supposed to get when someone was talking about them could reach across worlds. Where was Sam now? Had she tried to message him? What would she do when he didn't reply? How long would she wait for him?

"What about you?" he quickly asked, not wanting to go any further with the Sam talk for fear of jinxing something. "What are you doing out here? Do you have a home somewhere?"

Rufus glared at him. "Does my appearance suggest to you that I don't?" His tone suddenly serious.

"Um, no no! Not at all." He lied.

The homeless looking Santa Clause flipped his frown into a grin, and slapped Luke playfully on the back.

"I'm just havin' a laugh, lad. Of course I have a home. An apartment, even, if that's what you mean. In Tumblestone. But as you might have noticed before your night of fun, there's been some issues with the plumbing. It's what one might call..." His grin widened. "*A shitty situation.*"

Luke raised a brow, and forced himself to chuckle. They both chuckled.

"That's why I'm out here today. Washin' my clothes and myself in the stream."

Luke groaned inward. He had filled his canteen and drank from that stream earlier. Downstream at that.

"I had a wife once," said Rufus before polishing off his bottle. He produced another one from his backpack before continuing. "Several actually. Not all at the same time, unfortunately. Or *fortunately*, depending on how you look at it. Heh. But different ones, over the years."

"Eh, sorry to hear that," said Luke. "Hey, you wouldn't happen to know of any mages living in the city, would you?"

Rufus belched, then grinned. "My second wife was something of a magician. Let me tell you…"

The old man was going downhill fast. There were two other empty wine bottles where Rufus tossed the last one. From then on, the polite conversation devolved into a slurred, one sided dialog where Rufus regaled Luke of his exploits with his various ex wives in such a manner that belonged on the pages of *Penthouse Letters.*

After finishing *another* bottle of wine, the old man slouched heavily, and fell off the log in the middle of a description of his third wife, Martha's attributes. He began to snore almost immediately.

Luke sighed, and sat alone by the dying fire for a short while longer, nibbling on pheasant, and listening to several more songs about drinking beer after work on hot days. *Not one mention of trucks,* he thought. If this really was the Atlantean country music station, it was definitive proof that trucks didn't exist in this world.

It wasn't long before the songs began to repeat, so Luke got up to switch off the radio. He was startled when he felt the squirrel scamper up onto his shoulder. It shouldn't have surprised him. With Rufus passed out, the threat of being eaten had passed with him. What was more surprising, was the radio itself. At first glance, it appeared that the radio was sitting amongst a group of yellow flowers. When he approached, however, he saw that the yellow flowers were growing *out* of the radio. Here and there, they weaved in and out of it. They were miniature sunflowers. A thought struck him. He remembered the monkey village from the travel tome, and the city with the tall buildings that may or may not be Atlantis. There were sunflowers everywhere in those pictures, growing out of the buildings.

"Henry," he began.

"Yes Luke?"

"Do these sunflowers have something to do with the green energy you spoke of?"

"Indeed they do. More than something. Everything actually. They're the power source. The flowers absorb energy, and the roots of the flower deliver that energy where it's needed."

"But what about when it's dark? When the sun goes down?"

"Then they become star flowers, or night flowers. Well. Not really. They're still sunflowers, but at night they take energy from the moon and stars. Impressed?"

"Very. Power bills have been going nuts where I come from. What about when it's cloudy? And do you have to water them?"

"We'll have to find you a book at the library if you're so interested," chuckled Henry. "Perhaps we'll enroll you at the Triton College while we're in the city."

Luke smiled and shook his head. "I think we'll just stick to finding a travel tome for now."

Henry playfully pushed a tiny fist into Luke's cheek. "Of course. So we can return you to your lady friend."

His cheeks flushed. "I figured you heard that."

"Every word the man said, unfortunately. Tell me, how was your first human interaction in this world?"

"Not promising. But he did feed me, so I can't really complain."

Henry smiled. "I suppose not. Now I understand perfectly your motivation to return so quickly. I understand it far too well. We'll get you back to your lady friend, Luke, don't you worry. One way or another. It might not hurt to inquire with this Rufus fellow as to what state the local magical community is in. Many mages were killed during the purge, and those that survived were scattering to remote locations. It may prove difficult to find a mage in the city if they are still reclusive. However, I've been gone for a long time. Perhaps the population has bounced back."

Rufus's snores turned to something resembling a roar.

"Eh, well I did try to ask him. Didn't really get me very far. At least not in the direction I wanted to go. I don't really want to wake him up to try again, do you?"

"Gods no. Surely there will be less obscene folk to ask when we reach the city."

Luke nodded. "That sounds good to me."

By that point, the sun was on its way to bed, and the stars were coming out to play. There was little point in continuing his journey to the city in the dark. Coffee might only make him restless anyways, and he could really use the rest. Also, it would cost him none of the flattened coins he found in the backpack to sleep at Rufus's campsite.

Luke chatted with Henry for a short while longer, until his responses became shorter in words and longer in yawns. He found a rolled up blanket behind the log and placed it over the old man. His own pack was a little worse for wear since the deathwing attack, but the bedroll was still mostly intact. He spread it out under a tree and made himself comfortable. Henry, too, made himself comfortable, curling up at Luke's feet, like a tiny cat.

CHAPTER ELEVEN

"Hello moon! Hello stars! Hello... mouse? Oh, no need to run! Ah, how good it is to be free! Sweet sweet liberation!"

At full speed, the squirrel closed the distance between Rufus's campsite and the Riverview Inn in record time, shouting cordial greetings to any nocturnal creatures that weren't immediately frightened by his noisy approach. As he passed the inn, he chuckled to himself.

Some things never change.

The Riverview Inn had been in the Nikolaou family for generations. Friendly enough folks, but for as long as Henry had known of the inn, maintenance was restricted only to what was absolutely necessary for the building to remain standing. Judging by its current decrepit condition, there could be no doubt that the family still owned it. It was truly a wonder the building was still standing.

Oh dear!

His smile flattened. Generational negligence denoted that the inn would still be without a proper wastewater disposal system. The stingy landlords would have none of that. He would travel with a bit more distance between himself and the river from then on, but he felt terrible for not thinking to warn Luke not to drink from the stream. Hopefully the lad would not be too thirsty when he woke up. With any luck, Luke's trust in the river would still be shaken by Rufus's abuse of it the day before.

Following the stream further eventually brought him to another forest. He entered the forest and continued on close to the river until he came to a stone wall, about man height and barely recognizable for all the moss and vines. An easy leap took him to the top of the wall, and a short drop landed him within the boundaries of Mapleside, a village with a population of four thousand and five hundred, according to the sign that once marked the south entrance.

Henry didn't need to see the sign to know it had fallen to rot and been lugged off by ants long ago, nor did he need a new sign to tell him the population had likely doubled since the first sign was painted. Or tripled, it was impossible to count, for the new residents were trees, not humans, and they were everywhere. Appropriately, the majority of them were maple, and they grew up in the middle of the streets, through the shops and houses and through the park benches. When one fell and died, they grew up through that too.

The squirrel chuckled to himself. Mapleside was once a logging town. More than a dozen watermills lined the river in Mapleside's better days, when the river was truly a river, churning out lumber for the construction industry in the ever growing city of Atlantis and other neighboring communities. Among these neighboring communities that purchased lumber from Mapleside was the small but ambitious mountain town of Tiverton. Tiverton produced a dark beer that quickly grew in popularity, including amongst the loggers of Mapleside. To increase production, the people of Tiverton put in a substantial irrigation system which diverted the bulk of the river flow into a different river. With Tiverton situated upriver from Mapleside, this lowered the waters near Mapleside to such a shallow depth that it was impossible to run the water wheels, and shortly after, the village too, dried up.

Nature takes everything back, thought Henry as he passed the collapsed remains of a stone house and came to a bakery. A tree grew up through its roof.

He paused in front of the bakery to offer a moment of silence for the cinnamon rolls that were likely produced there back when it was in operation. It had been far too long since he had enjoyed a good cinnamon roll. Another thing for his to do list.

He frowned as the moment of silence was interrupted by the hooting of an owl. There was a pretty good chance it would want to eat him. A rustling in the foliage nearby told him there was trouble on the ground as well, but he couldn't take to the trees because the precious cargo he carried required both of his forepaws.

I must visit a cobbler when this is over, and have backpack fitted to me. Now that would be convenient. He continued along, only slightly concerned about the eyes he felt on him. Save for the hungry eyes of the owl, the others were only curious. That's what he told himself, anyhow.

In the center of the Mapleside Cemetery, the squirrel stopped in front of a mausoleum and breathed a sigh of triumphant relief. He had reached his destination at long last.

The mausoleum was rather extravagant in contrast to the simple grave stones that peppered the rest of the cemetery. It was a perfectly square framed structure, white, with a green domed roof, ornamentally supported all around by fluted pillars of marble. Much of the building was marble, save for the oxidized copper roof, and was roughly the size of a small house, made to serve as the final resting place for many generations of the Doukas family. They afforded this by founding the village, and the lumber mills with it. Their name was etched into a copper plaque above the doorway.

The mausoleum was in relatively untouched condition. In fact, Henry noted, it was *less* touched than it was when last he had been there. The moss and ivy that had covered nearly every inch of the white marble building had receded entirely, allowing it to practically glow in the moonlight. Trees and ferns had hindered entrance before, but they too, were gone. There were no trees within twenty feet or more of the place, nor grass either, only bare earth and mounds of decaying brush.

Curious.

The iron door in the recessed entry way was open, beckoning the squirrel into the mausoleum's dark mouth. This might have been creepy, had Henry not witnessed the amount of effort it had taken his companions to break the door open in the first place. It was propped open for his return, assuming he would be alone. Even unlocked, doors can be tricky for squirrels.

The glowing light of the apple he carried offered the squirrel limited vision within the mausoleum, but it was enough to find his way along the rows of covered coffins to one that was open. Although the lid leaning against the side of the coffin suggested its occupant was Alexander Doukas, Henry knew this was not the case. It was empty when his companions and he had first found it. Given the birth date, also marked on the lid, it was reasonably assumed that the centuries old Alexander had found a different bed for his eternal sleep.

Henry was pleased to see it was not empty now, the remains his companions placed within had remained within, untouched by vandals or necrophiles. He smirked at the statue of the region's patron God, Poseidon, standing in the back of the room, and wondered how much *his* vigil had to do with the safekeeping of the bones of the *blasphemous heretic*, Aradia. Aradia and Poseidon had never quite seen eye to eye, and not just because he was fifteen feet tall. What was it she called him? A *pompous pencil dicked prick?* Yes, that was it.

He did *not* like that.

Yet despite his blustering, he did not harm her. It wasn't until years later that she met her ultimate demise.

Memories flooded back.

Henry had found her, or rather, what was left of her, after the last of the terrible witch trials.

"Don't fret, my friend," she had said with a smile. *A smile.* "Everything will be fine, I promise."

She promised, yet she was willing to go to her doom. There was nothing fine about that. Henry had protested more passionately than he had ever protested anything in his life, until she had to lock him in a cage and seal it with magic to keep him from getting in her way.

She went with her captors without a fight, of course, for it could *not* have happened without her consent. How could she allow those savages to burn her alive? There had to have been a better way to end the oil giants' foolish crusade.

In the end, Aradia achieved her goal. She became a martyr. She was much loved. Her burning sparked a tremendous fire within her people, and even amongst the non magical humans. The burning of Aradia was a step too far. The oil giants fell from power not long after, and sunflowers began to spread throughout the land, but for Henry, the cost had been too great.

He lost his best friend. Would she still have gone if he had told her the truth? If he had told her... *everything?*

He felt bad for biting the girl who finally released him, angry that he had been freed too late to save his dear friend. The girl forgave him, and she and her husband were among those who helped Henry bring Aradia's remains to Mapleside years later.

Originally, she had been buried in an Atlantean cemetery, along with dozens of other mages. Henry visited her often in Atlantis, until one day Aradia's spirit spoke to him, and told him of a way she could be brought back to life with a magic apple from Morningwood.

"Does it have to be from Morningwood?" he had asked. Morningwood was cursed, after all.

There were likely more accessible Novarius trees in other parts of the world, but according to Aradia, the tree in Morningwood was the original and produced the most powerful fruit. She promised, however, that he would have her blessing. The curse within the forest would not affect him.

She also requested that her remains be removed from the cemetery and taken somewhere less public for when her resurrection occurred. Another cemetery in an abandoned village near Atlantis seemed private enough, though the initial act of bodysnatching was an awkward, nail biting affair.

Regrettably, so focused was he on the chance to revive Aradia, Henry questioned none of this. Her blessing had not been enough to avoid centuries of imprisonment. If not for Luke, he'd still be there.

Henry held the apple above the coffin and swallowed his nerves. The moment of truth. The golden apple glowed brighter and brighter, until the room couldn't have been better lit if the sun itself rose from the coffin. Everything was bathed in pulsing golden light. The apple grew warm as well, and then hot. Too hot. He held on as long as he could but eventually it fell from his grasp, into the coffin. Smoke swirled from his furry fingers.

A pale blue aura emanated from the bones. Henry watched with wide eyes as the aura detached from the bones and floated up, out of the coffin and over in front of the statue of Poseidon. The spectral aura hovered there for a time as a shapeless, swirling mass, until it materialized into the shape of something blissfully familiar. Henry blew on his paws and smiled wider than he had in centuries.

She was facing back to, toward the statue, but he knew it was her.

Raven black hair reached the middle of her back. She stood proudly, one of her pale hands rested on her shapely hips, the other, held to the side her favorite staff, gnarled driftwood topped with a flawless emerald. She wore her favorite robe, colored to match the gem of her staff and magically tailored to fit her form. She always liked to look her best.

She turned to him, and the breath he had been holding escaped in a gasp.

Her voice washed over him like a good song. It echoed off the walls.

"Henry," she said, smiling her cheeky little smile. Her large hazel eyes sparkled. "You did it."

"Of course, m'lady," he stammered, then, more confidently added, "Back before you even knew I left, eh?"

"I'm a patient woman."

Henry scoffed, playfully, "Not to my recollection."

"An acquired virtue, then."

"You did just rise from the dead. So I suppose anything is possible."

The witch laughed. She stepped towards the coffin and stretched her arm out to provide a ramp up to her shoulder, and the squirrel eagerly accepted. Her shoulder was cold, though one might expect someone who had been dead for centuries to be a little cold.

She reached into the coffin for the apple. "I'm so pleased you brought me the apple, Henry." She held the apple at face level. If it was still scalding hot, the woman made no fuss about it. "You've been a very good friend."

"Hmm. Well, you know. The least I could do. But I'm still mad that you locked me in that cage. Quite rude, I say."

Aradia smiled. The apple dimmed in her hand, nearly giving the mausoleum back to the darkness had it not been for the sun's intervention. The first rays of morning began to creep through the open doorway.

"You forgive me, though, don't you?"

Henry sighed.

If all the magic in all the worlds had disappeared entirely, there would still be those able to cast spells with just a look. A toss of their hair, a flutter of their lashes, a pout of their lips. Even the sound of their voice could cast enchantment. Certainly Aradia would be one of them.

The squirrel nodded. "Unfortunately, yes. I'm just glad you're back."

"I knew I could count on you to do this thing for me," she said, tossing the drained and shriveled apple into the coffin. "There are so few in this world who could have pulled it off, and even fewer, perhaps *no* others, who *would* have. But this was only the first step. There's just one more little thing I need."

"A hot bath and a bottle of wine?"

"Not quite, Henry."

"I must insist on the bath, at the very least. You smell like death, Aradia."

She giggled. "Yes. I would imagine I do."

"What is it that you need?"

"Where is the Otherworlder?"

"The Otherworlder? You mean the boy?"

"A boy," she smiled. "Perhaps, yes. The one who freed you from the forest."

"He's not here. How did you know he was from another world?"

"I know lots of things, Henry. Where is he?"

The question came out sprinkled with a hint of impatience. The squirrel laughed, "What happened to your 'acquired' virtue?"

"Tell me, *Henry.*"

He frowned. "You've only just woken, so I'll forgive your being cranky. Answer my question first, you owe me that much, don't you think? How did you know he was from another world?"

Aradia heaved a sigh. "Very well, *squirrel*. Only an Otherworlder could break the curse in Morningwood. Few other than the great Merlin could have freed themselves from Morningwood without the help of an Otherworlder."

The bottle. *That's why it wouldn't break for me.*

Henry narrowed his eyes, and, as casually as possible, hopped down from the witch's shoulder. "A simple enough deduction when you put it that way."

"Indeed. Satisfied?"

The squirrel stepped into the doorway and looked out at the brightening cemetery. He bobbed his head from side to side. "More or less."

"Good. Now tell me. Where is the boy?"

"I'm afraid I don't know where he is. We parted ways after we left the forest. Deathly allergic to squirrels, the boy."

"I'm not sure I believe you."

Henry moved out of the doorway to the dirt in front of the mausoleum, and turned back to face the entrance. "And why wouldn't you believe me? We're the best of friends, are we not? I'm not entirely sure I believe *you,* my dearest Aradia. What do you want with the boy? What are you playing at? He's far too young for you."

The witch, with a severe look in her eyes, stepped from the shadowy mausoleum and out into the sunlight.

Henry frowned. *Sunlight won't do it then...*

The witch blinked, and painted a more pleasant look on her face. "Henry," she said, sweetly. "Forgive me. It's like you said. I've just woken up. I shouldn't be so cranky. Forget about the boy for now. Let's go and find me that hot bath. What do you say? We can discuss this later."

"No. I think I might have been wrong, actually." Slowly, he began to back away from the witch. "You haven't just woken. I think, perhaps, you haven't slept at all for a very, very long time."

The witch followed him. She cocked her head to the side. "What do you mean, Henry?"

"Aradia, my dearest friend, sacrificed herself in an effort to end a great injustice. She is... *was* far too selfless to send someone to a potentially endless imprisonment, not if she knew the odds. I should have known better. My judgment was clouded."

"Oh Henry. I'd only figured it out after it was too late."

He sighed. "Sadly, I can say the same thing."

"Henry?" She stretched her arm out to him. He continued backing away.

"Yes? That is most certainly my name, but what of you? What is *your* name?"

The witch stopped her approach.

They were now amongst the tombstones. Dew drops were rising up from the earth around them to greet the morning sun, surrounding them in a misty fog. Nearby, bushes rustled ever so slightly, the sound nearly drowned out by the chirps of waking birds, but Henry's ears were keen.

The witch chuckled. Her voice was different, not at all the melodic pitch she had stolen from Aradia. It was deeper, darker.

"Casmolochasba Pantazis."

The words made Henry brace himself. He looked around, expectantly, but nothing happened.

"Come again?" he asked. "Was that some sort of spell? It didn't work, by the way."

"It is my true name!" spat the witch.

"Oh dear," said Henry. "I'm sorry for that, but you see, the forest robbed me of my ability to speak for quite some time. I presume you already knew that. So you should understand when I say that I'm afraid my tongue is not quite up to the task of untangling a knot like that. Beautiful name, though, really. Bonus points to your parents for creativity. Do you even have parents? Never mind. It doesn't matter. I'm just going to call you *Cosmo* if it's all the same to you."

Cosmo the witch, if she was a witch, snarled. "You will tell me where the boy is."

"Unlikely. I feel like your purpose is less than benevolent. How did you corrupt the bones of Aradia?"

"Foolish creature," Cosmo cackled. "Those were not the bones of Aradia."

It was the squirrel's turn to cock his head in curiosity. "Whose bones were they? Where is Aradia?"

Cosmo grinned. "They could have belonged to anyone. They are in remarkable shape for having been burned on a pyre, wouldn't you say?"

Henry's eyes widened. If she had really burned at the stake, much of her remains would have been turned to ash, charred at least. Foolish creature he was indeed, to think the perfectly preserved bones he found in the grave belonged to his incinerated friend. He shook the thoughts away. Too late now. "She's alive, then?"

"Oh yes. An immortal is incapable of dying, after all. You, more than any other, should have known this. You've done me a great service, squirrel." The witch bowed, and added with Aradia's voice, "*I knew I could count on you. You deserve a nice long rest after all your hard work.* Unless you tell me where the boy is…"

Henry remained silent. He gazed at the face of his dearest friend. Whatever the creature was, she had mimicked Aradia's form perfectly. She was just as beautiful to look upon as the real Aradia, even with such a vicious expression on her face. It was no wonder that he had been fooled. This was frustrating, but unimportant. Aradia was alive somewhere. And that was enough. He decided he was thankful for the small glimpse of his friend.

"It seems you've chosen death," Cosmo boomed.

Henry nodded. "It seems so!" He threw his arms akimbo. "Though I'm not entirely sure if it's possible. I guess you're just as foolish as I. Anyway. Ciao!"

When the body of Aradia reared back as if to leap at him, Henry waved goodbye and bounded off into the brush. A sound, terrifying to livestock and hikers everywhere, erupted behind him in several locations. It was typically the only sound made by a pack of raptors that was *ever* heard. The sound they made as they launched from their hiding places onto their prey. They had followed Henry, but found a more satisfying meal than the little squirrel would provide.

The witch with the complicated name screeched as the feathered fiends fell upon her. Her screech was so terrible and so loud that Henry became dizzy, and birds fell from the trees.

He glanced back. There were at least six raptors in the pack, each of them the size of an average human, but bent over. Their heads were long, with mouthes full of deadly sharp teeth. They moved swiftly on their hind legs, and had wings on their arms that, while unable to send the heavy creatures into the clouds, proved quite useful at enhancing their jumps. Both their legs and arms were equipped with fearsomely curved claws, and a long, feathery tail improved their balance. As stacked as their arsenal was, they'd likely need all of it in their current conflict.

It was not pleasant to watch the body of his best friend being mauled by the hungry raptors, even if it was a fake. He had somewhere else to be, anyhow. He left the cemetery as one of the raptors was sent crashing through the tombstones.

CHAPTER TWELVE

When Sam finished *resting her eyes*, she opened them to darkness. The sun no longer beamed through the windows of the cabin, and a peeping chorus of crickets told her it was nighttime. She wasted an entire day. Again.

The dream she had awoken from had been an odd one, of Luke and a naked old man sitting on a ridge line overlooking a dried up river. The dream might have been a nightmare had a flowing gray beard not concealed the old man's genitals. Their conversation, or rather, the old man's monologue, was rather nightmarish itself, but thankfully the details slipped quickly from her memory, like sand through fingers. Moments after waking, the only thing she remembered was something she'd rather not remember. Something about a woman named Martha.

She sat up slowly, giving her head a chance to catch up with her body. She felt better than earlier, but not perfect.

The children aren't here, she thought. At least not Lia. Surely the little girl would have pressed a jug of water into her hands by now if she were. Parts of her wished that were the case.

Voices floated in from outside. Sophie's, and then Gerald's. Her strange companions had not abandoned her.

Sam inched out of bed and crept slowly to the door, but it wasn't until she made it that far that she was confident she wouldn't fall over again. After a nod of self approval and a deep breath, she stepped outside.

The air was warm. A fire was crackling in the middle of a circle of rocks, and a billion stars peppered the sky. Save for the appearing out of thin air to an anthem of noisy vomiting thing, much was the same as the previous night. If the need to vomit suddenly resurfaced, however, there was at least less of a crowd to embarrass herself in front of. Sophie, Gerald, and Lia were the only people sitting by the campfire.

In the distance was a large house, distinguishable by the dim orange lights that flickered in its windows. As her night vision adjusted, a more focused view revealed a few other houses, smaller and unlit, scattered between Sophie's wagon and the larger house. It appeared as if they were parked at the edge of a farmer's field.

"She's alive," announced Sophie with a chuckle.

"Princess!" cried Lia. The little girl ran to help Sam down the wagon steps. This was slightly embarrassing, but probably necessary.

Gerald saluted her with his wine bottle. He was in far better shape that evening.

"I've returned, yes. Back from the dead." She bowed, and regretted it immediately. She stopped herself just short of vomiting.

Sam sat beside Sophie and matched the old woman's amused grin with a weak smile of her own. Lia was quick to scooch over to Sam's other side.

"Apple?" said the little girl, offering her own half eaten fruit.

"No, thank you, Lia."

"Wine?" offered Gerald.

"No!" Sam barked. "I mean, no thanks."

Gerald shrugged and tipped the bottle back himself.

Sophie laughed. The old woman was knitting. Her nimble fingers conducted a pair of needles over a half crafted sock that lay across her lap. The sight brought a *real* smile to Sam's face. It reminded her of her own grandmother, who was likely doing the exact same thing at that very moment in Austria. Then she remembered Luke's socks, and the little boy who now treasured them as mittens.

"Where's Oliver?" she asked.

"You don't remember?" chuckled Sophie. "You said goodbye to him."

"I did? When?"

"It was more of a moan or a groan, actually, then any sort of word," explained Gerald. "Oliver is in the house." He nodded to the closest building. "His family lives here. He tagged along while we traveled through Gaia."

"Oliver is my cousin," added Lia. "Did you change your mind about the socks?"

Sam shook her head. "No, no. I still don't want them. But... I *need* to go back to where you found them."

Sophie raised her head, and her eyebrows. Her hands continued, without supervision, to work in her lap. "Excuse me?"

"I need to go back. Luke is in that forest. I'm sure of it."

"You didn't tell us the wizard was with you yesterday," said Sophie.

Sam groaned. "He's *not* a wizard. I didn't know he had been there. Not until I saw Oliver wearing his socks."

"Little late for that now, princess," said Sophie, motioning with a needle to the darkness around them.

Sam groaned. Why didn't she just say no to the wine? What a stupid move.

"I have to go anyways," she said. "I'll walk. If you'll just point which way to go."

Sophie chuckled. "First you wanted to walk *here*, now you want to walk *back*. You must really like walking. But don't be ridiculous. It's mostly wilderness between here and Morningwood. You can't go stumbling around in the dark. It's not safe. There are many things that hunt at night."

"What if I took fire? A torch? You mentioned fire keeping those *raptors* at bay. Would you give me a torch?"

"We could, but the torch would burn out long before you reached your destination. We spent the larger part of the day traveling here with the horses. I don't imagine your little legs can move any faster than that."

"Please. I'll pay you. Just wait a minute."

Sam went back into the wagon and returned with her bag. After some digging, she found her purse.

"Here," she said, handing Sophie two twenty dollar bills. "Do you have more torches? How many can I buy with that? When one torch burns low, I'll light another."

Sophie squinted at the money and held it up for Gerald to see. "What funny paper this is. Who's this old woman on here? Your grandmother?"

Sam blinked in surprise. "It's Queen Elizabeth. Er, the Second. Haven't you seen money before?"

"We have. Though I'm not sure if *you* have, princess. Perhaps your servants do all the shopping for you."

"A picture of Queen Elizabeth, you say?" asked Gerald. "Huh. So that's what she looked like. Older lookin' than I imagined."

"So you at least know who she was, then?"

"Of course. I'm no historian or nothin', but everybody knows the tales of the warrior queen that died in the Battle of South Bridge, There's songs and everything."

Sam squinted. "What? A battle? No, no. She was nearly a hundred years old when she died. Her battling days were long over. She just passed away recently."

"*Recently?*" laughed Sophie. "Ridiculous. Even if she survived that battle, she'd be over five hundred years old now."

"Maybe she's a powerful witch," suggested Gerald.

"She wasn't a witch," said Sam and Sophie simultaneously.

Little Lia's eyes were nearly as big as the apple she was noisily munching.

"Am I in the future?" Sam thought out loud.

Society has collapsed. People are using horses and buggies and torches again. Robot Elizabeth was defeated in some bridge battle...

"Well, you're certainly not in the present," said Sophie.

She handed the bills back to Sam. "It's nice paper, to be sure, but I don't reckon you'll find anybody willing to trade you anything for it."

"Well, maybe I have something else you'd want. Strawberry lip balm? Not even opened. A half a pack of winterfresh gum? Hmm..."

Sophie waved a needle to stop her. "Enough, enough."

"The gum?" said Sam, hopeful.

"No, I don't want your *gum*. You wouldn't be able to carry the number of torches you'd need to find your way safely to Morningwood in the dark."

Sam shook her bag. "You'd be surprised how much stuff I can fit in this bag."

"It's a big bag!" agreed Lia.

Sam smiled at her and nodded. *This girl really is great.*

Sophie sighed. "Do I look like a torch merchant to you two? I don't have any torches left, nor anything to make torches with, which would make more sense, you know. To just bring some rags and resin along with you, and find new sticks on the edge of the forest as needed. Better than dragging around a cord of wood, wouldn't you think? Francesca could have fixed you up, but she's already in Atlantis by now, along with her people. We would be too, if not for you, sleeping beauty. Hard to return a rental wagon with someone still asleep in it."

"Oh, I'm really sorry," said Sam. "You could have thrown me out. I didn't know the wagon was a rental."

"Of course it was a rental. Have you heard what the insurance companies want for these things? Registration fees? Highway robbery if you ask me. But don't worry. We have a family discount on rentals. You can repay me, though, by forgetting this ridiculous idea of yours. You don't know for certain that your wizard went into that forest-"

"But we saw footprints, Sophie! Remember? From the socks to the trees."

"Quiet, Lia. If your wizard went into that forest, he's finished. You'll never see him again. Anyone in these parts can tell you about the Curse of Morningwood."

Gerald nodded his agreement. Of course he did.

"The *what?*" laughed Sam. "The curse of *morning wood? Now* who sounds ridiculous? Luke is a twenty-seven year old man. I'm sure he's dealt with morning wood before. He'll handle it."

"Many have thought so, but yet none have returned. Witnesses who've seen people enter, say they take only a few steps in before disappearing completely from sight. Can't call out to them neither. You'd get no answer."

"They should have taken a ball of yarn with them," said Lia. "Sophie has lots of yarn."

"Yarn, dear?"

"I'd suggest an axe, myself," said Gerald.

"No! Yarn," Lia insisted. "The people going into the forest should have taken a ball of yarn with them, and left one end outside the forest with the... witsis... the witsises. Then the people in the forest can't get lost. They can follow the string back out."

"You're a smart girl," said Sam. "That's like Hansel and Gretel, except Hansel left bread crumbs, and animals ate them."

"Well of course they would," Sophie scoffed. "*Bread crumbs.* Better to have a Lia than a Hansel I say, though I suspect the situation is more complicated than that. Surely someone would have thought of something like that by now. There's foul magic at play in that forest."

"I have to try," said Sam. "If he's in there I can't just leave him."

Sophie sighed. "Very well. Fine. I won't stop you from looking for your wizard. Your life is your own to live or to throw away, but I ask one thing of you."

"What's that?"

"You wait until morning. In the daylight, we'll take a horse and ride back to Morningwood. I won't have you torn to shreds by raptors or some other beast before you can throw your life away the way you wish."

"We?"

"Yes, we. I'll take you myself."

Gerald started. "Sophie, you can't—"

She silenced him with a needle. "Oh, don't worry about me, Gerald. I'm not stupid enough to enter the forest, but I can hold a piece of string and not be too frightened about it. What do you say, princess?"

"I think I can live with that. It's another wasted day, but if you're sure..."

"I'm *not* sure," said Sophie. "I'm not sure whether you'll *live* with that or not, but we'll find out tomorrow. For now, look through my basket here and pick out what color yarn you'd like found on your corpse."

Sam chose green.

"Third time's the charm, princess. Give me your hand."

Sam took a deep breath and tried again. This time she accepted Sophie's offer of assistance. She hooked her foot in the stirrup and used the old woman's surprisingly steady hand to swing herself up onto the horse. The saddle was only built for one, so she straddled the thing bareback behind Sophie.

It was a strange sensation to have a horse beneath her. She could feel the animals power, while she herself, felt small and delicate, vulnerable, as if the creature could decide at any minute it didn't want her on its back and she would be sent flying. Her concerns were imaginary, she knew. The big horse took her sloppy mounting attempts stoically, and remained perfectly calm when she finally succeeded. Still, Sam wasted little time wrapping her arms around Sophie's waist. She was grateful that Lia was sleeping in that morning, and that Gerald had went to the building she had seen in the dark, an inn, for breakfast.

"Thanks for your patience. I've never ridden a horse before."

"It's no trouble to me, girl," said Sophie. "I'm in no hurry to see you end yourself. We still have to wait for Gerald to finish stuffing his face so he can watch Lia."

They didn't wait long.

"Wait!" came a distant cry. "Waaaiit!"

The pair turned to see a cloud of dust making its way towards them from the inn. Ahead of the dust cloud was Gerald on the other horse, flailing one of his muscled arms in the air wildly."

"What are you on about?" scolded Sophie. "We *were* waiting, you dolt. You think I'd leave Lia here by herself? It's bad enough I'm leaving her with you."

Gerald ignored her. "Don't go."

"It's fine Gerald. I told you, I'm not going into the forest myself."

"Neither of you." He looked at Sam. "Come with me first, at least."

"Why?"

"Just trust me. I think you'll want to talk to the innkeeper."

Sam agreed, and took pride in the fact that it only took her two tries to mount Gerald's horse.

The *Riverview Inn,* "a drafty old dump that boasts a view of some damp rocks," as Sophie had put it the previous night when Sam asked. Daylight revealed the truth of her words. Many of the old fashioned windows were missing a pane or two, rotten siding fell away in places and a pile of missing roof tiles lay scattered on the ground. Sam imagined the vines and sunflowers wrapped around the building played a significant role in holding the place up. The maintenance budget was clearly spent entirely on a shiny new *Riverview Inn* sign posted beside the door, though even that looked suspiciously to be hiding a broken window.

Beside the inn was the questionably titled *river* that could easily be crossed in sneakers without getting wet feet, but there was a beautiful stone bridge that arched across for those willing to pay a toll. Not many, it seemed, if the snores of the toll operator and the tramped down bank on either side of the river next to the bridge were any indication. Beyond the bridge was a few miles of open farm land that ended at an enormous medieval looking wall. The wall looked to be in a condition similar to the inn, with here and there a section nearly completely crumbled, but an impressive gate framed by carved mermaids remained in the center of it. Fitting, if it really was the city of Atlantis. Far beyond the gate was a familiar looking castle, perched atop a high hill. Sam was in too much of a hurry to dwell on the view.

"I was dumpin' me chamber pots this mornin', I was," began the round bellied innkeep. "I always empty me pots down over the river bank as soon as I wake. The roosters ain't even crowin' yet at that time. It's usually right peaceful like, just me and the crickets. But not this mornin', no! I wasn't alone. This fella came crawlin' up over the bank in the pitch dark, no flashlight or lantern or nothin'. I damn near splashed him with me night soil. At first, I was struck with terror, you know, seein' this black shape come up outta nowhere. And I thought, *This is the end, Phil. This is the end for you. The Reaper's makin' his rounds early today.* But I had to say a silent prayer to Poseidon when I discovered the specter was just a man lookin' for *coffee.* Can you imagine? Had a blight of a headache he did, I guess. Claimed coffee was the only cure."

Sam's eyes lit up. "What did he look like?"

"He was younger than I, probably closer to your age, miss. Brown hair, a bit of a beard. Blue eyes, I think, but I *know* he was wearin' blue trousers, and was walkin' round barefoot. Say, you're wearing blue trousers too. Must be a new thing goin' round. Hmm. He was as red as a lobster, and asked a lot of questions about the sunflowers, like he never seen 'em before. Asked some questions about wizards too, but I don't know any. Never met one. Funny guy, but he was a nice enough fellow. He made no attempts to murder me, before, during, or after I served him his coffee. Even hugged me, he did."

"I'm sure it's Luke." Sam said to Gerald, though she didn't understand Luke's new interest in gardening. Gerald nodded his agreement. "He wouldn't happen to still be here, would he?"

The innkeeper shook his head.

"Did he say where he was going?"

"Aye. Said he was heading into Atlantis. Laughed about it. Then asked me several times if it really was Atlantis. As I said, he was a funny guy. Didn't say what he was going to the city for, so I don't know where to tell you to look. It's a big city, but a man with trousers like *that* is sure to attract attention. People haven't worn those in centuries. Ask around and I bet you'll track him soon enough."

Sam's eyes wandered to Gerald, standing beside her in a pair of tight leather pants and an open vest with no shirt beneath it. She suspected *somehow* that Gerald would raise fewer eyebrows.

"Thank you, Phil," she said. "You've been very helpful."

The innkeeper bowed. "Before you go, would you like to buy a blueberry muffin? Baked 'em meself, fresh this mornin'. Only a copper a piece."

"Absolutely!" said Sam. The lump of hard bread and water she had for breakfast had already left her. She began to dig through her bag for cash when the word "copper" registered with her. She looked to Gerald with pleading eyes.

Without hesitation, Gerald retrieved a handful copper coins from a pouch on his hip, and bought them a half dozen muffins.

Chapter Thirteen

The note was unsigned, but the very structure of it was signature enough. The message was spelled out in acorns. A considerable amount of acorns. *Catch up with you in Tumblestone,* it said.

Where would the squirrel have gone? And when?

Luke had slept terribly, and rose long before dawn, but somehow Henry had woken earlier, if he had slept at all. The squirrel had just been released from prison, basically, so maybe he had a lady squirrel waiting for him somewhere.

It didn't pay to dwell on the absence. Henry was free to do as he wished. He'd draw less attention to himself in the city without a chattering squirrel on his shoulder, anyhow. Who knew how the locals might react to a stranger from another world. He saw that *E.T.* movie, and countless other shows and books where visiting aliens were dissected and studied by scientists. *To hell with that.*

He hadn't lingered long at Rufus' campsite, quickly packing his things and yanking some cold meat off the pheasant for breakfast. He prayed that it wouldn't give him the shits, but before he could make it to the inn, he was squatting noisily in a copse of bushes. He was especially thankful then that Henry had taken a different route.

The layer of dirt caked to Luke's bloody soles was apparently a poor substitute for wearing shoes. Another grunt spewed from his mouth as his foot found the billionth pebble of the morning. His feet weren't alone in their suffering. His back, shoulders, and legs trumpeted varying degrees of protest, which resulted in the simulation of a thousand extra pounds in his backpack. Not to mention the dull ache that continued in his testicles.

He also suspected, based on the itchiness of his sunburned face, that if he announced himself to the citizens of Tumblestone as an alien from Earth, a good many of them would believe earthlings to be a race of humanoid lobsters. Minus the extruding eyeballs.

Despite the negatives, Luke was whistling cheerfully as he neared Tumblestone's gate. His mood was bright because his stomach was stuffed with blueberry muffins and saturated with coffee, and perhaps whatever bits of pheasant he hadn't left in the bushes. The coffee was great, and what was better, the coffee and five muffins only cost him six of the flattened copper pennies he found in his backpack.

Most of his journey had been made in the dark. It wasn't until about halfway through the stretch of sleeping farmland between the inn and the city gate that the sun poked its golden head up over the horizon, and the gentle chirping of crickets gave way to the obnoxious crowing of roosters.

He was in awe of the wall around the city, despite the decrepit shape it was in. Some sections were in such bad shape that if he wanted, he could just walk up the crumbled staircase its ruin had provided and bypass the gate entirely. He hoped, however, that someone at the gate would be able to direct him to a library, or a wizard.

The proper entrance was easily the most phenomenal piece of architecture Luke had ever seen, bumping the bridge he had crossed just a short while earlier out of the top spot. The gate itself was a huge wood latticed thing set between two enormous mermaids, expertly carved in stone. It was designed to appear as if it were the mermaids who raised and lowered it. The gate was still down when Luke arrived, but a light flickered in the window of the man door beside it.

Through the bars he saw a wide cobblestone courtyard that branched away in several directions through narrow gaps in a congestion of brick and stone buildings. On the far end of the courtyard, a man removed his floppy brimmed hat to shoo a rat away from the wagon he was in the process of uncovering. The rat bolted towards the gate, but, spying Luke, decided to shoot under a pile of rubble instead.

A group of scantily dressed women who had been chatting in a circle, witnessed this, and with a united squeal, disappeared into a building with a red light above the door. This left the courtyard occupied only by the floppy hatted rat chaser, and a pair of what Luke guessed were city workers, fussing over a statue in a small fountain. The statue was another impressive carving. Its likeness was that of Poseidon, judging by the trident raised proudly above its bearded head. A large plaque beneath the statue confirmed this, with *POSEIDON* etched in stone, and *SUCKS* hastily scrawled in black ink beneath it. Luke smiled and took a moment to watch the workers.

"Damn kids," he heard one of them say. "Why can't they just leave the statues alone? Look at this. They used witchworm guts to write it. That'll take forever to scrub out. And on market day, no less. The courtyard will be full to burst in a few hours."

"Ah but that's not the worst of it," said the other. "Look! His privates are missing. What would somebody want with Poseidon's privates?"

The first man let out a long and loud sigh. "Nothing," he said. "They've been doing this for months. Up on his head there, what do you see?"

"Goodness. That's his dick! Up there in his crown. How'd they get it up there?"

"Little monkeys they are. No, don't. Don't try to climb it. We'll have to get a ladder. We don't want to risk breaking anything else."

"And the sculptor? Should we call her this early?"

"Aye. That's why she's *on-call*. Full time job she has, fixin' penises. I imagine she's been wracking up a lot of overtime pay these days."

Luke shook his head and approached the man door. The large sliding peephole was open, and light still flickered within, but his first knock drew no response. After a moment, he tried again, louder, and was answered only by another obnoxious rooster somewhere behind him. He tried the door, but it was, of course, locked. When he poked his head in the peephole, the problem was clear. The gate watchman, if that's what he was, was asleep on a bench in the corner of the little room.

The watchman was a boy not likely out of his teens, wrapped in a coarse leather trench coat that was far too big for him, but appeared to make a good blanket. A top hat of the same tan colored material lay on his lap, and a rifle leaned lazily against the wall beside him.

Luke beat on the door again, and shouted in through the slot.

"Hey man! Wake up!"

The watchman woke with a start. His wide eyes shot Luke a look of pure fright before he stumbled up from the bench, knocking over the rifle and losing his hat to the floor. He composed himself admirably though, standing straight as a pencil, he asked in a tone too serious for his childish voice, "What business do you have in Tumblestone this early in the morning?"

"I'm looking for a library. Any one would do for a start. The biggest one, maybe?"

The boy blinked at him for a moment. "Aye, well I know of a few libraries, though I don't like readin' much myself. The biggest is the Knowledge House., but all libraries and museums are closed on Mondays. You'll have to come back tomorrow if you wanna see one."

"Of course they are," Luke frowned. "The Knowledge House sounds promising though. Well. I'm already here. Surely I could kill some time in the city, if you'll let me in. And then maybe I can find a hotel or something? Do you have hotels here?"

The watchman nodded. "Yes sir. Lots of hotels and inns in the city." He leaned in for a closer look at Luke through the slot. "Them's funny trousers you got on there. Where you coming from?"

Luke opened his mouth to say Halifax, but his tongue found the word *Ravenwall* instead. It was a place far from Atlantis, according to Rufus, where the old man met his second wife, Josephine.

The watchman nodded again. "I've never been there. Does everybody wear trousers like that in Ravenwall?"

"Yeah, pretty much. Can I come in?"

"You can if I open the door, sir. Er, sorry I didn't mean for that to come out rude. I just have one more question. Are you bringing any livestock with you today?"

Luke smiled. He wondered if Henry would have counted as livestock.

Probably best not to mention him at all.

He shook his head.

"A bit of a foolish question, I know. But I'm told to ask. Not an easy thing, to hide a chicken in your pockets. But chickens is allowed anyhow. It's goats we're after. Or, not after, I guess. Tristan, the King's brother, placed an... an embar... an embargo? Hmm. He says no trading of goats in the city until further notice."

"Goats? Really?"

"Aye. I know. Roast goat is my favorite. Me Pa says Tristan is a bit of a nut. While his brother's away on business in Camelot, he likes to make himself feel important."

"And banning goats makes him feel important, eh?"

"*He* says there was an illness bein' spread by the goats. For the public's safety, no goats until things are sorted out."

"Ah," Luke nodded. "Well, that sounds fair enough."

The watchman chuckled and leaned in close. "But word is that he had been eating *too much* goat cheese. Blocked himself up for days. My uncle was on duty in the palace when he finally managed to push one out of 'em, if you know what I mean. Said Tristan was howlin' somethin' fierce! But you didn't hear that from me. I figure the King hisself will lift the ban when he returns, but until then, no goats."

Luke laughed. "Understood. I didn't hear a thing, and I assure you I am goatless."

"Good. Oh, and one other thing. I don't know what it's like in Ravenwall, but here in Atlantis, public displays of magic are strictly prohibited to energy grid technicians only. People tend to get stirred up over such things, and there's a hefty fine."

"No worries of that from me. I'm not very magical, unfortunately, but I did want to ask if you knew of any mages here in the city. I have questions that I think a mage might be able to answer. Does this magic prohibition mean that mages aren't allowed in?"

"Oh they're allowed in. No problem there, but they'd need express permission from the King to be able to practice magic openly. Just a safety thing, is all."

"Fair enough. So do you know where I could find a mage?"

The boy shook his head. "Never met one, to tell the truth. At least none that came right out and said it. I don't think many mages come here to be honest. Can't say I blame 'em. What with that whole witch burning history thing we have here. Atlantis was the worst for it, they say."

Luke couldn't blame them either. "So it's probably unlikely that I'll meet one, huh?" He sighed, then shrugged. "Well, the library will have to do."

"It might just. Alright. You can come in through here."

The sound of metal scraping across metal could be heard as the locking bar was removed from the other side of the man door. The door swung open, and the guard waved him in and through the gatehouse to the courtyard. As Luke passed through the arched stone portal, the watchman placed a hand on his shoulder.

"Thanks for waking me up, sir, and not making a fuss of it. I've only started here a few weeks ago. These late nights are a bugger to get used to."

"Hey, no worries man. Thanks for letting me in."

"Ah, its just about time to go up and raise the portcullis anyhow. Anyone can get in after that. If I go up now, I might actually have it open before the farmers start in with their carts. It's awfully embarrassing when there's a crowd. Takes me three breathers to get the whole thing raised. People start shoutin' and hurryin'. It's a heavy thing, it is! Some of the pulleys have been broken and bypassed."

"I bet it's heavy! Is it just you here?"

The boy nodded. "Aye. Budget cuts."

"And this thing doesn't have an automatic opener?"

"I wish for that every day, I do. But this gate is the only one in all of Atlantis that has never been destroyed, probably because the Gaians to the south of here have always been too busy battling reptiles to bother waging war on anyone else. There's not even a point to closing it every night, other than tradition. Well, farmers have been claimin' lately they've seen raptors in their fields, but my pa says that's rubbish. The gatehouse has been labeled an historic property, you see. Everything has to be kept original, or the historical society will be cross."

"Ah yeah. You don't want that," Luke muttered, though his mind was struck by the mention of raptors. After the deathwing attack, it was difficult to dismiss the farmers' sightings as rubbish. Suddenly he felt that nearly being drenched by the contents of the innkeeper's chamber pot that morning wouldn't have been the worst thing that could have happened to him. Although really it would be a toss up between getting a face full of feces and having his face eaten off by a dinosaur. Maybe the dinosaur would be preferable.

"Do you want a hand with that gate?" he heard himself offer, though he wouldn't have been too upset if the gate remained closed behind him.

"Thank you sir, but I'll manage. I have some time, thanks to you."

"Good enough. Just think, each day you open that gate, you'll get a little stronger. A week or two from now, you'll only need two breathers to open it, and then one."

The young watchman puffed up his chest. "And then none!"

Luke slapped him on the back. "That's the spirit, man. I'll let you get to it. Take 'er easy."

"Take who? What?"

"Never mind. Have a great day."

The watchman tipped his hat, and disappeared into the gatehouse.

Luke barely had time to blink before a man was shouting to him.

"Have you heard the words of Lee Grover, my friend?"

It was the rat chaser he had seen through the gate. The man beamed at him from beneath the floppy brim of his straw hat. A mound of dark chest hair covered what the deep V of his white shirt did not.

Luke shook the offered hand. "I guess I haven't. What's Leegrover?"

"Not what, my friend. *Who*. You're looking at him." He threw his arms to the side. "The one and only Lee Grover, famous author and adventurer. Surely that rings a bell?"

Luke shook his head. "I'm afraid not." The man looked sad. "Eh, but I'm not from around here," Luke added.

The author and adventurer of questionable renown, Lee Grover, smiled again, somehow wider than before. "Me neither, me neither. I'm just passing through myself, as one might expect from an adventurer. Say, why don't you step over here with me to my cart and allow me to welcome you to this fine city with something that will rid you of your ignorance."

Luke narrowed his eyes and sighed, but did as the man asked.

The cart was similar to a small utility trailer one might tow behind their vehicle to haul a lawn tractor or an ATV. It was made entirely of wood, even the wheels, and was towed about by a long eared donkey. The donkey raised its tail in salute and promptly shit on the cobblestones.

"Elegant as always, Sabrina," said Lee to the donkey.

The cart contained some cookware and two small sacks. The rest of the space was consumed by no less than a hundred leather bound books, heaped up in careless piles. One of these books was forced into Luke's hands. Crudely etched into the cover were the words, *True Tales Of Triumph*, by *Lee Grover*. The other books appeared to be similar copies.

"A silver fox and three rabbits is enough to secure your enlightenment, my good man. What say you?"

Luke turned the book over in his hands.

It's probably trash, he thought, but it might make for a unique addition to his shelves at home, if he ever saw his home again. At the very least, it might help him get to sleep that night.

"Hmm." He hadn't counted the coins in his pouch, but he knew there were no silver ones. Assuming it was a *coin* the man was after, and not a dead fox or the head of George Clooney. It was likely the former, as he learned from the innkeeper that the flattened pennies in his pouch, of which he had probably a few dozen, were called "Copper Rabbits," or "Bits."

"I don't have any silver coins. What's it worth in copper pieces?"

Lee chuckled. "Not a mathematician, eh? That would be fifteen rabbits, my friend."

"That's a decent chunk of money. I don't know, man."

He opened the book to peruse the pages, and found himself holding only the cover. The pages fell and scattered onto the cobbles. One was carried away immediately on one of those breezes that only appears when it's inconvenient. Before Luke could frown, the shell of a book was snatched from his grasp and deftly replaced by a sturdier copy.

"Perhaps for you I can let it go for, say, twelve copper."

The replacement held firm when Luke flipped through the pages, a little too firm in places. A few pages were stuck together and had to be pried apart.

Luke sighed. "I don't know man. I don't think it's for me, but I'm sure you'll—"

"Ten copper," blurted Lee. "Ten copper, my friend. A steal of a deal, and you can put your savings toward some new shoes!"

New shoes sound pretty good. Of course, he would save more money for shoes by *not* buying the book at all.

He shrugged. "Sure. Why not?" and fished the coins out of his pouch.

Lee clapped his hands merrily. "Excellent. I applaud your decision. I'm sure after you've heard the words of Lee Grover, your only regret will be that you didn't offer twice the asking price."

"Oh yeah. Probably. Hey, since you're a traveler, do you know where I'd find the cheapest accommodations?"

"Indeed I do, my friend. I stayed at the Wooden Hearth Inn last night myself. A sort of boarding house set up. Cheapest rooms in Tumblestone. You'll find it on Reed Street, just off of Tumble Square, the heart of the borough."

"Sounds perfect. Er... which direction would that be?"

Lee pointed to one of the streets leaving the courtyard.

"That way, as the crow flies. You'll have to do some zigging and zagging the way these streets are laid out, but the square is quite grand. You'll reach it one way or another, I'm sure. Oh, and speaking of crows, watch out for bird droppings as you cross the square. The grackles are relentless this time of year."

"Thanks. I'll keep my head up."

"Eh, best to keep it down actually. Don't want that mess in your eyes, friend."

"Right."

Luke took one last look at the city gate before turning to the street Lee indicated. The gate was nearly raised. The watchman was working at the last few feet, just in time to welcome several horse and donkey drawn wagons, and the farmers walking beside them. Some wagons appeared to be pulling themselves, but then Luke saw the sunflowers, and nodded knowingly.

Lee wasted no time setting his sights on the new arrivals.

"Have you heard the words of Lee Grover?"

The sky above thinned to just a pale pink ribbon when Luke left the courtyard. Much of the rising sun was swallowed by the brick and stone buildings, close packed and several stories high. There, the narrow streets would rely just a little longer on the glow of lampposts, draped in sunflower vines, to push back the dark fingers of night.

The vines from these posts snaked down and between the cobbles to connect with the larger webs of vines that covered each of the buildings like enormous green nets. Many of the upper windows of these buildings had wooden shutters whose faded paint did little to diminish their charm. The street level windows Luke passed were fitted with iron bars over the glass, but nearly all of them had arrangements of flowers on display.

Rufus's stance on the city being a shit hole was not shared by Luke, though he could understand how others might be put off by the occasional piles of crumbled masonry on the street, or the rats that darted between them.

The man wanted to eat Henry, though. One would think he'd be thrilled with all of the small game running about. Some people were just never happy.

The view would have been better with Sam. He enjoyed seeing her face light up whenever she talked of her travels, of her walks through narrow cobbled streets in Europe. He supposed she'd rather drive though, once she saw the first rat.

I'd never get through this with my truck.

There weren't any trucks. Nothing that resembled a car either, but occasionally someone would pass him on a bicycle, or hum by on a scooter with sunflowers dancing on the sides of it. The streets were not built to easily accommodate anything larger, especially as the piles of rubble became more frequent. In some sections, the buildings themselves spilled out in dusty heaps to choke off the streets.

At a particularly narrow choke point, an older man and a younger man were busy chucking stones aside to make way for their wagon of furniture. Luke stopped to assist them, as much to be courteous as it was a necessity. They were in the way.

There were few shops in this part of the city, but no shortage of people selling nothing. If it wasn't rubble and rats, it was beggars. One street was full of them; men, women and children awake before the sun to stand or sit and ask for money. It seemed like a poor business plan, to saturate the market with so much *nothing* on one little street, but the bedrolls and piles of blankets suggested that this was just where the beggars had been sleeping. Likely, they'd move on to more lucrative locations.

As greasy and shoeless as he was, it was almost flattering to still be approached by the beggars. He might even have given one or two of them a coin, but with so many beggars within eye shot of one another, guilt would likely have drained his pouch by the end of the street if he started. It was best to save his coin for accommodations and food. Who knew how long he'd be stuck here.

After reaching the end of the beggar gauntlet, he was forced off the crow fly path and chose to turn right onto King Street. The left appeared to be populated by another wave of beggars.

The road to the right took him past a long row of statues tucked into alcoves. He stopped to read the plaque on the first one.

Atlas. First King of Atlantis.

A life sized image of the man was carved in stone, holding a real sword, brown from rust, in the air above his head. Luke wondered how the curly haired warlord felt about goats in his city. The artist of that statue, and of the other kings he passed, decided it best to immortalize the city rulers in the nude. Apparently, the Kings of Atlantis chose only the physically immaculate as their successors. Each new king was more muscular than the last, and somehow this progression of genetics extended to the dangly bits as well.

Luke held his arm up to the last statue in the row and shook his head.

"Wild."

If the sculptures were at all accurate, which he highly doubted, the current king of Atlantis was hung with an abomination the size of Luke's forearm.

The next street on the left began to slope uphill, and was surprisingly empty and quiet. There were no rats, beggars, naked statues or authors, nothing at all to distract him from noticing for the first time how nice the smooth cobbles felt on his ruined feet. He hadn't stepped on any jarring stones since he entered the city.

The moment of tranquility was a short one, annihilated in a symphony of shouting and splashing. Shutters above were flung open by people holding buckets, waving and shouting their good mornings to neighbors left, right, and across the way. Dozens of golden brown waterfalls spouted from their buckets, cascading down and splashing on the street below. Luke needed no explanation as to the contents of those buckets. The smell said plenty.

Rufus's words exploded into his mind. *The sewer system is backed up, and things are a little messy at the moment.*

Messy was right. He became fearfully conscious of his bare feet, and lost all appreciation for the smooth, splash conducive cobbles. He danced and dodged, desperate to avoid a direct hit or even a sideways splatter. He was mostly successful, but still felt violated as the rancid scent chased him into a side alley. He was lucky, at least, that nobody seemed to be emptying their bathrooms from the alley windows.

Luke removed his pack. Might as well wait for the danger to pass before continuing toward the city center. Besides, the reprieve gave him chance to realize his own needs for release. It was past time to liberate his morning coffee, and the setting was fitting. He relieved himself on a pile of dusty rubble to minimize splash back.

He barely stuffed himself back into his jeans when he heard a scraping on the stone behind him. Luke turned to see a small, red haired girl, with a red face to match, struggling to drag his backpack further down the alley. She might have been nine or ten years old.

"Ahem. Can I help you, young lady?" he asked, smiling. He was too amused by the thief's determination to be upset. She continued to pull on the pack even after he put his foot down on one of the straps. Her face turned a few more shades of red before she finally fell back in a huff.

Luke opened his mouth to ask if she was hungry or something, when a red haired man darted towards them and pulled the girl up by her wrist.

"Tsk tsk! I turn my back on you for two seconds and this is what happens."

The man had the red hair and green eyes of the girl, but where the girl's green dress and slippers could have passed her off as a princess, the man was more in line with the beggars he passed earlier. He wore a patchwork doublet that may once have been red, with a dirty brown waistcoat and matching pants. His feet were wrapped in rags.

Not a bad idea, thought Luke.

"I'm terribly sorry about this, sir," the man continued. "Kids these days, am I right? She will be punished properly I assure you."

The girl made a sad face.

Luke shook his head. "No, no. It's all good. Don't worry about it."

"I must insist on worrying about it, sir. She is my daughter and I wouldn't be much of a father if I let her carry on like this. She is young yet, and a young mind is still ripe for molding. There's hope for her." He turned to the girl. "Why were you accosting this man in such a way, darling?"

She pouted. "I was hungry, papa."

"Ah yes. Hunger. The bane of clear and rational thinking, right up there with anger, and just beneath those pesky pangs that come from one's heart when they're in love. An honest mistake dear, but patience is a virtue. The proper application of that will keep you out of the dungeons. You must remember this. Patience must be exercised when *choosing* a mark, but you must also not be scared to act immediately when an opportunity presents itself. You were a bit *too* patient. *Hesitation* was your downfall here, dear."

"Interesting advice," said Luke, his eyes narrowing.

"It's very *good* advice is what it is." The man winked. "Your sister has the right idea."

Luke twisted his body to follow the man's pointing finger behind him, and realized his folly too late. Another red head was on her hands and knees directly behind him, and the trap was complete when the man shoved Luke backwards over her.

He hit the cobbles with a grunt. The man was on him in a flash, pressing the cold steel of a knife under his chin.

"Not a very inventive trick, I'll grant you," the man chuckled. "But an effective one."

Luke started to get up, but the knife was deadly sharp.

"Careful now, lad. The girls are too young to see this get messy. Wouldn't you agree? Again, I'm terribly sorry. I don't like to do things this way, but the girls have many lessons to learn and I'll do what I must to teach them. Girls! What did I tell you about backpackers?"

"Never go for the whole backpack," said the girl who tripped him. She brushed the dirt off of her torn pants. This girl was more akin to her father in terms of fashion.

"And why is that, dear?" The question was directed to the girl in the green dress.

She looked at her toes. "Because they are too heavy."

"Exactly. As you have just proven. You'll have to triple up on your spinach intake if you want to tackle something like that. What else have I told you about backpackers?"

"Backpackers usually keep their coins where they can reach them while they are in town, like on their belt, so they don't gotta take off the backpacks when they buy stuff."

"Exactly. It's true for most people, really. You listen for a jingle. A keen ear is key here, girls. Of course, you can also watch them as they make purchases to see where they keep their coins. And please, substitute 'don't gotta' for 'don't have to'. You're respectable, educated ladies."

He prodded the pouch Luke had attached to his belt to show the girls the jingling sound.

"Once you have your target and the location of your prize, you must be patient and wait for the right moment. You were close with your moment, darling. Very close. But you would have found greater success had you chosen to go for the pouch on his belt, and done so when he *began* to water the stones here, not after. It's more difficult for him to give chase when he's messing all over himself. Convenient chaos. Purses are cut from belts swiftly, like so."

He motioned as if to cut Luke's coin purse from his belt, but only pretended.

"And then you fly, my little magpies! Fly fast and far. Race home now girls. Lunch will follow. Show me how fast a magpie flies!"

With that, the little red heads took off, shoving to get ahead of one another.

When they were alone, the man loosened Luke's purse string.

"You've been a great sport today, you know. Really I appreciate it. It warms my heart to know there are still decent folk left in this crazy world."

Luke scowled up at him. "I'm glad you're happy."

"Oh I am," he laughed. "The girls will learn one more lesson today."

"And what's that?"

The man opened Luke's pouch wide and gestured with the knife towards Lee Grover's book, laying on the cobbles next to them.

"It's a terrible thing for someone to be robbed twice in one day. We don't want people getting the wrong impression of our fine city. Here you are, lad."

He sprinkled a handful of copper coins into Luke's pouch and pulled the drawstring tight. "Consider yourself a teacher for the day. These are your wages for assisting in the tutelage of my magpies. Now, if you'll excuse me, I believe they require feeding. Goodbye!"

When Luke sat up, the man was nowhere to be seen. He shook his head and checked his pouch to make sure what he thought he saw actually happened.

"Amazing," he mumbled to himself, and looked up at the narrow sky. "Where the hell am I?"

Chapter Fourteen

"Have you lovely ladies heard the words of Lee Grover? How about you, sir? Little girl?"

Sam gasped when Sophie reacted to the beggar by winding back her walking stick as if to strike him. The man tipped his floppy brimmed hat to them, and fought through the crowd to turn his charms on less abrasive targets.

"Was that necessary?" Sam asked.

"Absolutely," said Sophie. "You have to be firm with those types, otherwise you'll never get rid of them."

"They have special noses," added Lia, clearly proud of herself for remembering another piece of Sophie's wisdom.

"Special noses?"

"She means they can smell weakness," explained Gerald.

Sam shook her head. "You mean *compassion.*"

Sophie harrumphed. "Was I not compassionate when I bought you that coffee you cried for? The coffee you *needed* to go with the muffin Gerald bought you? We can only sponsor so many freeloaders at a time, my dear."

Sam blushed and took a sip from the travel mug she conveniently carried in her tote bag at all times. The innkeeper was even nice enough to rinse it out for her.

The group traveled on foot, riding a wave of produce laden farmers through the city gates. There were many wagons pulled by animals, but there were plenty of others that pulled themselves. These wagons had no engines that Sam could see, nor compartments where an engine could be tucked away. She'd have thought them to be electric somehow, if Lia hadn't been so confused when she'd asked for an electrical outlet in the rental wagon. Curiously, the self propelled wagons were all riddled with sunflowers.

"That's brilliant," Sam cried, when she finally gave in and asked Sophie how the wagons operated.

Flower power, Sam named it. This explained the flowers that engulfed the Riverview Inn, and likely the vines strangling the buildings around them now. She remembered one of the pictures in Luke's book, the city with sunflowers on all the rooftops. *Is this that city?* The innkeeper said Luke was interested in the flower system. How much did he really know about this world? He was going to have a lot of explaining to do when she found him.

Precious moments were wasted admiring the dedication of a blond craftswoman who stood knee deep in a water fountain to repair the broken genitals of the fountain's permanent bather, Poseidon. These moments would have been better used in escaping the courtyard before the rest of the merchants flooded in through the mermaid gate, because shortly after their arrival, the wave of merchants met with an opposing force of customers so fiercely ready to shop that Sam could have sworn they hadn't ate in days.

The initial clash of consumer and producer was like something out of *Braveheart*. Sam expected at any moment that Mel Gibson would leap atop a vegetable cart and scream, *"Give us cabbages or give us death!"*

Did I mix my movies up? As Sam pondered the accuracy of her imagined quote, a wheel rolled off of a nearby wagon, tipping it just enough to lose a precariously stacked load of caged chickens. Several of the cages broke open when they hit the cobbles, adding a feathery element to the mounting chaos.

Lia was nearly trampled by a frantic chicken chaser, to which Sophie responded by hooking the man's foot and tripping him with her stick. The chicken he was chasing disappeared into the crowd. When he turned, furious, towards Sophie, Sophie was groping the air with one hand and tapping her staff to the cobbles with the other, as if she were blind. The man calmed, but another chicken chaser, who was running behind them, knew the truth of it.

"I saw that, you old hag!" he hollered, winding his palms back to push her.

He never had the chance. A quick jab to the face from Gerald's fist stunned him, and the following right hook leveled him to the cobbles next to his friend. The first man sprang from the ground towards Gerald's waist, but stopped abruptly, and finally, as his forehead collided with the driving butt of Sophie's staff.

Sam watched the scene through wide eyes, wide enough to see the third man.

She pulled Gerald aside just in time to see a brick sail through the space Gerald's head occupied a second earlier. The brick smacked into the back of a tall woman with long brown hair. The woman turned out to be a man, and that man may as well have been Mel Gibson. The rallying cry that erupted from the shaggy man's throat when he saw his attacker, highlighted by the second brick in his hand, whipped the entire courtyard into a violent frenzy. Fists and bricks and produce began flying every which way.

Sophie gave Sam a congratulatory pat on the back while dodging a rogue cucumber. "Good work, princess. Time for us to be off, I think. This way."

Gerald scooped Lia up in his arms and followed Sophie through the crowd. Sam paused long enough to notice the watchman emerge from the gatehouse, his mouth agape.

They were nearly out of the courtyard when a bearded man wedged himself between Sophie and Gerald, apparently thinking Gerald with his arms full was an easy mark. He was wrong. Gerald spartan kicked the man in the chest, sending him backwards and splitting the crowd to clear a smooth path to the street.

Sam looked over her shoulder at the carnage behind them. A cackling woman had risen above the crowd on a cart, and was firing apples from a basket at random targets.

"No wonder groceries are so expensive these days," complained Sophie. "Welcome to Tumblestone."

Sam laughed, pointing, "*You* started all that, you know."

"Pfft. I think not. That idiot should have watched where he was going. It's not like Lia is easy to miss. Atlantis is none too keen on displays of magic, even from children, and Lia has little control over her abilities."

"An emotional outburst might set her off," explained Gerald. "Not that her magic is really dangerous. It just might get us kicked out of the city."

"And land us a fine," said Sophie. "But worse, we wouldn't be able to find your wizard lover."

"He's not a wizard! And would starting a riot at the market really be less likely to get us kicked out of the city than one of Lia's magic bubble wall things?"

Sophie shrugged. "We're still here, aren't we?"

Sam sighed.

When they were a safe distance from the mob, Gerald set Lia back down. Lia, however, had enjoyed the special treatment, and requested a seat on Gerald's shoulders. He frowned, but obliged. Lia jingled happily from her new perch.

"I love these streets," said Sam. "The cobblestones. The buildings. It's just like Rome."

"Oh? Is Rome a shithole too?" asked Sophie.

"Sophie!" scolded Lia.

"Sorry, Lia."

"*No,* Rome is not a... not that. It's beautiful. Just look at those shutters!"

"I see them, princess. I also see a lot of rubbish. The buildings are falling apart."

"They just need to clean up a bit, that's all."

"Ha!" Sophie scoffed. "That won't happen. The Historical Society goes around marking everything as a Heritage Property. Everything has to be kept original, and there's so much paperwork involved in getting anything done that this is what happens. The buildings crumble to dust. But don't clean any of it. No no, not unless it's impossible to get around it otherwise. You'd be erasing history. If somebody *does* jump through all the hoops, they'll need those original bricks to put back in the wall. Nonsense, all of it."

"Sophie had a house in Camelot years ago. Same situation there, really," explained Gerald.

"Ahh, I see," said Sam. "Well, anyways... My grandmother took me to Rome once when I was little. This is something like that. I don't know about the heritage stuff, and my grandmother never started any market fights. Well, there was that guy with the bracelets... Hmm. Hey. Is Lia your granddaughter, Sophie?"

"She is."

"How come she calls you Sophie, and not grandmother, or grandma, or granny?"

"Because my *name* is Sophie."

"Sophie doesn't like to be called grandma," said Lia. "And she *really* doesn't like to be called granny. She says it makes her feel old. But she *is* old. She has wrinkles and everything."

Sophie shot Lia a scowl.

"You shouldn't be ashamed of it," said Sam. "You're in great shape, and you look really good for your age."

She instantly regretted her last three words, even before Sophie cursed her with a scowl as well.

"I look great for *any* age."

"You do. You're right. Really. You're lovely! Especially your eyes. You have very pretty eyes."

"That's more like it. Please continue. You haven't mentioned my heart shaped behind yet."

Gerald and Lia chuckled.

"I was *just* getting to that," said Sam. "Say, aren't you a little nervous walking through the city with that thing on your staff? I'm noticing a lot of, er, less fortunate people, eyeing it up."

"Let them look. Are you worried that I look like a witch? Witches are allowed in the city."

"Um, no. Well it does look kind of witchy, but I was thinking more like it might be tempting fate to walk around with a giant emerald on full display. I mean, I'm surprised nobody tried to swipe it back in the courtyard. Unless... Are emeralds cheap here? If so, I'd really like to get a couple before I head home."

Sophie and Gerald exchanged smiles, though Gerald's was more sheepish.

"Gerald here had a similar thought when we met, didn't you, Gerald?"

"I was just doing what I was told, Sophie..."

"What do you mean?" Sam asked.

Sophie chuckled. "Gerald and I met in this very city actually. Many moons ago."

"Before I was born!" said Lia.

"That's right, dear. Gerald was running with a gang of hoodlums back then, and I was traveling alone. I had been a stranger in several cities by that time, and was becoming quite accustomed to the lingering eyes and heavy jaws that followed me wherever I went. Such reactions are hardly avoidable when you cut a figure like mine."

Gerald sighed.

"When I added this little ornament here to my staff, the attention I received blended with the usual, so I admit to being a bit surprised when Gerald broke into my room at the inn."

"You broke into her room??"

Gerald was flushed. He nodded.

"The surprise was not that he broke into my room. I saw him making eyes at me earlier, and I knew he had followed me. I heard the click when he picked the lock on my door, so I pretended to be asleep when he entered. At that point I hadn't quite decided what I would do. He's comely enough, I thought. But does he deserve me? Of course, anyone willing to take someone in such a way by force is *not* deserving and should be castrated. However, I had needs of my own and a knife under the blankets to help steer the situation towards castration, if need be."

"What's castration, Sophie?"

"Never mind, Lia. Now, the real surprise came while I lay there, eyes closed, listening to his sad attempt at sneaking. The footsteps did *not* approach my bed, rather, they sounded toward the opposite corner of the room, where my staff stood leaning against the wall. When I opened my eyes, the moonlight shining in through those cheap curtains betrayed Gerald, fiddling with the fastenings on my staff. What happened next, Gerald?"

The red faced Gerald coughed nervously. "When I freed the ornament from the staff, I suspected it was not what I thought. I pulled open the curtain for a better look to be sure."

"The look on his face was priceless," Sophie laughed. "I have a good friend back home in the Summerfall Valley who runs a glass blowing shop. He supplied many of the local wineries with bottles for their product, still does. He's very good at what he does, but everyone makes mistakes, especially when they receive wine as partial payment for their talents."

Sam smiled and looked closer at the staff. It was obvious.

"So that's not an emerald at all. It's a—"

"Wine bottle." Sophie nodded.

"That's awesome. But still, you tried to rob her, and now you're traveling together. How?"

Gerald coughed again.

Sophie grinned. "Well I mentioned that I had some needs, but that's not a tale for little ears. Gerald had some redeeming qualities, we'll say."

A different light fell upon Gerald's *Village People* outfit, and the spry old woman. Sam was quite sure that traveling wasn't the only thing keeping her in shape. She smiled. *Good for her.*

She caught her mind wandering in warm directions, and coughed. "And you still carry the bottle with you like this, after that?"

"No, actually. There have been many other attempts to steal my bottle, and several have been successful. This isn't the original. I keep a few extras on hand."

"Why?"

Sophie shrugged. "It's good for a chuckle."

Sam shook her head. "Of course."

The group pinballed their way through a street nearly as crowded as the courtyard. They dodged women and girls in torn and dirty dresses. They squeezed past men and boys in dusty waist coats and flat caps. They might have been stylish had they not been so filthy. Every person they saw looked like they hadn't cut or washed their hair, or changed their outfit since they dolled themselves up for prom night twenty years ago.

Sam examined Sophie's witchy robe and Gerald's *Village People* outfit. "I'm a little surprised. Everybody in the city wears these old-timey clothes, you know. Well, I guess you probably don't know, but if you were from my world, you might. But you guys don't dress anything like these people."

"Why should we dress the same as everyone else?" asked Sophie.

Sam bobbed her head. "Fair point, actually. Never mind. Just an observation."

Many of the dirty prom dates tried their luck at begging, and many others offered some random thing to sell. One man insisted the belt buckle he had for sale was something they "couldn't live without."

Sophie waved her staff at him. "Are you threatening me, boy?"

The only successful entrepreneur of the lot was a young brunette with short hair that she appeared to have cut herself with a dull knife. The girl wooed Lia with an overarm display of "genuine fragments of Faron's star" made into necklaces and bracelets. Sam was no geologist, but was fairly certain the "star fragments" would match the pebbles found between the cobblestones. The jingling Lia was an easy sell though, immediately agreeing to purchase a necklace with Gerald's money.

A right turn at the end of the street bought them room to breathe. Aside from a few stray dogs and a couple people working to re-pin a wagon wheel, they had the street to themselves. Sophie assured her that it was the right way to the city center. The watchman at the gate had told them a "sun burnt guy with weird trousers" was looking for a library. Since the library was closed, the guy was planning to find a place to spend the night in the city.

Knowing that Luke had the same worthless money as she did, Sam suggested they find the cheapest possible accommodations. Perhaps Luke would beg for change to get a room. That thought was quickly banished. She smiled to herself. It would be more likely to find Luke sleeping behind a dumpster.

Still, they decided to seek out the Wooden Hearth Inn near the city center. It was notorious for being the biggest "shithole," as Sophie whispered, in the city. So it was probably the cheapest, and most often recommended as the cheapest, if he were to ask around. With Luke being a man, however, Sam held doubts as to whether he would actually ask anyone for directions.

They passed a row of statues that further reminded her of Italy. Naked depictions of men in various poses wielding swords, axes, hammers, and further down the line, rifles.

When Sam's slowing stride became noticeable about halfway along the row of statues, Sophie placed a hand on her shoulder and chuckled.

"Should we leave you alone for a moment, princess?"

Sam frowned at the cheeky old woman, and shook her head vigorously. She could honestly say the statues evoked no desires to be *left alone*. The sculptors of Tumblestone were far more generous in the 'between the legs' department than their Italian counterparts. Admittedly, the first few raised her eyebrows and conjured a silent "Wow!" but her expression melted into one of horror by the time she reached the last, and 'largest' statue.

Richard Stryker, the current King of Atlantis, had apparently eaten one of the Mr. Olympia champions. His muscle bloated likeness stood proud with a hand on his hip and a guitar over his shoulder. Sam held her arm up between the statue's legs and said aloud, "Ouch!"

CHAPTER FIFTEEN

The gently swaying spider web in the corner of the window was practically a bullseye to the experienced grackle. The bird swooped in, clung to the shutter just long enough to pluck the juicy treat from its web, and dropped down to the planter to consume it in comfort.

She was an old bird, and spent all of her years foraging amongst the stone nests of the earthbound creatures. She had seen many things, but the earthbound creatures were always full of surprises.

Earlier, she witnessed one such creature molt from the waist up in an alleyway, and tear its old brown skin into two pieces. It then attached a piece of the old skin to each of its feet and finished its strange ceremony by mounting a brown turtle shell to its back. Since then, the grackle kept a sharp eye on the curious creature, as had other grackles, watching from similar perches a safe distance above.

The creature was easy to follow. The skin of its lower region was as blue as the evening sky, and its face was as red as a cardinal.

It stood out like a beacon amidst the noisy grey-brown river of earthbound creatures below.

With the ingestion of the spider, the grackle was reloaded and ready for another fly by. She fluttered her wings, and dove.

Luke was developing a sixth sense, or rather, a staggering case of anxiety. Constant urges to look over his shoulder allowed him to survive the 'shit and fly' tactics so expertly applied by the local bird population. Without fail, every time he looked back, he saw them coming. Noisy little black birds, swooping and shitting on everything in their wake. Everything except Luke. So far, his dodges had kept him out of harm's way, but he was getting tired.

These must be the grackles that Lee guy warned me about.

He had to be getting close to the city center.

Luke's new sense tilted his head to the sky just in time. He flinched violently, throwing himself away from the sticky white missile and into the side of a moving wagon. Embarrassed, he issued a quick apology to the wagon driver and his mule. The driver nodded his understanding. When he did so, the man revealed the brim of his gray hat to be peppered with white blobs.

"Ahh!" Luke smiled, and pointed a finger at the man. "Look at you! Clever guy."

The attacks made him regret his decision to destroy his shirt in favor of his feet, but the man's shit covered hat gave him an idea for a solution. He paused for a moment, keeping a watchful eye on the skies, to remove his backpack and unfasten the bedroll. He strapped back into the pack and pulled the bedroll up over his head. It wasn't much of a shield, and he probably looked ridiculous, but at least his sore feet and legs could have a break from all the dodging. He was also less likely to be run over by a carriage this way.

Aside from the shit raining from the skies, Luke had made his way into a much cleaner part of the city in comparison to where he entered. He saw his first trash bin in this section, and he witnessed people using it. No trash littered the cobbles here, nor any piles of rubble. People were sweeping the streets in front of shops and, inside, others were taking great care in how they displayed their merchandise in the shop windows. The paint on the buildings was smooth and bright, and where it was not, painters were in the process of making it so.

The people themselves were dressed perilously nice as well, like how he imagined everyone in London to dress. It seemed unwise to him, though, that everyone would be wearing frivolous dresses and fancy suits and hats with the threat of shit stains constantly swooping over them, but they were remarkably adept at dodging. A painter, in slacks, with a black vest over his white button up shirt, was painting a window sill, when, without even looking back, he casually stepped to the side just as the cobbles where he was standing were bombarded. He must have seen the birds coming in the reflection off the window.

With the class change came an increase in stares. Now it wasn't just his out of this world jeans that drew the eye. He was outclassed. A greasy mess. His feet were wrapped in rags. His bare chest was pasty white, with here and there a brown bruise courtesy of his fall from the tree. His arms and face were burnt red, and the brown bedroll flowed down from over his head to trail behind him. He could hardly blame the gawkers. He probably looked like an animated lump of half melted neapolitan ice cream shambling up the street.

He tried to make the best of the situation. He began to think of himself as Medusa from Greek mythology. While many people were polite enough to smile before turning away from him, those that did stare made no secret of it. They turned completely to stone when they saw him, all of them frozen with wide eyes and slackened jaws, like each was a statue chiseled by the same uninspired artist.

He smiled and nodded at anyone he made eye contact with. Occasionally, these gestures would break the paralyzing spell cast by his image, and people would either turn away shyly, or take ridiculous fright. One man was struck so hard by Luke's smile that he tumbled backwards, knocking over a child peddling apples from a wheelbarrow. The wheelbarrow and apples went down with them, a splash of rolling red on the gray cobbles.

The street he was following met on an angle with what was clearly a main thoroughfare. The connecting road was considerably wider and busier. There the horses and wagons traveled in the center of the road, and pedestrians were routed along the sides on raised flagstone sidewalks. It was just like a normal city road, except, of course, for all the horses and wagons.

There were plenty of self propelled vehicles as well. Luke saw his first car then, or at least the closest thing he had seen to a car. It looked as if someone had taken a four door sedan and equipped it with jungle camouflage. It had the usual four wheels with rubber tires, and windows on the sides, front and back, but the rest of it was wrapped entirely in vines and bristled with sunflowers. It was hard to tell how the doors opened.

He failed to register that he was staring at the car while it was stopped, waiting for the light to change. Children in the backseat looked back at him with wonder in their eyes, while the mother in the front seat had her head craned around, shouting at them. The back window began to wind up slowly.

The mother was protecting her children from the ice cream monster on the sidewalk.

Luke sighed and looked elsewhere. Fewer grackles patrolled the skies, so he took a moment to pack up his bedroll after smearing some of the droppings onto the sidewalk. This was slightly depressing, but his heart soared when across the busy street he saw an *actual sign*. A directional sign, indicating Tumble Square was to his right.

Beautiful.

Besides the King Street sign he saw earlier, the most he saw of street signage that day were the empty poles where street signs should have been.

Luke followed the wide road to the right and passed something of a transit terminal. There was one large bus on the lot that was wrapped in vines like the sedan, but the majority of travel options consisted of wooden wagons and carriages hitched to mules and horses. It was strange that so many people were still using animals to pull their wagons when they could power their vehicles with sunflowers. Perhaps the animals were faster, or maybe the operators just enjoyed their company.

The animals were calmly blinking at passersby while their handlers were desperately vomiting out various destination services so fast and loud it was nearly impossible to understand them, not that Luke recognized any of the locations. One of them might have been screaming "Tiverton!!" but the man was not consistently intelligible. The majority of these people were screaming in English, or *Arthurian,* but there may have been some Spanish and German as well. Whatever they called Spanish and German in this world, anyways.

The drivers pounced on anyone that glanced in their direction, eager to be on the road and earning coin. Luke made the mistake of waving to one of them and the entire lot swarmed over him like ants on sugar. One of the ants indeed spoke Spanish. Luke knew the Spanish word for no was the same as in English, but none of them, not even the English ants seemed to understand him.

When a particularly excited driver screamed all over his face about how fast his mules were, Luke swore that even if he broke both of his legs he would rather drag himself anywhere in the world than travel with any of *them*.

After breaking free, with great difficulty, from the wagon ants, it was not long before Luke reached Tumble Square.

Lee was right about it being hard to miss. The square was massive, like a football stadium with at least six streets branching off in each direction from a roundabout that circled an attractive park. Tall buildings framed the square on three sides, while the fourth showcased a flowing river. A wide bridge spanned the river, directly in line with the castle from the travel tome. The castle was perched beyond the river atop a hill with more cityscape surrounding it.

Luke entered the square with a side view of the park's centerpiece; an enormous marble statue, rising above a scattering of neatly spaced poplar trees. It stood in the middle of a crescent shaped fountain. The statue was, of course, carved without the detail of clothing, but unlike all the other statues he'd come across that bore the supposed likeness of ridiculously hung kings or gods, this one was chiseled into a rather shapely woman. Perhaps she was a queen or a goddess.

Two geysers spouted continuously on either side of the marble giant, adding a fine mist to the air that tickled his skin with cool kisses as he approached. He closed his eyes to bask in the sensation as he crossed the roundabout to the park, but snapped them back open when a carriage driver shouted for him to watch where he was walking.

One of many narrow gravel walkways took him on a meandering path towards the fountain, past rows of fragrant rose bushes blooming beneath the shade of the trees. Wherever there was grass instead of shrubbery, the space was filled by people. Picnickers, readers, people tossing balls back and forth. Merchants carrying or pushing their wares loitered about, holding up a necklace or a piece of fruit to passersby. Others laid out blankets to display their goods. Some of the beggars from earlier had made their way to the park as well, but they didn't pester him. Wealthier prey was plentiful.

A red squirrel crossed his path and stopped halfway up a tree to look back at him, on the chance that Luke might offer a snack, no doubt. When Luke turned his empty palms up, the squirrel chittered and continued on its way.

The squirrel was the wrong color, and spoke the wrong language to be Henry. Where was he now? Henry would never find Luke in the city. He'd been walking all day, and probably couldn't even find his own way back to the gate where he entered without getting lost. Not that the squirrel *needed* to return to him, but his company was kind of nice.

Another chitter from the red squirrel drew Luke's gaze upwards. He couldn't see where it had gone, but the grackles, whose warbling, screeching racket had blended into the background noise lately, cackled amongst themselves from the squirrel's tree and many others, likely planning another shit and fly.

Luke braved a seat on one of the convenient benches next to the fountain. The rest and mist were wonderful, though he kept a watchful eye to the trees in respect for the grackles. With his other eye, he beheld for a moment the fountain's naked marble guardian. A shiny plaque proclaimed her as "Lady Luck."

An elderly man stopped to seek the lady's favor by tossing a silver coin into the water at her feet. He removed his hat and said some sort of prayer before walking away. Apparently, the favor he sought was not for himself, but for the dirt faced boy who dove, fully clothed, into the fountain after he left. The boy emerged with a cleaner face, and held the sparkling silver wish between two of his fingers.

Others paid homage to the fountain's patron saint by following her lead, stripping their clothes and bathing naked in the foamy pool. Several men and women were splashing about, scrubbing themselves with rags and rinsing off beneath the geysers. Occasionally, they waved at familiar faces, and received casual waves and hellos in return. A beat cop of sorts strolled by, merely nodding at the indecent exposure.

Their courage was admirable. Some of them, for multiple reasons, were a bit too admirable. Not unlike the human statues who gawked at him earlier, Luke froze, wide eyed and slack jawed, when a long haired brunette who looked exactly like Sam came bouncing over to his edge of the fountain. He swallowed hard, and was about to shout out to the beautiful woman, but Sam shouted first.

"David! David, come in! The water is *perfect* today!"

David?

A curly haired, olive skinned man rushed past him, throwing his shirt off as he ran. The woman, whose face in no way at all resembled Sam's, leaned out of the fountain to kiss him. Before Luke knew it, the man was also naked, and splashing about in the fountain with the woman.

For a second, the idea of stealing the man's shirt and shoes played out in his head, but he thought better of it. Instead, he coughed, and turned his attention elsewhere.

It was just as well. The grackles were beginning another round of bombings throughout the square.

Better to give them a moving target, he thought, and left the bench to seek out Reed Street and the suspiciously titled *Wooden Hearth Inn* that supposedly existed there.

No surprise, the adjacent streets were marked only by empty sign posts. Street signs were too much to ask for in this city.

He peered down three of the streets, hoping the inn would jump out at him. No luck, and as he might have expected, the streets peered right back at him. He poked his tongue out at a gawking blonde boy and felt quite satisfied about it, until he turned to see himself walk into an elderly woman wrapped in colorful shawls. The woman and her two heavy buckets of overripe bananas tumbled backwards onto the cobbles.

Luke rushed to help her to her feet, apologizing profusely. The old woman didn't seem too concerned. In fact, she was all toothless smiles as the accident made it impossible for Luke to refuse purchasing one of the mushy black bundles. A doubly unfortunate mistake. By purchasing the bananas, he alerted the other banana vendors, hovering nearby, to his great need of bananas. They shouted and tripped over one another, each boasting the best banana prices in the city.

He learned caution from that incident. So much caution that he had no room for stubbornness. He stopped to ask for directions.

A group of people in clothing more closely related to that worn in Halifax were doing exercises in an open area behind the giant statue. A burly bald man in a sleeveless *COFFEE* shirt was taking a breather, and was the first to stare at him, so Luke chose him for directions.

He caught himself mirroring the stunned look on the man's face when he noticed the *COFFEE* shirt was actually a burlap sack. It was likely filled with coffee beans in a previous life. Being shirtless, the coffee sack had a certain appeal. He was curious how it smelled, but hadn't lost enough of his mind to take a whiff of the stranger's shirt. Perhaps tomorrow.

He flashed the bald man a smile. "Hey buddy! Any idea where Reed Street is? I can't seem to find a sign for it. Is it one of these streets?"

The bald man glanced over his shoulder to confirm himself as the intended target of Luke's inquiry. With a glint of fear in his eyes, the big man answered with a grunt.

Luke's smile vanished, but reappeared when the man nodded and began speaking with a slow and deep cadence.

"It's ova dare," he said, pointing.

"Beautiful. Thanks man. Here!" He pressed the bananas into the man's hands, carefully, to avoid smushing them. No easy task. "For your troubles. No need to thank me. Have a great day!"

He left the man staring dumbly at his new old bananas.

After a few minutes of walking on the relatively quiet Reed Street, Luke's eye was caught by a peculiar building. He tilted his head hard to the left to match the three story structure's lean. At first glance, it seemed as if the foundation had settled badly on the left side. A closer inspection revealed that to be accurate, but the sill had rotted away as well. The wooden structure was relying completely on its stone neighbor to remain upright, like a drunk might lean on a sober person.

"Ugh" he groaned, his eyes wandering along the trail of dead cockroaches leading up the steps to the sagging porch. There he saw the worst part.

"Shit."

A faded sign with the barely discernible words, "*Wooden Hearth Inn,*" lay on the porch next to the entry way. The rusty chains that once held it up now swayed pointlessly above it. There was a porch swing in a similar state, with one side suspended and the other being used by the wind to slowly scrape through the deck.

He sighed. *Beggars can't be choosers, I guess.* If only he had been *robbed* a few more times, perhaps he could have spent the night in that castle across the river.

Rusty hinges groaned in complaint when he shoved open the old door, followed by the crunch of a cockroach under his, thankfully, wrapped foot. Still, the feeling was enough to make him cringe.

A terrible stench smacked him in the face the second the door was opened. Instinctively, he reached to pull his shirt over his nose, but of course, his shirt was wrapped around his feet, covered in cockroach guts. He settled for pressing his bicep into his face instead, and was not pleased by the smell he found in his arm pit either. Perhaps he'd visit the fountain later. After dark. There'd be no bathing here, even if he survived the smell.

The room was dark, unlit save for the sunlight filtering in through the dirty windows and around the shadow he cast from the open doorway. When his eyes adjusted, he stepped gingerly around a pile of blankets laying in the center of the foyer, and approached the messy front desk. The pale receptionist offered no immediate reply to his greeting. No grunt. Not even a blink. He stared absently ahead beneath the brim of a dark bowler hat.

"Hello?" he offered again. "Are you deaf?" The incredibly gaunt man looked ancient enough to have serious hearing issues, so for the third "Hello!" he yelled.

Still nothing. Something stirred behind him, but when he looked he saw nothing.

Probably a rat.

"Something on my face, maybe?" he asked, running a hand over his forehead. "Oh. Of course there is."

He rubbed the grackle shit from his hair onto his jeans.

"Sorry. I know I look like... well, shit."

But so does this place.

It looked an awful lot like his own house when he first bought it. Filthy cracked windows, dust over everything, water damage everywhere, holes in the baseboards, holes no doubt used by rats or mice to sneak around the building. He should have been pleased, at least, that there had been no cockroaches in his house. Most of them scattered when he entered the inn, but the dead ones laid about the floor like toys in a toddler's playroom.

The receptionist remained unresponsive. He just sat there, unmoving, with his pasty white jaw hanging open, his crooked yellow teeth on full display.

What's wrong with this guy?

A cockroach appeared on the man's shoulder. Its tiny legs carried it casually across his neck and chin, before stopping to rest on his cheek. The cockroach answered Luke's unspoken question.

"Perfect," he groaned. "You're dead. Beautiful. That certainly, um, explains the lack of upkeep here. Ugh."

But that Lee guy said he stayed here last night. Did he kill him? No. The receptionist had clearly been dead for some time. It wasn't difficult to imagine Lee simply squatting in a derelict building and paying no heed to the corpse.

Before Luke could think on what to do about discovering a corpse, another rustling sounded behind him. The pile of blankets was moving, rising up from the floor as if by a specter. It belched, long and loud.

"That man is *not* dead!" argued the blankets. With a shimmy, the blankets fell back to the floor, leaving a *slightly* less cadaverous looking man standing in their place. A curly clump of graying black hair grew from his head, and a wild, bushy beard hung from his chin. The smell of stale booze and body odor overtook the smell of death. It was not an improvement.

The drunk continued. "That man is my great, great, great grandfather. Harry Delbridge."

"Right," said Luke. "Well, I'm pretty sure your... great, great, great grandfather *is* dead."

"Impossible."

"Look at him! He's fucked!"

"Hmm. Admittedly he does look terrible. But the man is *immortal.* He *can't* die. Hold on a moment."

Luke pressed his arm tighter to his face as the rancid man walked by him to one of the windows. He picked up a watering can, and poured some water onto a plant sitting on the window sill. Then he approached his triple-great grandfather to repeat the action. He shooed away the cockroach, tilted the man's head back, and poured a generous amount of liquid into his open mouth. Luke stared gape mouthed at the procedure.

The corpse moved. A shoulder twitched. The other shoulder twitched. Then the head tilted slightly to the left, and the lifeless eyes *blinked.*

But that was all. The movement stopped there.

"Hmm," said the grandson. "Sometimes it's like this. Another moment please."

Luke nodded and spoke mechanically, "Yes. My truck is the same way sometimes."

The grandson poured another shot of water into his triple-great grandfather's mouth, much of which came back out and trickled down his chin. This drew a raspy moan from somewhere deep in the old man's throat. His mouth moved. He began to slowly chew at the air, spilling more water.

What the hell am I watching right now?

He watched the old man's chest rise as he took in air, and saw and smelled the chest fall, as it exhaled the potent stench of death. His eyes fell shut. When they snapped back open a few heartbeats later, they were looking directly at Luke.

Luke shuddered.

The old man's head slumped. Lifeless again.

His grandson pouted. "Ohh we almost had him that time! One more shot should do it."

He raised the watering can again, but Luke held out a hand to stop him.

"You know what? I'm good. I believe you now, and that's enough. Let him rest. Clearly he's exhausted."

"Are you sure? It's no bother to him at all. Really. Let's try again."

"No! I mean... yes, I'm sure. Please. Let him rest."

"Oh. Well alright. I suppose he did have a pretty late night. Very well. Perhaps *I* can be of assistance. Are you looking for a bed?"

With some reluctance, Luke nodded his head. "Yes. I am."

"Splendid," the grandson beamed. "Let's just check the ledger here and see what's available, hmm?"

Luke didn't need to see the ledger. He knew the entire building was vacant.

The grandson sucked air through his teeth, "Oh, sorry lad. We're all booked up at the moment. But we should have a room free up later today if you'd like to come back this evening. Should I pencil you in?"

"Sure. Why not..."

Luke glanced around the room, avoiding the grandson's awkward smile for a moment.

Really should have said no.

The grandson snapped him from his lamentation with a wave of his hand.

"Sir? Your name, please. I'm sure *I'll* remember your face, but if it should be granddad who checks you in, he'll need a name. He's becoming forgetful."

"Right. Of course. Luke. Luke Fletcher."

"Splendid. Done! That'll be three coppers upon check in. Don't worry about it now. We'll fix up later."

As the grandson closed the ledger, a bright eyed young man emerged from the hallway behind the front desk and flipped his stove pipe hat to them.

"Good day, Spencer!" said the man to the grandson.

"Good day to *you*, Charlie!" Spencer retorted, then to Luke he added, "Unfortunately, that doesn't mark a vacancy. Charlie is one of our full time residents."

Luke's eyebrows disappeared into his hair line. "Full time residents. *Full time,*" he mumbled. He knew people could adjust somehow to foul smells, but he found it difficult to imagine adjusting to the smell of a rotting triple-great grandfather. His eyes were watering.

"What was that, sir?"

"Nothing, nothing. I'll see you later, I guess."

Several minutes of dry heaving in front of the Wooden Hearth Inn reminded Luke that he hadn't eaten anything since breakfast. It seemed high time that he changed that.

CHAPTER SIXTEEN

S am's shirt went up over her nose the second she entered.

"Ugh! Gross! *What* died in here??"

Gerald pinched his nose, and Sophie cursed as she crunched a cockroach into the floorboards with her stick.

"By the gods, Gerald. Prop that door open," Sophie ordered, "before *we* die in here."

A lantern sparked to life, illuminating the desk it sat upon further into the foyer with a flickering glow.

Lia screamed.

Something *did* die in the inn, and that something had lit the lantern. A wrinkly white corpse in a dark bowler hat smiled a gummy smile at them from behind the desk. It tried several times to blow out the match it held before the flame reached its fingers and guttered itself out.

"Welcome... to the Wooden Hearth... Inn," came the raspy, breathless voice of the corpse. Its cracked lips stretched with effort into another gummy smile.

Sam had no words.

Lia screamed again.

The eyes of the corpse widened. "What... is it... little girl?" Its head turned slowly to the left and to the right. "Do you... see another... cockroach? Dreadful things."

Lia hid herself in Sophie's robes.

The corpse reached out and picked up a watering can. It appeared to use every ounce of strength it had to tilt the can to its mouth, but it managed, successfully filling its mouth and soaking its pea coat in one motion. The corpse swallowed the water with a noise similar to a clogged sink drain.

Sam remained speechless.

"Harry Delbridge?" said an incredulous Sophie.

"You know that thing? Um... him?" asked Gerald, with equal surprise.

"Indeed... it is I, Harry Delbridge," said the corpse. Its speech had improved slightly after the drink. "Forgive me if I... don't recognize you... darling. Many people come and go."

"I wouldn't expect you to. I've changed a bit these last, what, fifty years? I stayed here once with my father as a girl. I wasn't much older than you, Lia. But *you*, Harry... You haven't aged a day."

"Really?" Sam managed.

"You... flatter me, miss?"

"Sophie Saddler. So it must be true then. My father told me you were immortal. I didn't believe him."

Harry the immortal corpse laughed, though if he hadn't been smiling, and immortal, Sam would have assumed he was choking to death.

"Your doubt was... reasonably placed. Immortality becomes... more and more... difficult to achieve. It seems my kind are a... dying breed." Again, Harry gagged happily.

If that's what immortality looks like...

Gerald's gag was not as pleasant. "If you're good here, Sophie, I think I'll run back to that, uh, that kid selling the bootlaces in the square. I just remembered that I need a new pair for my spare boots. I should hurry before he sells out."

"I'll help you Gerald!" cried Lia. She bobbed her head enthusiastically, sending her necklaces into a jingle.

"I like... her style," said Harry, watching Lia rustle away.

"Yes. She seems to as well," sighed Sophie. "Never takes those trinkets off. Even sleeps with the bloody things."

Harry smiled. "My own son... insisted on dragging a stuffed bear with him... everywhere... until he was... eleven. For years... it was like having a... one armed child. Ah... children."

"Indeed. I keep telling her she's going to turn herself into a hunchback, wearing all those necklaces. But she 'doesn't care'. Loves her necklaces. Reminds her of the places we've traveled."

"Better to collect memories... than things. They weigh less."

"Well. Not always, though Lia says 'I can collect both.'"

Harry gagged heartily.

"Ahem!" Sam coughed, as much from impatience as from lung pollution. "I hate to interrupt, but we did come here for a reason."

"Of course, madam. Business... first. Are you seeking... a room?" Harry bent forward to eye the ledger.

"Not exactly. We're looking for someone. We believe he may have been heading here to find lodging for the night."

"Then he may very well... have done so, but you... don't look like members of the watch."

"We're not members of any watches," said Sam. "I'm just looking for my friend."

"But perhaps he is not... looking for you. I wouldn't... know. I'm... I'm..." Harry held up a bony finger, then raised the watering can to his lips again, drinking and spilling greedily. "I'm sorry but I can't... give information on guests unless they... give me permission themselves, or if you are members of... the watch."

"Fine. We *are* members of the watch. Official business and all that. Is a 'Luke Fletcher' staying here?"

Another amused gag. "I wasn't born yesterday, dear. Do you... seek this, Luke... on charges of infidelity?"

"What? No, no, nothing like that. He's just lost."

"Hmm... Not all who wander... are lost, my child. Perhaps he seeks to... find himself."

"What? Is that a guest ledger or a book of inspirational quotes? Luke and I..." Sam hesitated, but only for a second. Telling her strange story of teleporting through a book to the ancient corpse would be no more ridiculous than talking to an ancient corpse in the first place. She told him.

Harry listened to her tale with his hands clasped across his brittle chest.

"Hmm. Interesting," he said when she finished. "You found a... travel tome. Another rarity these days. Many were... burned... during the Great... Purge. Nothing great about those days. Such a thing in your... possession could get you killed... back then. Mage or not."

"The Purge ended centuries ago, though, right?" said Sam, looking to Sophie for correction. She had spoke of the Purge earlier. She was grateful to have arrived long after such events.

Sophie nodded.

"Thank the Gods... for that." Harry took another drink from the watering can. "But the books are still... rare. It requires a great... expenditure of energy... to create the portals within. With all the advances made... in the transportation sector, after the...purge, because of the photoaradiac energy development, railways and... automobiles... allow people to go further than...

ever before with less cost and effort. Travel tomes are... used far less now. People have learned to... slow down. To enjoy the beauty around them as they travel."

More from his inspiration quote book, no doubt.

Sam was doing her best *not* to enjoy the *beauty* around her at that moment. Her eyes stayed fixed on the talking corpse in front of her. Somehow, he was the lesser of the evils in the room, but she still caught odd glimpses of cockroaches in the corner of her eye, crawling about.

"Well, unfortunately I don't have the book anymore. I came through after Luke. The book stayed behind when he came through, and it didn't come with me. Everything else I had on me did, but not the book."

"How would you know?" asked Sophie. "There's more junk in that bag of yours than in a merchants warehouse."

Sam shot her a look. "I *don't* have the book."

Harry nodded. "There is a trick... to make such a book travel with you, though I... know not what it is. You will... figure it out... next time, perhaps."

"I just want to find Luke and get back home. So, could you just tell me if you've seen him or not?"

The ancient man sighed. "I suppose it won't hurt. Your story seems... genuine. I'll tell you... what I know about your... missing husband."

"He's not... whatever. Go ahead."

"Your husband is... not here, Mrs. Fletcher."

Mrs. Fletcher. Great. The next chat with her mother was going to be an awkward one. "So, what have you been up to, Samantha?" "Not much, mom. Work's been slow, found someone to take over my apartment, oh, and I got married. To a wizard. Yes. The hocus pocus kind." "Oh."

"My grandson made a note... in the ledger regarding... a shirtless man with blue trousers... and feet wrapped in rags... who bore the name you seek." He examined Sam, from head to feet, and back up again. "Clearly... the noble Luke sees to... his wife, first and... foremost. An admirable quality."

"Shirtless?" smiled Sam.

"Keep your trousers on, girl," warned Sophie. "We haven't found him yet."

"Yes... I agree with... Lady Saddler. Please keep them on. My heart... wouldn't stand it."

"But you're immortal, are you not?" argued Sam, though she had absolutely no intentions of taking her jeans off in a room crawling with cockroaches.

"I am. But knowledge of ones... imminent survival... does not equate... pleasure... during a heart attack."

"Fair enough. I promise. I'll keep my pants on."

"Thank you. As I was... saying. We did not have any... rooms available when Luke... was here. However... He was promised a room... set to vacate before the... end of the day. He left... but voiced his intent... to return. You may wait for him here... in the lobby... if you like."

"No, thank you. We'd love to, really, but we should probably, um, go check on the others. And maybe we'll run into Luke in the square."

Harry smiled. "Perhaps you may."

"It was... interesting to see you again, Harry," said Sophie. "But Sam is right. We should go. My granddaughter could be buried in trinkets by now."

Harry chuckled and bowed his head. "Be well, children."

His head didn't return from the bowed position. Before Sam and Sophie reached the doorway, Harry started to snore.

CHAPTER SEVENTEEN

A decision to buy a cup of wine from a boy who couldn't possibly be older than eight turned out to be a bad one. With a deposit of one copper rabbit, Luke was able to rent a dirty tin cup from that same boy. Another copper had the boy fill the cup with red wine and sediment. Mostly sediment. One regrettable mouthful later, the wine was slopped in a chunky heap on the cobbles, and Luke returned his cup for the deposit. A pair of stray dogs cleaned up his mess.

It was a decision borne of desperation to wash the taste of onions from his mouth, but he succeeded only in replacing one horrid taste with another. Onions were a blight on the food industry, and he had trusted the previous street vendor when she promised that there would be no onions in the soft taco she prepared for him.

His trust was sadly misplaced.

Sometime during the moments when he was distracted by a dapper group of acapella singers, snapping their fingers and singing for change in front of the Lady Luck fountain, the street vendor maliciously stuffed his taco with white onions. She snuck them in there, under the chicken, so he couldn't immediately spot the danger. He managed three bites before that too, was left for the dogs.

He considered at first to try a nice sit down restaurant, but after seeing his greasy sun-burnt reflection in the glass front window of *The Tumbled Tart*, and all the well dressed people inside, the phrase 'No Shirt, No Shoes, No Service' rang in his ears. He chose to be kind and not put the restaurant staff in the awkward position where they would have to kick him out.

His tongue was still squirming from the earlier betrayals as he looked about the square for a more trustworthy street vendor. This time he swore not to take his eyes off them for a second, not until the food was in his hands. He'd have to be quick, though. The square was getting busier by the minute. Lineups were beginning to stretch out in front of each of the vendors. There were even a few people lined up to drink the little boy's wine sediment.

He shuddered, and picked his way through the crowd toward a booth with a sign above it that read, *KEBAB*. It would be difficult to hide an onion in something served on a stick.

While waiting in line, his eyes fell upon a familiar long haired terrier. The white dog popped out from between the feet of a tall blond woman, and targeted Luke immediately. It was one of the stray dogs who had finished off his onion taco.

"Well hello again, little buddy," he greeted the dog.

Curiosity often outweighs good sense, but in this case, curiosity outweighed *bad scents*. The mop haired creature fearlessly approached and thoroughly whiffed both of Luke's undoubtedly foul smelling feet.

"Where'd you come from, anyways? Do you have an owner?"

He scratched the dog's neck and scanned the crowd for such a person, but nobody stood out. Did people in Tumblestone even keep dogs as pets? There were lots of dogs in the city. They were everywhere, walking the crowded streets, sniffing at trash cans, sleeping in alleyways. Sometimes they traveled in packs of six or more, but he had yet to see a dog on a leash or even wearing a collar.

The terrier was scrawny, filthy, and losing fur in patches. Likely, it belonged to the streets, not exactly the kindest or most loving master.

Luke unfolded the wrapper he had been saving for a garbage bin, and shook out the few remaining crumbs and bits of onion in front of the dog. Its dull eyes brightened at that, and made quick work of the offering, but it didn't stop there.

"Hey! What are you doing??" Luke cried.

It appeared that a hard life on the streets had no effect on the dog's libido. A few neck scratches and a mouthful of onions was enough to light a fire in the dog's loins. The rogue latched onto Luke's forearm and began pumping its hips with reckless abandon. This gave new merit to Luke's opinion that nothing good ever came from onions.

"No! Bad dog! Bad dog!"

He pushed the dog away with his free hand, but the dog bounced back. Consent meant nothing to it.

"You don't give up, do you?" he laughed, though his laughter petered out after several unsuccessful rounds of rejecting the assault. However, the laughter continued, as it was taken up by the crowd around him. Luke shook his head and smiled awkwardly at his audience. The dog would not give up.

One blessed onlooker stepped in to pull the dog off of him, but as soon as he released it, it was back again, sinking its claws and teeth into Luke's leg for a tighter grip.

He broke free again and ran, pushing through the laughing crowd, toward and around the dapper singers. There he found an opening.

"Shit."

The dog found the opening as well. Now an even larger number of eyes witnessed his embarrassment, and even more mouths roared with laughter. The dog was not letting him go this time, pumping furiously even as Luke kicked his leg into the air. He kicked again and again, but the dog had a death grip.

The crowd parted, and Luke made another run for it, awkwardly dancing and weaving through the laughing crowd with the dog quite literally *hot* on his heels. He made it into the roundabout, and barely avoided being struck by one of the vine cars while crossing over to the sidewalk. The dog was equally lucky.

He ran right into, and nearly knocked over, a severe looking man in a green tailcoat. The man and his incredibly bushy eyebrows scowled fiercely.

"Terribly... sorry, man," said Luke, jumping back to his feet. The collision separated the dog from his leg, just long enough for him to bolt into the nearest building and slam the door behind him.

The dog made a few attempts to paw its way through the door before it gave up. When Luke peeked through the door's window, he was pleased to see the dog had turned its affections onto the dick in the green coat.

He breathed a sigh of relief.

Sit down restaurant it is, then.

Hearing the door slam, every patron in the place stopped what they were doing and turned toward the sudden intruder. Luke offered them a sheepish grin.

He was fairly certain that the sign outside the door had read, *The Silver Fox Tavern,* but in his haste, perhaps he had read it wrong. Or perhaps the lighting provided by candle studded chandeliers was just bad, but from what Luke could see, the dimly lit faces staring back at him begged a different title. Not one of them looked a bit like George Clooney. Their less than handsome faces were further soured by the angry expressions they bore towards him.

Awkward seconds ticked by in silence, until Luke answered the "Who the hell is this guy?" question he imagined was on everyone's mind.

"I'm Luke," he said, stretching his smile wider across his right cheek. "Er, sorry about that." He motioned to the door. "It's fine though. The door's fine. No harm done. The dogs here, eh? They uh, they get excited, don't they?" He chuckled nervously.

Some of the men looked at each other and murmured something not meant for him to hear, and then looked back at him, and at the rags wrapped around his feet. The only clear sound in the tavern was that of *Cryin' Ryan Hobbs* wailing pathetically through speakers mounted throughout the room. His mournful "New Hit Single: Don't Wanna Stop Drinkin' About You" was playing, as it had played several times the night before next to Rufus's fire. That decided it.

"Right. Well..." Luke turned to leave, but a cautionary peek out the window stopped his hand from turning the door handle. The terrier was still out there, pacing back and forth, its eyes searching the crowds. The dick in the green coat had failed to satisfy. No surprise there.

Luke sighed, and turned back to the crowd. The room was a maze of tables. He looked quickly about for a free table in a private corner, but of course there were none. Each table was occupied by at least one rough looking character. Not wanting to risk further disapproval by bumping someone or someone's drink with his backpack, he unstrapped it and held it in front of him as he navigated the gauntlet of patrons on his way to the bar at the back of the room.

He noticed on his walk of shame that nobody in the tavern was eating. All the tables were cluttered with clear mugs of golden beer or glasses of harder stuff. The smell alone threatened to intoxicate him before he reached a stool. With crossed fingers, he sat at the bar and asked the glaring bartender if there was any food on the menu. Thankfully, the bartender nodded and handed him a menu.

The bartender was a powerful looking man who looked especially brawny in a tight fitting white sweater with the sleeves rolled up. A pair of thick brown suspenders stretched down from his shoulders to his pants, but they were likely snug enough that the suspenders weren't necessary. He was possibly the closest thing to a silver fox in the room, but could someone still be called a silver fox if they didn't have any hair to turn silver? The man's eyebrows, now lowered in suspicion, were gray. Maybe that was enough.

"That's gonna be coin up front," the bartender insisted.

"Not surprised," said Luke. He threw his arms to the side and looked down at himself before looking back at the bartender with a grin. The faintest hint of a smile pulled at the man's lips.

As in any restaurant Luke had ever been to, there were many things on the menu he simply didn't have the patience to understand. He searched the menu until his eyes fell upon an old faithful.

"A beef burger with cheese," he read aloud. "No onions, please."

"You want somethin' to drink with that?"

"Um, yeah. Just water please."

He dug from his coin pouch the five copper coins he needed for the burger, and another one when the bartender told him that water would be a copper as well. The meal would set him back twice as much as the room he was still considering at the *Wooden Hearth Inn*. He shuddered at the memory of those cockroaches.

The bartender was very nearly smiling now that Luke had proved he wasn't as destitute as he appeared. "Ale's the same price, if you'd rather," he offered.

Luke shook his head. Again he gestured down at his ragged self. "No thanks. I think I'll stay away from ale for awhile."

The bartender *smiled* and nodded his understanding, though his understanding was probably quite far off from the reality of the situation. Pouring beer down his dehydrated throat and into his empty stomach would simply be a terrible choice. Still, Luke took the bartender's nod as a win.

He watched closely as the man scribbled down his order. His heart surged with happiness when he saw *NO ONIONS* written in big letters with a circle around it.

Electronic payment, such as credit or debit, didn't appear to be an option. The bartender took Luke's coins and deposited them into an old fashioned looking cash register. A monstrosity of a thing, trimmed in brass, it even made a ka-ching noise when he operated it. After depositing his money, the bartender disappeared through a door behind the bar that must have led to a kitchen.

The candles in the chandeliers turned out to be imitations, light fixtures with bulbs shaped like candles and powered by the same green energy that seemed to power everything in the city. How nice would it be to switch his own home over to this flower power? Although, it probably wouldn't work so well in the winter, unless maybe he built a solarium. Did it ever snow in

Atlantis? Maybe snow wouldn't kill the flowers anyways. Were there any electricians in this world? Or were they all magicians?

A toilet flushed somewhere down a hallway next to the bar. *A working washroom.* One could assume the plumbing to be working in this part of the city, provided a flood of toilet paper didn't come rushing down the hall in the next few moments. Perhaps there would be less chance of golden precipitation in the forecast the next morning when he made his way to the library.

Amongst the many fox related knick knacks and alcohol posters that decorated the tavern were street signs. It wasn't uncommon to see street signs in bars back home. Usually they were of fake streets, or replicas of ones from famous places, but these ones looked suspiciously authentic. Was this where all the street signs in the city had gone to? He narrowed his eyes to focus on a particular one on the wall above the opposite end of the bar. *REED STREET.*

No wonder he couldn't find the thing. He couldn't help but chuckle aloud and shake his head.

Chuckling and shaking his head in that particular direction proved to be yet another mistake. Seated at the other end of the bar was a rather large man, easily twice the size of the bartender. At first glance, Luke thought the impossibly large man was just a decoration of some sort. Unfortunately not.

While many of the other patrons had returned to their beers, this man had continued to stare, and he seemed quite unhappy about the way Luke was looking at him.

Shit.

Luke had seen this type of man before. Rough, dumb and drunk, and looking for any reason at all to pick a fight. He was not at all surprised when the man rose from his stool, tilted his body to the side to avoid bumping his head on the ceiling as he walked, and sat down next to Luke. A storm was brewing in the man's dark blue eyes.

Luke sighed. Of course, he hadn't seen that type of man, or *any* type of man for that matter, in *that size* before. Could he be one of the oil giants Henry had mentioned? There had to be an exceptional Big & Tall store in the city somewhere to provide him with an outfit that fit him as well as it did. A brown blazer with enough fabric to blanket a king sized bed clung to his torso, and a navy blue flat cap topped his thick skull. Curly gray hairs spilled out from his cap to join the bushy bird's nest beard that framed his face. His crooked nose had been severely broken at one time, and never reset properly. He stank of rum.

"You find somethin' funny about me, boy?"

The bartender returned and set a glass of water in front of Luke, and for an instant Luke imagined smashing it into the funny man's face and running out the door. The urge passed quickly. The man might very well catch the glass in his teeth, spit it back in Luke's face and strangle him to death before he could get up from his stool. Besides, Luke was thirsty. And starving.

He fixed his gaze on the selection of liquors on a shelf behind the bar and took a sip of water before saying, "Nope. Nothin' funny about you, man."

He could still see the man's glaring eyes boring into him out of the corner of his own.

The man scoffed. "Are you mad, then? Laughing at nothing?"

"No, no. Well. Probably a bit crazy, yes. I was just looking at the signs above your head over there. That's all. Was off in my own little world."

The man turned back to look at the signs. "Nothin' funny about those. Can you even read?"

"Well enough, I think. But maybe I misread them. Either way, I wasn't laughing at you. Promise. Sorry to bother you, really."

He took another sip of water. The man continued staring.

"Where did you steal that coin from?"

"What makes you think I stole it?"

"I can tell just by lookin' at you. And you're not denying it, are you?"

It probably wouldn't help anything if Luke told him he *found* it. It was clear that he needed to choose his words carefully with this brute if he hoped to live long enough to eat his burger.

"I didn't steal anything." *I just took it from a corpse that was buried by a squirrel.* "But I understand..." He turned to meet the man's glare. "It's easy for you to mark me as some kind of degenerate. I mean, look at me. I look like shit. And believe me, I feel it too. It's been a rough couple of days. Maybe you've been lucky enough to never have had a bad day in your life? If so, please, I'll buy you a beer if you tell me your secrets. Two, if you'll leave me be. I just want a damn burger."

"I just want a damn burger..." the man repeated. For a second, it seemed the man was going to snap, but then the storm in the man's eyes eased off, the sun began to peek through the clouds. He chuckled. "I just want a damn burger."

Luke smiled. "It's true."

Right on cue, the bartender was called to the kitchen and returned with Luke's burger. It smelled amazing. There was even an unexpected side of rice and vegetables.

"Thank you," he said, when the bartender placed cutlery, wrapped in cloth, next to his plate.

The real test, though. He lifted the top bun. Some lettuce, a slice of tomato, melted cheese and *no onions*. He could have reached across and hugged the bartender, but decided against it. Instead, he asked him to get a beer for his friend, and pushed a copper across the bar.

He took a bite and chewed very slowly. He wanted to savor at least one bite before devouring the thing. It was a little under-cooked, still faintly pink in the middle, but he wasn't about to complain.

"I *knew* you were alright, kid," said the big man, elbowing Luke playfully in the ribs. He raised his new drink. "Cheers!"

Luke raised his glass of water to clink with the man's beer. He nodded, and took a sip. He still didn't really like the man, but enjoying a meal trumped suffering a beating any day.

"Well, there's your burger," said the big man. "I can see in your eyes that your day's already gotten better. I'm sorry for hasslin' you, lad. Truth is, I've had a bad day myself."

"Oh yeah?" asked Luke. It was probably in his best interest to pretend to care.

"Aye. Somebody cut my purse today. Still a little pissed about it."

"Mmm," Luke nodded and moaned his sympathies, while shoveling rice into his mouth.

"It was on a metal chain, too, it was. Little bastard must have used some sort of magic to do it. Turned the chain to rust." He pulled at a thin chain attached to his belt to show Luke. The chain looked shiny and new where it attached the belt, but the last few links at the tip looked like they'd been laying in a damp basement for years. Reddish brown flakes fell to the floor.

Luke shook his head. "Terrible," he said. *Impressive,* he thought.

"I almost got him. I was *this* close to nabbing the little bastard but he was just too quick. I'll remember him though. Don't you worry." The big man took a sip of his beer. The mug looked tiny in his hands. "Street urchin. Rags on his feet."

Luke's eyes widened. "It wasn't—"

The big man slapped him on the back and laughed. "It wasn't you. I know that. Though I honestly hoped it was when you walked in. Your hair's the wrong color though. Face is all wrong."

"What's wrong with my face?" Luke grinned.

"Well it's burnt to shit, for one. You ever hear of sun screen? And what the hell happened to your clothes, anyways? Were you robbed as well?"

Luke thought to say yes, but didn't figure his robbery story would offer much in the way of commiseration with the big man. "Nah, I was attacked by one of those deathwing things on my way to the city."

"Really?? I was talkin' to a guy the other day who mentioned seein' those flyin' bastards out by the Twins. You came Gaia way, did you?"

"Yes." Luke guessed. "I was lucky though. It picked me up and tried to carry me back to its nest, or whatever they do, but I was too heavy for it. It crash landed into a tree and killed itself. I fell, but didn't get hurt too bad. Well, not as bad as the deathwing, anyways."

"If it struggled with a little guy like you, I shouldn't have anything to worry about."

"Maybe not. But their claws might do a number on that fancy jacket of yours."

The big man guffawed. "What? This old thing? I suppose anything would be fancy to you right now, wouldn't it?"

Before Luke could answer, a thin man in a murky green colored uniform burst through the front door. A dark blue patch was stitched above his chest pocket, showing in gold letters, *TPD*.

"Sir!" he shouted, "Mestorphemus, sir!"

Luke's eyebrows raised at that. *Mestorphemus. Wow. What a name.*

"What is it, Malcolm?" the big man replied. "Can't you see I'm busy?" He raised his mug.

Malcolm removed his hat and bowed slightly. "Sorry sir, but you'll want to see this. We have the thief, sir. The one that swiped your coin."

Mestorphemus's eyes bulged. His face twisted into a sinister smile. "Are you sure, lad?"

Malcolm nodded. "Yes sir. Very sure. Based on your description."

"Ho ho!" the big man bellowed. He downed the last of his beer and slammed the mug triumphantly on the counter. This painted a concerned look on the face of the bartender, but wisely he said nothing.

Luke nearly spit out a chunk of hamburger when Mestorphemus slapped him on the back, much harder than last time. The big man was practically shaking with excitement.

"Come on, lad," he said to Luke as he rose from his stool.

"Me?" said Luke, "What for?"

"Somebody's about to have a far worse day than you."

"Oh, thanks. But that's fine. I don't need to-"

He barely managed to swipe the remains of the burger from his plate as Mestorphemus yanked him to his feet.

"Nonsense. It'll cheer you up."

"I'm really quite fine."

The big man wasn't hearing any of it. Luke had no desire to watch him tear another man's head off, but he had even less desire to get on the man's bad side. He'd like to keep his own head where it was. With a groan, he shouldered his backpack and reluctantly followed Mestorphemus and Malcolm out of the tavern.

He stepped gingerly out onto the sidewalk, his eyes darting this way and that, and stuck close to the other two men as they crossed the road. He breathed easier when they reached the other side unmolested, though he kept glancing over his shoulder. It seemed as if the white haired terrier had ventured off.

The square was really packed now. The grassy areas and the gravel paths leading to the fountain were crawling with people, but Luke's passage was easy following the big man. Most people were more than eager to get out of his way, and those who moved too slow or weren't paying attention were chucked aside like rag dolls. He finished his burger as they came to an opening at the fountain.

A queasy feeling swirled around in his stomach when he saw that the fountain area was occupied by a dozen or more men, uniformed like Malcolm. Many were keeping a large crowd at bay, while three of them detained another man in the center of the opening. Luke recognized the detained man at once.

The man wore a patchwork doublet, with a dirty brown waistcoat and matching pants. His feet, wrapped in rags, had been the very same feet that had given Luke the earlier idea to wrap his own. Unmistakably, this was the same red haired man that had *robbed* him earlier. His arms were held behind his back by two of the uniformed men, while the other interrogated him. It was a small consolation that Luke couldn't see his daughters anywhere nearby.

When the uniformed men noticed Mestorphemus approach, one of them said, "Took a knife off him sir, but no sign of your pouch on him. No coin at all. Stashed it somewhere, most like."

Another said, "What do you want us to do with him?"

Mestorphemus snarled. "That's him, alright," the big man bellowed, and charged, closing the distance between him and the prisoner faster than a man his size ought to be capable of. He struck the prisoner with a thunderous blow across his face, dropping him to the ground and knocking his captors backwards.

Luke's jaw dropped to the ground as well.

"Sir?" One of the uniformed men dared to question the raging giant.

"You'll find a bonus in your pay if you can keep the crowds back, boys. Leave the thief to me."

The uniformed men exchanged looks, but nodded and backed away to police the crowd.

Groggily, the red haired man rose to his knees, and *smiled* up at the giant towering over him. "Oh, hello. Do we know each other?" he asked.

Points for having balls. Luke smiled, but the smile was quickly chased from his face by a mighty roar from Mestorphemus. He gripped the red haired man's throat, and with ridiculous ease raised him to his feet and further, up in the air above his head, with one hand. The red haired man kicked helplessly at his attacker before being flung backwards into the marble edge of the fountain. His back hit the corner with a grunt.

Mestorphemus raised his catcher's mitt hands to the air and swept his gaze over the horrified crowd. "This is what happens to thieves in *my city*," he roared. "I am *Mestorphemus!* Remember that name next time any of you think of breaking the law in Tumblestone."

With that, he stalked over to Red, who had somehow managed to rise to his feet, swaying and bloody. Red put his hands up to block a strike, but Mestorphemus punched straight through his defenses, shoving his hands back into his face and knocking him backwards to the ground. This time Mestorphemus didn't wait for him to rise. He smashed him several more times before picking him up and chucking him into the side of the fountain.

Luke was stunned. Were the uniformed men supposed to be police officers? Were they really just going to ignore this? Many of them looked uncomfortable, a few were looking elsewhere, but not one of them seemed to be considering lifting a finger against the big man's brutality. He was huge, sure, but even if just half of them stepped in, surely they could stop him. Instead they monitored the crowd, dissuading anyone else from stopping the senseless act.

There was a big splash as Mestorphemus tossed Red into the fountain. He crawled in after him. Luke looked away, focused his attention on the person next to him instead. It was the boy who sold him the wine sediment.

This kid shouldn't be watching this.

Remarkably, the cauldron the boy had dipped his wine out of was empty. He had sold it all somehow. Or maybe he spilled it. Either way, it was empty. The cauldron sat in a wheelbarrow, making it easy for the boy to move it around when it was full.

Mestorphemus held Red under the water for far too long and gave him just seconds to breathe before repeating the process. Still, the uniformed men did nothing. Nobody was going to stop it. Mestorphemus would kill him.

A little girl shouted from the crowd, "Gerald! Gerald! He's hurting him! He's hurting him! You have to do something." Luke caught a glimpse of the girl, small and blond and ridiculously bedazzled in necklaces. The girl was trying to push her way through the crowd, but couldn't squeeze through. Several of the uniformed men responded by pushing the crowd back in that area.

Luke sighed. *Shit.* At least he had gotten to eat his burger. A last meal.

"Hey kid," he said to the wine boy.

"Yes, sir?"

He fished a couple of copper coins out of his pouch and pushed them into the boy's palm. The boy looked at him quizzically.

"Can I borrow your cauldron? I won't go far with it, I promise. You'll be able to watch me the whole time."

The boy was clearly confused, but agreed. Luke picked up the cauldron. It was lighter than he expected. He glanced at the scene playing out in the fountain, thought for a second, then placed the cauldron on the ground next to the boy.

"On second thought," he said, untying his coin pouch, "Can I borrow the wheelbarrow instead? And here, hold this." He handed the boy the pouch. "If I don't come back, it's all yours.'

The wide eyed boy nodded enthusiastically as he jingled the pouch.

Luke twisted his hands tightly around the wheelbarrow's handles and swallowed hard. Most of the uniformed men were giving their attention to the little girl's section, so nobody moved in time to stop him as he wheeled his barrow across the gravel toward the fountain. It was heavier than the cauldron. But not *too* heavy.

Mestorphemus had just brought Red's head up out of the water for another breath of air as Luke reached the fountain edge. Seconds before he reached it, he broke into a run, and shouted, "Hey asshole!" at the top of his lungs.

Mestorphemus turned.

Still running, Luke changed his grip on the barrow. Grabbing it by the front and back of the rim, he hoisted the barrow over his head, leaped onto the edge of the fountain and dove straight at the wide eyed Mestorphemus. Every member of the crowd gasped in unison.

In the air, Luke wound back, and, with all his hamburger fueled might, drove the nose of the barrow downward into the giant's face and splashed into the fountain. Mestorphemus staggered backwards and fell, nearly crushing Red under his huge bulk, had the man not found the energy somewhere inside him to move out of the way.

The giant's fall made waves in the fountain, sending water racing away and splashing up over the sides as if it were desperate to escape. The crowd was frantic now. The uniformed men were completely occupied with holding them back. There'd be no better time to bolt, but Red was taking too long to rise, so Luke hooked his arm under the man's shoulder and lifted him to his feet.

He coughed and sputtered, and looked up at Luke as he drug him out of the fountain. His green eyes, what were visible of them, sparkled with recognition. "You!" He smiled. He still had all of his teeth, at least. "You needn't have done that, you know. I had it all under control. All part of the plan."

The man's eyes were nearly swollen shut. He looked like a drowned rat.

"Right. Sure looked like it." Luke scanned the crowd for the easiest exit point. He frowned. It would have been better to exit the fountain on the other side. He wasn't going back in.

A mighty roar cranked his head around to the fountain.

The crowd gasped.

Luke cursed.

The big man was stalking through the fountain, roaring and unbuttoning his blazer.

Red sputtered out a half cough, half chuckle. "Oh, he's really ticked now."

Not wanting to find out just how *really ticked* Mestorphemus was, Luke, dragging the redhead along beside him, pushed into the crowd.

But the crowd pushed back.

Another batch of uniformed men had arrived to hold the perimeter. Luke and Red were shoved back into the opening.

"What the hell? Why are they helping him?"

Again the redhead chuckle-coughed. "Mestorphemus is captain of the watch. He's their boss!"

"Of course he is," Luke muttered. "Why would you rob the captain of the watch??"

The redhead shrugged. "Why would you help me?"

"Because nobody else was."

"Exactly," said the redhead with a smile.

"That is some shit logic, man."

"I can say the same to you."

Mestorphemus stomped out of the fountain, tossing a ball of clothing to the side. He was shirtless now. Beads of water glistened down over his chest and arms from his soaked hair, highlighting his massive chiseled physique in a golden shimmer. The row of statues on King Street didn't seem so exaggerated at that moment. When he cracked his knuckles, his chest muscles popped.

Luke groaned. "Was that really necessary?"

"Thick as thieves," the big man spat. His stormy eyes were raging tempests. "I KNEW you stole that coin!" Like a bull, he charged.

Red nearly fell over when Luke detached himself, but he couldn't worry about that. Grim faced, Luke charged to meet Mestorphemus.

Like the football running backs he had seen on television, at the last second Luke strafed and spun to the left to get around the big man, but it didn't happen quite like it did on television. The big man was *big,* and his arms were long. Mestorphemus's arm stretched out and smacked into Luke's chest, effectively leveling him to the gravel.

The blow knocked all the wind from his sails. The kitchenware in his backpack drove painfully into his back. He felt like a turtle, flipped over on its shell. *Well, shit.*

In an instant, Luke was back on his feet, but not by his own power. Mestorphemus yanked him up, only to kick him in the chest. He practically flew backwards into the edge of the fountain. With a grunt, he managed to push himself back up to his knees as his opponent closed the distance between them. The big man wound back to strike him again as he approached. But he stopped, suddenly blind.

Red had found the wine boy's cauldron, and the cauldron found its way onto Mestorphemus's head. His roar echoed out from the iron mask. Before he could take the cauldron off his head, the redhead dropped low, and slammed his fist up into the big man's groin. The metallic roar turned into a metallic howl as Mestorphemus fell to ground, squirming wildly and clutching his wounded manhood. Red grinned like a fool.

Luke was up. A burst of hope sent his hand over his shoulder. He flipped open the flap on his pack and reached in, grabbing the first handle his hand touched. He didn't check to see what he had grabbed, he just swung it as hard as he could. The cooking pot banged off the cauldron with a satisfying twang, again and again and again.

The big man roared inside the cauldron, but Luke wasn't about to let up. He wound back for another swing, and nearly connected when his ankle was ripped out from under him. He was on his back again, cursing.

Mestorphemus tore the cauldron from his head as he rose and swung it wide around to catch Red, taking him out at the knees. "No more toys," he growled, and hurled the cauldron recklessly into the crowd, hitting one of his own men.

Nobody dared reproach him. The crowd stepped back of their own accord, widening the arena.

Luke kicked at the big man's leg as he tried to push away, but he may as well have kicked a brick wall, and he had just given the man his leg. Mestorphemus reeled him in like a fish on a hook.

"You're done now, you little bastard."

Stars sparkled in the sky and danced around the big man's face. Stars sparkled *everywhere* after a fist struck Luke's face like a meteor. His head lulled to the side. Red was moving, but slowly, on his hands and knees. Mestorphemus spat insults at Luke, but he barely heard him.

He heard a bird cry though. A piercing screech. An eagle, maybe? He read a book once, where an eagle carried the heroes to safety at the last minute. It was a popular book, but the title escaped him. Another meteor landed on his face, and then a third.

He saw an object sail from the crowd. Not an eagle. Something purple. It landed in the gravel in front of Red. Something wrapped in cloth.

Another meteor fell, and Luke saw nothing but black for several seconds. When his vision returned, he saw and felt Mestorphemus's huge hands around his throat. Huge knees were driven into his chest, pinning one of his arms beneath them as well.

His free hand clawed helplessly against the vice-like grip. He couldn't breathe. His eye lids grew heavy. His arm stopped.

His eyes shut.

Another cry rang out, decidedly not eagle-like. "Luke! Luke!"
Sam??

But when he snapped his eyes open, he realized it was a different voice he must have heard.

The hands choking off his air were needed elsewhere. He could breathe again. Sweet, sweet air.

Mestorphemus roared curses and swatted violently at his own face, as if a hornet's nest had fallen on him, and in a way, it certainly had.

"Luke!" the squirrel cried. "I was worried I'd— Oh!"

The squirrel wriggled free of Mestorphemus's clutching hands and continued, "I was worried I'd never find you, but what a smoke signal you've set off! How *have* you been, my dear boy? Keeping well I trust?" He offered a wink before disappearing over the big man's shoulder and down his back.

Mestorphemus threw his head back and howled. He flailed about wildly, even slammed himself into the gravel to try and free himself of the biting, scratching squirrel. Henry was impossibly fast.

Luke sat up slowly, but still far too quickly. His head was spinning like a top. He nearly flopped back over but a freckled hand steadied him, despite being shaky itself.

"Hey," said Red. "Luke, is it? What interesting friends you have. Can you stand?"

"I think so," he nodded. With the redhead's help, he managed.

"Marvelous. Now here, take this."

The redhead pulled the cork out of a thin glass vial and handed the vial to Luke. A cloudy silver liquid sloshed inside. It was *smoking*.

"What—"

"Drink half of it and hand it back. Just half. Quick!"

"But—"

"Just do it. Hurry. Your squirrel friend won't hold him for-ever."

Mestorphemus seemed hopelessly preoccupied with his furry new opponent, but Red was probably right. It was unlikely the big man would impale himself on anything, no matter how hard he thrashed.

With a sigh, he tipped the vial back and drank the mysterious liquid he received from someone he didn't know. He'd never have done something like that at a college party.

It tasted awful, but still better than onions. A strange and wonderful sensation swept over him. It started from the top of his head and spread quickly to his toes. He shivered. The full body orgasm felt amazing, but after it passed, the pain of the beating he had endured remained. It wasn't a health potion. Whatever it was that he swallowed, it drew another gasp from the crowd.

It took several tries to give the vial back to Red. In the end, he had to push it directly into his palm. Red laughed, all grins now.

He turned and bowed theatrically to the crowd, "Sorry to ruin the evening's entertainment, ladies and gentlemen! But we really must be off!" He tipped back the remains of the vial, and was *gone*. Nowhere to be seen.

An invisibility potion!

Something slapped his elbow, and slid down his forearm to his wrist. A hand.

"Time to go!" came the redhead's voice.

"Luke!!" came another voice, not Red's, nor the squirrel's, but he couldn't pinpoint where it came from.

Sam?

It couldn't be. He was probably heavily brain damaged, after all.

There was no time to find out. Red's invisible hand pulled him by the wrist, guiding him toward and onto the fountain ledge.

He looked back as they traversed the ledge away from the crowd, and smiled. Henry tore the back out of Mestorphemus's pants, exposing his floral print underwear to the crowd. The crowd roared with laughter and Mestorphemus roared with rage. The squirrel, much like the redhead, bowed, and disappeared into the crowd.

When they reached the other side of the fountain, the hop back down to ground level sent sharp pains through Luke's back. He bit his lip, and forced himself to keep step with the now running redhead. Every step was agony as the shock faded and his back became increasingly aware of the trauma it had endured.

To make matters worse, being invisible placed all responsibility for avoiding collisions with them. The pair, still joined at the wrist, side stepped and dodged as one as best as they could, but there were just too many people moving too erratically to avoid them all. This resulted in some rather puzzled and horrified expressions when collisions did occur.

Somehow, they made it to one of the adjacent streets, though Luke lost his foot wraps in the process. He barely noticed. His heart was pounding and his lungs pained with each breath. His back was nearly done.

"Cardio... is so... important," he croaked.

Red agreed, though his breathing was fine.

Suddenly, a woman in a pink dress, hurrying by with a basket of eggs, screamed. She dropped her basket. Yellow yolk oozed over the cobbles.

Luke looked at her and she was looking right at them. *She could see him.* At that second, Red appeared as well. He held out a hand to calm her, but she screamed again and ran away.

"Well, that didn't last very long."

"The dose was only meant for one," Red explained. "You weren't part of the plan." He yanked Luke into an alley. "No matter, we're here anyways."

"Here? There's nowhere to go. It's a dead end."

"Is it?" the redhead smiled. He dipped his head and directed Luke with his eyes.

A manhole cover. The sewers. Red crouched to pry it open.

"No..."

The burning fury of Mestorphemus reached them even in the alley.

"WHERE THE HELL DID THEY GO!? SOMEBODY SPEAK!! NOW!!"

Luke groaned.

The grackle glanced over at his brother and nodded.

His brother nodded back.

Hundreds of other birds were performing similar preparedness checks in the sky around them. The target was confirmed. The earthbound creature below was without a doubt the same creature that had been witnessed tossing food in such a way as to lure seagulls into oncoming traffic. The grackle had no special love for the larger, dumber, sea birds, but they were still *birds*. Such atrocities could not be permitted.

And besides, the target was huge. An incredibly easy target to hit. The grackle swooped, as did his brother and the hundreds of others.

In seconds, the giant earthbound creature was covered head to toe in their white missiles. Had he not been so intent on letting the world hear his rage, perhaps he might have avoided getting it in his mouth as well.

The grackle's eyes sparkled. If it could have twisted its beak in such a way, it would have smiled.

CHAPTER EIGHTEEN

Luke was *there*. So close she could have hit him with a rock.

Sam had spied him moments before, from a tree she had climbed for a better chance of spotting Lia and Gerald. She didn't see Lia or Gerald, instead she saw two men taking a savage beating from a shirtless giant by the fountain. The giant was straddling one of the men, hiding him from view and smashing him so hard that Sam could feel it in her soul.

The blows hit her even harder after something happened to drive the giant into a frenzy and away from his victim, revealing the identity of the bloody punching bag.

Sam's eyes had bulged, and "Luke!" exploded from her lips, but he made no indication of hearing her.

By the time she weaved herself through the tangled mess of limbs and bodies to get near the front of the crowd, it was too late. Her breath caught in her throat.

Luke and the other man disappeared, leaving the giant alone in the clearing. They vanished into thin air.

Like wizards.

The crowd gasped, and a moment of hushed questions ensued.

"Where did they go?"

"Was that...?"

"Magic?"

"Mommy can we go? I need to pee!"

The giant roared. The sky darkened.

Hundreds of screeching grackles, a flapping black mass, blotted the sky as they descended on the square. As one, they opened up on the giant, painting him from head to toe with the rejected contents of their stomachs. His ferocious roar died back to a sickening gargle. Remarkably, the giant seemed to be the main target.

Was this another part of Luke's magic trick? Could he command the wild?

Her question was answered, hopefully with a no, when the birds decided there was just as much fun to be had in splattering the bystanders as well. The whole place erupted in chaos, like someone kicked an ant hill. People rushed to get as far away as possible from the fountain, the raging giant, and the shitty birds, but mostly they tangled and tripped one another.

Sam was more methodical in her escape. She didn't run or scream. She moved at a brisk pace with her hands clapped over her ears against the cacophony of screeching birds and screaming humans. She did, however, curse, when side stepping around a flailing man put herself in line for one of the sticky white missiles to land on her head. Luckily, Luke's ball cap took the brunt of it and she was able to shake it off. If the shitting birds *were* his doing, a soiled hat was his just dessert.

"Princess!!" came a familiar cry.

"Lia!" Sam called back, but the little girl was nowhere to be seen.

She fought through the crowd, searching. What she found was the cobbles, up close, after being tripped by an excited white terrier.

"Shit," she spat. And shit she saw. A wide volley, hurtling in her direction. Too fast. There was nothing to do but curl up in a ball and pray that *some* of it missed her. She'd need some teleportation magic of her own to avoid it all.

She heard Lia cry again, but she didn't dare look up, not until the third cry, seconds later. The volley should have reached her by then.

It was like she had teleported after all, into a poorly lit room, but the cobbles were still beneath her. She was inside of an igloo. An igloo made of bird shit. The area outside was barely visible through tiny windows the birds had missed. She was still in the square.

Lia stood beside her with trembling fists. Her face a world of worry in contrast to the happy jingling of her jewelry. Several other confused people were with them inside of Lia's protective dome.

"Are you okay, princess?"

"I am, Lia. You wonderful little girl."

Lia beamed, but she was swaying. Now would be a poor time for her to fall asleep. The mountain of shit building above would crush them.

"Stay focused!" Sam begged, "I'm going to carry you, okay?"

Lia's jewelry continued to jingle. She nodded, sleepily.

Sam picked her up by her arm pits, not wanting to change the girl's position too much in case her stance had some effect on the bubble shield. The shield held.

"Do you think you can hold this thing until we get somewhere where it's not... raining?" Sam asked, already moving toward a nearby merchant's stall.

"I think so," Lia yawned. Not promising.

Sam carried the little girl away from the fountain, issuing encouragement all the while to keep her awake. The bird shit igloo moved with them, keeping them always in the center of it. The random people trapped with them were less than appreciative of the protection the igloo offered them. They shouted, fearfully demanding their freedom. Some flung themselves uselessly against the sides. One man bounced backward to the ground and was drug along by the force of the bubble.

Serves him right, Sam thought.

"You're doing great, Lia. Really great. Just a bit longer. You can do it."

The chaotic crowd outside had no affect on their passage. The igloo effortlessly pushed aside anyone who didn't immediately get out of their way. But it was getting darker. Each splattering from the birds blocked out a little more of the sunlight, until soon the igloo was fully *bricked in* and nothing of the outside world could be seen.

Sam held a steady course in the direction she knew the merchant's stall to be, and soon it emerged from the edge of the globe as if passing through a thick fog.

Lia yawned.

Shit.

Her eyelids fell shut.

"Shit!"

Sam sprang toward the stall as the igloo collapsed, setting Lia on the counter before falling in front of it herself, just beneath the shelter of the stall's awning. Safe.

The randoms who were trapped in the igloo with them were not so lucky. The disgusting white ceiling fell on them with enough force to flatten them. Their following groans and moans indicated both that they were alive, and that they were very disappointed about it. They were drenched.

"Sorry!" said Sam. "Should have told you my plan, I guess."

She smiled at her little hero, now curled up in a ball on the merchant's counter, snoring softly. A look behind the counter made her laugh. *How fitting*. They had taken shelter in a booth selling souvenirs and jewelry. No one nearby jumped out as the proprietor of the shop, so there was no one to stop her from plucking a cute beaded bracelet from a display rack. Lia deserved that much at least.

The birds continued to swoop and screech overhead, but mercifully, their bowels were not bottomless. Fewer projectiles rained down on the crowd. The crowd was thinning as well. The giant remained by the fountain, sitting alone, wailing in rage and misery. He tore a thick glob from his beard and chucked it aside.

Sam frowned. An urge to confront the man pulled at her. Why was he assaulting Luke? Did he have any idea where he could have gone? Maybe she should just run up and soccer kick him in the groin.

"Samantha!" came a distracting shout. "Samantha! Over here!"

At the mouth of one of the adjacent streets, Gerald was shouting through his cupped hands. Sophie stood beside him, waving her wine bottle staff in the air. Sam waved back.

With Lia nestled in her arms, she trudged through the sloppy moat surrounding the stall, over the squirming bodies of the unlucky randoms, until she reached her companions.

Sophie frowned from within her raised hood. Several gobs caked her emerald robes. Gerald had removed his vest and was wiping gunk from his hair.

Sophie noticed the sleeping bundle Sam carried. She nodded. "I saw the bubble." Her attention returned to Sam. "That was a fine mess your wizard got himself into."

It was hard to dispute the wizard comment now. Luke literally disappeared right in front of them. Although it could have been that the redheaded man was the wizard, not Luke, but Luke *did* have a book for doing just that in his house. He could be there now, for all she knew, drinking his primitive instant coffee and trying to ring her on her cell phone. Her phone was long dead, of course, and she didn't even want to imagine what the roaming charges in Atlantis would be.

"I don't understand," she said. "What was that all about?"

Sophie shrugged. "Men are stupid."

"The giant started it," said Gerald. "Something about a theft. Luke stepped in to help the redhead."

"Well, that I can believe," said Sam.

Sophie shook a splattering off of her robe. "A noble idiot. Why didn't they just disappear from the start?"

"How should I know? I had no idea he could *disappear* at all."

Gerald tossed his soiled vest in a trash bin. "I don't know if either of them is a wizard. Somebody threw the redhead a flask, and they both drank from it. That's when they disappeared."

"Ah," said Sophie. "Alchemy then. An invisibility potion. Then they couldn't have gone too far, not in the shape they're in."

"But there are so many ways out of the square," said Sam. "They could have gone anywhere."

Shadows were creeping out from the tall buildings as the sun began to pass its torch to the moon. True dark was still a long ways off, but sunlight wasn't going to make it any easier to find an invisible person anyways. Where to start?

A shimmer drew Sam's eye to the cobbles. A slimy mess marked the stones, but it was different from the bird shit. Clear and dotted with yellow... yolks? Eggs. Busted bits of shell lay scattered throughout. She smiled stupidly, and flushed when she noticed Sophie's eyebrows raised in her direction.

"Some of that bird crap make its way into your brain?" Sophie asked.

Sam laughed. "No, no. Just a silly thought. Stupid really. I just... You don't suppose the birds started chucking their babies at the crowd when they ran out of poop, do you?"

"Wouldn't surprise me," said Sophie. "But I'd say that basket over there is a more likely point of origin. Somebody lost their groceries."

"That... yes. That probably makes more sense." Sam pursed her lips. "But the birds were mostly in the square, weren't they? That's why you ran over here, isn't it?"

Gerald nodded.

"What's your point, princess?" asked Sophie.

"Don't you think it's odd that somebody would get so spooked over here?"

"I think it's odd that we're standing here discussing a mess of broken eggs instead of looking for your wizard."

"I'm just wondering if it wasn't the birds that spooked this person into dropping their basket, maybe it was something even more sudden. Like someone *suddenly appearing* in front of them? That would be enough to make me drop my groceries, I'd think."

Even if that had been the case, Luke was certainly not there now.

"That is an excellent deduction, my dear girl!" came a male voice, startling them all.

The source escaped them. Nobody in the immediate area seemed to be focused on their little group. A handful of people were gathered here and there along the street, but they were clearly chatting amongst themselves. An elderly woman carrying a dead rooster smiled a toothless smile at them as she walked by, and nearly tripped over a gray squirrel. *Poor rooster,* Sam thought. *One less voice for the morning choir.*

"Ahem," came a cough from the cobbles. The squirrel was right beside them now. It stood on its hind legs, with its hands clasped together across its puffed up chest.

Nobody said anything for several seconds. They looked at the squirrel, and the squirrel looked back, its head tilting towards each one of them in turn. When still nobody responded, the squirrel nodded.

"Right. Yes," the squirrel chuckled. "Well I suppose this rude behavior is to be expected. I take no offense."

"Are you... Are you talking?" Sam asked. She turned to the others. "Are you hearing this too? Or have I lost my mind? Are talking animals a normal thing here?"

"I was under the impression you lost your mind when you started fussing over the eggs," remarked the old woman. "But yes, I hear the rodent too, and no, it is definitely *not* normal, though nothing surprises me these days."

The squirrel's oil drop eyes bulged. He gasped. "Rodent! No manners at all. And from someone impersonating someone else. Unless... No. No you're not her. She doesn't age. I won't be fooled twice in one day."

"What are you talking about?" Sophie asked.

"Nothing of immediate importance," said the squirrel. He cleared his throat again. "Pardon me. Let's start again. Were my ears correct in marking *you,*" he gestured with a tiny hand in

Sam's direction, "as the one shouting for Luke in the crowd back there?"

It was Sam's turn to gasp, "You're not... You can't be. *Luke?*"

The squirrel chuckled. "Oh no, my dear girl. Merely a mutual acquaintance, it would seem. My name is Henry. Henry the Squirrel. It's a pleasure to meet another who has had dealings with the Master of Morningwood. Though I must admit some surprise. It was my understanding that Luke was not of this particular world. How, may I ask, do you know him?"

Sam smirked. "Wait. The Master of *what?* Does *he* call himself that?"

"A recently acquired title. We agreed upon it together. It seemed quite fitting."

"Ah, not sure if I want to know how the *two of you* came to that agreement. But anyways, I'm also *not of this particular world*. Luke and I came from the same place. His house, actually. Still not entirely sure how. Does he come here often?"

Henry shook his head, smiling. "No, I believe he was just as surprised as you to find himself here. And I dare say he'll be surprised again, and quite happy to find out you are here as well, *Sam.*"

"How do you know my name? Did he talk about me?"

The squirrel's grin touched his eyes. "Talk about you? My dear girl. His mouth practically never opens without a praise cast in your direction. *The most beautiful girl in the entire world*, he says, and says and says again. Now that I've seen you, I can say with all certainty that you are the most beautiful girl from his world that *I've* ever seen."

Sophie and Gerald snickered.

Sam rolled her eyes. "Right. Well, did he also tell you where he disappeared to just now? Do you know where he is?"

"Sadly, no. Not precisely anyhow. But if I did, we wouldn't be having this lovely rendezvous. You were correct with your broken egg theory. They were definitely here. I followed their scent into the alley, but it's a dead end, unfortunately. It seems they went down into the sewers."

"Then what are we doing?? We need to get down there after him! Come on. Let's go."

Beyond a string of trash cans, the alley indeed ended abruptly at a brick pedway connecting the two buildings. A rusty raised manhole cover marked the sewer entrance. Sam gave her arms a rest by placing Lia on top of a wooden crate. The little girl snored away.

With a nod from Sophie, Gerald yanked the heavy manhole cover to the side. The regret came instantly.

"Oh god!" Sam gagged. "That is awful!" She took an uncontrollable fit of coughing.

The smell was worse than anything she could ever have imagined. It was easy to believe the tidbits of conversation she had heard throughout the day about the city's wastewater problems. Francesca and her gang should be given the castle if they managed to sort *that* out.

A choking Sophie demanded the cover be replaced. Gerald didn't argue, and Sam didn't try to stop him.

"I'm sorry princess," the old woman said. "Your prince is surely dead. And if he's not, I wouldn't be so eager to jump in bed with him after he's been through there."

Sam was inclined to agree. The smell continued to assault her nostrils and tickle her throat, even with the cover replaced and her shirt pulled up over her nose. "I don't think I can go down there."

The squirrel had wisely remained at the entrance to the alley. Even he had his tail pulled around and held to his nose. "My thoughts exactly."

Sam removed her borrowed hat and ran her fingers through her hair. She sighed. "Now what? He has to come up somewhere. Maybe we could check the exits."

"*If* he comes up," pointed Sophie, "we can just follow the screams and retches of those who witness them."

"The sewer system here is a veritable labyrinth," said the squirrel. "There are entrances all throughout the city. They could come back up anywhere. It's a great way to sneak around if you don't have a nose."

"Maybe he'll show up at the Wooden Hearth," Sophie suggested. "He made a reservation. We could wait for him there. Suddenly the inn doesn't smell so bad."

"We could give it a shot. But it's not very far from here," said Gerald. "If they were running from that ogre, I'd think they'd want to get as far away as possible."

Sophie nodded and raised her eyebrows at him. "Well, you would know best about sneaking around, wouldn't you? You are the expert here, after all."

Gerald sighed. His face flushed.

Sophie narrowed her eyes and added, "I hope you never used the sewers during your escapades back then."

"No. Never. They didn't smell much better twenty years ago. Hey! Where did Lia get to??"

Everyone exchanged frightened looks. The little girl was not on the crate where Sam left her. Maybe it was for the best that she had given up on teaching. If she couldn't keep track of *one sleeping child*...

"Lia?" the squirrel asked calmly. "I presume this little devil hiding behind that box is Lia, then. Fear not. I have my eye on her. And she has *both* of her eyes on me. You're not thinking to eat me, are you, child?"

Lia peered out from behind the crate, and shook her head. Her neck jingled.

"Oh thank goodness," said Sam, rushing to her. In the span of a few moments, the girl had gone from dead to the world to hiding herself between the crate and the building behind it. Her eyes were indeed locked on Henry. "I thought you were sleeping!"

Lia crinkled her nose. "The smell woke me up. And then I saw *him*." She pointed at the squirrel.

"Fair enough. But why are you hiding from him?"

Not that she could ever successfully hide from anything, wearing as much jewelry as she did. Lia didn't hear her. She sprang from behind the crate towards the squirrel and fell to her knees before him. The squirrel reacted calmly. He tilted his head up and smiled back at the vibrating child. Her fists were held in front of her, shaking. Sam braced herself for another burst of magic.

Henry chuckled. "Well? What are you waiting for? Go on."

Nothing magical occurred. The little girl squealed happily and flung a hand forward, but stopped suddenly just before Henry's head. She continued forward, gently, with one finger, and stroked the back of the squirrel's neck. He leaned into it, like a cat. Sam half expected him to purr. Instead, he scurried up Lia's arm and perched right on her shoulder, drawing another happy squeal out of the girl.

Sophie sighed, "What happened to being tired?" She shook her head. "You have a princess, *and* a talking squirrel now, girl. Anything else you'd like this week?"

Lia was beaming. The very definition of pure happiness.

"Just watch out he doesn't shit on you."

"Sophie!" cried Lia.

Henry scowled. "The audacity! I would never do such a thing. Do you truly think me a savage?"

Sam stifled a laugh. "This is all very adorable, but Luke is missing. I think the idea of staking out the hotel is as good as any. And the kid at the gate said Luke was asking about libraries, but they were all closed today. He was probably going to check out the... Hmm. Knowledge House? That was it, wasn't it? Is it close? Even if he doesn't show up at the inn tonight, there's still a chance he might head there in the morning when it's open."

"Ah yes," the squirrel bobbed his head. "Good lad, that Luke. He took my suggestion. It's not far from here at all, no. I know exactly where it is. Unless it has been moved since I was last here, but I doubt it. The Knowledge House is the oldest and largest library in the city. A good choice."

"Why would he want to go to the library?" Sam asked, and then she remembered the book in his house. "Ah! Of course. *Magic books.* He's looking for a magic book. To go home."

"Correct," Henry agreed. "Although, to be more precise, he was particularly keen in finding a way back to *you*. Yes, blush if you must. A little color looks good on your cheeks. Anyhow, Luke and I arrived at the thought that it must have been a travel tome that brought him to this world. Apart from finding a mage in possession of one, we decided a library would be a reasonable place to start looking." He nodded in Sophie's direction. "What about you? You don't have one tucked away in that robe of *yours*, do you? Mages are always losing things in their robes. All those magical pockets. A real nightmare when it comes to automobile keys."

"There's no such book in *my* robes, I can assure you, squirrel. I'm not a mage. Just a traveler."

"Truly? But you're dressed just like Aradia. Emerald staff and all. Hmm. No… Is that a… That's a wine bottle. A melted wine bottle." Henry chuckled. "Clever girl. I'll have to introduce you to the *real* Aradia someday. She'd be quite tickled to have such a devoted fan. And after so long an absence!"

Sophie cocked her head. "Introduce me? Aradia was burnt at the stake a few hundred years ago."

"Oh yes, I'm well aware," said the squirrel. "Excuse me, but I think I hear that large man stomping in this direction. Perhaps we should walk and talk, if that's alright with you folks. I have a feeling he won't be very happy if he sees me, or anyone associated with me. Just a feeling."

The squirrel was right. When they left the alley, the large man was just crossing the roundabout and walking toward their street. He was fuming, shaking his head and cursing. Not that anyone could blame him, being covered head to toe in bird shit and feathers like he was.

They began walking up the street at a slightly quicker than normal pace. They had no reason to fear the big man so long as he didn't spot Henry. The squirrel relocated himself to Lia's palms, which she held close to her chest to keep out of sight.

"Can we keep him?" Lia pleaded, casting her best puppy dog eyes at Sophie.

"I've told you many times, Lia. No pets."

"No. You said *no dogs.* Henry is a squirrel. He won't ruin your carpets. Just feel him, Sophie. Feel how soft he is."

"That's quite alright. I believe you. Keep him over there. We don't want that buffoon behind us to see him."

Henry coughed. "Yes. And I should like to think that my own opinion has value in the matter."

While everyone was in agreement that the best course of action was to track Luke to the inn, or to the library the next day,

Sam insisted they try searching at least a few of the nearby alleys for other sewer entrances. "We might find some slimy footprints or something."

If *she* had been the one down in the sewer, she would have wanted to pop back up at the first opportunity. Unfortunately, Luke proved more tolerant than her. At least she hoped that was the case, and that he wasn't dead like Sophie kept suggesting. After more than a dozen fruitless entrance checks, Sam's growling stomach reminded her that food consumption was vital to human life.

"I think I know where we should look next," said Gerald when the growling persisted. "Why don't we look in there?" He pointed to a round sign hanging out from a brick building. *The Tumbled Teapot* was written along the top, above the image of a chipped and cracked tea pot pouring tea into a chipped and cracked tea cup. *Circa 11441* was written along the bottom of the sign.

Sam didn't argue. She'd never find Luke if she starved to death.

The diner was small and empty of customers, but full of charm. A cozy, hole in the wall sort of place with half a dozen round tables spaced comfortably apart throughout the serving room. Every table had a green tea pot filled with daisies at its center, and two green tea cups, one on either side of the pot. Each held a short candle, just waiting to be lit. Paintings of happy people drinking from tea cups of every color smiled at them from every angle. One painting depicted a happy *dog*, a pug, drinking tea in an armchair with a book across its lap. The perfect number of stools for Sam's party paired with a smooth wooden counter that spanned the length of the arched picture window in the front of the diner, so they chose there to sit. In the unlikely event that Luke should wander by, they would see him.

Henry made himself at home in Sam's tote bag, which she laid on the counter, to stay out of side. They were all unsure how strict the Food Health and Safety laws were regarding squirrels in Tumblestone restaurants. It was better to be safe than sorry.

"This is somehow worse than a mage's pocket," the squirrel remarked. "Oh my."

Sam smirked. "Be careful what you get into in there." *Seriously.*

As if on cue, Sam's tote bag started vibrating noisily. Her face felt like it had been shoved in an oven.

"What's that?" asked Lia. "Is it Henry? Is he alright?"

"Yes!" Sam barked. "Yes it's just Henry, and he's fine."

She reached in the bag and pushed the furry snoop away from the vibrator and fumbled for the power button to turn it off. It was still inside its velvet storage pouch, but she would make sure to wash it, and the pouch, before using it again. She shook her head at her own stupidity. She had kept the vibrator on her person to *avoid* such embarrassments, just in case the rental office needed to poke around again in her apartment while she was gone. Of course, she wasn't planning on taking the thing on a tour of another world.

The waitress showed up with menus just in time to rescue her from any further possible questions on the matter. With any luck, the incident would be forgotten. Gerald would probably just blush or laugh, but Sophie would never let her hear the end of it. She could handle that, but she didn't want to be the one to explain its purpose to Lia.

Sophie ordered a round of teas to start, and the waitress left to give them a moment with the menu.

A hallway in the back of the room caught Sam's eye. The sight of the sign next to it reminded her of yet another necessary human function. It promised washrooms. It was a good thing *somebody* was looking out for her.

Before she left the counter to take advantage of the facilities, she snuck the vibrator out of her tote while the others were busy with the menus and put it in her coat pocket. She couldn't risk having the ever curious Lia, who was seated next to her, get hold of it. Henry, perhaps, might turn it on again, or knock it out onto the floor. She shuddered at the thought.

She told Sophie to get her whatever she was having if she wasn't back before the waitress. After listening to another teasing about freeloaders, Sam hugged her benefactor and went to do her business.

It was a slight disappointment to find that the bathroom was much like any other public washroom she had ever been in. There was an ordinary toilet, and an ordinary sink with an ordinary mirror over it. The soap bar, at least, was sitting in a cute little teacup shaped tea tray. She was hoping for something more, not entirely sure what exactly, but something *different.*

She washed her hands and face in the sink, and checked her reflection. Her nose and cheeks were a little burnt from the sun, but not too severely. Her hair was a mess, as expected, but a few quick tosses soon set it to rights.

When she went to dry her hands, a smile stretched across her face. "Perfect," she whispered.

While looking for something to dry her hands, instead of a roll of paper towel or an electric air dryer, she found a basket filled with soft *leaves.* They were large green leaves, about the size of a dinner plate, and remarkably absorbent. That was it. The something different. Beside the toilet was another basket, containing several *rolls* of leaves.

She sat down to do her business, grinning foolishly. The rolls were even better, hand sized leaves held together by a thin plant membrane of sorts. The leaves broke apart just like normal toilet paper into individual pieces. And they were soft. Incredibly soft. It was like wiping herself with cashmere.

"What are you grinning about?" Sophie asked her when she returned from the bathroom. It could have been an embarrassing question, had Sophie known about the vibrator in her pocket.

Sam laughed, and from her *other* pocket, produced one of the green toilet paper leaves.

All three of them shot concerned looks at her.

"You don't have to steal bathroom foliage to cover your tab, princess," said Sophie.

"Bathroom *foliage!*" Sam laughed. "You can't get any greener than that, can you? It's fantastic. I love it."

Sophie shook her head in disbelief. "I guess the princess has never taken a shit before."

"Sophie!" cried Lia.

Sophie sighed, "Yes. I'm naughty today, aren't I, Lia? Well anyways, I ordered you a cucumber sandwich with cream cheese. If you don't like it, you can give it to the squirrel."

"I do enjoy cucumber," said the tote bag. "It's been so very long since I've tasted a good cucumber."

Sam patted the bag and promised to share.

The service was quick and the meal delightful. They ordered another round of tea after the food was gone, and listened to Henry describe in detail his meeting with Luke. A few concerned glances from the pretty young waitress resulted in the tote bag being moved to the end of the counter, in front of Gerald, to provide a more believable body for the male voice floating from it.

Henry told them of Luke's luck in the forest, and his unlucky fall after. He told them of Luke's second brush with death the very next day, when the pair were attacked by a deathwing. And he told them of their parting of ways at the camp of a nearly naked old man. He had no explanation as to how Luke had infuriated the giant into throttling him in the park.

Sam listened to it all and started sipping on her third cup of tea. She was typically a strictly coffee girl, but after experiencing the Tumbled Teapot's house brand, she vowed to reevaluate her position. After some thought, she asked, "Why were you imprisoned in the forest?"

The squirrel didn't seem in any way a malevolent being. He had rescued Luke on more than one occasion, once right before her eyes, but she couldn't help but remember a cartoon she once saw, where a bunch of adorable woodland animals tricked a child into defeating a predatory mountain lion so that they would be safe and free to perform a blood orgy ceremony in the name of Satan. She did not share these thoughts with the others, and happily accepted Henry's story of entering the forest despite the risk of imprisonment, with the hope of bringing his best friend back to life.

After guiding Luke safely out of the forest, the squirrel took another chance, and went back in for the golden apple he had sought to retrieve centuries before. Apparently the squirrel was much older than he appeared. As it turned out, he timed the theft perfectly. He had fled the forest with murderous faeries singeing the fur on his heels, but managed to escape just as the curse's power returned, trapping the faeries on the other side of the trees. At first, he buried the apple, but returned for it later after Luke knocked himself out, and hid the apple in his backpack for easy transport. He later regretted this, when he realized there was a good possibility that the deathwing might have been drawn to it. So he parted from Luke in the night and made his attempt to revive his dear friend, who turned out to be a demon of sorts.

Images of the woodland blood orgy flashed back into Sam's mind, but she shook them away, and took another sip of tea to drown them.

"And you're sure the raptors finished her off?" she asked.

"Eh, well, probably they did," said Henry, "I didn't stay to witness the outcome."

"So," Sam began, stopping to wet her words with another splash of the addictive tea, "basically, you're saying that not only is there a pissed off, er, sorry Lia, *angry* giant out there thinking about murdering Luke, but there's also a possibility that some sort of demon ghost thing is floating about out there looking for him as well?"

"I won't deny that it is a *possibility,* yes" Gerald pretended to say as the waitress and her tea pot made another round with re-fills. Gerald did a terrible job lip syncing, but aside from raising her eyebrows at him, the waitress said nothing.

"Great," said Sam. "Let's hope we can find him before one of them does." She set her cup down. "Maybe we should head to the inn. He should be there by now, if that was his plan. Listen. You guys don't have to follow me there. You can get yourselves nicer accommodations. You've already done so much for me, I don't want you to suffer another trip to that smelly inn."

Sophie waved a hand. "Nonsense. We'll see this through."

Gerald and Lia both nodded their approval.

"Thanks guys. Really. For everything. You've been way too good to me."

"We know," said Sophie.

Lia scooped up the tote bag before Sam had a chance, eager for the honor of carrying the squirrel. Sam didn't argue. There was nothing left in the bag to embarrass her.

Sophie paid the bill, and everyone said their thank yous and goodbyes to the waitress. She tilted her head at Gerald's goodbye, and asked, "Did you always sound like that?"

"Yes. Always," he muttered, and everyone rushed out of the diner laughing.

The sun had disappeared completely by the time they left the diner. Vine wrapped street lamps guided them, paving the streets in golden light. When they started walking again after sitting down for so long, Sam's feet had figured out how to tell her they were sore. Terribly sore. And she was exhausted. The entire day had been spent walking. She could only imagine how Luke felt, walking just as much, no doubt, but without any shoes. She saw the remains of his shirt around his feet, but that couldn't have helped much.

A cool breeze whipped through the streets. She shuddered, and hoped that Luke had found somewhere warm to spend the night. Maybe he was already back at the inn, wondering what took them so long, but she had little hope for that.

There were far less people to be found wandering the city by the time they rounded the corner onto the bottom of Reed Street. A sharp *crack* sound was what pulled their eyes to the fountain. It was a small fountain, similar to the one they saw when they first entered the city, but tucked away in an alcove. They hadn't seen anyone in several minutes, so they were surprised to catch someone who wasn't a statue in the middle of the fountain. Streetlight glistened off the rippled water around the person's knees.

When the person turned to them in surprise, the naked statue was not the only familiar sight. The woman was dressed shabbier, her clothes dirty and torn, and she wore a flat cap, pulled low over her eyes, but Sam still recognized them. They were the deep blue ocean eyes that belonged to the blond craftswoman she saw that morning working on the statue of Poseidon. She had no tool bag with her this time, just a hammer in one hand, and a severed marble penis in the other.

Sam opened her mouth to say something, to accuse her maybe, but she held her tongue as the woman saluted them with her hammer and stepped out of the fountain. Her pant legs dripped onto the cobbles, leaving a dark spotted trail behind as she approached them. She had the same cheeky smile on her face that she had flashed them earlier in the day when they watched her work. Her teeth were flawless. She was a real beauty. Similar in age to Sam. Perhaps a little older.

"Nice night for a walk, innit?" she said, her arms wide. Her voice was thickly accented. She sounded much more English than Luke. Sam would have to review her opinion of his accent.

Lia spoke first. "What are you doing with that man's..." She shied over the word. "Thing."

So she knows a bit of anatomy, Sam thought.

"Oh, just takin' it for a little walk, darling. Don't you fret," replied the vandal craftswoman. She shot a wink at Sam. "Saw you mates earlier by the gate before the big kerfuffle. What a show that was, what? Happens all the time here. Tumblestoners love a good scrap. Enjoying yourselves in the city, though, I hope?"

Before anyone could respond, she said, "Hold on a second." Then the vandal reached in her ratty coat pocket, deposited the marble penis, withdrew a small handful of copper coins, and startled Sam by pushing them into her palms. She nodded at the grown ups, and crouched down with her fist out to Lia for a fist bump. Lia happily met the woman's fist with her own, giggling.

"Drinks on me tonight, mates. Don't even mention it. Seriously. Don't. I'd love to take you out meself, but I'm completely knackered. Time for bed, I reckon."

Then the woman casually began to walk away.

Sam gave Sophie and Gerald a *what the hell was that* look, but they both just shrugged.

A few seconds later, the vandal turned around and lifted her cap to them. She flashed a big perfect smile, and disappeared around the corner.

"City people," said Sophie, shaking her head. "It's the same in every city. They're all lunatics. Every one of them."

CHAPTER NINETEEN

The water was nearly scalding, spraying into his face and cascading down his entire body like a river of lava. It was excruciating, but Luke didn't care. He fiddled with the hot water knob, trying in vain to further raise the temperature. He wanted nothing more at that moment than to watch his tainted skin melt away, to swirl around his blistered feet and disappear forever down the shower drain.

Only time could truly cleanse his body and soul of the horrifying ordeal he faced down in the sewers. The experience would haunt him for days to come. He would feel and smell it all every time his mind wandered back there. He knew this, and he knew it would get better eventually, but now he'd do just about anything for a fast forward button. Anything, except go back down in that sewer. He thought of tempting fate with the fireflies. The *faeries*. How beautiful they looked floating about, and how easily they could have killed him. He replayed the sounds of the deathwing, shrieking above his head as it tried to carry him away, its death cries. He saw the watch captain, huge and angry. He felt the knobby fists.

He tried to focus on his face, now throbbing and hideously swollen. To savor the sting of the soap as it found each of his wounds. But it was no use. His whole body shivered as the memories, still fresh and strong, clawed their way back to the surface of his mind despite his efforts to push them back.

They had traveled by the dim light of tiny mushrooms that glowed an eerie blue in the otherwise perpetual darkness. The mushrooms grew in the dirt spilling from holes left by failed bricks that had cracked and crumbled out of the tunnel walls. There were raised sidewalks of a sort that ran parallel on both sides above a trough where the sewage was meant to flow, but the sewer had been plagued by recent drainage issues. The sewage had risen far above the trough, so when Luke and the redheaded thief, Jacob, climbed down into the sewer and stepped onto the sidewalk, they were up to their waists in cold and chunky liquid.

The sewer had become a slow moving river of human feces with nowhere dry to step. Dead rats and clumps of who knows what floated by, and more often than not, collided with them. There were live rats as well, out for a swim, that squeaked greetings or warnings as they passed. Sometimes the rats would cross in front of the mushrooms, and project themselves as enormous black shadows on the walls. Treasures lurked beneath the surface as well, semi solids that refused to float, frequently squeezed their way up between his bare toes. Occasionally, something like a fish or an eel would blindly bump into him, and frantically wiggle and squirm to get away, splashing sewage in its wake.

The feeling and knowledge of what was soaking through his jeans and lapping at his bare stomach was terrible. The fact that his dick was also submerged was the worst. Enough to make him cry, or it would have, had his vision not already been blurred with tears brought on by the smell when the manhole was first uncovered. He waded along with his backpack in front, hugged close to his nose, but several times throughout the journey he had to move it aside to vomit.

Luke and Jacob barely spoke within the sewers. Only a quick introduction and Jacob's directions, which were usually given as hand gestures. At the time, Luke thought the man must be insane for having been in the sewers enough to know his way around so confidently, but later Jacob explained that it was not always so bad, that usually the sewage remained in the trough. A simple rag over the face was normally enough to pass through with reasonable comfort. Perhaps this tidbit was meant to make him sound less crazy, but the man *had* chosen to bring the wrath of probably the biggest man in the city down upon himself for the sake of a few coins and a laugh.

The sewage levels had receded by the time they reached a long straight section that took them away from Tumblestone and under the river. The going was easier there, across the river beneath the streets of the High City district, the area around the castle, but the damage to Luke's psyche had already been done. There was little chance the big man would find them. Even if he did, surely the smell would keep him at bay. But they chose to keep to the sewers as long as possible, until they reached the Old City district where Jacob lived. Neither of them wanted to be seen in public with their lower halves drenched in chunky human waste.

A secret knock gained them entry to Jacob's apartment. An obscene number of latches and deadbolts were released by his daughters, waiting inside. They were horrified by the sight and smell of their father and his companion, but they obediently laid out newspapers from the front door to the bathroom, and another paper trail for Jacob to wait outside on the balcony after he graciously insisted Luke be the first to shower. He was told to leave his clothes outside the door.

That doorway had brought him into the center of the bathroom, where his cold feet were warmed by sparkling sand colored tiles. He felt a terrible pang of guilt stepping on them with his filthy feet, but Jacob promised they would clean up easily. The room was incredibly spacious, and entirely devoted to self cleansing. A toilet, assuming Jacob had one, was kept elsewhere. Several steps straight ahead from the door were two white sinks set in a long brown counter, with cabinets and drawers beneath, and above was a grand mirror which Luke couldn't bare to look into. To the center right was a three step pyramid of tiles leading into a white soaker tub. A tall window stretched wide beyond it, offering a view of the city lights through louvered vertical blinds. Stars twinkled down on the tub from a skylight in the high ceiling directly above. A similar skylight looked down on the open shower area on the left side of the room.

It was all lost to him now as another shiver brought him back to the present. He could see nothing beyond his own reach, the rest of the bathroom had been swallowed up by the dense gray steam from his extra long, extra hot shower. When he had entered, Jacob handed him a brand new fist sized bar of soap. It was now the size and thickness of a quarter. *Time to get out,* he thought. Hopefully Jacob had another bar of soap somewhere for himself, and hopefully the hot water would hold out for a second shower.

He fumbled through the haze until he found the towel rack. His towel had made an attempt to soak up some of the steam, and had done quite well at it. It was too wet to properly dry himself, but he managed at least to stop his hair from dripping everywhere. With no clothes to change into, he had little choice but to push open the bathroom door and enter the living room with just the towel wrapped around his waist.

The steam snaked out around his nearly naked form, and an upbeat pop song was playing on the radio. It would have made a grand entrance to a boxing match surrounded by screaming fans, but it was an especially awkward way for a stranger to enter a living room occupied by two children lounging on the couch in their pajamas. The girls exchanged looks, and laughed. One of them, the one who had tripped him, jumped up immediately and brought him a bundle of clothes.

"Papa said they should fit you," she said. "We threw your trousers in the garbage. I hope that's alright."

"Absolutely, yes." Luke nodded, "I hope I never see them again. Thank you."

"You're welcome!" she said, cheerfully.

Not wanting to risk any wardrobe malfunctions in front of the children, Luke nodded again and quickly ducked back into the bathroom to make himself decent.

He hesitated a moment with the underwear. They were something similar to boxer shorts, but he had never worn another person's underwear before. The thought of Jacob's dangly bits being inside of them before his was slightly unnerving. He had, however, just crawled out of a sewer where far worse things had come in contact with his junk. He shuddered and put them on. It wasn't so bad.

He slid into the pants next, and was amazed by the fit. He didn't even need a belt. They were light and comfortable dressy type pants, much easier to move about in than jeans. Luke didn't own anything other than jeans. He might have to diversify his wardrobe if he ever made it back home. The similarity in color of the olive green pants to Sam's coat was not lost on him.

Next, he threw on and buttoned up a crisp white dress shirt. It looked brand new, and felt silky smooth on his skin. He narrowed his eyes and grinned at the next item. An olive green dinner jacket to match the pants, or maybe it was a sport coat, or a blazer. Whatever it was, he'd never owned one of those either, but he had to admit he'd been quite struck by the amount of well dressed people he saw in the city. Now he could try the look for himself. He normally wore his shirts loose, but for this ensemble, he felt compelled to tuck his shirt in.

He cleared a block of condensation from the mirror and nodded smugly at his reflection.

Ohhh yeahhh, he thought, dragging out the single syllables in his head. He tugged at the jacket and stretched out his arms. The sleeves were the perfect length. *Sharp Dressed Man* played in his head, and he felt quite sharp indeed, save for his messy hair and lumpy, purple monstrosity of a face. Smiling was painful. The next day, no doubt, would be worse.

Last came the socks. Nothing particularly special about them, just ordinary black socks, but it felt heavenly to have a soft buffer between his feet and the world for a change.

The children were quieter upon his return to the living room. This was a plus, though it might have had less to do with his clothing and more to do with their own shirts, which they had pulled up over their noses. Their father had come inside from the balcony and brought the smell of the sewer with him.

Luke, too, scrunched up his nose as Jacob walked the newspaper carpet to take his turn in the shower. The thief paused to admire Luke's new look.

"You clean up well," he said, smiling, and might have said more had his daughters not shouted in unison, "Papa! Get in the washroom!"

Jacob chuckled. "Right. Well then, if you'll excuse me... Make yourself at home. The girls will—"

"Papa!"

"Alright!" He disappeared into the washroom.

Shortly afterward, he cracked the door open long enough to toss out his filthy clothes, and the *tripping daughter* rushed to collect them. She tied them tightly inside a cloth bag and placed the bag inside of a closet next to the apartment entrance. Or maybe it was a condo? Whatever it was would definitely be out of Luke's price range if he found its equivalent in Halifax.

On its own, the living room wasn't much bigger than the bathroom, but the lack of separation between it and the kitchen and dining area created a feeling of substantial loftiness. Two long couches and an arm chair formed a partial square frame around a large, low coffee table. On the table were two suspicious piles of coins, some loose, some spilling from stuffed pouches. The girls giggled when they noticed him looking. He just shook his head.

The couches weren't pointed at a television, as with most living room set ups. In place of a television were several rows of shelves spanning the length of the outer wall of the bathroom. The shelves were filled with books and board games and various decorative knick knacks. The radio continued to play its upbeat pop music at a low volume from an end table between the two couches.

A dining table and four chairs were situated by the sliding glass exit to the balcony. Through the glass, a mass of black high rise buildings was visible, each speckled with tiny squares of golden light. The buildings spread out from the base of an enormous hill, higher still than the high rises. The castle from the book, the same one he saw earlier from the square, was perched there. Its silhouette loomed over the city, hauntingly beautiful.

The girls shifted to either side of the couch and offered him a seat between them. They were both in pajamas, the *tripper* in a gray and black two piece, and the other in a purple onesie with the hood pulled up over her head. It would have been obvious to anyone that they were sisters, or at least closely related. They were nearly identical at a glance. They both had the same red hair, straight and of shoulder length. Their eyes were deep set and green, though the tripper's eyes were a shade closer to blue. Her nose was also smaller, more pointed, and on the couch she sat a few inches taller. She was probably the oldest.

A hint of mischief glinted in their eyes as Luke moved to take the offered seat, but in his experience, most girls their age always looked like they were up to no good. Besides, he had nothing for them to steal, and there was nothing they could do that would be worse than his trip through the sewers.

"Er, nice to see you again, ladies," he said.

The girls giggled. "A pleasure to see you as well, *sir*" said the youngest in a teasingly pompous voice. They both laughed.

"How *do* you *do?*" continued the tripper. More laughter.

Luke shook his head, smiling. "I'm not quite sure how I'm doing. But I'm still alive. I suppose that's alright. My name's Luke, by the way."

"I'm Cassie," said the tripper.

"And I'm Chloe," said the youngest. "Would you like some water?"

Luke nodded, "Yes please. That would be great."

He swept his hand over the piles of coins on the coffee table. Two small mountains of copper and silver, each with a draw string bag next to them. One might expect a similar display on Halloween when children returned home to show off their bounty of candy. "That's, uh, quite a haul you got there. Did you get all that today?"

Cassie grinned devilishly, but shook her head. "No. That's just from this evening."

Luke blinked. "This evening? *Just* this evening? Did you, er, collect more during the day?"

"We did, but not so much. Papa's plan worked great. Nobody was paying *any* attention to us. He didn't tell us that you'd be working with him though. Were you working with him in the morning too? To test us?"

"Er... Sure, yeah. You weren't at the square, were you?"

Cassie nodded, and Chloe, returning with Luke's glass of water, said "Yep. Both of us. Papa said he would make sure that nobody was looking at us."

"Ah," said Luke. "Well, he definitely did that." He took a sip of water and wondered if drowning in the fountain was also part of their father's plan, like some twisted sort of life insurance policy scheme to provide for his children, but he decided not to ask.

"That pile is mine," said Cassie, pointing proudly to the slightly larger pile. "And the other one is Chloe's. *I* won."

Chloe stuck her tongue out at her sister and the two began to bicker and tease one another about thieving methods. *Typical children's argument,* Luke thought. He sat between them, listening and sipping his water, and was generally just enjoying the comfortable couch. As soon as his glass was empty, however, the girls stopped their bickering and turned on him.

"Will you read now?" asked Chloe. She clasped her hands together and held them out to him. Her sister nodded, as if to show Luke the proper answer to Chloe's question.

"What?"

Cassie hung her head. Wrong answer, apparently.

"You finished your water. Will you read now?" Chloe repeated. "Papa always drinks a glass of water before he reads to us. It's good for his voice, he says."

"Oh. Well, I'm sure he'll want to read to you himself when he gets out of the shower. He shouldn't be too long."

"*You* were in there forever, though," Cassie groaned. "Papa said you'd read to us if we asked nicely."

"He did," Chloe confirmed.

"I see. Well—"

"Unless you *can't* read," said Cassie.

"Hey hold on now. I—"

Chloe cut him off. "Yeah, you're probably right, Cass. We shouldn't have asked."

"Hey! Hold your horses. I was just about to say yes. What do you want me to read?"

The girls exchanged victory grins. Chloe went to the bookshelf and returned with a thick book. She placed it on Luke's lap. His eyes narrowed when he saw the title.

"How did you get this?" he asked.

"We didn't steal it!" Chloe insisted. "We don't steal books."

"No, that's fine." He shook his head. "I don't mean that. Sorry. Where did you get it? That's what I meant."

"It was mom's book," Cassie explained, "from when she was little."

Maybe he shouldn't have asked. "Is your mother, um..."

"She's working," said Cassie. "She'll be home later."

"Ah, good," said Luke. "That's good. Is she a bartender or something?"

"She works for the king. She's a fixer person," said Chloe.

"A fixer person? What, like an assassin?"

The girls giggled. "No silly," said Chloe. "She fixes things."

"She's a mason," Cassie added. "She works with bricks and stuff. And she fixes the statues."

"Oh really? That sounds like a good job. But isn't it a little late to be out fixing statues?"

Chloe shook her head. "She fixes them during the day. At night she—"

"Enough Chloe. He'll never quit if you keep going. Are you gonna read or what?"

"Maybe he really can't read," said Chloe.

Luke sighed. "That's a little rude, ya know? Is this where you left off?" He opened the book to where a red ribbon marked the sixth chapter.

The girls nodded, so the illiterate Luke began to read aloud from an ancient copy of *Robinson Crusoe* by *Daniel Defoe*. He was a bit shy at first, nervous that his reading voice would be too quick for his speaking voice and he'd mess up the words, but after just a few pages, his confidence increased. The girls were hanging on his every word as he told them about Robinson's first day after surviving a shipwreck. The crafty guy went right to work scavenging the wrecked ship for food and supplies. He even fashioned himself a raft to haul his goods back to shore.

Several pages in, Chloe laid her head against his shoulder and closed her eyes, but insisted she wasn't sleeping and that he should continue. He obliged, until the secret knock rapped at the front door.

"That'd be mum!" said Cassie, and hopped up to begin the lengthy process of unlocking the door. Chloe began to snore softly.

A tall woman in a dusty gray overcoat strode into the room and was immediately caught by her daughter in a hug. During the embrace, she cast a curious look at the newspaper trail still littering the apartment. Unlike the rest of her family, her wavy hair was a golden blond. It fell to about the bottom of her chin from beneath a gray flat cap. Her eyes narrowed severely when she saw Luke on the couch with her other daughter snuggled up next to him.

She separated herself from her daughter and moved towards Luke. She spoke sternly as she did so, her eyes fixed on him. "Who's this dodgy tosser on my couch and *what* are you doing with my magpies?"

Chloe woke then, blinking. "Oh hey, mum."

Luke gulped. "Uh, well—"

The mother, who was probably no older than Luke himself, stood close enough now that he could see the blue of her eyes. Before he could say anything, she pointed a hammer in his face and said, "If you have an issue, you can bloody well settle it with me. You'll leave them out of it, thank you. And why are you wearing my husband's clothes? Did you bump him off?"

So this was where the girls learned to speak without waiting for answers. Luke smiled, on the inside. On the outside he remained straight faced. "No no. Nothing like that. He's in the shower." *Hopefully still alive.* It had been awhile, but as the girls said, Luke was in the shower for forever.

"He was helping papa tonight, mum," explained Cassie. "His clothes were ruined."

The mother relaxed then. Her eyes softened. "Ah, so you're one of Jacob's nutters. Sorry about the dodgy tosser thing, mate."

"It's okay. I have no idea what that means."

The mother laughed. "I'm Melody. Please don't call me *m'lady*, like Jacob does, or I'll smack you."

"She really will," said Cassie.

"I have no doubt." Luke chuckled. He introduced himself.

"What's all this newspaper layin' about for?" she asked as she opened the closet to hang her coat. "Oh bloody hell. What in the blazes is that stench? What's in those bags?"

The girls laughed and set themselves to cleaning up the newspaper since it was no longer necessary. Luke explained to Melody the situation with Jacob and the watch captain and their trip through the sewers, while she made them some tea. When the girls were finished with the newspapers, Melody sent the girls to bed. They thanked Luke for reading to them.

He smiled, "My pleasure, *ladies*," and bowed. "Goodnight!"

"Goodnight *sir*," they giggled, and curtsied, before disappearing down the hallway to the bedrooms.

Melody shook her head as she handed him a plate and tea cup.

"Now you've done it," she said. "They'll think they're proper princesses from now on. Right fancy like."

"Sorry about that," he said, blowing on the hot beverage.

"I added some ginger to the mix, and a pinch of verbena. Let it steep a little first. It won't make your ugly mug any prettier, but it should help with the pain."

"Thanks."

Melody took a seat in the arm chair across from him with a cup of her own. She surveyed the treasure horde on the table.

"So these are the fruits of their father's thick idea, then? Not bad really. But still stupid."

Luke couldn't disagree.

At that moment, Jacob emerged from the bathroom, alive, ahead of a thick cloud of steam, with a towel around his waist. His battered face lit up when he saw the mother of his children.

"M'lady!" he cried. "Home so soon? I thought to have myself all cleaned up before you got back. Oh well. Any chance of getting a cup myself?"

"Oh you'll get a cup," snapped Melody, setting her tea down on the table. She stormed over to the bathroom. "The watch captain? Hmm? Mestorphemus? What the hell were you thinking? And involving the girls, no less!"

Jacob smiled foolishly, and looked to Luke, "Sometimes it's best to leave certain details out when talkin' with the missus." He turned back to Melody. "Oh love, the girls were never in any danger. All eyes on me. You know how I like to make a spectacle of myself."

"The girls were so in danger." She pushed a finger, roughly into Jacob's bare chest, knocking him back a step. Thankfully, his towel was snugly tied. "In danger of losing their stupid father. Mestorphemus is part god or something. You should know that. It's never wise to be messin' with divinity."

Jacob chuckled, "Oh! *Really?* That's solid advice comin' from a woman who spends her evenings snapping the knobs off of all manner of divine beings."

Melody sputtered her lips. "The statues don't make no fuss about it. A marble Poseidon isn't gonna reach down and smite me, but one of his living, breathing nephews might very well take a crack at it. Look at you. You look like hell, and look at me. I—"

"You look the very picture of a goddess, darling."

Melody groaned, but something of a smile tugged at her lips. "Go in and put some trousers on, will you? We have a guest."

Jacob grinned. "You sure you want me to put them on right away? You know, my back's a little sore. I might need a hand." He bobbed his fiery eyebrows at her.

Melody swung her hand around to slap him, but stopped before his cheek, and pinched his ear lobe. "I'd slap you, I would. But it looks like you've had enough of that already. Anyways, the girls have only just gone in for bed. *Somebody* let them stay up past their bedtime, so it'll be awhile before they're sleepin' proper." She waved him away. "Get on with you! *By yourself.*"

Luke watched this while blowing and sipping at his tea. Regardless of whether or not the tea had any actual healing properties, just the thought of it at work as it warmed its way down to this stomach had a certain effect of its own. The throbbing in his face and back became less intense.

"I should tell you," said Melody to him as she returned to her chair and tea, "that you are just as much of an idiot as Jacob is for getting yourself involved in that mess."

Again, Luke couldn't disagree. He wondered how Sam would react if he never returned home. If he just up and got himself beat to death in some other world without saying a word of goodbye. They were only just getting to know one another. She was funny, and smart, and a total babe. Of course, she'd find someone else, no problem. But it'd still be a dick move on his part.

"But I'm glad you did," Melody continued. "Mestorphemus is not known for his... control. He would have killed Jacob, most likely. My father died when I was young. It was difficult for a long time. The kids don't need to be dealin' with that. And, you know, I might miss him a little bit myself."

Luke smiled, and nodded, "So how is somebody like that even in power? He's a psychopath."

"He's not the real watch captain. Just a temp. A filler. He steps in when the real captain is away with the king on business. Law enforcement gets a little extreme when he's in charge. *When* he's in charge. He's usually drunk most of the time. Anyways, he only looks after the Tumblestone district. Don't have to worry about him over here."

"That's right," said Jacob, fresh from the bedroom in a cozy looking pajama set. "Forget about him. Everything is *fine*. Look how well the girls did, Mel. We'll just stay out of Tumblestone for a little while. Keep our heads low."

"Yes you will," Melody agreed, glaring at him from behind her tea cup.

Jacob chuckled, and set about making himself a cup of tea. "So, Luke! Tell me about yourself, why don't you? Didn't have much chance to speak on the way here, on account of the vomiting and whatnot. What brought you to Tumblestone? I can't imagine that it was divine intervention on my behalf. I spend too little time praying for that."

As Luke went through the details of his journey so far, Melody and Jacob listened in much the same way as their children did with the tale of Robinson Crusoe, but Jacob stopped him when he got to the part where Henry spoke to him on the hill.

"Aha!" he cried. "I thought it was just my head going all whoozy from the smackings, but I *did* hear that squirrel in the square talk. Maybe my brain's not damaged after all."

Melody scoffed and raised an eyebrow at him. He chuckled and bade Luke to continue.

A moment later, Jacob interjected again with a laugh. "Rufus, you say? Tall and lanky, beard down to his knees?"

Luke nodded.

Jacob exchanged a smile with Melody and continued, "I'm sure that's Rufus Brackenreid, the politician. He's on the Tumblestone Council. You can thank him for the sewage problems as of late. The sewer workers went off the job when their pay didn't come on time. Turns out he had been losing heaps of city coin at the gambling dens in Camelot. What a fellow. Ah, sorry lad. Go on."

Moments later, it was clear that Jacob wanted to interrupt again, but he held his tongue and waited until Luke had brought them up to their second meeting at the fountain.

"You didn't happen to find any of that deathwing's teeth lodged in your backpack, did you?" he asked.

"Er, no," said Luke. "Why do you ask?"

"Deathwing teeth are one of the ingredients in the potion I gave you in the square, after my lovely daughter Cassandra finally found the time to get around to tossing it to me. I suppose I should be happy she thought to toss it at all. I had a flask of my own, but it didn't survive one of my falls. Anyways, you have to grind the teeth up and boil them first, of course. Wouldn't go down very easy otherwise."

"You mean the invisibility potion?" Luke asked, "So that's like.. a thing here?" It wasn't an entirely difficult thing to believe, given some of the other things he had seen. And it had, in fact, actually made them invisible. That would be enough to drive doubt from anyone.

"Indeed it is, though the secrets to making such a thing are not common knowledge. The ingredients aren't too complicated, really. Some shavings of mandrake root, the yolk of pretty much any egg, deathwing teeth, ah and a few drops of faerie blood. That gives the liquid that smoky effect. It's the preparation of the thing that is difficult."

"Faerie blood? *Faeries*?" Did those things exist outside the forest too?

Jacob chuckled. "Don't worry. I didn't hurt any faeries. The blood has to be given freely or it doesn't work. As I said, the process is rather finicky. Sometimes faeries will sell it. Sometimes they ask for favors. I prefer to buy it. Well, that's pretty much my only option now, being married and all. I don't suggest going the favor route. The favors they ask can vary *quite* wildly depending on the faerie."

"I see," said Luke, imagining some shady behind-the-dumpster-out-back kind of deals to acquire faerie blood. He pushed the image aside. "Kind of. But aren't they like... this big?" He spread his thumb and forefinger apart to indicate the small size of the faeries he knew of. "The ones I saw in the forest just floated around like little yellow light bulbs. And they didn't say anything. I would never even have assumed they were faeries had Henry not told me about them."

"Oh the wee ones!" Melody said. "My nan used to tell me stories about the wee ones. The green and blue faeries are supposed to be quite friendly, but the golden ones are said to be nasty little creatures."

Jacob nodded. "Yes. Very nasty. I've never seen any of those ones myself. Luckily, the recipe is not so sensitive in that respect. Any faerie will do."

"What kind of faerie did you, um, use?" Luke asked.

"The more human-y kind," said Jacob. "There's one that runs the coffee shop around the block from here. He's good to deal with. Oh, and Mel. You would know. Your friend that writes children's books. Janelle. She's a faerie, isn't she?"

"Half fairy, actually," Melody corrected.

"Ah yes, half faerie," said Jacob, bobbing his head. "The city used to be swarming with faeries and other magical beings before the purge, I've heard. But they're slowly starting to make a comeback. Good for them, I say."

"Speaking of books," Luke held up the book he had been reading to the girls. "I wanted to ask. This book. Robinson Crusoe. Where did you get it?"

"Do you like it?" Melody asked. 'It was my mum's book when she was young. She gave it to me when I had Cassie."

"It's good, yeah. I've read it before actually. Do you know where she got it? Because the author wasn't from *this world*. Or at least, I don't think he was. It's an old book. Something like three hundred years old."

"Ah yes, this other world of yours. I've never heard of such a thing," said Jacob. "Have you, Mel?"

Melody shook her head. "Can't say that I have. I don't know where my mother got the book, but she's never been one for traveling. I don't think she's ever left the city, let alone visited another world. Most likely she picked the thing up in a thrift store. Loves those, she does. Her apartment is full of useless junk. I don't know how she moves around in there. I *have* heard of books that could whisk people away to other places right quick like though. There used to be an old fellow on Spring Avenue in High Town that ran a travel agency, for when people wanted to go on vacations and getaways and whatnot, you know. He had a list of destinations with pictures and information that a customer could choose from, and once a choice was made and he was paid, he could send you there in the blink of an eye. All you had to do was look long enough at the picture in his little book. Made a killing, he did, sending people down south to Gaia during the colder months."

"That sounds exactly like the book I found," said Luke, "but how did his customers get back home? Did they have to find some other way back?"

"I think he had round trip options. Arrangements could be made to meet back up at the drop off point at a certain time. Something like that."

"Nice," Luke nodded. "Maybe that guy can help me. Is it far from here? This Spring Avenue?"

Melody shrugged, "It's a bit of a walk. But you could get there by bus quick enough. Like I said, though, He *used to be* on Spring. A few hundred years ago. Before the Purge. Suppose I should have clarified that."

"Oh," said Luke with a sigh. "That is unfortunate." He told them of his plans to visit a library in the morning, in hopes of finding some clue as to how to get home, but even as he spoke he felt the chances were probably slim. Jacob agreed with him.

"I wouldn't say it would be *impossible* for them to have something like that. But as your squirrel friend said, a librarian might be able to help. Who knows? The Knowledge House would certainly be your best bet in that approach. I'll be happy to guide you there, first thing in the morning. If I can walk."

"Oh no you won't," snapped Melody. "The Knowledge House is in Tumblestone. You and the girls are staying on this side of the river until Mestorphemus is gone, remember? I'll hear nothing of you doing otherwise. I can take him. I have a feeling I'll have a few service calls in that area to deal with in the morning anyhow."

"Well then I can at least ask around the neighborhood about these other worlds. See what I can turn up."

"Fine. So long as you stay out of Tumblestone. I'm serious, Jacob."

"Yes, m'lady. Have no fear," he grinned, throwing his arms to the side. "Ooh." He groaned, feeling at his back. "That's getting a bit stiff."

Melody wagged a finger at him. "And don't you dare complain. You did it to yourself."

Luke could definitely relate with Jacob. He had been doing his best to move as little as possible. The tea helped only to slow the inevitable onslaught of muscle soreness. He was exhausted, physically and mentally. It had been days since he had a proper night's sleep, and apparently, his body decided it didn't want to wait much longer, because the next thing Luke knew, Melody was placing a blanket over him.

She smiled, "We're losing you, what?"

He apologized for crashing, but she sputtered her lips and waved a hand at him. "Nonsense. It's about time we went to bed ourselves."

Jacob handed him a pillow. "Sorry, we don't have a spare bedroom. I hope you don't mind the couch."

"Not at all," said Luke. "I'm quite familiar with them."

The couple bid him goodnight, and made their way down the hall.

"I'm still mad at you, ya know," he heard Melody say as the bedroom door closed.

Luke fluffed up the pillow and made himself comfortable, which, other than the pain involved in shifting himself into a horizontal position, was remarkably easy. Jacob's couch made his own couch feel like sleeping in a ditch.

A noise down the hall caught his ear as he was falling asleep. He cocked his head to listen closer, and quickly confirmed what he had thought the noise to be.

Melody can't be too mad at him.

He closed his eyes again and drifted away to the sounds of spirited reconciliation.

Chapter Twenty

S am pushed the incredibly soft, incredibly pleasant smelling blanket away from her and stepped barefoot onto the impeccably clean hardwood floor beside her bed. She wasn't afraid that an enormous cockroach might take her out at the knees, nor was she urged to hold her breath against any cadaverous odors. By some strange miracle, the dorm room Sophie had acquired for them held none of the horrors that haunted the common areas of the Wooden Hearth Inn.

The room was quite charming, actually. Spartan in furnishings, but clean and comfortable. Four single beds, each with a small dresser at its foot, lined a wall with two windows in between them. The windows were nearly kissing the building next door, which seemed to be the only thing keeping the Wooden Hearth Inn from falling over. If Sam had to make a complaint, it would be that the floor was dangerously sloped. It would be a terrible room to book if one had plans to go out drinking. The group ended up switching the pillows from where they were placed on the bed, to what was intended as the foot of the bed. Otherwise it would have been like sleeping upside down.

Morning appeared to be a while off yet. It was still dark outside, and everyone else was sleeping peacefully. Sam would have preferred to be doing the same, but her bladder had decided to be a dick. She shambled towards the amber glow of the fireplace on the opposite wall. It was still full of wood. Either she hadn't been sleeping long, or someone had recently tossed in a few fresh logs. The fireplace, contrary to the name of the building, *thankfully*, was not wooden, but built with bricks. The sheer enormity of it made the room extra cozy.

The bathroom door was to the right of the fireplace, but before she reached it, she stopped, and turned back to the mantel above the fireplace. The cupcake was gone. And so was the candle.

The cupcake, with its pink frosting and red sprinkles, had been placed on the mantel in front of a wax candle when they first arrived. The cupcake was given to them by the ancient receptionist after they paid for the room, with specific instructions regarding its placement in front of the candle that was already there waiting for them. It was meant for the cleaning staff, Harry told them. Sam had laughed at this peculiarity. Apparently, a kobold, whatever that was, would be showing up at some point to do some cleaning. When they found the room to be spotless, Sam figured this must have been some kind of joke, and had even put some thought into eating the cupcake herself, but she had decided against it. Now it was gone. One of the others must have eaten it.

The bathroom door was closed. She looked back. Everyone else was asleep in their beds.

Was it closed when we settled down to sleep?

She couldn't remember. Her heart began to thump a little quicker in her chest, but she took a deep breath and approached the door. She knocked, lightly, perhaps too lightly for anyone to hear. She didn't want to wake the others. Another breath, and she turned the handle.

Her jaw dropped in the same instant that the little boy in the bathroom dropped his wet rag. It hit the floor with a squishy splat. He had been scrubbing the toilet by candlelight. The candle from the mantel was on a shelf above the toilet. What was a small child doing scrubbing toilets in the middle of the night?

Child labor laws must be pretty lax in this city.

As she blinked away her shock, however, she realized that while the thing she saw before her was the relative size and shape of a three year old boy, and wore human clothing, that was where the similarities ended. Its skin was rough and gray, like a statue come to life. Its ears, long and pointy, stuck out from its head at odd angles. The left ear slanted upward, the right drooped towards the floor. Both of them bounced a little as the creature breathed. At the base of its long crooked nose, like a bent carrot, were the creature's enormous golden eyes. It was looking at her, blinking.

If she hadn't heard the receptionist mention a strange creature coming to do the cleaning, she might have screamed. She might have screamed anyways, had the receptionist himself not been a scarier sight than the creature before her. As it were, she was reasonably prepared for such things, and endeavored not to wake her sleeping friends unless it became necessary.

She whispered, "Hello?"

The creature opened its mouth, a mouth full of tiny pointed teeth, into a slight smile. It whispered back with enthusiasm, "Hallo!"

"You must be the kobold, I take it?"

The creature looked at her sadly and held his bony hands out at a loss. "Es tut mir leid, meine Dame. Ich spreche kein Arthurisch."

She was taken aback. The creature spoke German.

"Oh," she whispered, "Hmm. Let's see." She reached into the back of her mind and pulled out the file labeled, 'Vacations At Grandmothers In Austria' and said, "Glauben Sie, es ist ein bisschen spät für... umm.. dies?" She couldn't remember the words to ask whether the creature thought it might be a little late for *cleaning*, so she settled for *this*.

The creature's eyes and smile broadened at that, and prattled off, far too quickly, several long and complicated German sentences. A German sentence did not need to be long to be complicated enough already. She had no idea what the creature said. It was her turn to apologize for a lack of understanding.

She asked the creature to speak slower, and with simpler language.

His name was Felix Langhahn, and he was indeed the kobold in charge of cleaning the rooms. There were two others, his brother Lukas and his sister Monika, working elsewhere in the inn that night. Together they formed the company Langhahn Cleaning Services. He expressly mentioned, however, that they were not paid to deal with the corridors and lobby, and asked Sam not to think them lazy. She assured him that she did not. "The room is excellent."

Through a series of hand gestures and terribly pronounced words, Sam was also able to discern that the kobolds placed a charm of sorts on the doors to each of the rooms, preventing rodents and cockroaches from crossing the threshold. Felix articulated this by mimicking a crawly critter with his right hand, and making it 'explode' as it crossed the pointer finger of his left hand. She thanked him for that, and he bowed. It was nothing, he said. He hated cockroaches.

The room door had been locked, and the chain pulled across. Even with a key, it would be impossible to enter without anyone knowing. She asked him how he was able to get in. She couldn't understand his answer, until he took her outside the bathroom and pointed at the chimney. Her eyes widened.

"But the fire!" she blurted in English, unthinking, before repeating it in German.

Felix chuckled softly into his hands, and did a twirl. The seat of his pants was charred black.

Sam laughed a little too loudly, but when she looked behind her to the beds, nobody had stirred. Even Henry remained silent, curled up in a ball like a small cat, nestled on top of the blanket between the outline of Lia's feet.

They returned to the bathroom where there was less chance of disturbing the others. There she had a thought. If Felix and his family could use magic, maybe they would know something of magical books or other worlds. Unfortunately, her vocabulary was not structured around such things, and she had to resort to asking him if he had ever heard of Canada, or North America, or Europe, along with a slew of other random countries and cities that popped into her head. Felix shook his head in response to all of them. He had never heard of any places from her world, so there was a fair chance he wouldn't know how to get there. It was worth a shot.

She was enjoying chatting with the creature, but her bladder was starting to realize that the longer she kept him talking, the longer she would have to wait before she could use the toilet. She also didn't want to use the toilet and watch him resume his cleaning immediately afterwards. It just felt like a rude thing to do. Instead, she thanked him for his 'excellent service' and bid him goodnight. He bowed and smiled before disappearing behind the bathroom door.

Blessedly, she didn't have to squirm in her bed very long before Felix finished his duties. She heard him mutter something unintelligible in front of the fireplace, and wave his hand at it. After a few seconds, nothing had happened. The kobold sighed and shook his head. Then repeated the process. This time, after he waved his hand, Sam gasped. The fire disappeared completely. Logs and all. Felix punched the air in a celebratory fashion, and shimmied his way up the chimney.

She waited a few more moments before getting up to finally use the bathroom, and very nearly pissed herself just as she reached the door. The fire returned in a startling blink. The logs crackled away as if they had been burning there all along.

CHAPTER TWENTY-ONE

The next day brought no further arguments from Jacob as to whether or not he'd accompany Luke to the library. In fact, he didn't even get of bed for breakfast. He just groaned something incoherent when Melody asked him if he was coming out. Chloe took him some buttered toast.

Luke was more determined. Despite the agony of simple movement, he drug himself to the table for a delicious breakfast of eggs, sausage, toast, and coffee. It might not have been a particularly unique moment in his life, but it was easily his favorite experience of the last couple days.

While he was helping Melody to dry the dishes, he peered out the window over the balcony. The castle was even more magnificent in the daylight. Long teal colored strips of fabric stretched out and flapped in the wind from dozens of poles along the sprawling outer wall. The crenelations along the top of the wall gave it the 'classic' look that Luke always associated with castles growing up. Beyond the walls were towers of varying heights and shapes. Some round and some square. A few rose up and ended with flat crenelated roofs similar to the wall, while many others were capped with green domes. Tarnished copper, maybe. A pretty expensive roof, but if he were unfortunate enough to be their roofer, he'd want to use a material that would last long after he was dead, whatever the cost. He shuddered at the thought of working at such a height.

More interesting than the castle, were the streets below the apartment building. Specifically, how the paved streets ended after a couple of blocks and gave way to a series of waterways between the buildings. The traffic crawled steadily along like ants, and didn't miss a beat as it transitioned from ground travel to amphibious travel. Were those the same green vehicles he saw yesterday? The scene gave off a Venice/sunken city vibe. He'd never been to Venice, but he'd never seen any photos of people driving their cars into the waterways. Instead, he imagined all Venetians traveled throughout the city by little boats, paddled by handsome, well tanned men who sang romantic songs and wore deep v neck shirts that allowed their chest hair to blow majestically in the breeze. This was probably a ridiculous stereotype, but one he hoped was true.

"That's the Lower Quarter," said Melody when she noticed him looking. "Pretty neat, huh?"

Luke nodded. "It is, yeah. But it seems a little crazy to build part of the city in the water though, don't you think? Wouldn't it have been easier to just expand the city further on the mainland?"

Melody handed him another plate to dry and smiled, "Wasn't planned like that, so they say. Somethin' like ten thousand years ago, or probably more, the entire Lower Quarter and some of the Upper Quarter sank into the ocean after a mighty big explosion. Wiped pretty much everything out, though somehow the buildings that sank stayed sturdy enough that when people came back, they built on top of them. Don't ask me why. Probably for the tourists. But I like it."

"Must have been some explosion. What happened?"

"They called Atlantis 'The City of Lights' back then. Well, in some other language, I guess. We were the first to have automatic lights and hot water. Thousands of years before Camelot even. Though it don't pay to take too much pride in it, since it ended up killing everyone. It was just the Upper and Lower Quarters of the city in those days, on this side of the river. Actually, most people call them the High City and Old City districts now, but I'm partial to the Quarters thing. And Tumblestone wasn't even thought of until the settlers came back to rebuild. An energy station was located somewhere in the heart of the city, and things were all fine and dandy, but as the city grew it became harder and harder to power everything. Nobody knew what they were doing back then, I don't think. How could they? It was all new. Some poor bloke had the daft idea to amplify the energy output with magic, without thinkin' things through. I don't know the details. You'll have to find a book for that. But what happened was the energy station up and exploded after whatever they did. It must have been wild. They say shock waves from the explosion were felt as far away as Ravenwall, even knocked a few buildings down in villages in between. Nothin' of the like has ever happened since." She rapped her knuckles on the wooden dining table for luck. "Yeah, so Atlantis was abandoned for a long time. A *long* time. It wasn't until King Arthur's time that people started coming back. They were scared to. Some idiots actually thought that it was Poseidon who sank the city. They said he cursed the place for some reason or other, and drove it into the water himself in a tiff one night. Pfft. *Poseidon.* I'll tell you right now, mate. He wouldn't have the balls."

She smiled broadly to herself then, and seemed to be thinking on something.

"Ah, but that's enough history for the day, don't you think? We should get a move on if we're to get you to that library. I've got work to do."

"Hey, I'm ready when you are. I'll just go get my backpack."

His backpack had been placed out on the balcony overnight. It hadn't been submerged in the sewage like his legs had, but nevertheless, it absorbed its fair share of stench. The night air did little to resolve the issue. Shouldering the backpack instantly wiped the smile from his face. He would be reminded of the sewers all day, every time he took a breath. That was simply unacceptable.

"You know what," he said, "You can keep this. I'll just leave it out here."

He set the pack down and took a moment to search it. There was really nothing in it that he needed. He still had the bedroll, and there were a few cooking implements left, minus the pot he lost in the scuffle with Mestorphemus, but it wasn't likely that he'd actually end up cooking anything, and if he had to sleep in the city again, with any luck he would be allowed to sleep on Jacob and Melody's couch. It was all just dead weight. The book he bought when he entered the city, *True Tales of Triumph*, gave him pause.

It would be kinda neat to bring a book home from this place.

His eyes narrowed as he read the cover title a second time. True Tales of *Trumph*. The 'i' was missing. He sighed. The guy must have hand made all of them. Impressive actually, but he decided to leave the book behind as well. If he could make it home, he could make it back, and surely Lee Grover would find him again. His type always do. The only thing he kept from the backpack was the pouch of coins, and the spoon he brought from home. It had come all this way. It deserved to return home with him. Plus, it fit neatly in his back pocket.

The girls attempted to join them, but Melody stopped them when they reached for their coats.

"Not today girls. You're to stay here and look after your father."

Chloe pouted. "But papa's gonna be in bed all day, mum. I know it."

"And you'll be here to fix him snacks." She smiled, and kissed the girls on their foreheads.

"Yes mum," they both sighed.

Melody looked Luke over for a moment, thoughtfully, before reaching into the closet and grabbing a gray flat cap, similar to the one she was already wearing. She did this quickly, not wanting to let the smell from the bags of soiled clothing out.

"Fancy a cap to go with your outfit, mate?"

"Uh, sure? This outfit, I..."

"It's all yours."

"What? Really? But it's so... *fancy*. I can't just take it."

"Well, I'll tell you right now, I'm not taking you *anywhere* if you plan on wearing your old clothes. Don't fret about it. Jacob's got plenty of clothes. Consider it a gift. Fits you proper enough, yeah?"

She pressed the cap down over Luke's head and angled it slightly to the left. She nodded. "A proper gent you are, now."

Luke stepped in front of a tall mirror above the shoe mat. He hardly recognized himself. The suit was a little ruffled from being slept in, but he was dramatically closer to *a proper gent* than he was yesterday. He could use a shave though, he thought, as he scratched his scruffy cheeks.

"I could get used to this," he said, turning to check the angles. "But I'm sure I'd end up ruining it next time something breaks on my truck. Er, my automobile."

Melody smiled, "A messy suit is still a suit." She tipped her ragged cap at him. "Let's be off then, shall we?"

They traveled by boat. The view of the city was fantastic, but there was no exotic singing man doing the paddling. Luke was paddling, and he had no breath to spare, so he wasn't singing either. There was a bit of a breeze working against him. He wasn't used to paddling, and yesterday's injuries were not helpful. Melody relaxed in the front with her feet over the side, occasionally correcting him verbally when he veered off course.

As he approached, the ants flowing along the waterfront slowly grew and formed into people, bustling this way and that. He was thoroughly exhausted by the time he brought the boat near the dock. Just another moment and he could give his weary arms a rest, but there was one ant at the end of the dock that remained an ant much longer than the others.

Luke cursed. *It couldn't be.*

"What is it?" Melody asked. "What do you see? Is it Mestorphemus?"

"No," Luke swallowed. "No. Something worse."

He dipped his paddle to slow and stop the boat from reaching the dock.

"Let's try another dock," he said.

"I don't see anything," said Melody, scanning the dock and shoreline.

Luke pointed to a scruffy, white haired terrier pacing back and forth along the dock. Its tail began to wag when it saw him.

"What? The dog? Are you havin' a laugh?"

Luke shook his head. "I'm not landing here. There's more docks further along, aren't there?"

"Well, yeah, alright. It'll be a bit more of a walk, though. You serious?"

The dog began to bark.

"Deadly serious, Melody."

Chapter Twenty-Two

Everyone agreed with Sophie's suggestion to skip the complimentary breakfast offered by the Wooden Hearth Inn. Although the room had surprised them pleasantly, none of them trusted the basket of muffins sitting on the front desk in the rancid, roach infested lobby. The immortal Harry was not offended.

"More... for me," he gasped.

Instead, the group opted for breakfast out in the fresh air. In the square, they found a friendly old man running a coffee stall, and a sweet young girl selling her mother's equally sweet and sour gooseberry pies. They enjoyed their meal on a bench beneath the shade of the enormous Lady Luck statue. Sam was sipping her coffee and making a solid effort to appear as if she *wasn't* staring at the people bathing in the fountain. Gerald was not trying quite so hard.

The fountain reflected the morning sun in a sparkling shimmer, and a warm breeze swept through the square, occasionally giving her cause to snap her hand to her head to keep

Luke's stained cap from blowing away. The square was buzzing with life. People loitered about the fountain area, chatting and drinking coffee. Others were in more of a rush, passing through quickly with the tools of their various trades under arm. A briefcase here. A tool bag there. People selling things. It was really not so different from her world, aside from the naked people in the fountain. Two children were kicking a ball back and forth in the spot where just last evening Luke was being savagely beaten by a giant asshole. The kids were shouting and laughing in blissful ignorance.

Sam's group was split up between two benches. Gerald was weakly defending himself from Sophie's accusations that he was being a pervert on one bench, and Sam was sitting next to a beaming Lia on another. Lia was beaming down at the squirrel sitting between them, gorging himself on his own slice of gooseberry pie. His furry face was a sticky purple mess.

"Oh my," he mumbled, "This is truly wonderful. I'm a mess, aren't I?"

Sam smiled and gave a sarcastic "Noooo," in response. "You look fine, Henry. A real class act."

The squirrel scoffed, and chuckled, "I appreciate your dishonesty, young lady."

"Young lady," Sam laughed. "I suppose I'm still a young lady. But how young am I, really, in relation to you? How long do squirrels live, anyway? Like, five, ten years?"

Henry held up a tiny clawed finger as he devoured another face full of pie with alarming aggression. Lia giggled. Several people slowed their roll when they saw the squirrel sitting between them. Their eyes inevitably rose to Sam and Lia as if to ask, "Am I seeing this?" Sam smiled and waved.

"Well," said the squirrel, licking the berries from around his mouth, "I'm a fair bit older than that."

"Ah, right right. You said you were trapped in a forest for... *centuries?* Is that right? That can't be. Or can it?"

"Oh it is most certainly something that *can be*, my dear. To my great displeasure." He sighed.

"I'm sorry. Being trapped somewhere for that long must have been maddening. I shouldn't complain so much about airline delays."

"Airline delays?"

"A thing back home. Air travel. Flights get delayed. Layovers. Basically, you can get stuck in a building with overpriced food for hours. Sometimes for days. Er, but that's not really comparable at all. *Centuries.* That's crazy." Sam shook her head. "So then... Are you immortal? Like Harry?"

"Not... quite like... Harry," the squirrel rasped mockingly. "If I were to hazard a guess, I'd say that our friend, the innkeeper, found a particularly spiteful djinn sometime in his younger years. What's that saying? Be careful what you wish for?"

"A djinn? Do you mean a genie? The wish granting kind?"

"Yes, that's the kind. I'd suggest avoiding them, though. Most of them are less than fond of granting wishes. Please choose your words very carefully if you ever do have dealings with one."

"Noted."

"Good. And to answer your question, yes. I am immortal. At least, I still seem to be. I'm not about to throw myself under a carriage wheel to test it."

Sam laughed. "I'd rather you didn't. So you *think* you're immortal. You lived in a forest for a couple hundred years. We'll go with it. And you're in much better shape than Harry. I'd certainly prefer whatever your version of immortality is."

The squirrel looked thoughtful. "Better than Harry. Yes, I suppose so. Everything is relative. There are different methods of achieving immortality, or a form of it. Each with varying results. *Wildly* varying." He curled and uncurled his tiny fingers. "Each one has a catch. A cost of some sort."

"What's the downside for you? I mean, besides the imprisonment. A squirrel who gets to talk and live forever sounds pretty great to me."

Henry smiled, but there was sadness in his oil drop eyes. "Everything is relative," he repeated. "A man who gets to live forever as a talking squirrel might see things differently."

"But you're... You weren't always a squirrel, then. Were you?"

"I was not. Humanity for immortality. That was my cost. Of course, nobody tells you these things in advance."

"Oh, I'm sorry, Henry. For what it's worth, you're the finest squirrel I've ever met."

"And the prettiest!" chimed Lia. "I wish I could be a squirrel like you."

Sam scanned their surroundings on the off chance that one of the passersby might be a genie. What did a real genie look like anyways?

"I bet it's really fun climbing trees," Lia added, unchanged. She remained a human jewelry stand.

The squirrel laughed. "Once you get the hang of it, yes. I suppose it is. There's a bit of a learning curve."

"So how did you go about it?" Sam asked. "Becoming immortal, that is. Fountain of youth? Holy grail? Magic... fruit?"

Henry shook his head and chuckled. He gazed up at the statue of Lady Luck. "Foolishness, actually."

Lia's eyes widened. "Then... Then do you think I'm immortal too? Sophie says I'm foolish all the time!"

"Perhaps! Have you ever broken into any Gaian tombs?"

"No," said Lia, a little deflated. "Do I have to do that?"

"Yes, you do, but it's best if you don't, my dear. An ancient Gaian king was said to have been buried with an artifact that could grant immortality. The object in question turned out to be an acorn, a glass one, tucked away inside of the king's tattered robes. We can all see the significance of *that* now, cant we?" He wagged his bushy tail. "In hindsight, an immortality granting object in the possession of a *dead* king should have raised a few red flags."

Sam smiled. "*Probably.*"

"The acorn *did* work, however. And quickly! The very first test of its function came immediately after activating it. As soon as I kissed the acorn, the room was suddenly much larger, and I was suddenly much furrier. I likely would have died of shock right then, had I been able to die."

"You kissed an acorn?" Lia laughed.

"Yeah, really," said Sam. "Kissing something you found on an ancient corpse sounds more like the *very first test* of immortality than the shock part does. Sounds like the beginning of the next *Mummy* movie to me."

The squirrel shrugged. "It may not have been necessary, to be honest. But as with all magic, thoughts and feelings and intent are essential. Kissing it was... hmm... Well, it was a way of focusing my intent."

Sam raised her eyebrows.

"Don't look at me like that. It was just a peck. It's not like I took the thing to bed. It was important to me that it worked on the first try."

"Lia doesn't have to kiss anything to create magic bubbles."

Lia shook her head. "Nope."

Henry sighed. "These are two completely different things, ladies. I'll have you know I was thinking of Aradia when I kissed that acorn."

"Aradia? The woman you tried to raise from the dead?" asked Sam.

"Yes," the squirrel frowned. "Although she wasn't dead at the time. She wasn't supposed to be able to die at all. She was immortal. That was the whole point of it all."

Sam gasped. "And you loved her, didn't you? That's why you wanted immortality. That's why you kissed an acorn. That is like the sweetest thing I've ever heard."

His furry cheeks might not have been able to show a change of color, but Henry was obviously blushing. "I see you missed the part where she did eventually die. Or so I thought. But yes, that was my reasoning. Sadly, I never did reveal myself to her after I changed."

"What do you mean?" Sam asked. "You told me you were there the day she was taken away. She stuck you in a cage."

Henry nodded sadly. "That I was. But as a friend she had met little more than a year before. I sought out the tomb on my own. I wanted to surprise her with my immortality, but when I was turned into a squirrel... I couldn't expect her to maintain a romantic relationship with me. I reintroduced myself as a squirrel who just happened to have the same name as her missing lover. I'm quite fond of the name, you see, and it would have been very confusing for me to go by any other. Naturally, we became fast friends. It was better than never seeing her again. After a time, she came to think that I, the human me, had either perished or decided I couldn't be with someone who I couldn't grow old with. And I let her believe it."

"So in the span of moments, you've just told me the sweetest and saddest things I've ever heard in my life."

"You're welcome."

Sam tapped him on the back with her fore finger. "Hey. Chin up. You said the bones you found weren't hers. If she's immortal, she's probably still out there somewhere. Maybe she just disappeared, ran away somewhere in search of her Human Henry?"

Henry hummed thoughtfully. "A nice fantasy. But that was hundreds of years ago. Human Henry would have died long ago, and she would have given up looking and moved on, if that were even the case." He shook his head. "Perhaps I will try to find her, but not now. Never mind all of that. We should make our way to the library. Luke might already be there. We don't want to miss him."

The squirrel stood up straight on his hind legs and nodded, then scampered up onto Lia's shoulder.

"Well then," he said, "Shall we be off?"

"Oh Henry," Sam sighed. He was right, though. The library was her last lead on Luke's whereabouts. She rose to her feet. "Ready if you are."

She looked at Sophie and Gerald, who she only just noticed had stopped bickering and were strangely quiet. Sophie was no longer complaining about Gerald's shameless eyeballing of the bathers, although his eyes were still very much glued to the fountain. However, now there was a healthy balance of male eye candy splashing about. Sophie was staring too.

"What a cute couple you are," Sam remarked, but her comment fell on deaf ears.

The Knowledge House was quite literally a *house of knowledge*, in two ways. One, it was a library. And two, it was a library shaped like a row of giant books. Eight giant stone books made up the row, with a ninth spread open across the top with its spine up to create a pitched roof. A wide set of marble stairs ascended the front to a grand entryway built into the spine of probably the largest copy of *Arthurian Chronicles: Volume 1* in existence. As with most of the buildings in the city, it would not have been out of place if it had been stumbled across in the middle of the deepest jungle. The dull gray of the stone was complimented nicely by the green net of vines draped over it. Since the vines apparently were what powered the buildings, Sam had taken to calling them 'Power Vines', and thought she was quite clever in doing so.

The library stood as the main feature in a circular courtyard, framed by expensive looking shops with fabulously decorated display windows. Signs and barricades prohibited vehicles, leaving the space relatively safe for pedestrians to wander and bump into each other. Cyclists passed through, dinging their little bells whenever they needed to part the crowds. Adding to the population was a generous smattering of the naked statues that the city seemed far too fond of. Sam noted that each of the male statues they passed still proudly displayed their original penises. The body parts were all faded evenly. Blondie hadn't gotten to those ones yet.

Sam and her group passed through the great doors of the library into a small reception area. Immediately, the aroma of coffee hit her like a scalp massage. She took a deep whiff, and the sensation spread to her soul. A cheery librarian was standing at a coffee percolator, conveniently located on the corner of her desk, as there should be on every desk. A green vine ran from the percolator to an outlet on the floor beneath it.

The librarian had just poured herself a fresh cup, and Sam was probably drooling over it in the exact same manner that Sophie and Gerald were drooling over the fountain bathers. When the librarian noticed this, she smiled and raised the pot questioningly at her. Sam nodded vigorously.

"Yes, please!"

The others politely refused.

While the librarian was pouring, Sam looked beyond her to the library proper.

The reception area was a sort of viewing platform, looking down on a narrow seating area with dozens of round wooden tables and several couches. This stretched the width of the building, from wall to wall. On the back side of the seating area were the books, and there were lots of them. Three floors of tall shelves beginning on the seating level were visible from the librarian's desk. The floors were connected by six spiral staircases spaced evenly apart, and a powered lift in the center. It was currently letting an elderly woman in a wheelchair off on the top floor. The shelves were high enough to require sliding ladders, and were so equipped. The entirety of the structure was well lit through a generous application of powered light fixtures, and two enormous sky lights above. Amongst the throng of silent patrons, Sam noticed none that were shirtless. If Luke was there, he would have to be somewhere further in the back.

"It's so big," she muttered, and imagined Luke's ridiculous "That's what she said" response that he took amusement in using at every unnecessary opportunity. It always managed to draw a smile and a head shake out of her though, even now, when he wasn't there to say it.

"I know, right?" the librarians voice broke through Sam's daze. "You should try dusting it all!"

The woman's voice took Sam back to Austria, when the shopkeepers would switch from German to accommodate her English. She was tall and slender, with long brown hair down to her waist, and matching doe eyes that smiled along with her mouth as she awaited a reply.

"I can only imagine," said Sam, "Ah! Thank you so much." The librarian handed her a green mug filled with steaming black coffee.

All eyes fell to Lia when the little girl gasped and rushed to the desk. "What did you *dooo?*" she cried.

"Excuse me?" asked the puzzled librarian.

"Your hair is *green!*"

"Is it really?" said the librarian, dropping her jaw and widening her eyes in exaggerated shock. "Are you sure?"

She smiled and pushed the bulk of her hair to the side, showcasing two braids that were nearly hidden before. Woven into the braids were lengths of green string. She leaned forward over the desk for Lia's inspection, and stoically accepted the little girl's poking and pulling of her hair.

"Looks like you have some competition now, Henry," said Sophie.

A muffled chuckle came from Sam's tote bag, drawing the librarian's attention. Lia quickly pulled it back. A sign at the entrance had read, "Sorry, No Pets."

When she was satisfied, Lia, with saucer eyes, turned to Sophie. "I want green hair too!"

"Of course you do, dear. I'm sorry about that, miss...?"

"Elisabeth," the librarian said, bowing slightly. "And it's quite alright. Is there some way I can help you?"

"You could color my hair!" suggested Lia.

Elisabeth laughed.

"Have you seen anyone in here today wearing blue jeans?" Sam asked, "Blue trousers, I mean. Like these? And he probably didn't have a shirt on, either."

"Hmm. No. I can't say that I've seen any trousers like that, but I like them! That's a no on the shirtless men as well, unfortunately. Sorry."

"That's okay. Thank you, though. It's just that a friend of mine is supposed to meet us here today, but we forgot to agree on a time. Is it okay if we browse for awhile?"

"Oh yes. Of course. The library is free to the public. I just have to ask you not to remove any books from the library without checking them out first. There is a reading area with plenty of comfy chairs in the back. Oh, and obviously, please keep your voices down. It *is* a library."

"We will, thank you," said Sam. "Oh! While we have you... Do you have any books that, well, take you places?"

"Oh my, yes. What book doesn't? I strongly recommend *Gulliver's Travels*. It takes you to some *amazing* places. Lands of tiny people and lands of giants. I've read it twice myself."

"*Gulliver's Travels*? Isn't that an earth book?"

"An earth book? What do you mean?"

"Er, never mind."

"What she means to ask," Sophie cut in, "is whether or not you have any books that actually physically send you places when you open them. A travel tome. Do you have anything like that?"

"Wow, I wish we did. That'd be fantastic, wouldn't it? Took me nearly a full week last year to get to Las Arenas in Southern Gaia by train and bus. Oh but it was worth it, though. You should have seen the turtles coming ashore on the full moon. It was *magical*. Well, a different sort of magical. Now if I had a magic book like this tome you speak of, I could lay on the beach every night after work..."

Elisabeth stared off into the distance, clearly reminiscing. Sam could almost see the sea turtles crawling in her eyes. After a moment, the librarian shook her head back to the present and smiled, "I think you've just given me the travel bug again.

Where is it you'd like to go? Perhaps I can point you in the right direction."

"Oh, I don't know about that," said Sam.

"Try me?"

"Okay. Have you ever heard of Halifax?"

The librarian blinked. "Hmm. Nope! I have not. That's surprising. I'll have to look it up. Where is it? *What* is it? A village? A mountain?"

"It's a city, actually, in an entirely different world, if you can believe that. The same world where *Gulliver's Travels* was written. I think..."

Elisabeth cocked her head to the side, her eyes wide. "You mean that book was *non-fiction?* Really? Do they really have giant wasps??" She held her hands apart as wide as they would go.

Sam laughed, "Totally. Except we call them Murder Hornets. It's the rats you really have to worry about, though. Much bigger. And they show up at the worst possible times."

"Oh dear. Why would anyone want to go there??"

Chapter Twenty-Three

Before Luke and Melody parted ways at a safer dock, she wished him luck, and let him know that her couch would still be available if he couldn't find his magical book. He thanked her for that, and again for the new clothes. They were a true blessing, as much for comfort as for camouflage. Of course, his change of outfit somehow had no effect on that terrier's ability to spot him from the docks. He could only hope that Mestorphemus had no such tracking skills.

Several packs of stray dogs crossed his path during his extended walk, but none of them spared more than a passing glance in his direction. He kept his hat low to shade his lumpy, purple face whenever he passed a member of the city watch. They paid him no mind either.

Luke reached the Knowledge House happily unmolested. It was going to be a good day.

A smile spread across his face as he tipped his hat to the pretty librarian behind the front desk. A little blond girl who resembled something of a jewelry stand was sitting on top of the desk, facing the librarian and away from Luke. She was chattering excitedly about princesses and squirrels. The squirrel part gave him pause, and he realized the little girl was the same one from the crowd at the fountain. She must have saw Henry.

The librarian seemed thoroughly engaged in braiding the girl's hair, so he didn't push for conversation beyond the polite welcome he received. It was just as well. Although there wasn't likely to be a section labeled, "Magic Spell Books" or anything like that, it was, regardless, his habit to look for things until he achieved a frustrating level of failure before asking someone for assistance.

He walked down the wide staircase past the desk, his footfalls echoing softly on the grated metal steps. He scanned the awesome collection of books beyond the seating area as he descended, looking for some hint as to where he might begin. Three deep levels, full of bookcases. It could take all day to explore it all. There were worse ways to spend a day.

In the seating area, he found a desk with an arrangement of leaflets with information on various points of interest throughout the city, as well as maps of the library. He took one of these maps, and decided to begin on the bottom floor and work his way up.

Great care went into the organization of the library. Hand painted signs with pictures relating to their respective subjects hung above every aisle, and in the aisles themselves every bookcase and individual shelf was labeled. There was even a leaflet to go with each bookcase, with a list detailing which books could be found on it. This would be particularly helpful for the books on the higher shelves, as a rough estimate put them at about fifteen feet tall. Of course, the option to simply climb and browse was made available also, by means of rolling ladders fixed on tracks that could be slid to the left or right as needed. A library wasn't a *fancy* library unless it had ladders.

But for all the structure of the place, where would he find a travel tome? In the geography section? With the travel guides? Or perhaps under fantasy? Spiritualism? Mysticism?

Ah, Erotica! That's the one.

The geography aisle was close, and seemed as good a place to start as any. There he was bombarded by walls of place names that rang no 'Earthly' bells in his memory. Names like Alessia, Everus, Tolles Tal, Weeping Rocks. These places meant nothing to him. Ravenwall. The gate guard had mentioned it, but he knew nothing beyond its name. Gaia seemed to him to be a sort of continent, or some other broad area of land. Not one that he wanted to visit, however, as he imagined it to be crawling with pterodactyls and other murderous prehistoric beasts that would love to eat him.

Curiosity led him to grab a book called *Camelot: Through The Ages.* He flipped through it quickly, as if a few cursory glances at its pages would tell him how Camelot, apparently a real place here, became such a fascinating legend in his own world. If Merlin had really been on Earth, how did he get there? Did he just paint a picture of a place he'd never been, and say to the magic gods or whatever, "Yeah, take me there!" And if he'd been there, maybe other people had as well, like the guy who wrote *Robinson Crusoe.* After a minute or two went by, Luke was none the wiser, and put the book back where he found it.

Probably nothing in this aisle. Where next?

He wandered deeper into the library, hoping something would jump out at him. Something did. In a casual, not at all jumpy way. However, he did freeze when a woman in her fifties or early sixties, stepped into view at the next intersection. They exchanged friendly nods, and she continued on her way, but Luke was struck by her appearance. She was wearing a slim fitting robe of a shiny green material, and carrying a staff with a similar colored gem crudely fastened to the top with bits of twine.

Very witchy.

Was she a witch? Perhaps she knew something about teleporting. He rushed to the intersection, but she was already gone down another aisle out of view. She couldn't have gotten far, unless she *teleported*. He followed the direction she traveled and soon enough, found her seven aisles down. He stepped towards her into the aisle, and was suddenly bothered by a nagging awkwardness. How do you approach a witch? Is it even okay to approach a witch? From the look on her face, there was *something* wrong with his approach.

Her eyes were as green as the gem on her staff, and they were narrowed into a scowl. He realized then that it was probably quite obvious that he had followed her.

"See something you like, boy?" she asked.

"Er, no. I mean... Hey, how ya doin'?"

The woman's scowl disappeared, replaced by confused blinking.

"Uh, yeah. A bit weird. I know. Sorry, but I just saw you, and, well, you know." He waved a hand at her clothing.

Her eyes narrowed again, and her head fell back slightly. "So you *do* like what you see, is that it? Can't say that I blame you, but you could be a little more subtle about it, don't you think? You remind me of my Gerald. He's a pervert too."

"What? No no. I didn't mean— I meant your clothing. The robes. The staff. Are you a witch?"

"Oh is that what you're after. Well that's disappointing, but I can disappoint you in turn. I am *not* a witch. I just like the style."

"Ah. I see. I'm sorry to bother you, miss. If it's any consolation, the robe does look good on you. You wear it well."

The woman smiled. "I'll take it. Wait a moment." Her gaze turned suspicious. "Your face is all lumpy. What happened?"

Luke swallowed. Did she work for the watch? She didn't look she did, but maybe there were wanted posters out for him. "Uh, just allergies. Bee sting, you know. Don't worry about it."

He tipped his hat to her and turned to continue his quest elsewhere, but at once he found himself looking at another oddly dressed character. A man of about forty years walked into the aisle with the appearance of someone who had gotten lost on his way to a bachelorette party. He wore tight fitting leather pants and his hairy chest and muscular arms were on full display beneath a skimpy brown vest. Yet as they passed, it was the lost stripper who had the quizzical look on his face. Luke tried to avoid eye contact after nodding to him, but an outstretched hand stopped him in his tracks.

"Excuse me?" he said to the stripper.

"Have I seen you before?" the stripper asked. "Yesterday, in the square?"

Luke was unsure how to answer. The guy certainly didn't look like he had anything to do with the city watch. His eyes were dark, but friendly.

Before Luke could respond, the man continued, smiling. "It *is* you. I'm sure of it." He looked Luke up and down. "The clothes threw me off a little, but it's definitely you. We've been looking for you. How's your face feeling today? You took *some* beating yesterday."

"Uh..."

The old woman was beside them now. She eyed him as well. "Luke?" she asked.

"How do you-" the words were lost in his throat. They could have seen him in the square. There could even be posters, but how could anyone know his name? Did they hear Henry calling to him?

"Didn't you recognize him, Sophie?" the stripper asked the witch.

"Well I didn't get much of a look at him yesterday, myself," she said. "The lumpy face should have given it away, I suppose." She sniffed. "And he still smells a bit like the sewers."

"Hey," said Luke, "Who are you guys? How do you know my name?"

"I'm Gerald," said the stripper.

"And I'm Sophie," said the witch. "We share an acquaintance."

"An acquaintance?" Luke asked, his head cocked in interest. "Do you mean Henry? The squirrel?"

Sophie chuckled. "Oh yes. Him. Well I suppose that's *two* acquaintances we share."

"And the other? Don't tell me it's Mestorphemus."

Sophie squinted. "Who? What kind of name is that?"

Gerald shook his head. "No. We're talking about Samantha. She's going to be thrilled. I can't believe you're actually here. I thought you'd have hopped the first train out of the city."

Luke's mouth flopped open. "Sam?"

"Indeed," said Sophie. "She's been looking for you."

"She's *here?* How's that possible?"

Sophie shrugged. "Apparently the same way you came here. A travel tome."

The book. It didn't come with him, not like the spoon and the peanut butter jar. It must have stayed in his chair. She could have went in looking for him and found the book instead.

"If you've seen her, where is she now?"

"Historical Romance, perhaps," said Sophie. "That's where I left her anyhow, but the girl does have legs."

Yes she does. "She's here?? In the library?"

Gerald grinned. "Yep. She is. Come on. We'll take you to her."

Suddenly the weight of Sophie's comment on his smell hit him like a ton of bricks. He sniffed his shoulders and checked his breath on his hand. The results were not satisfying. Even with the second shower he took that morning, the sewer stench lingered. It was faint, but still wretched.

They walked for an eternity through the enormous library. The soft echo of their footsteps kept time with the drum pounding in his chest. When at last they arrived at Historical Romance on the third floor, Sam had transformed into a middle aged bald man with a large stomach. The man was perusing a book titled *Tie Me Up: Henrietta's Affair*.

"It fell off the shelf as I walked by," he claimed, and beat a hasty retreat.

"Hmm. Now where did she go?" said Sophie.

She led them to the end of the aisle and looked about thoughtfully for a moment before deciding on a left turn. Luke followed at the rear, and saw when he glanced to the right, another woman in a green robe similar to the one worn by Sophie. *Must be a pretty popular style.*

The condition of this woman's robe, however, was worth another glance. It was filthy, caked in mud as if the woman had rolled around in a pasture, and a pasture housing particularly violent animals at that. The robe was utterly destroyed. Tattered and torn, with thin strips of fabric dangling outward in many places. It was a wonder that it didn't just fall apart entirely onto the floor. Despite her ragged appearance, a broad smile sparkled beneath the shadow of her hood. It was pulled low down over her eyes, concealing much of her pale face. Two thin red lines, cuts, ran from under her chin and up along her cheek before disappearing into the hood.

Luke offered her a polite smile, tipped his hat, and stepped quickly to catch up with the others.

They found her in the art section, of course. Gerald and Sophie stopped at the end of the aisle, and waved him past so that he could introduce himself alone. He took a deep breath as he approached the woman who wore Sam's coat. The coat she bought the day after they met. She was facing a shelf with her nose in a large book, but it was *her*. It was really her. And she was wearing *his* hat. Backwards. He smiled at that, not just because she looked good in it, but also because it had obviously shielded her from the city's pesky grackles.

Her entire face lit up when she looked from the book to see him walking slowly towards her. It had only been a few days, but at that moment it felt like an eternity since they had last saw each other.

"Luke!" she cried. She shelved her book and ran to him.

Just like in the movies.

Luke was too sore to run, but she closed the distance quick enough for the both of them. Sam locked her arms tight around his neck when they collided. Her hair, flowing over her shoulder from the left side of his ball cap, smelled of lavender. He could have cried.

Why does she have to smell so good?

"Sam," he coughed nervously. "Don't take this the wrong way, but I hope... I hope your nose is broken. The smelling part, anyways."

She pulled back to look him in the eyes. Her nose was scrunched up. Her beautiful brown eyes narrowed.

"I think it is now," she said. "You smell..." She bobbed her head thoughtfully, "You smell like shit. Yep. Shit."

"That's very accurate," he sighed. "Two showers just wasn't enough."

She smiled. "Why'd you have to go into the sewers, dummy?"

Before he could ask how she knew he was in the sewers, the words in his mouth found the exit blocked by her lips. She was a brave woman, to kiss him so deeply. It had been days since he brushed his teeth. She, of course, tasted like peppermint.

This time she scrunched up her lips. "Hmm. Morning breath with a hint of coffee. Not as bad as I was expecting. Here, have a mint."

"You brought mints??"

"I brought everything, Luke."

Including a furry gray squirrel, which scurried up her arm when she reached into her tote bag, and found a perch on Luke's shoulder.

"My dear boy!" cried Henry. "I'm so very glad to see you. And look at you! A man of taste after all. I apologize for not rushing to greet you the second I caught your scent, but I didn't want to interrupt. Oh, but your poor face..."

"Henry! It's good to see you too, buddy. Thanks for the hand yesterday. Or the paw, I guess. I thought that was gonna be the end of me."

"Oh, think nothing of it, lad."

Sam took a good look at Luke's face and shook her head sadly.

Luke noticed her concern and assured her, "It's not as bad as it looks." *It's probably worse.*

It was clear she didn't believe him, but she changed the subject. "I like the new hat. Very classy. I brought your ball cap though." She turned and tilted her head so he could see the bill pointing backwards. "Would you like to trade? I know how much you like it."

He laughed, "Ah. Maybe not right now. I think it looks better on you."

"Well, yeah. Everything looks better on me."

He pinched his lips and nodded. She wasn't wrong.

Sam raised her eyebrows and said, "So Henry here tells me that you've *repeatedly* told him that I'm the most beautiful girl on Earth. Is this true, Luke? He says you wouldn't shut up about it. That's why he had to leave you when he did."

"Uh..." He frowned at the squirrel.

Henry turned so Sam couldn't see his face, and whispered into Luke's ear, "Just go with it, boy."

He sighed, and sucked thoughtfully on his mint before mumbling, "Um, yeah well. You know, I mean, you're not *terrible* looking."

Henry scoffed.

Sam shook her head, smiling, and leaned in for another hug, sending Henry leaping for the safety of the nearest shelf. "I can't believe we found you. If we didn't find you here, I wouldn't have a clue where to look next."

"How did you even get here?" he asked. "Was it the book?"

"I'm sure of it. It's a magic book, you know."

"You knew?"

"No. Of course not. But it doesn't take a Sherlock to figure it out, does it? So tell me the truth. Why did you have it? Are you a wizard?"

"What? No," he laughed. "I'm not a wizard. Ask Henry. I had no idea the book was in the house. It must have belonged to the previous owner."

"But the book was so clean. Everything else in the room was filthy."

Luke shrugged, "I can't explain that. I thought you cleaned it off yourself. Maybe magic things just don't get dirty?"

They both looked to Henry. His chest fur was slicked down with a sticky red substance. "Hmm?" he hummed. "Oh, yes. Well that's partially true. Objects of a magical nature tend to repel dust particles, so in a dusty room, such objects often stand out. Mind you, if you toss something magical in the mud, it will still become dirty."

Footsteps drew their attention to the approaching Sophie and Gerald.

"Is it safe?" asked Sophie, a cheeky grin on her face. "You're not about to start fornicating, are you?"

Luke blushed.

"No," laughed Sam. "Not with Henry watching." She winked at Luke. She turned her palms up and spread them aside. "Although, a library could be fun?"

He didn't doubt that. The effects of her suggestive comment were instant, stirring a sensation below his waist that would have been far less awkward had they been alone, and not in the presence of an old woman, a squirrel, and a male stripper. He chose to deflect, by pressing a finger to his lips and issuing his best librarian "SHHHH" towards her.

"So how did you meet these people? And Henry?" he asked.

"I entered the book through the same page as you. It was open in your chair. Sophie and Gerald, and some others were already there by the forest, camping out. Apparently it's a traditional resting place for travelers coming from Gaia, some sort of tropical place, before the last push to Atlantis. I guess my timing was just a little luckier than yours."

"I'll say. It started to rain like hell when I arrived, so I ran for the forest. Lost my socks in the mud."

"I know. I saw them."

"Really? Do you have them?"

She laughed, "I'm afraid not. An odd little boy laid claim to them before I could. And they aren't socks anymore. They're mittens. He liked them so much, I couldn't bring myself to take them from him. I'm sorry. You'll have to get your grandmother to knit you a new pair."

"Ah, well." He shook his head. "She's gone now."

"Oh, I'm really sorry. I didn't know. But you know, you never really talk much about yourself. I do all the jabbering and you just sit and listen. Well, listen here. From now on Mr. Fletcher, you're gonna have to start telling me more about yourself. No more secret worlds and secret relatives."

He nodded. "I'll do my best, Miss Vale. But what if the mystery is the only thing attracting you? What if I told you I'm actually very boring?"

"I'd say you're full of shit, wizard. I promise mystery is not the only thing I'm attracted to." She grinned and smacked him on the ass.

"Oh to be young again," said Sophie, smacking Gerald just the same, though hard enough to make him jump.

Henry was beaming, his smiling mouth filling his tiny face. "What a wonderful reunion. Though I must repeat the librarian's words to you, Luke. We won't find the means to return you home here in this library."

"Well that will save me a lot of looking," he replied.

Sam was quick to point out that, "Asking the librarian would have saved you some looking, as well."

"I would have asked *eventually.*"

"Do you think maybe a second hand book store would have been a better option? Or like, a thrift shop?" Sam asked. "Assuming there are any here, that is."

Luke had never thought of that. Each probably would have been a better option than a library. People die all the time, and what belongings that didn't get scooped up by relatives or friends would have to go somewhere. All it would take is for someone to not realize what the book was, for it to get pawned off. Clearly nobody had realized what the book in his own house was before he bought it. Unless there were some missing real estate agents that he didn't know about.

He was about to agree with Sam when the hanging lights around them flickered twice, then went out completely. If not for the huge skylights above, the aisle would have fallen into total darkness.

"A power outage?" Gerald asked.

"Leave it to Tumblestone," complained Sophie.

"No," said Henry, his voice was grave. "Something else. Something is draining the power from the grid. And I think I know what it is."

Everyone looked to the squirrel for further explanation, but he looked at Luke and merely said, "I'm sorry, boy." Without another word he climbed to the top of the bookcase and was gone.

"Okay," said Luke. "That's not creepy at all."

"Um, Luke?" said Sam, tugging his shirtsleeve.

She pointed to the end of the aisle where a shadowy figure had entered and stood, facing them. The tattered cloak gave the shadow away instantly as the woman he saw earlier, just before meeting Sam. Perhaps it was the poor lighting, but something about the way she stood there now put the cheeky smile she had flashed him earlier into a more sinister perspective.

"Okay. That's *more* creepy," he admitted, then called nervously to the woman, "Hello? Can we help you?"

The woman chuckled, a melodious sound, far daintier than he expected, and spoke with a similarly pleasant voice. "Oh darling, you have no idea how much you can do for me."

She took a step toward them. A feeling in Luke's stomach seemed to tug at his feet, urging him to back away. He did so, nudging Sam to do the same.

"Tell me that's a friend of yours, Sophie," Sam whispered. "She's dressed just like you."

"She's a friend of mine," said Sophie, though she too, started to back away.

Sam sighed, "She's not actually, is she?"

"Nope," said Sophie. "Although she does look a bit like someone who died hundreds of years ago."

"That's comforting," said Luke.

"Oh no," Sam gasped. "Henry's demon took on the appearance of Aradia. She died hundreds of years ago, supposedly. Is that who she looks like, Sophie?"

"Hmm. Why yes. Maybe its actually her, and not a demon."

Sam shook her head. "No. Henry said she was attacked by raptors, remember. This woman *definitely* looks like she's been mauled by raptors."

Luke frowned. "Henry told me I *wasn't* releasing a demon when I freed him..."

"Well, *Henry* isn't a demon. He released it himself after you freed him," Sam whispered.

"That makes it so much better," he groaned. Where did the squirrel run off to?

For each step they took backwards, the woman matched it with a step forward. The folds of her robe concealed her legs, making it appear as if she weren't stepping at all, but floating toward them.

Luke swallowed his fear, and stopped his retreat. Maybe they were overreacting. Maybe this woman was just looking for loose change.

"What is it you want?" he dared to ask.

He saw the white of her teeth before she answered calmly. "Just your seed."

Luke snorted. "My *what?*"

Sophie laughed. "Sounds like you're going to have some competition tonight, princess."

Sam elbowed her.

"My seed, eh? Is that all?" Luke chuckled nervously. She couldn't be serious. Could she?

The woman snuffed out his chuckle with full blown laughter of her own. He started to laugh himself, when she stopped, abruptly, and spoke with undeniable seriousness. "That is all I require of you, yes. Will you give it willingly?"

Luke adjusted his cap and scratched the stubble on his chin. What do you say to something like that? A moment ago, he was toying with thoughts of a similar scenario with Sam, but this ruined the fantasy completely. This woman, with her scratched face and shredded robe, looked like she'd play a bit too rough for his fragile state.

He opened his mouth to tell her as much, but Sam spoke first. Her face was stern, her jaw set in defiance. "Sorry. He's taken," she said.

The woman flashed her deadly smile. "We can share."

"Oh wow," Luke blurted, and placed himself in front of Sam. "That sounds great and all. I'm flattered, really. But I'm going to have to pass. I can only handle disappointing one woman at a time. Two would just be too much for my ego." He stepped backward, nudging Sam to do the same. The woman stepped with them.

"Gerald?" said Sam. "Sophie? You guys sound like you might be into that sort of thing."

"Is that what you think of us?" asked Sophie, scowling.

The woman shook her head. "It is the Otherworlder's seed that I require."

"You'll get no seed here, weirdo," spat Sophie. "Go check the farmer's market. Buy yourself a papaya."

The woman stopped her approach and shook her head. "A pity." She held her hands out in defeat. "Well, I tried."

With a flourish of her right hand, the bookcase to Luke's left toppled over. It was startling, but harmless as the bookcase fell away from them into the next aisle. Only when the second bookcase, to his right, began to fall inward did he realize the point of the first action. There would be nothing to stop the second bookcase from crushing them.

Luke and Sam dove forward, flattening themselves to the ground. An avalanche of books crashed onto them, but the bookcase never came. Sophie had dove forward as well, to her knees, and sacrificed her emerald staff by planting it as a brace to hold up the bookcase.

Luke didn't need the following shouts from Sophie to convince him to "get his ass moving." Desperately the group clawed their way through the piles of books to get out from under the precarious bookcase. Luke pulled Sophie to safety just seconds before the staff kicked out and the bookcase dropped with a crash. Gerald was the first up and made quick work hauling everyone to their feet.

"I guess she's not gonna take no for an answer," Luke groaned.

The woman merely laughed at her failed attempt to crush them. Luke looked back to see her walking atop the fallen bookcase, doing another twirly thing in the air with her hand. He didn't wait to find out her purpose, he fled as fast as his stiff and aching legs would carry him, but he had asked far too much from his legs lately. He was lagging behind the others considerably when they rounded the turn at the nearest intersection.

He didn't make the turn.

Something big smashed into his lower back, and sent him crashing to the floor. The *something big* was a chandelier.

"Shit," he muttered.

He struggled to crawl out of the aisle, out of the robed woman's line of sight, while Sam shouted to the others and turned back towards him.

Too slow.

He knew she was standing over him even before she clawed at his waist band. The robed woman cackled in a deeper, more appropriately murderous tone. With incredible force, she ripped him backwards.

But her hands flew from him. Momentum alone slid him into a bookcase. She howled in pain.

Luke's ass was *hot*. Something in his back pocket was burning up. He dug the object out and twisted himself up into a seated position. There he found himself staring in bewilderment at his peanut butter spoon. It shimmered, catching the light from the windows above. It was cool now. Ordinary. Yet the robed woman was screaming and clutching her wrist in the background.

The woman snapped her head to the right, at Sam and the others, and her deadly hand followed. She flicked her wrist, just flicked it, a simple movement that drug a heavy bookcase out into the aisle and slammed it against a bookcase on the other side. It was like shutting a door, effectively isolating Luke from the others. They would have to go around if they were to get to him.

Then she swung her arms this way and that, conducting a magical orchestra that shifted the bookcases around them, boxing them into a prison of literature. There was nowhere to run, unless he were to climb the shelves. He wouldn't be quick enough. The crazy woman would never allow it. If she wanted his seed, she might very well have it by the time anyone could help him.

Maybe it wouldn't be so bad. He'd wasted tons of it into the folds of tissue paper over the years. Why put up such a fuss now when someone was willing to kill him for it? Unfortunately, he wasn't feeling up to his new "Master of Morningwood" title. There was nothing sexy about being hit with a chandelier.

How did she plan to get it out of him? Clearly seduction was not on the table. Luke gulped. The victorious shape of her smile told him he'd soon find out.

But the smile faltered when she looked directly at him, or rather, at the spoon he held defensively in front of his face.

It was just an ordinary spoon, wasn't it? Identical to the others he found in a drawer in his kitchen after he bought the house. He planned on tossing them out, but they weren't rusty and they cleaned up pretty well, so he kept them. They were nice spoons. This woman, however, was not fond of his cutlery.

Perhaps she wouldn't have his seed after all. He rose to his feet, shaky, but oddly confident his spoon would protect him.

"Suddenly he's brave," spat the woman.

"Suddenly she's afraid of a spoon," said Luke, grinning. He feigned a few thrusts in her direction, satisfied by her flinches. "What do you want me for anyway? You're not completely hideous. Find someone else."

The woman growled. "I want my body back."

"Er... What? How is getting pregnant going to help you with that?"

She lunged for him, but Luke swung the spoon. She backed away, hissing.

"Fool," she said. "This is not *my* body. My body is in Midgard."

"Well there you go. I have no idea where that is, but it sounds like you do. Go get it back. Get away from me."

She snarled. "You are *from* Midgard."

Luke shook his head. "Nope."

"Yes. Midgard has the most connections to this world. You think you are speaking *English*, yes?"

He narrowed his eyes. *Was* he from Midgard? It would be news to him.

The woman smiled. "Only an otherworlder from Midgard could break the curse placed on Morningwood. I must bare your child. With it inside me, a soul from Midgard, I can go there myself to retrieve my body. I can become whole and finally fulfill my purpose."

"And what purpose is that, if you don't mind my asking?"

"Vengeance," she said. "The woman whose image I bare brought me into this world to slay its rulers in retribution for a great injustice."

"I see. Okay. Well, you seem more than capable of that already. Why come after me?"

"Without my body, my time is too limited. I would be forced into dormancy before I could complete my task. Again. That is simply unacceptable." She closed her eyes and sighed. "So you see, I must have your seed. I ask once more, will you give it willingly? I will *not* ask a third time."

She wasn't kidding. Of that, there could be no doubt. Running off a load would surely have been the easier route, but instead he said, "No thanks. I don't think I'm ready for kids just yet. And I don't think regicide is something I want to tie my name to, either. You did better this second time, though.

Explaining *why* before, you know, just straight up demanding seed right out of the gate. *Seed.* Who even says that?"

He could hear the others, shouting and grunting as they tried to move the heavy bookcases. There was no give to them. He was alone. The only thing between him and the wannabe mother of his child was a little silver spoon.

"Put down the spoon," the woman demanded.

He squeezed the spoon tighter. "I'd really rather not." He took another warning swipe at the woman, but this time she didn't flinch.

Her smile flashed again. "A pity it isn't your decision to make."

She raised her hand towards him, and to his horror, the fingers of his spoon hand started to unclench, and he was powerless to convince them otherwise. Quickly, he fortified his grip with his other hand, but that too, he lost control of. He nearly released the spoon, when suddenly his hands clasped tight again. They were his. He looked in confusion to the woman, who was looking at him the same, though her confusion was mixed with frustration, and then rage.

She threw her head back, her arms wide, and screeched. A horrible, blood curdling sound that nearly made him drop the spoon anyways. He fell, dizzy, into the bookcase behind him. There was no warning crack to be heard from the skylights above, not over the piercing screech, just a shower of glass over the whole of the library to say that the windows had shattered.

A stream of expletives gave Luke the fortitude to toss a heavy book into the raised chin of the woman. She staggered back, silenced.

Luke gasped. When her head snapped back, her hood fell, revealing the full length of the scar that ran from her chin. Whatever had scratched her chin had traveled up the length of her face and tore off the left side of her scalp. The wound looked fresh, as if it would still be wet to the touch. Her remaining scalp produced ebony black hair that streamed down behind her right shoulder in stark contrast to her moon pale skin.

Her eyes opened, and Luke's strength left him. Though they were large and hazel and beautiful, her eyes were full of hatred and promises of nothing good.

She lunged.

In a flash she was on him, pinning him to the shelves and holding his wrist to the side, rendering the spoon useless. He pushed her back with his free hand, and tried reaching to aid his trapped one, but she caught it halfway, shoving his own hand into his throat. Her strength was unbelievable. She pressed her body against him in a way that might have been pleasant, had she been Sam, and not some cold zombie thing trying to get herself pregnant.

"It'll all be over in a moment," she purred. "Don't move."

Her words were laced with the putrid smell of rotting meat, and completely unnecessary. He couldn't move anyways, not his arms, nor his legs. He could only squirm his neck from side to side in vain as she brought her face closer to his. Her smile was a pretty thing, but with ugly intentions. She pressed it to his lips.

Her tongue pushed into his mouth like a wriggling eel, and an aggressive hand found his lower bits. He couldn't have been more flaccid. The only thing rising within him was his breakfast to meet the rancid smell and taste of her breath.

He choked. The spoon clanged to the floor.

He felt weak, as if he hadn't eaten for a day. She wasn't just terrible at foreplay. She was *draining his energy*.

Something fell on his head. Something soft. The sharp toes gave it away as Henry even before it continued downward in front of his eyes.

"I'm sorry, dear. I can't allow it," said the squirrel before biting down on the woman's lip.

She broke from Luke, howling with rage. Luke collapsed to the floor as the woman drove Henry into a bookcase.

"I should thank you, Henry," she said with a laugh. "You were most helpful in finding him. I had only to follow your scent."

"Yes, well, I regretfully underestimated you. It's a wonder you can smell anything over that breath of yours. You really should have taken my advice and freshened up, Cosmo. How can you expect to seduce someone in such a state?"

The woman snarled. "It's *Casmolochasba!*"

Henry chuckled, "Ah yes. Casmala... Casmolo... Nope. Cosmo will have to do. Sorry."

And he leaped at the woman, Cosmo, beginning a ridiculous game of cat and mouse between them.

Luke yawned, blinked sleepily, and yawned again, longer and drawn out, bringing tears to his eyes. *A nap would be so lovely right now.* He shook his head. He'd be no help to Henry if he stayed on the ground, napping.

He found the spoon, and tried to stand but only made it to his knees before weariness took him, and he needed a rest. He could still breathe, but poorly. So he knelt, and took long, deep breaths that seemed to get lost somewhere along the way, like pumping up a tire with a hole in it.

Sam and the others continued to shout beyond the makeshift arena. Another voice had joined them, a familiar one, but not one he was fond of.

Oh come on. You gotta be kidding me.

Suddenly, there was a mighty grunt, and a pair of bookcases parted. Between them stood the hulking Mestorphemus. His bearded face was covered in welts and scratches from his last encounter with the squirrel, and before him must have appeared to be another victim of the savage critter. Cosmo was flailing about wildly, much the same as he had, trying to catch and destroy her assailant. Then his eyes fell to Luke, and they narrowed in angry recognition. Luke smiled and waved lazily.

Henry separated from Cosmo, and scurried atop the bookcases, out of her reach.

Mestorphemus boomed, "What's going on here?"

Cosmo answered with a hiss, and charged him.

The two could have joined forces, the big man and the dead woman, and ended Luke right there. But apart from being an asshole, Mestorphemus was still a law man, and Cosmo was a crazy succubus.

Mestorphemus banged her with his right fist, sending her flying backwards into the shelves. Dozens of books fell over her crumpled form. She practically bounced back up in a spray of books and hurled herself again at the confused giant.

They met in the center of the arena. Mestorphemus fired another enormous fist in her direction, but she *caught it* in her dainty little hand, stopping him as suddenly as if he had hit a granite boulder. Her face was a sneer. His was horrified.

"What the hell *are* you?" he grunted.

Cosmo cackled. "Casmolochasba Pantazis."

"What the hell does that mean?"

Cosmo swung him into the books as easily as if he were a pillow, but he landed with the weight of a comet, knocking over a domino of bookcases. She laughed maniacally.

Mestorphemus pulled himself up from the wreckage and snarled. "A demon." Then he smiled. "I got just the thing for you."

A pair of pistols were holstered on his hip, but it was from somewhere else on his person that Mestorphemus produced a weapon of a different kind. A thin blue and white striped rod with a yellow star on the tip. A magic wand?

The big man was grinning as he aimed it at Cosmo. The whole rod glowed red, dimly at first, but brighter and brighter until it fired a beam of energy at the dead woman. This, the woman also caught, with her palm and a grin. The beam concentrated in her hand, forming a blinding ball of light before shrinking and fizzling out to nothing. Her hand was glowing, as if she had absorbed the light into her being.

That's what Henry meant. She stole the energy that powered the lights, and now she'd just absorbed the energy from Mestorphemus's wand.

As if to clarify this, Cosmo thanked Mestorphemus and helped him, violently, to his feet with a wave of her hand. With her other hand, she willed the wand from his grasp and snatched it out of the air. The wand glowed intensely when Cosmo gave it a flick, smashing Mestorphemus into a bookcase on the left. Another flick, and he was hurtling to the right.

She repeated this action several times. The arena was a mess of scattered books, broken glass and tottering bookcases. Finally, as Mestorphemus was grunting to his feet, Cosmo battered him with chandelier after chandelier until he dropped, and proceeded to bury him beneath half a dozen bookcases, laughing all the while.

Sometime during this, Gerald snuck around the distracted woman and helped Luke to his feet. With Gerald supporting his weight, the pair hobbled their way back to the entrance Mestorphemus had created. But it was not to be. Finished with her burial ceremony, Cosmo returned to her prey. She threw the wand, striking Gerald in the side of the head. Luke tumbled with him to the floor.

And then she was on him, straddling his chest and filling his mouth with more of her rancid breath. She didn't bother to pin his arms. He was too weak to struggle. Her leg shot out and dished another blow to Gerald's head as he tried to rise, laying him low and lifeless.

Energy flowed from Luke by the second. He couldn't shove her off, but a pitiful thrust of the spoon up into her side was enough to break her concentration.

The spoon flared with heat when it made contact, almost enough to make him drop it, but clearly nothing compared to whatever Cosmo felt. It burned through her cloak and into her flesh. She reared back, screaming, and swatted the spoon aside.

The world froze. Everything moved at a crawl. Luke's body no longer took orders from his brain. For the second time in as many days he was destroyed. Maybe it would be easier, better, to just close his eyes and slip away from it all, but he couldn't even do that.

Cosmo recovered and leaned in for another deadly kiss. "I've waited too long to fail at this," she hissed. "We need some privacy." Then she smiled. "Don't worry. I don't need you alive."

She didn't kiss him. Her teeth pierced his neck, though he barely felt more than a pinch. When she pulled back, her lips and chin were stained with his blood. She grinned wider, her fiery hazel eyes locked on his, until a furry blur landed on her face. When the blur bounced away, a chunk of the angry zombie woman's lip bounced with it. She screamed and tore off after the squirrel.

Someone was tugging on his coat, shouting. *Sam?* But her voice sounded too far away. Then he saw his blue ball cap and the faded round stain of grackle shit. It felt like moments passed before her face appeared, full of worry. He wanted to tell her not to worry. To run.

She started to drag him, and Sophie did the same with Gerald. His head lulled to the side, changing the channel of vision to Henry attacking the zombie woman with a fury Luke had never seen. The squirrel was everywhere and nowhere. Ripping and tearing. If his entire world hadn't slowed down, he might not have been able to follow the furious creature at all. He smiled weakly as another chunk of Cosmos's scalp hit the floor beside him.

The light flooding in from the skylight above took on a more physical form, shrouding the flailing woman in a rectangular beam of yellow. Occasionally, glimpses of her arms or legs or face would pop out from the beam as she struggled with Henry. Cosmo howled. Books tumbled and fell from the shelves. The librarian was going to be so pissed.

The skylight pulsed brighter and brighter until he could barely see anything but yellow light.

Don't go into the light, his voice echoed inside of his head. *Don't go into the light.*

His eyes fell shut.

When he opened them again, the yellow beams were gone, but his vision was blurred. Sam had left him propped up against something. He saw her walking towards Cosmo. Henry was gone. Cosmo stood alone in the middle of the arena, wiping blood from her eyes.

What are you doing?? He wanted to scream, but couldn't.

Someone was beside him and put a hand to his forehead. The librarian from the front desk. She didn't look pissed. She looked worried. Sad. He saw her lips move, saying something that he couldn't hear and patted him on the cheek, then disappeared from his vision.

Suddenly his hearing returned in full, as if he had come up from underwater.

"No kids for you," Sam insisted. "You'd make an awful mother." Her voice boomed too loud. It spooked him, like when he'd start his truck the day after shutting it off with the radio volume left up too high. The responding laughter from Cosmo was deafening.

Get away from her!

There was nothing Sam could do. There was nothing anybody could do without the spoon.

Sam *had* the spoon. Luke could see it, behind her back, but Cosmo could not. What Cosmo could see was the purple penis Sam held out in front of her, threateningly.

Is that a vibrator?

"Play with this instead, *bitch*."

Cosmo cocked her head as the vibrator roared to life. What he was hearing had to be wrong, but his addled mind amplified the vibration to an enormous volume. It sounded like a race car engine.

She shouted a suspiciously Harry Potter themed spell, ending with "Eat a dick!" and tossed the vibrating vibrator at the wide eyed Cosmo, who fumbled to catch it, even as Sam quickened her pace to a run. Cosmo had the vibrator in hand for only a second when Sam reached her. She whipped the spoon out from behind her back and jammed it in the dead woman's gaping mouth. The two of them tumbled to the floor, with Sam on top, still pushing down with the spoon.

Cosmo's head began to smoke. She screamed a gargled scream, and flailed desperately to no avail. The smoke wisps grew thicker and thicker until her whole body looked like a brush fire. Sam held the spoon in her throat long after the smoking corpse stopped moving, just to be sure.

Everything went black for awhile. When Luke's eyes worked again, Sam was kneeling beside the blackened corpse, and the librarian stood over it, holding a stack of encyclopedias. She dropped them on Cosmo's head, shattering it into dust. A lesson to all who disrespect the library's code of silence. Sam got up and stomped and kicked at the rest of the body, until it was nothing but a pile of ash.

Luke's gaze landed on a thick brown braid dangling down one side of the librarian's face, against her cheek. The braid was entwined with green string. The green of it shown like a beacon, pulsing brighter and brighter, like the skylight above. Soon he could see nothing else. He closed his eyes, but there too, the green chased him.

When Luke opened his eyes again he was looking at the floor, at the back of someone's boots. Someone's leather pants. That stripper guy. Gerald.

"This way! This way!" came a voice like a distorted audio recording, something like the creepy voice criminals use on television shows to hide their voice. It was impossible to tell where sounds were coming from.

"You're gonna be fine."

Briefly, he saw the little girl from the front desk, her blue eyes wide with concern. The jewelry on her wrists jingled as she waved up at him. Then she was gone.

Hands cupped his cheeks. He saw, but couldn't feel them. He couldn't feel anything.

Another monstrous voice called his name. "Luke, you're *not* dying. Luke. Don't be an idiot. Luke. Just a second, please."

Gerald stopped moving.

The owner of the voice and hands crouched and raised Luke's head. It was Sam. Seeing her face allowed his brain to properly tune in to the frequency of her voice and hear the way he knew she should sound.

"Luke," she smiled. "You have to do what I say. You know why? Because I'm a *princess* now. Can you believe it? It's true. And I can command you to stay alive, and you have to do it. Are you listening to me? Luke?"

His eyes fell shut.

"Luke!" she called, "Damn it, Luke."

His eyes wouldn't open.

"It's a command, Luke." Her voice was fading. "You have to."

Her lips pressed against his. He felt *that*. Soft and hard at the same time. She kissed him deeply. A tingling warmth spread from his lips, seemed to swirl around inside of his head and then shoot through his body to his toes. It was a wonderful feeling, and seemed to revitalize him completely, long enough to kiss her back, gently.

And then he felt nothing.

He heard nothing. And thought nothing.

He was gone.

Chapter Twenty-Four

The third floor of the library was largely a disaster. Bookcases were strewn about everywhere but where they should be. Some were simply knocked over, some leaned into others like dominoes, relying on the next in line to keep from falling completely, yet still they spat the contents of their shelves in messy heaps beneath them. Steel chains dangled and swayed gently above, free from the burden of the chandeliers they once held. Bits of broken glass from the shattered skylights crunched underfoot.

The big man was groaning. The mountain of bookcases atop him started to tremble and shake as he gathered the strength he needed to drag himself from the wreckage. Strength that he no doubt had. Sam had doubts, however, as to whether the giant would react positively to the sight of Luke and the woozy squirrel, so she suggested the group leave the library immediately.

Everyone else, aside from the librarians and other operational staff, had already fled when the ruckus began. Members of the city watch began to fill the void, but Elisabeth was kind enough to help them avoid questioning by showing them a private exit through the staff lunchroom.

Sam apologized for the mess, but Elisabeth would have none of it.

"It's no fault of yours, miss," she said. "Besides, I used to work in a daycare. This is nothing."

They parted with hugs. Lia demanded and received a particularly long squeeze. She had missed the fight entirely, utterly distracted and elated with the fancy new braid in her hair, adorned with green string just like the librarian's. Sam imagined it wouldn't be long now before the rest of her hair was as bedazzled as her neck and wrists.

The mood was less cheerful when they left the library. The thrill of victory gave way to bitter reality as they passed through the pedestrian courtyard, wasting no time on the beauty around them. Their passage was swift, unheeded by the crowds as most people moved courteously aside when they saw their cargo. Luke hung lifeless and limp, slung over Gerald's shoulder. Henry was merely dizzy from hitting his head when Cosmo managed to snatch and throw him. He was recovering in Sam's tote bag.

At the first opportunity, they cut into a quiet alley and found a doorway hidden between a stack of crates and a barrel. A wide step in front of the door offered a seat to rest. Luke was placed in a seated position on the step with his back to the barrel. He slumped forward like one of the sleeping beggars they had passed earlier that morning. The cap he had looked so good in had been lost somewhere in the library. His hair poked out at messy angles.

If Gerald was at all winded from carrying Luke, he didn't show it. She offered him a smile of gratitude. He nodded grimly in return, and placed a hand on Luke's chest, and in front of his mouth.

"I don't think he's breathing, Samantha," he said, and pressed an ear to Luke's chest. "I can't hear a heartbeat either."

"What?" Sam snapped, a little sharper than she intended. "He's breathing. He has to be."

Gerald moved aside to allow her to check for herself. A moment later, she confirmed that Luke was indeed *not* breathing. Her own breathing turned shallow and rapid as the results drove her towards panic. Sophie placed a gentle hand on her back, relaxing her slightly, enough to retain her senses. She stretched Luke out onto his back and, for the first time in her life, put her CPR training to use.

The others watched in silence as she went through the motions once, twice, three times. After the fourth round of chest compressions and a fourth failed attempt to breathe life into him, she collapsed on his chest, too exhausted to even fight the tears welling up in her eyes. They streamed freely down her cheeks and onto his shirt. This time it was Gerald who gave her a comforting pat on the shoulder.

"I'm sorry for snapping at you," Sam told him.

Gerald smiled. "That was snapping? I've been following Sophie around for twenty years. Her compliments are more venomous than that."

She smiled a little at that.

Sophie scoffed, but didn't argue. Lia was hiding in her robes, sniffling.

"He can't be dead," cried Sam. "We *just* found him."

She kissed him. His lips were dry, but still warm. Aside from the swelling around his eyes, which he had before the encounter with Cosmo, the only new injury appeared to be a set of bite marks on his neck. She wiped away the fresh blood from where the teeth had pierced his skin. Sickly blue lines branched out an inch or so from around the wound. Poison?

Her breath caught. What if Cosmo was a vampire? Was Luke going to wake up and kill them all? She could live with that, sort of, so long as he woke up.

She laid her head back down on his chest and sobbed.

Her tote bag wiggled to life, and Henry scurried out. She watched him through blurry eyes as he crawled onto Luke's shoulder, next to her face. He smelled like the forest. He was sniffing and moving his head about in the sporadic, impossibly fast way that squirrels do. He conducted himself the way any squirrel would, except instead of chittering away, he repeated a *hmmm* sound as he examined Luke's body.

Thump-thump

Sam sat up like a rocket.

"His heart!" she cried. "It's beating! Henry! What did you do?"

She pressed her ear to Luke's chest again. For a long moment, there was nothing. Was she just hearing things?

Henry cocked his head and gave her a thoughtful look.

"Hmm," he hummed again. Then he smiled. "Excellent work, my dear."

Sam narrowed her eyes at him. "What are you talking about? I didn't do anything. Tell me he's alive. I really thought I heard his heart beat, but I can't hear it anymore. Maybe I was just- Oh! There it went again. It's so... slow!"

The squirrel nodded. "Indeed it is! And we should be thankful for that. I don't know what type of demon Cosmo is, but Luke was failing quickly after she bit him. Likely she infected him with some sort of poison, or paralytic. I believe it would have killed him."

"But it didn't? It *won't*, will it? We stopped her. Maybe she didn't have time to finish him."

"*You* stopped her, my dear," the squirrel smiled. "But she did succeed in poisoning him. See the blue lines. It's in his blood."

"Then why are you smiling?" Sam asked, rather pointedly. But how could he be so pleasant while Luke lay before them, barely alive?

Henry was unaffected by her tone. He began cheerily, "Because, the decelerated heart rate is a blessing. By some *miracle*," He gave Sam a curious look before continuing, "the boy is in a state of stasis. Frozen, if you will. A most fortunate scenario, as it may give us some time to sort him out."

Sam nodded, hopeful. "Okay. That's good, right? Let's get him to a doctor." She blinked. "You... You do have doctors here, right?"

"Of course there are doctors," said Sophie, "What kind of world do you come from?"

"I'm afraid ordinary doctors won't cut it," said Henry. "Cosmo was a demon. Her affliction would be of a magical nature. A magical ailment requires a magical remedy."

Sam looked to Lia. "Healing magic wouldn't happen to be in your arsenal, would it?"

"What's an ar-sen-ull?" she asked.

Henry shook his head. "Only the most advanced of magical healers could handle such a thing. His very soul would be under attack."

Sam twisted her lips. "What about the cleaner at the inn? The kobold? Last night I saw him using magic to put out the fire. Do you think he could help Luke?"

Again the squirrel shook his head. "Kobolds aren't known for their healing abilities."

"Well, what *is?*" Sam sighed. This world was too much. "Is there some like, healing spring we can take him to? Some kind of magical *soul fruit* we can pick? Should we take him to a *soul food* restaurant? What about a unicorn? They heal people, don't they? Is there anywhere around here offering unicorn rides? Oh, the holy grail. Maybe you have that here somewhere."

"Oh, clever clever girl," said Henry. "You're brilliant."

Sam frowned. "Am I? Don't tell me you know where to find the holy grail?"

"Never heard of such a thing, no. But you're on to something with the unicorns. No better healers in all the land. If any creature can mend him, it would be a unicorn. Silly of me to not have thought of it myself."

"Didn't they sell Unicorn Water near the castle at one point?" Gerald asked Sophie.

Sophie snorted. "Yes. I remember that. That was years ago. And they shut that guy down. Turned out he was just selling ditch water at extortionate prices. Unicorn water doesn't keep. If we want unicorns, we're going to have to find a ride to the Torpid Valley. There are herds of them there."

Unicorns. Really? Sam looked at Luke, and brushed his cheek. "Unicorns it is, I guess." She held back a laugh. The absurdity of it.

"Yes," said Sophie. "But we can't very well wander through town with the boy slapped over Gerald's shoulder like a sack of grain. Sooner or later, the watch will ask questions, and that big ogre they work for might make a less helpful appearance."

"Right," said Sam. "What about this?" She stood up and walked a little further into the alley where a large wheelbarrow was tipped up and leaning against the bricks. "We could push him in this? It's big enough that we could curl him up, and hide him with my coat."

Gerald nodded. "No arguments from me. Let's give it a go."

Carefully, Sam and Gerald lifted Luke and moved to place him in the barrow, when Lia pleaded they stop. Sam gave the girl an inquisitive look.

"That won't be very comfortable for him, will it?" asked the girl.

"I suppose not," Sam agreed, "But it's not like hanging over Gerald's shoulder is any better. What else can we do?"

"He needs blankets. The wheelbarrow is so cold and hard."

Sam smiled at her. "It's very sweet of you to say, Lia, but we don't have any blankets. Luke's not about to complain."

Lia shook her head and turned to tug on Sophie's sleeve. "Blankets, Sophie. Please?"

"Alright girl, alright. Don't tear the thing. Hold on."

Sophie reached into her robe and pulled out a wad of thick fabric. Sam's eyes grew wider and wider as Sophie pulled out more and more of a red and black checkered blanket. Soon she had a queen sized quilt in her hands, enough to wrap Luke in a cozy cocoon.

"Ah," smiled Henry, "so I was correct."

"How did you do that?" Sam asked. There was no way the woman could have concealed a blanket on her person without her noticing, and she didn't appear to have gotten any smaller after shedding so much mass.

"I'm not a witch," Sophie insisted. "But it's not just the style that I appreciate. Magic robes are very convenient. The pockets are bigger on the inside."

"Oh I see," said Sam, excited. "Like in Doctor Who."

Sophie shot her a puzzled look. "Doctor what?"

Sam shook her head. "Never mind, never mind. Let's just get him wrapped up. He's getting heavy."

Shortly after, the group left the alley by the end opposite which they entered, and found themselves on a relatively quiet street lined with tall and colorful vine covered residential buildings, and the cute shutters that came with them. Automobiles were allowed thoroughfare, evidently, but only a handful were to be seen. Their green engines propelled them silently by. A small scattering of pedestrians traveled about, some stole curious glances into the wheelbarrow as they passed, but most of them said nothing. One elderly woman asked what they were selling, but she was turned away quick enough when Sophie told her it was a body.

"So does this suit you, Lia?" Sam asked of Luke's new bedding arrangement. He looked like a red and black checkered taquito. They were careful to leave a breathing tunnel at the top for him, in case he decided to actually breathe. Henry was also in there somewhere, probably curled up on Luke's shoulder.

Lia nodded vigorously. Her jingling neck raised the eyebrows of a passing couple, holding hands.

Sam smiled. "Snug as a bug in a rug, eh?"

Lia giggled.

They made good time on their way back to the transit depot they passed the previous day, until Sam spied a sign up ahead that promised *BOOKS AND COFFEE*. Several black iron bistro table and chair sets were parked out front.

Her stomach growled. Demon slaying was hungry work. She pouted her lips at Sophie.

Sophie rolled her eyes, but failed to hide her smile. "Yes, my little freeloader. For the road."

CHAPTER TWENTY-FIVE

T he ambitious shouts and screams of the taxi drivers could be heard long before they reached the transit depot. Sam was wary of getting in a wagon driven by one of these crazy people, but Sophie insisted it was their best option. A train could get them close, but although it moved much faster, it would take a roundabout route around a mountain range to get there, which would take too much time and cost too much money. The wagons could take the road right through the mountains. Quicker and cheaper.

Finding a driver that was going there, however, proved difficult. There were lots of drivers offering dozens of destinations, but they all screamed and shouted over each other. It was as if they thought the one who screamed the fastest and loudest was going to win a customer's favor, regardless of where a potential customer actually wanted to go. After some time, they picked their way through the noise to find two men shouting two different, but both utterly butchered, versions of the words representing the place Sam and her party wanted to go. Torpid Valley.

Shouts of "Turpedvaleee! Turpedvaleee!" exploded from one operator's mouth, while passersby of the other were assaulted by a constant barrage of "Tupvleeee! Tupvleeee! Tupvleeee!" Lucky for anyone interested, the operators also waved about signs that listed their destination without the verbal butchery.

When Sam made eye contact with the closest operator, his eyes lit up. He had a target. He rushed towards her, shouting again "Turpedvaleee! Turpedvaleee!" inches from her face. Apparently he had the impression she was deaf.

"Come come! Into the wagon. We leave right away for Turpedvaleee! Turpedvaleee!" He hollered these last words to another passing group, who all but ran from him. He was a well tanned man in his late fifties, with short black hair and a bushy black mustache. He wore a threadbare sweater of cream color with the sleeves rolled up, exposing hairy forearms.

Sam and her companions shrugged, and were about to get in when the other driver cut in front of them. A man of similar appearance, though his hair was almost completely gray. Likely from the stress of shouting all day.

"Oh no, friends," said Driver Two, "You don't go with him. His horses old and slow. My mules fast! You'll see."

Driver One frowned.

Both drivers were towing similar flat deck wagons with short railings and a canopy. A handful of passengers were already seated on the benches. The decision was easy.

"We'll go with him, thanks," said Sam, referring to Driver One. Maybe his horses were old and slow, but he made no attempts to bad mouth Driver Two's mules.

"Oh thank you, thank you. You won't regret your choice," said Driver One, bowing appreciatively. He ushered them over to his wagon and began to count heads.

"Ah, two, three, four of you. Twenty rabbits a piece. Ah, but half price for the little one."

"There's one more," said Gerald, unfurling the blanket to show Luke to the driver. "He's not feeling well."

The driver's expression was sympathetic. He nodded, "Ah, you seek the unicorns. I'll get you there quick. No problem. Ninety rabbits, por favor."

Ninety rabbits! Sam was starting to become an expensive burden on Sophie and Gerald. She really had to find a way to repay them. Sophie fished her coin purse from the folds of her robe and counted out seven silver and six copper coins. When she turned to see the guilty look on Sam's face, she only winked.

Driver One bowed again, and helped Sophie onto the wagon.

"Thank you. My name is Hector. If you have any problems during the ride, you need only shout. If I don't hear you, throw something."

When Gerald stepped forward with Luke over his shoulder, Hector was quick to lend a hand in getting him situated on a bench. Lia was next to enter, squeezing in between Sophie and Gerald while making an obvious effort to show off her new hair braid to the other passengers by twirling it in her fingers. Sam took a seat on the end of the bench with Luke's limp body wedged upright between her and Gerald. His head, poking up out of the blankets, rolled over onto her shoulder. Something that might have been cute had she known for certain he wasn't dead.

She put an arm around him, and pressed her lips to his hair to whisper, "Are you still in there, Henry?"

"Indeed I am, my dear," came the reply.

She smiled and nodded at the people across from her. They responded politely, but were otherwise engaged in quiet conversation. None of them seemed to notice the voice that emanated from Luke's chest while his mouth remained closed.

When everyone was situated, the driver urged the horses into a trot, and the wagon began to roll along the cobbles and out into traffic. The steady clip-clopping of hooves was relaxing, though the hard wooden bench was not. She almost envied Luke for his cozy blanket and lack of consciousness, until Sophie began passing out more of the blankets, impossibly produced from her slim robe.

Traffic was light on the wide street, allowing them a steady pace once the driver managed to squeak by a wagon accident. Two men were engaged in a fistfight over the matter while their entwined horses sniffed each other affectionately.

"Are we going to Three Goats, Sophie?" Lia asked.

"I suppose we are, little one."

"Oh lovely. I love Three Goats. I have a bracelet from there. See? You'll like it too, princess."

This title drew curious looks from the other bench. Sam made a show of rolling her eyes and shaking her head, and the other bench smiled knowingly.

"Oh, I'll like it *a lot* if we can get Luke the help he needs, Lia. Is it full of goats?"

"Ummm. I don't know. I don't remember any goats, but I'm sure there's at least three."

Sam laughed. "You think so?"

"Yep! And there's a really pretty lake with a beach! You'll love it."

She smiled, "I'm sure I will, Lia. I'm sure I will."

The wagon approached an enormous wall, identical to the one they crossed when they arrived in the city, minus the gate.

The wall simply ended on either side of the wide road in a staircase of rubble. There was no gate house, no guards, just smooth sailing out into the countryside. Miles of farmland stretched out ahead of them before turning to forest at the base of a wide mountain range. Sam closed her eyes and took in the smells and the fresh air. Her butt was quite comfy with a blanket beneath it.

The leisurely bounce over the dirt roads through the first few miles of farmland was a false prelude to the rest of the journey. All hell broke loose when the wagon left the populated region and began the mountain pass on the other side of the forest. Contrary to Driver Two's rude comment, Hector's horses were anything but slow. The ride became a white knuckle affair, and preventing Luke from bouncing off the bench was a full time job for both her and Gerald. Luke flopped forward into the center more than once as the driver pushed his horses to reckless limits along the twisty mountain path.

Hector seemed to make a game out of hitting as many bumps and potholes as possible, and he was very good at it. He hardly slowed down over the holes and washouts, and on the rare occasion that he failed to hit one of his targets, if he swerved to the right, Sam was slapped by outreaching trees.

She took the slaps and bumps stoically, even when a particularly aggressive branch scratched a red line across her throat. The faster they found the unicorns the better. The other passengers stared indifferently ahead. They'd done this before. Whenever they were jolted from their seats, they repositioned themselves without complaint.

When the wagon cleared the first mountain pass and pulled into a small village, everyone was allowed off for a bathroom break while the driver exchanged his two horses for four fresh ones. The necessity of the extra horses was revealed a short distance later, in the next village.

A large crowd was gathered at the edge of the village. Several people were waving their arms to flag down the driver. The benches were already filled, but to Sam's surprise, Hector stopped the wagon and started collecting fares.

Hector was short and stocky, with laughing eyes and a perpetually enormous grin. This grin was somehow wider then, likely a reflection of the coin he stood to earn from such a payload. Sam could only gape as each person funneled aboard.

First came a middle aged couple. They found seats on the deck at the front of the wagon, flanked on either side by their luggage, two heaping sacks of vegetables. Then a younger couple closer to Sam's age hopped on. The woman, with a sleeping babe clutched to her chest, squeezed herself onto the bench between Sam and the tailgate. She flashed Sam a shy, appreciative smile. The man sat in the middle of the deck on one of the great sacks he carried with him.

Next came an elderly gentleman, who was nearly trampled by a flock of half a dozen children. They filled the rest of the gaps, one child even wedged himself aggressively between Sam and the nursing woman, forcing Sam into an awkward half standing position. Her seat was forfeit, but now Luke was wedged in so tight it would take a great earthquake to dislodge him. She turned and saw that three more people remained in the queue to board, one of them an especially large woman holding the reigns of a donkey.

There's no way, she thought.

But the driver thought different. The grinning driver ushered the large woman *and* her donkey on, copper coins practically beaming in his eyes. The donkey was directed to flop down on the nursing girl's toes, while the large woman plunked herself down on the deck at Sam's feet. Two of the children found new seats on top of the large woman, thoroughly blocking the way aboard for the remaining two.

Then, to Sam's relief, Hector, in a moment of compassion or sanity, closed the gate. Instead, he coaxed the remaining would-be passengers, a tiny pair of ancient ladies and their knitting bags, into the hide covered cab up front that separated him from the rest of his living cargo.

An entire family tree fell onto the wagon, but the added weight did little to slow the roll of the inexhaustible horses. It did, at least, keep the wheels grounded on the sharp corners. Still, nobody complained or showed any sign of discomfort in their cramped conditions. They swayed and bounced along without a care. The large woman was constantly rolling backwards into Sam's legs, and each time she bellowed a hearty, contagious laugh that set the other adults smiling and the children giggling.

A smile crept across Sam's face. This was a far cry from her typical public transit ride.

Her smile remained, hours later even, as she looked up at the twinkling night sky. Her legs were tired and her face was badly burnt by the day's sun and the wind, and she needed to pee. Blessedly, the driver began to slow the horses in the middle of a little village, apparently the last one before the final push through another mountain range to Three Goats.

The houses appeared relatively modern compared to those in Tumblestone, with wood siding and metal roofs, though she wasted little time in admiring them. When the wagon came to a halt, she leaped over the tail gate and ran for the washroom to a chorus of chuckles from Hector and the other passengers. She freshened up while smiling to herself, still amused by the baskets of leaves used for toilet paper.

When she made to get back onto the wagon, she had to blink. Everyone was gone, aside from her companions. Luke was placed seated on the deck in front of Sophie, braced up between her knees.

"What happened?" Sam asked.

"They all got off here," said Gerald. "I guess we're the only ones heading to Three Goats."

"Oh that's great. Some leg room."

Sophie's face was grave. A sick feeling sprang into Sam's stomach.

"Have you... How is Luke?"

"I checked him again," said Sophie. "I couldn't find a heart-beat."

"I checked too," said Lia. The happy jingle of her necklaces were at odds with her watery eyes. "And he's really cold, like my bunny Juniper was."

"Juniper ran away, dear."

Lia shook her head. "No he didn't. I saw mom bury him."

"Did you now? Hmm."

A tiny yawn emerged from Luke's blanket. Henry poked his head out and looked around to make sure they were alone.

"My condolences for the loss of your rabbit, my dear," he said.

Lia perked up at the sight of him.

"But please," he continued, "Don't put any thoughts into burying the boy. He's not dead. Not very lively, I give you. But he *is* alive."

"I hope you're right. But how can you tell?" asked Sam.

"The wound on his neck has not gotten worse. The infection hasn't spread. Sure he's cold, but aren't you all? These midnight wagon rides are the worst things for catching colds."

Everyone nodded thoughtfully.

Sam couldn't bare to check his vitals herself. Henry's theory was preferable. "So you really think he's still in this stasis thing, then?"

"I do. Have some faith, my dear."

"I'm trying."

"We're almost there," the squirrel assured her.

Sam nodded. "Okay. We'll go with that. Tell me about these unicorns. We're not gonna have to..." she swallowed. "*Kill one?* Are we? Or like, cut off their horn or something?"

By the horrified expressions on the other faces, she guessed the answer was a no. She was going to have to start reading better fantasy novels.

"I wouldn't suggest it," said Henry. "I doubt they'd be willing to help us if you tried such a thing. They're rather fond of their horns."

Sam let out a sigh. "Well that's good. It's not like I *wanted* to cut off one of their horns. Sorry. Again, *this world*, ya know. So how *does* it work?"

"Unicorns respond better to offerings of carrots or apples, as opposed to mutilation," Henry explained. "Once you've earned their favor, they'll be only too happy to help. You'll see."

"Okay. Yeah that's *much* better," said Sam. "Hmm."

"Something else, princess?" Sophie asked.

"Er, well, is it a thing here that, um, that unicorns only appear before virgins?"

Sophie raised an eyebrow. Gerald chuckled, while Henry merely smiled, a twinkle in his oil drop eyes. Lia had a look on her face that asked the question "What is a virgin?" before her mouth asked it.

"Clearly not the princess," Sophie mused. "Fear not. Any fool with eyes can see a unicorn. Why should a unicorn care what goes on beneath your bedsheets?"

"I guess that's kind of silly, huh?"

Sophie went on, "And what do you think unicorns do all day in the woods? You think they don't do that sort of thing? That's all they do really. Eat, sleep and-"

"Sophie!" Sam shouted, and nodded her head towards Lia. "I don't know how this poor girl handles you."

Hector returned from the rest stop, eating a sandwich. His eyes bulged when he saw them. Henry scurried back into Luke's cocoon.

"Passengers!" he cried. "I thought everyone heard."

"Heard what?" asked Sophie.

"I'm afraid this is the end of the line for me and my wagon."

"What? But I paid for you to take us to the Torpid Valley."

"Ah yes, yes. You did. But unfortunately the road is blocked. There has been a landslide in the pass. Happens from time to time. They say it is Three Goats's turn to clear the road, and they haven't done it yet."

"Of course."

"I'm very sorry madam. My wagon just cannot go to Three Goats at this time. But it is not far! You can walk there in a few hours."

"But I *paid* to be carted there, so I wouldn't have to do any walking."

Hector coughed nervously. "Ah, yes. Well, if you mention my name to Sara inside the rest stop, he will give you a great deal on mule rentals to get you the rest of the way. You can get there no problem without a wagon."

"Could we not just unhitch your horses?" Sam asked, "And continue on horseback?"

"Oh no," said Hector, shaking his head. "These horses won't like climbing over landslides. A mule is what you want."

"Perhaps we should have chosen the mule driver then," said Gerald.

"No," said Sam. "He was a dick."

"A dick that could have gotten us to Three Goats," pointed Sophie.

"Not so," said Hector. "The pass is not fit for any wagons. The end would have been the same. I am sorry. You will need to rent mules to carry you over the pass, or walk. But I'll tell you what." He dug out his change purse, which was now bulging with coins from the day's fares. He picked out a silver coin and handed it to Sophie.

"Here. Go inside, enjoy a bit of downtime in the rest area. It's very comfortable. And have yourself a sandwich, on me. Then you rent your mules. Half price, I am sure. You'll be in Three Goats before you know it."

Gerald shrugged. "I could eat."

Sophie sighed. "I suppose that's it, then. Fine."

Sam looked at Luke. Her lips tightened.

Hopefully the delay would not be the final nail in his coffin.

CHAPTER TWENTY-SIX

The roast beef and cheddar was a terrible choice.

Luckily, Sam didn't have to experience the consequences of that choice. She chose to quiet her hunger pangs with an apple and a squished granola bar she found in her tote bag, to reduce her burden on Sophie's purse.

Lia, wanting to be like her favorite princess, also chose an apple, and Sam shared her granola bar. Because of this frugal decision, Sam and Lia were sitting comfortably in the rest stop lounge while Sophie and Gerald were dry heaving over the toilets in their respective bathrooms.

"I'm gonna kill that Hector next time I see him," groaned Sophie.

Luke's condition remained the same, which Sam took for a good sign, but she was worried that Sophie and Gerald's predicament might eat up whatever time he had left.

"How much longer do you think Luke's going to last, Henry?"

She spoke quietly, though the only other person in the rest stop was the young attendant, and she was slumped over her counter, snoring.

"Truthfully, it fascinates me that his stasis has lasted this long."

"I see… That doesn't sound promising."

"Indeed. This roast beef fiasco is an unfortunate setback. We must hold onto the hope that the magic lasts a little longer. The sooner we get him to the unicorns the better."

A flurry of curses drifted out from the bathroom.

"Sophieeee!" scolded Lia.

Sophie responded with a wretched hacking sound.

The attendant stirred, but merely switched which side of her head laid on the counter.

"Maybe we should go to this Three Goats place ourselves?" Sam suggested to the squirrel. "Hector said it wasn't far, and surely someone can point us in the direction of the unicorns."

"Ah! That's the spirit. Yes. I have to agree with you, but do you think you can carry the boy on your own? I'm afraid I'm not much good for heavy lifting." Henry flexed his tiny arms.

"Definitely not," said Sam. "I had a difficult enough time with Gerald's help just placing him in the wheelbarrow. And we left that back in Tumblestone. But… let's see."

She went to the bathroom.

"Sophie?"

The older woman was kneeling in front of the toilet. She turned her head towards Sam, and grunted, "Yes? What can I do for you, princess?"

"Oh my," said Sam. Sophie was deathly pale. "Well, since you asked… I think the best thing you can do for me right now is stay here and recover from that awful sandwich. Um, and also, maybe, if you could lend me a little more money to rent a mule…

Just one! To carry Luke to Three Goats. I'll walk. I don't think riding is really my thing anyway."

Sophie nodded, reached into her robes, and slid her coin purse across the floor to Sam. Sam looked at it in disbelief.

"Um... Well, okay then," she said. Not all, but a small portion of the guilt she felt over spending Sophie's money slipped away when she felt the weight of the purse. Sophie was *loaded*, and amazingly trusting of someone she had recently met, although at the moment, it looked like she might expect to keel over before the night was through anyway.

"Thank you. I'll bring this right back."

She approached the counter.

"Hello?" she said, loud enough to be heard over the snores of the attendant. "Excuse me? Miss?"

"Huh? What? Oh. Hi there. What's up?" The attendant stretched her arms out wide and yawned. *Sara* was the name on her shirt.

"Sorry to bother you. Is it possible to rent a mule at this hour?"

"Yeah, sure. Absolutely. Come with me."

Sara popped up out of her seat with surprising energy. A second later, she nearly tumbled over.

"Oops," she said with an embarrassed smile. "Not awake enough for that yet."

Sam followed the groggy teenager outside to a pen behind the rest stop.

"Take your pick."

A quick scan for a mule that wasn't sleeping proved fruitless. There were more than a dozen mules scattered throughout the pen, and all of them were sleeping. Sam picked one of the three standing sleepers because the ones on the ground looked far more comfortable. A standing sleeper was basically awake anyways, wasn't it?

"Good morning Jasper," said Sara, scratching the mule's neck. "An *early* morning for you today, bud."

She led the mule over to Sam.

"Where ya headed with him?"

"Three Goats."

Sara nodded. "It's thirteen copper a day for this guy. The first day you pay up front. And it's thirteen copper and a finger a day if you abuse him."

"A finger?"

"Oh yeah. Probably more than one, actually. He'll bite your hand right off if you strike him. He's done it before."

"Um.."

Sara laughed. "Nah I'm just playin' with you. Jasper's actually one of the friendlier ones. But seriously, be kind. I love these mules."

"Of course I'll be kind to him."

"Good. Anyhow, we have a stable in Three Goats as well, so you can actually drop him off there if you plan on staying any length of time. Save yourself some coin."

"Sounds perfect. Thank you. Oh! Hector said something about a discount?"

"Who's Hector?"

"He was— Eh, never mind. Here."

She paid the girl the full amount and led Jasper around to the front of the rest stop. She tied him to a pole while she went inside to get Luke. With considerable effort, she and Sara hoisted Luke onto the mule's back and secured him with a length of rope.

Sophie and Gerald didn't leave the bathroom to say goodbye, but vowed to catch up with her as soon as they were feeling better. Lia hugged her. She had one request.

"Wait! Before you go..." She smiled at Henry. "Can I scratch your neck again?"

"My dear girl, you know you needn't even ask!"

Lia was thrilled.

"Take good care of them, Lia. Just like you took care of me when I was sick."

Lia bobbed her head. "You can count on me, princess!"

The sun was stretching its sleepy fingers across the land as Sam traversed the wooded pass between the two mountains that would take her into the Torpid Valley. Jasper proved quite adept at navigating the landslide. In fact, he made it over the rough terrain without slipping once, which was more than Sam could say.

The rest of the pass had been reasonable, though the constant uphill climb had Sam winded when they finally reached the crest overlooking the valley below. If she had any breath left, the view would have taken the rest away.

A mountainous bowl of broccoli florets with a giant blueberry in the center is what came to mind. A feast for the eyes. If there was a place where unicorns roamed, this would be it.

"Amazing," she gasped.

"Quite lovely, isn't it?" said the squirrel.

"It really is."

Henry had scampered up onto Jasper's head for a better view. Sam smiled at the pair. It seemed the mule was warming up to the squirrel. Jasper was none too happy to have the tiny passenger on his back in the beginning.

There was no sign of a village near the lake, or anywhere for that matter. No rising smoke to betray its location. No boats in the water. But the road continued down into the forest, and she had to assume it would lead her to it. Maybe she'd get lucky and stumble across a unicorn along the way.

So enthralled was she by the view that she jumped a little when a voice called out to her from just below the crest. "Hello there, madam! Have you heard the word of Lee Grover?"

The chipper voice belonged to a smiling man in a floppy brimmed straw hat. He was leading a donkey, who carried on its back a large lumpy sack. Jasper was the first to greet them, or rather, the donkey. The two exchanged happy brays.

"Er, hello!" said Sam, "What's this about Lee Grover? Oh! Are you the guy I met at the gate in Tumblestone? The one Sophie chased away."

"Ah, how nice it is to meet such a lovely vision on this trail. The trip hasn't been a total loss after all. But alas, I cannot claim to be my famous cousin. It's likely that *he* is who you met in the city. My name is Ben Grover. I'm on a pilgrimage."

"Really? Interesting. What sort of pilgrimage?"

"Honestly it's more of a sales thing, really. I've been traveling from place to place, selling my cousin's books. Now tell me, darling, have you heard the word of Lee Grover?"

"I can't really say that I have."

"I see. I see. Well fear not. I have just the cure for your ignorance. Have a gander at what my dear friend Charlie has on his back."

Sam frowned at the "ignorance" comment, but indulged him anyway.

As Ben loosened the draw string on the donkey's cargo, he asked, "Is there not somebody else with you? I swore I heard another voice as I approached. *He* doesn't look very talkative." He nodded at Luke.

"He's sick." Sam explained.

"Ah" he laughed, "Too much drink, I bet. I've been there. Oh yes. I've been *there*. Has somebody else gone off to squat in the woods then, perhaps?"

"Er," Sam began. Maybe it wasn't wise to let this man know she was alone in the middle of nowhere, but a swift kick to the groin should put him down if necessary, and Henry had proven to be quite feral when provoked.

"No," she decided. "Nobody else. Just me, chatting with my mule."

Ben smiled and nodded. "I often find myself doing the same with Charlie here. He never has much to say, but he's a great listener."

He produced from the sack a thin, roughly bound novel and handed it to her.

"True Tales of... *Umph?*" she read aloud. "By Lee Grover."

"What? Oh, sorry about that."

He swapped her copy for another. This one contained the missing letters that transformed *umph* into Triumph.

"A silver fox and three rabbits is enough to secure your enlightenment, miss. What say you?"

"I say that's a little steep. I don't even have that much money. Sorry."

It was the truth. She had returned Sophie's pouch to her, and only kept one silver and two copper coins, to purchase some food and possibly accommodations when she arrived in the village.

"How much *could* you spare?" he persisted. "I'd love to see you walk away from here with something to read down in the village. You'll need it."

Sam sighed. "I don't know, really. Two copper, maybe? But that's it."

Ben frowned. "How about seven?"

"No. Really. Two is all I can possibly give. Sorry."

It was Ben's turn to sigh. "I'll tell you what. Just so I can say I sold *something* on this trip to Three Goats, I'll let you have the copy with the incomplete title for two bits. It's a steal of a deal miss."

Sam couldn't argue. Perhaps Luke might need some time to recover after they found the unicorns, and he'd enjoy something to read. She paid the man.

He bowed appreciatively.

"You really didn't sell anything in the village?" she asked.

Ben nodded sadly, and removed his hat to wipe his forehead. With the shade of the hat removed, Sam noticed his face was peppered with thin red scratches.

"Not a single sale! Oh but I assure you that speaks nothing to the quality of the material. The problem was that there was nobody around to sell to. There was not a soul to be found in the entire village. I knocked on every door, and loitered about the village for three days, I did. I'm ashamed to admit I even resorted to peeking in windows. But, nothing! Might as well change the name from Three Goats to *A Hundred Chickens* now. Plenty of those strutting about."

"Are you sure? Nobody at all?"

"Nobody."

"What happened to your face?"

The scratches were nearly disguised as Ben's face flushed. "I, um…"

Sam raised her eyebrows.

"T'was the chickens," said Ben to his toes.

"Really? Chickens? They attacked you?"

"They did. At least a dozen of the little monsters. Scratched me up good. My hands too, see. Never seen chickens band together like that before."

"Hmm." Her eyes narrowed. "What did you do?"

"Eh... I might have tried to eat one. I didn't though! Couldn't catch it. Don't judge me. I was looking forward to a hot meal when I arrived, and after three days, I couldn't resist. I know it's stealing. But there's lots of 'em down there. I thought, 'who's gonna miss *one* chicken?' The other chickens, that's who. I've learned my lesson. Won't ever happen again. I can promise you that."

"Interesting," said Sam. She wouldn't judge him. It sounded like she might have to *borrow* some food without permission herself.

"Hey! Would you look at that!" Ben grinned. He pointed at Henry, who was sitting quietly on Jasper's head. "My, if I had a picture box with me. What a sight. A squirrel, sitting on a mule's head like it's nothin'. Animals are full of surprises these days."

"Tell me about it. But hey, I should get going. I wanna see these murderous chickens for myself."

"Indeed. Quite a sight they are. They really aren't too violent though, so long as you don't try to harm one of 'em."

"Thanks for the book, Ben. I hope your sales improve."

"They can only go up!"

Ben tightened the draw string on his cargo and left Sam with a handshake, and made her pledge to spread the word of Lee Grover should she enjoy his writing. Jasper and the donkey also exchanged goodbye brays. Henry waved when Ben wasn't looking.

When they began their descent into the valley, Henry again became a talking squirrel.

"Ah, a village full of chickens. Sounds a bit fishy, don't you think?"

"Not at all," said Sam. "Sounds feathery, though. Where do you think the villagers went?"

"I have my suspicions, though we can determine nothing until we arrive."

"Right. I just hope that whatever happened, we can still find a unicorn. Man. It feels weird saying something like that. Unicorns are supposed to just be fairy tales, you know."

Henry chuckled. "Do you really not have such things in your world? My knowledge of your world is slight."

"As far as *I* know, we don't. But does that mean you *have* heard of our world? I mean, before you met Luke?"

"I have. It's not common knowledge, but over the centuries there have been travelers between the realms. Most have been fairly secretive about it. I, myself, have not had the pleasure."

"Well, when this is over, and we find a way home, I think I can speak for both of us, Luke and me, when I say you'd be more than welcome to come visit."

"I would like that, Samantha" he said, though with little enthusiasm.

Sam knew by the look on his face that he had fell into thoughts of his lost witch woman. It was too bad that she couldn't help him find her, if she was even still alive, but if she wasn't home by Christmas her parents were going to have a fit. She decided to help take his mind off things while they made their way down to the village by enthusiastically reading aloud to Henry from her new book.

Right off the bat, the legitimacy of the word True in the title was questionable. She had her doubts as to whether the traveling book salesman had ever actually woken up naked in an undersea mermaid brothel after a night of drinking, but really, who was she to question the things of this world?

Chapter Twenty-Seven

As Sam and Henry left the forest trail and passed through a narrow section of cultivated farm land, they both noted an absence of laborers. The fields outside of Tumblestone had been full of workers toiling away in the dirt and sun, but here there was no one, just as Ben had said.

Leaving the farm land, they entered the village proper, a scattering of small houses with plastered siding and slate roofs built in the shadow of tall pine trees. Muddy streets weaved between them. All was quiet, save for the chirping of birds in the trees and the gangs of chickens clucking about on the ground.

They crossed the village by way of one of the main streets and found on the largest building in the village a wooden sign dangling on chains above its door way. The sign read *Two Goats Coffee and Lodgings,* and pictured a pair of elderly ladies in rocking chairs with coffee cups in their laps. The suggestive picture was so enchanting after a long morning of walking and no coffee, that Sam barely noticed the dozens of chickens and roosters she had to wade through to get to the door. She tied

Jasper off to a lamp pole and went inside, with Henry on her shoulder.

Inside she found another group of chickens, some strutting about and shitting on the floor, others perched on wooden chairs in front of rustic tables set with empty plates and coffee mugs. There was a counter to her left, with a little sign next to a bell that said "Ring For Service". Sam rang the bell and walked through the café to one of the three wide picture windows in the back, scattering frightened chickens as she did so.

There were more tables outside, where one could sip coffee in a private garden hidden from the world by a tall yew hedge. Just enough sunlight filtered in from the pines above to flower a brilliant magnolia tree in one of the corners, and lilies and hydrangeas added further color throughout.

Sam sighed at the beauty of it, and was thoroughly disappointed when, after several minutes, nobody answered the service bell. She thought briefly about drinking some of the cold coffee in the pot on the stove behind the counter, but left it as a thought.

Sam and Henry continued down the main street with Jasper and Luke in tow, and made it all the way to the lake without seeing a single human. Jutting out into the lake were a couple of long docks with enough fishing boats tied off to them to quickly rule out a mass fishing trip as a cause for the absence of villagers. Some ducks waddled and quacked along the sandy shore line.

Near the docks, they found a couple of cushioned sun chairs beneath the shade of a cluster of birch trees. It had been a long night, and Sam's legs were tired. Here she insisted on resting, but first she unfastened Luke from Jasper, and nearly done herself in hauling him off the mule and onto one of the chairs. She arranged him in a comfortable position and kissed him on the forehead. If he woke up in his new position, he'd have a lovely view of the lake.

After some time, Sam shook herself to keep from falling asleep in the other chair. If not for Luke's condition, she'd happily have given in and slept there forever.

"I think we should leave him here while we look around some more," she said. "These chairs are pretty comfy. Certainly more comfortable than being slung over Jasper's back."

"Indeed," agreed Henry.

She looked around, at the ducks, the water slapping against the shoreline, and the puffy white clouds above. There were worse places to die, though of course, Luke was *not* going to die. She would find a unicorn with or without help from the village.

"There has to be somebody here," she said. "Somewhere."

"I have to agree with you again, my dear," chuckled Henry. "Look at that. I believe we've been followed."

At least a dozen chickens were warbling and wobbling down the main road towards them, seemingly on a mission. Sam stood up to face them, not wanting to be caught lying down if the chickens decided she was in league with Ben.

The chickens came to a stop under the birch trees. A couple of them seemed to be sizing Sam and Henry up with heads cocked to the side. Most of them were simply pecking the ground.

"Er, hello?" said Sam, offering a slow wave.

The staring chickens blinked. The others continued pecking.

Henry hopped forward to greet them, and when he spoke, *all* of the chickens focused their gaze entirely on him. They slowly backed away as the squirrel approached.

"A pleasure to meet you all," he said, bowing. "I hope you don't mind us making ourselves comfortable. The hospitality at the local inn left much to be desired."

When Henry stopped moving, the chickens did also.

"I don't think they like you, Henry."

"Seems that way, doesn't it? Please, my feathered friends. We come in peace. We are in no way associated with that book salesman who left your village today."

There was something creepy about the way the chickens stared, unmoving, at Henry. Yet they completely ignored Sam as she knelt down before them. Cautiously, she extended a hand to one of the chickens. Not until the hand was inches from the chicken did it acknowledge her. It looked at Sam, then back at the hand. The chicken gave her finger a gentle peck.

The peck tickled in a sensational way, a rolling wave that flowed from the hand where the peck landed all the way to her toes. She shivered. Strange. The effect was the same each time the chicken pecked her.

"There's something odd about this chicken," she said, shivering again.

She turned to Henry, who was grinning up at her.

"Tickles you all over, doesn't it?"

"Why, yes. That's exactly what it does. How did you know?"

Henry chuckled. "It is as I suspected. I thought I'd have to chase one to be sure, but I'd rather take your word for it. I'd like to think chicken chasing is beneath me."

"What do you mean? What are you sure of?"

"Magic, my dear girl. That tingling you feel, is the magic affecting these poor chickens. I believe the villagers we seek are right here in front of us, scratching the dirt and eating ants."

Sam gasped and snapped her hand away from the chicken. "Why didn't you say something?? I don't want to turn into a chicken!"

Henry chuckled again. "Oh no, you don't have to worry about that. It's not contagious. The tingling just alerts us to the presence of magic. Nothing more. This confirms the suspicions I had when Mr. Grover explained that he was attacked by the chickens after trying to eat one of them. Normally, chickens don't possess such chivalry, but chickens who were once humans might."

Sam made an O with her mouth. "Ah. So do you think these people gave up there humanity to become immortal? Like you? Sorry if that's a touchy subject."

"Not at all, Samantha. Worry not. But I believe this case is quite different."

"Can we help them?"

"Perhaps. Someone must be responsible for this. They might still be around."

Sam looked back at the chickens, all of which were now looking at her and waddling closer, clucking softly.

"Ah," said Henry. "I think they can still understand us. That's why they were apprehensive. Never seen a talking squirrel before, I suppose. Hypocrites."

The chickens became very quiet as they closed in around Sam and the squirrel. They just stood, staring and blinking, some with their heads cocked to the side. They really *did* seem to be listening to them.

"Hmm. Can you understand us?" she asked. "Wait. *If* you can understand me, cluck once for yes, or twice for no."

Though they all clucked at different times, it appeared as if the chickens understood. To be sure, Sam addressed one chicken specifically. The chicken clucked once.

"Amazing," said Sam.

"An excellent system, Samantha!"

"Thank you Henry, but let's just try it once more. This time, three clucks for yes."

Three clucks rang out.

"Perfect," she said, smiling proudly.

Henry addressed the chicken ambassador Sam had chosen. "Now, my dear villager, if we can just get beyond your distrust of talking squirrels, I'd like to ask a few questions myself. What do you say to that? Again with the one and two cluck system, if you please."

One cluck.

"Excellent! Thank you. Let's start with this. Was it the book salesman who turned you into chickens?"

Two clucks.

Henry nodded. "Do you know of any mages living in the village?"

The ambassador clucked twice. While Henry paused to scratch another question out of his chin, one of the chickens in the back waddled and clucked through the crowd until it stood before the squirrel.

It clucked once. The ambassador and all the others turned their eyes on the new speaker.

"Ah," said Henry. "Yes, I suppose not everyone would be privy to that knowledge. Perhaps we can convince this mage to change you back."

Two clucks.

"Hold on now. I haven't asked a question yet. Can you take us to this mage?"

The chicken clucked twice, and began clawing at the dirt, stopping briefly to consume an ant.

"Are you trying to tell me something?"

One cluck. The chicken dug a small trench in the dirt, and then filled it back in.

Henry groaned.

"What is it?" asked Sam.

"He's dead, isn't he?"

One cluck.

"Oh dear," said Henry. "I would like to point out that I asked if there were any mages *living* in the village. Anyways. That is most unfortunate." He renewed his chin scratching.

"Well," said Sam. "Somebody had to do this, right? What about... Did this mage have any surviving relatives in the village?" Maybe magic was hereditary.

The second ambassador devoured several more ants before answering with a single cluck.

Sam smiled triumphantly, "Great. Could you take us to them, or their house, maybe? Er, but please finish your meal first."

The second ambassador clucked once more, and after another helping of ants, began to lead Sam and Henry back towards the village.

"Marvelous. This is going better than I'd hoped," said Henry. "Let's be off then."

"Wait," said Sam, tying Jasper's lead to the tree. "Is it safe for us to leave our friend here?"

One cluck.

"No water hags or mermen lurking about, are there?"

Two clucks.

"Okay. That should cover the bases. I guess we're off to see the wizard, then."

She kissed Luke goodbye and promised to return as soon as possible, and she, Henry, and a flock of chickens made their way back through the village.

The odd fellowship moved slowly toward its destination, as their path was constantly blocked by barriers of insects demanding to be eaten. The fellowship grew in size and sound each time they passed another group of chickens, including the large group that had been loitering in front of the coffee shop.

By the time Sam and Henry reached the mage's house, they were accompanied by at least fifty clucking hens and roosters. The insect population was devastated in their wake.

A few hunks of flagstone offered a visually appealing walkway to the front door, and an excellent practical surface to kick off the mud from the streets. The house itself was as plain as the others, but beautifully adorned by well kept window planters of purple geraniums and neat rows of shrubbery. Not surprisingly, no one answered Sam's knock, and there was no movement in the window. The door, however, was unlocked.

Henry turned on Sam's shoulder to address the flock, "If you'll please just wait for us out here, we'll see what can be done."

As Sam slowly turned the handle and pushed inward, a sudden loud movement inside frightened her into slamming the door, but after a deep breath she opened it again, laughing.

"So sorry," she said to the startled hen inside. "I should have knocked louder."

The chicken had squawked and took flight around the room, bombarding the floor and furniture with sloppy white missiles in the process.

"I take it you must be the mage," said Henry, bowing politely. "Please relax. We aren't very hungry."

"Speak for yourself. That apple was gone hours ago. Er, but yes. We haven't come to eat you, chicken lady. Um, actually. Why *are* we here, anyways?"

"For this, my dear girl."

Henry hopped from Sam's shoulder and scurried up onto a desk in the corner of the room. On the desk was a large open book. Her hopes soared when she saw that the text on the pages was in Latin.

"Is that a Travel Tome?" she asked.

"Not quite. As far as your quest goes it offers little significance, but I'm sure it is of great interest to our feathered friends, though they don't likely know it. Hmm."

Henry tried to push the tome into the beam of light from the window, but after some grunting, turned to Sam and smiled pleadingly. She finished the task for him, receiving another mysterious tingle through her body when she touched the book.

"Thank you, Samantha."

He began to scan the page.

"Can you read that?"

"I can," said the squirrel. "Hmm. Ahh! There's nothing in the text that allows for the caster to be excluded from the spells effects. That would have to have come from the original owner of this book's memory. A sort of safeguard if the book fell into the wrong hands. Or maybe just poor planning."

"I see. So it's a spell book."

"Indeed it is. And I would say..." he turned around with an amused smile. "Our magician can likely be counted amongst these chickens." He nodded to the hen watching them from the dinner table. "Given this ones close proximity to the book, I think we can confidently deduce *this* is our culprit. Hmm."

Henry started looking around the house, sniffing at drawers and cupboards. The chicken clucked rapidly, and fluttered its wings, when Henry went under the bed.

"Is there a problem?" asked the squirrel.

"Umm. You are just rooting around someone's house right in front of them. It's kinda rude, don't you think?"

"Oh dear!" said Henry. "Terribly sorry. Please forgive our invasion of your privacy, but I assure you it is necessary if you wish for your legs back."

The chicken relaxed.

Sam began helping the squirrel in his search by opening drawers and cupboards, "Hey. What exactly are we looking for?"

"A source. Simple spells may be conducted through the gathering of energies from nearby plants, fire, running water, things like that. A certain amount can come simply from within the user, but that can be quite taxing."

Sam nodded. "Like how Lia falls asleep after her magic bubbles."

"Precisely. With proper training, she could harness the energies around her instead of using her own. But that is a different matter. To conduct the amount of magic required to turn an entire village into chickens, however, the caster would need a direct source. A powerful one. Something close by."

Hunger drove Sam to closely examine a bowl of shiny red and green apples sitting on the fireplace mantle. She was a bit disappointed to discover they were fake.

"Hey. One of these apples is glowing," she exclaimed, digging a golden one up from the bottom of the bowl. "Ahhh!"

A jolt went through her body when she grabbed the glowing apple, causing her to jump. She knocked the entire bowl of apples on the floor, scattering them in all directions. Her body trembled. The sensation was similar to that of touching the spell book, or being pecked by the chickens, but *much* stronger. Her face flushed when the apple's strange effects reached certain sensitive areas. One could make a fortune in the adult toy industry with something as potent as the strange apple.

"Brilliant!" Henry beamed. "Hiding in plain sight. That, my girl, is an apple from a novarius tree. A younger tree than the one in Morningwood, but that apple is still quite powerful. You won't find a better source than this."

Sam took a deep breath and steeled herself to retrieve the apple from the floor.

"Oh my," she gasped.

The apple glowed and pulsed in her hands. She held it for a few long seconds, enjoying the sensation a bit too much, before finally forcing herself to set it on the table next to Henry. All the fur on the squirrel's body lifted upwards.

"Indeed. Positively humming with power. More than enough to poultrify a small village like this."

Sam was mesmerized, unable to take her wide eyes off the pulsing apple.

"Incredible things, these apples," continued Henry. "They produce vast amounts of energy, and can last for decades after being plucked from their tree. It's capable of recharging itself, and will do so, so long as it is never drained completely, destroyed, or eaten. I don't recommend eating it. You'll get an awful stomach ache. And when it comes out—"

"I don't need to know that, thanks. I won't eat it. But how could they have one? I thought you said Luke was the first person ever to make it out of Morningwood?"

"There are novarius trees in other parts of the world, my dear. Certainly not a common tree, but there are many that are more accessible than the one in Morningwood."

"This makes your trip into the cursed forest a lot more foolish you know."

The squirrel laughed, then sighed. "I know, Samantha. I know. But the tree in Morningwood is the oldest. Its apples are unmatched power sources."

"I was only picking, Henry. So, can you change the villagers back? Um, break the spell or whatever? Now that we have the apple."

"I believe the spell can be broken, so long as the spell wasn't cast too long ago. After a certain amount of time has passed, the magic can't be undone. The transformation would be permanent."

The hen clucked and flapped frantically.

Henry issued a calming gesture with his paws.

"Please, my dear chicken, hope is not yet lost. Surely there must be something in this book to help us. I need but a bit of time to work out a remedy for the situation."

"I have faith in you, Henry. You know, in a world where innkeepers can live well past their expiration date, and people can turn invisible, and things are powered by sunflowers, and... and *unicorns,* I don't understand why anyone would be put off by a talking squirrel."

"Simple human nature, my dear. People often stare at things that are out of the ordinary. Most types of magic are rare enough these days to merit a second glance, and my speaking might reasonably be attributed to magical persuasion. You might agree that these chickens have a particularly good reason to be a little wary of magic right now."

"Fair enough."

"Our chicken friend is looking a bit flustered. We should get on with our task. I think I've found what we were looking for here. I'll need you to repeat after me, unless you can pronounce these words correctly on your own, of course. Forgive my assumption, but Luke's spell recital in the forest did little to inspire faith."

The thought of Luke trying to read Latin brought a smile to her face. "Wait, you want *me* to perform the spell?"

"Yes. Of course."

"Why can't you just do it? I can't do it."

"Can't you?" the squirrel raised a brow, smiling. "I'm afraid I can't do it myself. My ability to conduct magic was lost along with my humanity. Unfortunately, this is not the same as the scroll Luke read from. There is no magic spell loaded into this book, waiting to be released. It must be conjured. While I've retained the ability to sense magic, I am no wizard."

Sam laughed, "Well, I'm not either, Henry. We might have to wait until Lia gets here."

"Nonsense. By then, it may be too late. You feel the tingling, don't you? When you touch the book. The apple. You felt its power, did you not?"

"Sure, but what of it? You say you can feel it too."

"You remember the kobold at the inn?"

"Yes."

"Only magic users can see and hear a kobold, Samantha, unless they absolutely *want* to be seen. While I could sense its presence, and knew better, it still sounded to me as if you were talking to yourself in the bathroom."

Sam shook her head. "But you were sleeping."

Henry smiled. "One eye open, my dear. There's also the matter of you enchanting Luke into a stasis."

Sam frowned. "But—"

"No more buts. Just humor me. For the chickens' sake. You have to try, unless you're fine with leaving these villagers as chickens."

The hen hopped up and down on the table behind them, flapping its wings like mad.

"Okay, okay," she said. "I'll try. But if I burn your house down or something, don't be mad at me."

"Everything will be fine. Just follow my lead and think hard on what it is you want to accomplish. A village of humans. Not chickens. Keep that in your mind's eye."

"This is foolish," Sam mumbled, but she did as she was asked.

She really did want to help the villagers. She imagined the gang of chickens outside poofing back into humans, one by one, and held that thought as Henry cleared his throat and began to speak. He spoke in a slow, prayer-like cadence, stopping in short intervals to allow Sam to parrot the strange words in her own less confident tone. She was careful to repeat each phrase exactly, though she had no sweet clue what she was saying. She just kept repeating and thinking of the chickens. As each word left her lips, however, the apple pulsed quicker and brighter, and the sensation within her grew to dizzying heights. *Something* was happening. At a certain point, the apple dulled to almost nothing, like a light bulb that had been turned off, but as the last word was spoken, the apple's glow began to return.

Henry turned and bowed his head to her, and smiled.

"You did fine, my lady. That should do it."

They both turned to look at the hen, who was still a hen, and looking back at them with its head cocked.

"Are you sure about that, Henry?"

Henry scratched his chin. "That *should* have done something. I could feel it. Perhaps I read something wrong."

"Should we try again?"

"At the moment, no. We must wait for the apple to recharge, though that could take quite some time. In the meantime, I'll try and figure out what went wrong."

"Okay. Well, well maybe I'll just step outside and sit in the garden for a bit. I'm a bit dizzy, and everything in here is covered in chicken shit."

Henry nodded, his nose pressed to the spell book.

"Wanna join me?" she asked the hen. "Some fresh air might do you some good."

The hen protested at first, but quickly surrendered to Sam's gentle hands. She set the hen down outside with the others and sat down on a large granite rock decoratively placed amongst the shrubbery. To her surprise, the hen rejoined her, hovering up into her lap.

She laughed, "Nervous, are you?"

A thought struck her. She lifted the chicken for a few seconds to examine her lap. Her suspicions were correct.

She frowned. "Yes. Yes you are."

With a sigh she began to stroke the back of the chicken's neck. "It's okay," she told herself as much as the chicken, and closed her eyes until the magical tingling left her. Though it wouldn't entirely leave her so long as the chicken rested in her lap, it became manageable. She watched the others for awhile, methodically purging the yard of insects.

How was Luke doing? If a breeze came in off the lake, would he get cold? Was he already cold? No, he had the blanket. It was a warm enough day. He should be fine, but was he still alive? How were Sophie and Gerald feeling? How would she pay them back? Where would she live when she made it back to Halifax? *Would* she make it back to Halifax? She felt anxious. She wanted to hurry and find a unicorn and a new place to live, but she couldn't. Not now. Her burdens felt heavy. So heavy that she *grunted*.

The hen on Sam's lap swelled rapidly, each of its spindly legs stretched out into something rather shapely, and in a matter of seconds, Sam found herself looking down into a pair of big green eyes. The young woman beamed up at her.

"You did it!" shouted the young woman, and pulled Sam by the neck to plant a kiss on her cheek. "Sorry for shitting on you."

"Oh, t-thats fine," Sam stammered. "But it wasn't—"

At that moment, Henry shouted down from the roof line.

"Samantha! I believe we've done it after all."

He stood proudly on his hind legs, with his front paws on his hips, surveying the chickens-turned-humans gathered in front of the house. Many of them were looking with bewilderment at their new hands and shuffling their new feet.

Sam nodded. "Yes I think you're right, Henry, but what are you doing up there?"

"Had to come up through the chimney, my dear. It's awfully hard to turn door knobs when you're this size. It seems the only thing our little performance was missing was patience. A body needs time to read the blueprints, if you will, before making such radical changes."

"Seems fair," said Sam.

"There was a delay when I turned them as well," said the young woman. "Oh sorry, I suppose I'm crushing you now, aren't I?"

"A little," Sam smiled.

The young woman rose, and Sam took stock of the others. The crowd whooped and laughed happily. Tears of joy strewn down many faces. They exchanged hugs and handshakes amongst themselves, and with Sam. A few even nodded their approval to the talking squirrel on the roof. Children darted this way and that, squealing and flapping their arms as if they were still chickens. A head count was suggested to be sure everyone was turned, and it was agreed they would gather everyone by the lake to do so. Some of the chickens, it seemed, were always chickens, as a handful of the feathery creatures continued to strut about.

The young woman stole Sam into the quiet of her home. Henry dropped back down through the chimney to join them, churning up a small ash cloud when he landed. His gray fur was tinged with black soot. The woman shot him a curious look at first, but quickly shrugged away any apprehension.

"Thank you both *soo* much," she said. "I thought I was going to be stuck as a chicken forever. And it was all my own fault too. If I had more time with my grandfather, perhaps I would have known better."

Sam placed a comforting hand on her shoulder. "It's okay. Everything is back to normal now, I think. So it *was* you who changed everyone?"

The young woman nodded sadly. "Yes. This was my grandfather's house, and that was his spell book on the table. I didn't even know I could use magic until about two years ago, when I came to visit for the summer. My grandfather offered to teach me, but he passed away a few months later. Clearly, I didn't learn enough. I'm Fiona, by the way."

"It's nice to meet you Fiona. My name's Sam. I'm sorry to hear about your grandfather, and I can understand the magic thing. A little. I definitely wouldn't have been able to help you on my own. Henry here deserves all the credit."

Henry bowed his head. "My dear Samantha is too kind. I merely nudged her in the right direction."

"In any case, the problem is resolved," said Fiona. "I never should have toyed with such a spell in the first place."

"Chin up, Fiona. I dare say your grandfather would be quite amused. No small feat, that!"

"But I turned myself into a chicken! With no voice to change myself back."

Henry chuckled. "A minor technicality. Still an impressive feat, to turn an entire village into chickens. May I ask *why* you wanted to do such a thing in the first place?"

"I didn't *want* to turn the village into chickens. There was a— Oh no!"

"What is it?" Sam asked.

"A monster! In the village. It showed up one day, and I ran back here to look for a spell. I found the chicken spell, and I thought I could memorize it. I have a very good memory, you see. But I made the mistake of reading it out loud, which I guess wouldn't have affected the end result anyhow. I'd just have turned into a chicken at the coffee shop instead of here."

"What kind of monster?" asked Sam. She gasped. "Luke is out there!"

A scream from the middle of the village split the air, followed quickly by dozens more.

"It's still here..." said Fiona.

Sam gulped.

Chapter Twenty-Eight

With Henry on her shoulder, Sam rushed through the village, toward the screams of terror and through the throngs of panicked villagers running the opposite way. She had zero desire to face or even see a monster, Cosmo had been plenty, but the screams, the beach, and Luke were all in the same direction. Luke would be helpless. Even Jasper would be limited in his ability to defend him, if the mule so wished, since he was tied to a tree.

When she turned onto the main street, she saw it.

Her jaw dropped.

A black bear stood on its hind legs in front of the coffee shop, yet only the short black fur, and the size of its body resembled that of a bear. The head was of an entirely different creature. Its large face was gaunt and hairless, with pale wrinkled skin. It had a pair of curved goat horns, pointy ears, and a glamorous mane of thick red hair that fell from its scalp to its chest. Several locks of its hair were braided and adorned with...

Sam squinted.

Pink ribbons?

Lengths of pink ribbon were indeed tied in pretty bows near the tips of the creature's rope braids. The braids *jingled* when they swayed. Lia hadn't turned into a monster, had she?

The creature tried to grab one of the villagers as he fled the coffee shop, but the sight of the creature's deadly claws spurred the young man into a breakneck pace. He escaped. The creature *sighed*.

The creature opened its mouth, revealing two rows of predatory fangs that made Sam shudder.

"Es tut mir Leid!" it yelled. The thing spoke German, just like the housekeeper at the Wooden Hearth, but the voice was distinctly feminine. "Bitte nicht rennen! Ich bin ein Freund!"

"What the hell is it saying??" screamed a bald headed man.

"It's casting a spell!" screamed another through his bushy orange beard. "A curse! A curse! Another curse!"

A blond woman tripped over her own dress, rose to her knees, threw her arms up to the sky and screeched, "It's going to kill us all!!! The end times are upon us!!"

Sam gave the creature a wide berth, and crept towards the lake, though she didn't dare take her eyes away from it. The creature noticed her, and raised a claw in her direction.

Shit.

"Entschuldigung!" shouted the creature.

Wait a second. Sam paused. She had seen a creature like that before, long ago when she was maybe six years old. She was with her parents visiting her grandmother in Austria. Wasn't there a tradition in Austria at the beginning of December that involved locals dressing up in monstrous costumes as a way of scaring away evil winter spirits? Yes. The creatures were called Perchten in plural, or Percht, in the singular. They roamed about their towns and cities, jangling bells and chasing and whipping people through a haze of smoke and spooky red lighting. At six, she had been terrified, even though her grandmother insisted the creatures weren't real. This time, at twenty-eight, she asked the squirrel on her shoulder to tell her the same thing. He did not.

"Oh she's quite real, I'd say," chuckled the squirrel, clearly not concerned.

Sam reached inside for the same courage. The Percht didn't seem to be hurting anyone, despite its capable size and appearance. She didn't run when the creature addressed her again, instead she greeted her in German. The Percht gasped, again displaying its terrifying teeth.

"Very good Samantha!" said Henry. "You can speak Grimmish. Impressive. Not an easy language."

"I'm not really all that good at it," she admitted.

"Then allow me to begin the peace talks."

The squirrel hopped from her shoulder and bounced confidently towards the creature and began weaving some German, or Grimmish, of his own.

"Gestatten Sie mir, Sie nun ordnungsgemäss in Two Goats willkommen zu heissen, mein lieber Percht."

Henry stopped and extended a paw to the creature, and the creature did not reach down and squish him. Rather, it lowered itself and offered a finger for the squirrel to shake. It *giggled* when Henry obliged. The sight was ridiculous. The two exchanged several more volleys of German words before Henry guided the creature toward Sam. She noticed then that the jingling sound came from tiny silver bells fastened to the bows in its hair.

Henry introduced the creature as "Heidi".

"Hallo!" said Heidi, offering a clawed hand to her. With a deep breath, Sam took the hand and engaged in a surprisingly gentle handshake. The fur made her hand quite soft, and Heidi was careful with her claws.

For a moment, Sam was speechless, staring dumbstruck into the creature's cornflower blue eyes. Heidi waited patiently for her reply, but it was not until Henry returned to her shoulder that her mouth started working again.

"Hi," she answered in a small voice, and then cleared her throat to say, "Hallo!"

Heidi curled her frightening mouth into a smile, and bowed her horned head.

"You see," said Henry, "Despite appearances, she's really quite friendly."

"She's a Percht," she and Henry said at the same time.

"Well now," Henry bowed. "You are full of surprises, Samantha. As you may have gathered from all the screaming and running in opposite directions, knowledge of the Perchten is rather limited in the more remote Arthurian speaking regions."

"There are traditions in Austria and Germany that involve dressing up as these creatures. But I guess you've probably never heard of those places, eh?"

"I have not," said Henry, "but perhaps Heidi has. She's a long way from home, just like you. Her kind are more commonly spotted in the mountain towns and villages of the Greytooth region, or the Fangs, as some might say."

Sam eyed the smiling Heidi's own fangs. "Seems appropriate."

Heidi spoke again, and Henry responded, smiling. Heidi laughed.

"What?" asked Sam, wishing her German wasn't so rusty.

"She wanted to know why you bare the image of a chili pepper on your chest. She asks if it is a local tradition to venerate vegetables in such a way. I told her she's not the only peculiar tourist in Three Goats today."

"Oh. Yes." She said, looking down. Her coat was open, revealing the shirt she had been wearing for too many days in a row. She smiled at Heidi. "It's my favorite band actually. They're musicians."

"What?" cried Henry. "No, that can't be true. There are singing vegetables in your world?" He relayed this misinterpretation to Heidi, whose toothy jaw dropped and eyes bulged.

Sam sighed. A talking squirrel and a Percht were acting as if they weren't the oddest things in the street at the moment.

"No," she said. "They are just people, human people, who play music and call themselves the Red Hot Chili Peppers." She did her best to repeat this to Heidi, who responded with an understanding "Ah."

"Why would they do that?" asked Henry.

"I don't know, Henry. You can call yourself whatever you want when you play good music. Can we just get back to this Percht situation, please?"

"Ahem," came a cough from behind them.

It was Fiona, peeking out around the corner of a building. Heidi greeted her with a wave. Fiona offered a timid wave back.

"Is... Is it safe?" she asked.

"Of course!" said Henry, waving her over. "It always was. Come out here."

Fiona approached with caution, smiling meekly at the Percht. Sam shrugged when the girl looked to her for assurance.

"Hallo!" said Heidi.

"Hello," Fiona managed.

Henry nodded approvingly. "Excellent. Not so bad, is she, my dear?"

"I guess not."

Heidi said something to Henry, and he replied.

"What language is that?" asked Fiona.

"Heidi here speaks Grimmish," Henry explained, "It's a language spoken most frequently in the Fangs and the Toller Tal. She wishes to learn Arthurian, but until today, couldn't find anyone who spoke both languages. And here in these little out of the way villages, where people who know of her race are few and far between..." He made a sweeping gesture to highlight the empty streets, "things are even worse for her."

Suddenly, Sam was saddened by her initial reaction to the creature.

"So is everyone who speaks Grimmish one of these creatures?" asked Fiona.

"No, not everyone," said Henry. "There are likely as many human settlements of Grimmish speakers as there are of Arthurian speakers. The current name of the language was actually changed some time ago to honor a pair of traveling journalists who elevated the written form of it. They were humans. The Perchten live mainly in the mountains in villages of their own. There was a time when they kept entirely to themselves, only coming down from the mountains to stock up on supplies before winter, but these days they can often be found living in human settlements as well."

Sam scratched her chin. The Perchten costumes were donned at the beginning of winter in Austria. Perhaps there was a connection between the Perchten here and the Perchten in her world.

"Why would you choose to come here? To risk, well, being treated like a monster?" she asked Heidi directly, momentarily forgetting that she wouldn't be understood. *I really have to stop doing that.* She repeated the question in her language.

Heidi smiled and held up a finger to signal patience, and then slipped free from a pair of straps that secured a pack to her back. It was a bit of a surprise, as the straps blended perfectly with her black fur. From the pack, Heidi produced a book. She flipped it open to a page marked with a crow feather, and held it up for everyone to see.

Sam nodded. "Ahh!"

"Einhorn!" said Heidi.

"A unicorn," repeated Sam. Her thoughts returned to Luke. "I need to find a unicorn as well."

"Ah, see," Henry smiled, "just a harmless tourist. I believe you owe this lady an apology, Fiona. I know you have your physical differences, but I doubt there is a culture in the world that classifies being turned into a chicken as anything but rude."

"You're right. Tell her I'm sorry, please. And if she must eat someone, let it be me."

Henry frowned, but repeated the message.

Heidi laughed and answered.

Henry coughed. A grin pulled at the corner of his mouth. "Um. She says thank you, and um... that you have lovely eyes and are in general quite pretty but she doesn't... er, swing that way. She has some friends that do, however, if you are interested."

Sam burst out laughing.

Fiona's eyes narrowed, and then bulged in understanding. She blushed.

"Yes," said Henry, "If I didn't know any better I'd assume she'd been hanging around with that Luke of yours, Samantha. I dare not repeat the things he said he'd be willing to do for a bagel during our first morning together."

"I think I could guess."

Heidi continued.

"She says she's kidding, and that at any rate, she is a vegetarian. She says she left her home for new experiences. Living as a chicken for a few days was certainly a new experience, and one that she will never forget. She bares no grudges. Instead, she thanks you. Hmm? Ah, yes. Since you offered to feed her, she says a hot bowl of vegetable soup to wash the taste of ants from her mouth would be greatly appreciated, but she's not holding you to it."

Fiona bobbed her head. "Absolutely. I think that's a great idea. Come, the three of you, back to my place. There's plenty of carrots and beans out back, and if you're interested, my grandfather left a few bottles of wine in the cellar. Then, if you'd like, we can track down some unicorns. They can be pretty tricky to find during the day, but just around sunset I know a spot where a few gather regularly."

"That sounds great," said Sam. "I'm starving, but... could I get one of you to give me a hand first? My friend is laying down by the lake, and he's quite heavy. I'd hate to leave him outside all day while I eat soup and drink wine. It'd be a bit rude, I think."

"Of course. Show us the way," said Fiona.

Jasper, though frightened at first, was thrilled to have Heidi accompany them to Fiona's home. The Percht, as big and as strong as a black bear, easily hoisted Luke over her furry shoulder, and relieved the mule of its burden. Apparently, she believed the mule deserved a rest, and Jasper did not argue.

The cellar beneath Fiona's home was at least twice the size of the main level, with a dirt floor and messily finished brick walls. Four tall storage shelves spanned the length of the room, dividing the space into three aisles. Each shelf was filled, front to back, with more than *a few* wine bottles. Martin Swyft, Fiona's grandfather, had lived a long life, and had amassed a diverse collection of wines from every corner of the world. Some were made from plants Sam had never heard of, while many more were made in *places* she had never heard of. Given enough time, a fair bit of geography could be learned in Martin's cellar. There were even bottles from the Tolles Tal, *Beschwipst,* they were labeled, and Heidi was quick to give the brand a thumbs up. They selected two bottles of Heidi's suggestion to wash down their soup.

The soup was prepared in a cauldron over a fire in the hearth, with potatoes, carrots, and a sprinkling of basil. Sam hadn't realized just how hungry she was until she was devouring her third bowl of the stuff.

Then she sat on Fiona's bed next to Luke, and sipped wine while listening to Henry act as a translator between Fiona and Heidi. Fiona was a generous host, quick to surrender her bed to Luke for as long he needed it, though she apologized profusely for not having any clean sheets prepared, and reminded Sam that she had been sleeping in the bed as a chicken for at least a week.

"I don't think he'll mind," Sam had assured her.

Heidi was curious as to how the village came to be known as Three Goats. Fiona told Henry, who told Heidi, the story of a hunter who built a small cabin on the lake in the Torpid Valley, long before anyone else. He lived for many blissful years in the valley, hunting and fishing to feed himself, and traveling over the mountains to Jasmine, the village where Sam had procured her mule, when he needed extra supplies. But eventually the hunter grew old and tired of making the trek over the mountains to Jasmine. On one of his shopping trips, he decided he wouldn't make the trip back. He traded the key to his cabin to a young family in exchange for three goats. The deal was remembered as the family attracted other families to the valley, and everyone agreed it was a fitting name for a budding village.

Heidi in turn spoke of her own home, Nefrew, a town of rock and timber houses nestled high in the Greytooth Mountains. It snowed often, as it was quite cold, but the Perchten were built for such weather, what with all the fur. The town also boasted of several hot springs that attracted many human visitors, and a large castle made of ice higher up in the mountains, above the clouds, where a giant named Hymir lived.

As amazed by talk of giants and ice castles as Sam was, she expected her description of things such as cell phones and televisions to be just as intriguing to the others, but her expectations fell short. Radio was king there, it seemed, radio plays and live performances. They had never developed television or computers. Maybe the resources didn't exist. Either way, they seemed happy without those things. It didn't sound so bad to her either.

"Verdammt!" muttered the Percht, clearly louder than she intended.

Everyone turned to Heidi, who had just spilled her glass of wine. She was trying to mop it up with her furry forearm when she noticed that she was now the center of attention.

She lowered her head and said, "Entschuldigung." After a thought, she added, "Sorry. Excuse me."

Fiona laughed and took her by the hand to stop her cleaning. "Please. It's no problem. You're not the first to spill wine in this house, I assure you. And look! There's chicken shit everywhere. I'll take care of the cleaning tomorrow. You just enjoy yourself. I have about a week of atrocious hospitality to make up for. Ah, but look at the time! We should head out. Why don't I go down and fetch a few more bottles for the road."

Sam was about to ask Heidi for help getting Luke onto the mule, when Henry stopped her.

"That won't be necessary, Samantha. A pail of water will be easier to carry than a grown man."

"What do you mean?"

"We merely need to convince a unicorn to drink from a pail of water, and bring the leftovers back to Luke."

"Really?"

"Yes. They'll drink some of your water, all of it actually, if you don't bring enough. So make it a decent sized pail, and make sure it's full. Their saliva will mix into the remaining water and there you'll have a potent healing remedy."

"I assumed it would have something to do with the horn. So they just slobber into a bucket of water? That's it? That's disgusting."

"Agreed. But neither of us will be the ones to have to drink it." He smiled.

Fiona returned from the cellar with three full bottles of wine, passed them around, and ushered everyone out of the house. Sam shook her head incredulously, and reluctantly accepted the additional bottle. She hadn't yet finished the first, and knew how she would feel in the morning if she were to drink both of them. It was a wiser move to just continue nursing the first bottle, and leave the new bottle behind. Maybe she'd share it with Luke when he returned from the dead. Instead of wine, she took with her a wooden pail filled with tap water.

Fiona led them into the forest and along a narrow footpath. The path was steep, but short. Soon they emerged at the top of a grassy knoll, overlooking a small clearing split in two by a babbling brook. The sun was on its way to bed behind the mountains ahead of them, and the sky was beginning its evening light show.

"Oh my," Sam gasped. She took another swig of wine. "Unicorns and sunsets, really? So romantic."

"Spectacular viewing spot, isn't it?" smiled Fiona. "I come here often. It won't be long now. Let's sit."

They sat, and they drank. Two humans, a Percht, and a squirrel. Even Henry had a few capfuls. There could have been five humans, but three people who made the trip up to the hill after them decided to turn back when Heidi saluted them with her bottle. She sighed and shook her horned head, and tipped the bottle back to drown her sorrows.

Sam gave her a pat on the back, and the Percht looked to Sam, bells jingling in her hair as she did so. She smiled her frightening smile in return.

When the sun had dipped almost completely behind the mountains, and the sky was lit aflame, a horse as white as snow stepped out of the forest below them and lowered its head to drink from the brook. Its *horned* head. They watched in silence for several moments as the unicorn drank and tossed carefree glances their way. The sheen of its coat seemed to absorb the last rays of sunlight, for as the light waned and the shadows grew, the unicorn remained illuminated. A bright aura pushed back the shadows around it.

Sam and Heidi exchanged looks, their eyes bright with wine and wonder.

"Ah," said Henry. "As fine a beast as ever."

"It's beautiful," Sam agreed.

Heidi produced a small wooden box with a metal cylinder protruding from it. It looked an awful lot like a camera, and when the Percht raised it to her face with the cylinder pointing towards the unicorn, Sam heard the click, and saw the flash, and knew her first impression was correct. The unicorn looked up, swallowed, and dipped its head for another drink.

Fiona chuckled at Heidi's gasp as another unicorn joined the first at the brook. And then another. Finally, a unicorn half the size of the others, with just a tiny stub of a horn, trotted out into the clearing.

The new unicorns glanced up at their audience, but like the first, weren't bothered by their presence. They were unfazed even when Fiona rose to her feet.

"Come on," she said, taking a wide eyed and gape mouthed Heidi by the wrist. She passed Heidi a bundle of carrots and led her down the hill. Sam and Henry watched in awe.

The unicorns either saw Heidi in a different light then the rest of the Torpid Valley residents, or they only saw the bundle of carrots the Percht had to offer them. Whichever it was, the enormous toothy grin on Heidi's face was plain to see even from the hilltop.

Sam took a picture with the camera Heidi left behind, then made her way down the hill with her bucket of water.

CHAPTER TWENTY-NINE

Three of the unicorns, two of the adults and the foal, were occupied by the Percht and her carrots. The remaining unicorn watched Sam's approach intently.

She felt suddenly naked. She hadn't brought anything to feed it, yet Fiona had thought of her as well. The young sorceress stepped up beside her and discreetly pressed an apple into her free hand.

"You're amazing," said Sam.

"I know," said Fiona, smiling.

The unicorn stood patiently before her, its pale coat shimmering, its tail happily flopping.

Sam swallowed. Her heart raced. This was the moment where the unicorn would bless her bucket of water and Luke would live, or the unicorn wouldn't, and Luke would die. Those thoughts felt foolish when her eyes met those of the unicorn. They were purple and soothing, like orbs of lavender, and seemed to say that everything would be alright.

It's a trifling thing, for me to slobber into your bucket, came a thought that may or may not have been her own.

And then she felt its hot breath on her cheek. It was curious about the squirrel on her shoulder, and sniffed and poked at him with its nose.

"Stop that now," barked Henry. "That tickles. Enough."

The unicorn drew back, and looked again at Sam. She held up the apple.

The unicorn sniffed it, and took a gentle nibble. It took several of these test bites while Sam's hand acted as a dinner plate, before snatching the whole apple into its mouth and crunching it into oblivion. After, it bowed its head and snorted at the bucket. She offered the water, and it drank, and drank, and drank, until the bucket was empty.

"Oh my," said Sam. "Thirsty girl, you are."

It was a good thing the meeting took place at a brook. A few short steps was all it took to refill the bucket. It was a wonder that the unicorn bothered drinking from it at all.

"I believe this one is a male, actually," Henry corrected, "judging by the dangly-"

"Don't ruin the moment."

"Ah, yes. Sorry. I suppose it is I who has spent too much time with Luke."

Sam laughed, "I'm sure he'd be proud to have corrupted a squirrel."

She offered the unicorn another drink and it accepted, though this time it only vacuumed up three quarters of the bucket.

"Do you think this is enough?" she asked Henry.

"Just a sip will be all he needs, my dear."

"Thank you, sir unicorn," she said, bowing politely, "for your, um, blessing."

Don't mention it, came another questionable thought in her mind, and the unicorn cantered over to the brook and continued drinking.

She squished her lips together and scrutinized the unicorn for a moment. She shook her head.

Heidi and Fiona were engaged in a language lesson, each pointing out a part of the unicorn and labeling it in their respective languages. Sam heard her say that "the ear" was "das Ohr, " and "the nose" was "die Nase" before she interrupted the lesson.

"I think I'll head back to the house now, if that's okay," she said. "The sooner I give this to Luke the better. But you guys don't have to leave. Enjoy the unicorns, please. I can find my way back."

Fiona smirked, "Want some alone time with him, do you?"

"I'm just going to revive him, that's *all*," she insisted. "You're not related to Sophie, are you?"

"I don't know any Sophie's. But alright. We'll be along shortly. And we'll knock first," she winked.

Sam flushed. "Henry is going to be with me anyhow. You're terrible."

"I know. See you soon, and good luck."

The narrow forest path was decidedly more malicious in the absence of light. She was glad for Henry's company. It felt as if every dark bush or branch had something nefarious in mind for her. The exposed roots on the ground did more than threaten. Several times the roots attacked, grabbing her feet and tossing her forward into an awkward stumble. But each time she caught herself before she fell, and the forest did not win. She arrived at

Fiona's house without spilling a drop of the precious medicine in her bucket.

Luke was still there in the bed where she left him, illuminated by the dim glow from the still red coals in the fireplace. She chose not to flick on the light switch, instead she found and lit a candle to place by his bedside table. She kissed his forehead and was relieved to feel that he was still warm. He was alive. Since it would be pretty hard to swallow anything while laying on his back, she propped him up in a semi-seated position with a pillow behind his back and head against the headboard.

"Do I need to do anything special?" she asked the squirrel, who had taken a seat at the foot of the bed. "Any chants or magic words?"

Henry bobbed his head from side to side, thoughtfully. "No, no magic words so far as the water goes, at least. Perhaps use a cloth at first, dab some on his face and neck, especially around that bite."

She found a face cloth in a closet in the bathroom and did so. She looked at Henry, who nodded.

"That should do," he said, "Now perhaps soak the cloth again and leave it on his forehead."

"Are you just making this up as you go, Henry?"

"Yes," he admitted. "I only know that people usually drink it. It needs to be absorbed into his system in some way, but as he is not conscious, getting the boy to drink might be a bit troublesome."

"This is where a doctor and an IV might come in handy," she said.

"You're probably right. Did we pass any hospitals or doctor's offices out there in the village?"

"Eh, nothing obvious, no. I guess this will have to do."

"I'm sure it will be fine, my dear. Now, for the next step, you're going to need a little faith. You're going to have to bring him out of his stasis."

"What? How do I do that?"

"The same way you placed him into it, Samantha."

She shook her head. "That's crazy. I really didn't do anything. It must have been Lia."

The squirrel smiled. "You did *something*, my dear. Surely you believe by now that you can use magic."

"Sure, I guess. I used it to turn the chickens back. But I had a spell book, and you reading it to me. I don't know a thing about magic. I wouldn't even have known what a stasis was."

"Let's take a trip back, shall we? Back to the library. What do you remember about our escape? What interaction did you have with Luke *before* we exited the building? He was already in his stasis by the time we collected ourselves in that alley."

She searched her memory, and was slightly embarrassed by what she found there. She had told Luke she was a princess, and she *commanded* him to live several times. Then she kissed him.

"That was it," she cried.

"Hmm? I can't read thoughts, Samantha."

"Sorry. Um, well I kissed him, like you did with than glass acorn... and I told him that he had to live. And there *was* a feeling, a tingling sensation, like there was with the chickens and the spell book, and... but there was too much happening. It slipped from my mind entirely until now. But, that's all I did. I'm sure I didn't say any magic words."

"Words aren't always necessary. Think, for example, of how you look at someone. Even if you don't speak the same language, you can tell that person without saying a single word, that you are happy, or angry, or sad, or that you want to tear their clothes off."

Sam raised her eyebrows.

Henry continued, "Words are just another way of getting your point across. At the core of it, all words are completely meaningless sounds. It's the feelings or ideas that you associate with the words you speak and hear that give them meaning. Any combination of words would have put Luke in a stasis, or no words at all, because it was your will that Luke live. You wanted him to live long enough for you to fix him, so you made it so, by pausing his life before it could end. You wanted it, and you expressed it rather deeply. I believe now the stasis would have lasted as long as you wanted him to live. Lia operates her invisible barriers on a similar principal. Raw emotion. It can be mastered with practice."

Sam nodded, though still not entirely sure of everything.

"So what do I do now?" she asked.

"You'll figure it out," he smiled. "I'll just make myself cozy over by the fire."

Sam frowned, and sighed. "Okay. Right. Well, let's see."

She breathed into her hand to smell her breath. Not exactly winter fresh. She thought to brush her teeth, because, of course, she carried a tube of paste and a toothbrush in her tote bag, but she settled for a stick of gum instead. Then she fixed her hair, which was a bit greasy, but there was nothing she could do about that. When she felt she was reasonably presentable, she leaned over and pressed her lips to Luke's.

There was nothing, just the pleasant feeling of kissing him sprinkled with a tinge of awkwardness from not being kissed back. It felt very much like kissing a dead thing, she assumed, but his lips were still warm. This was *not* necrophilia.

She pulled back and watched for movement. Nothing. She traced the purple swelling around his eye lightly with her finger, and then the blue veins on his neck. Her lips pouted. Her own eyes became watery.

She grabbed his cheeks and chin and kissed him again, harder, pressing her lips to his with more need. Perhaps that was the way. She really *did* need him. She needed him to wake up, to not die, to wake up and return her kiss. She needed him to live and see the unicorns with her. They had to find a way home. Together.

Sadness washed over her while she kissed him, like waves eroding a shoreline, her hope began to fade, and the tears in her eyes began to stream down her cheeks. Nothing was happening. She stopped kissing him. What was the point of all this? Why was nothing happening? She grabbed his shoulders and shook him.

"Wake up you idiot! Enough screwing around. Come on."

She smacked his chest, then gasped. What was she doing? He'd been smacked around enough. Her cheeks flushed.

She kissed him again.

The coals in the fire, already dim, blinked out entirely. The candle on the bedside table flickered.

And there it was. The tingling. It rose from the tips of her toes, through her legs, her chest, her lips, and into his. She shivered. She felt *him* shiver.

She pulled away. Life flickered in his face, a small twitch of his eye lids.

His chest rose, fell, and rose again. He was breathing.

His eyes opened lazily.

"Luke!!"

He smiled, heavy on the right side of his mouth, like he often did.

He was alive, but his eyes fell shut and he made no further movement, save for the gentle rise and fall of his chest.

"Okay," she said, mostly to herself. "Now he should be able to drink the water."

Henry gave her a nod of approval from the fireplace.

She gasped when she saw the blue lines creeping further from the bite wound on his neck, fast enough for her to notice immediately. She took a deep breath. She needed to stay calm. Everything was fine. She had the water.

She reached for the bucket, but thought better of it. Rather than come this far only to drown him, she found a more manageable cup to dip with. While holding his mouth open with her thumb, she poured a small amount onto his tongue. After many heart beats, he swallowed. She repeated this process until the cup was empty, and washed his face again with the cloth. Would one cup be enough?

Contrary to his earlier comment about not being able to read minds, Henry rejoined her at the foot of the bed and said, "That's plenty. You've done all you can. Just give the boy some time."

"Thanks Henry."

She turned away. Out of sight, out of mind, or so she hoped. It proved impossible to think of anything else while waiting to see if Luke would awaken. Not even when Henry found the radio, tuned to a station playing a sort of smooth jazz music could she relax. It was not until later, when Fiona and Heidi had returned, and they were sitting by the fire listening to Henry's retelling of the story of his and Luke's meeting, in Arthurian and Grimmish languages, that she began to feel at ease. Giving in to the second bottle of wine might also have played a role in that.

The Master of Morningwood, she smiled to herself when Henry brought up Luke's ridiculous new title. *Of course.* She couldn't wait to hear him proclaim that to her some morning with a towel around his waist.

It was hard to imagine Heidi being frightened of anything, but when Henry got to the part where he and Luke were being chased by a deathwing, she gasped, a clawed hand pressed to her chest dramatically.

Sam shook her head. Her face flushed with this reminder that while she was nursing a hangover the morning after a night of drinking wine with Sophie and Gerald, Luke was running from flying dinosaurs. And what was she doing now? While Luke lay in bed recovering from a zombie witch attack, she was drinking wine again. She took another sip, hiding her embarrassment behind the bottle.

"Ah, but our dear boy refused to stay still for long," Henry went on, "so adamant was he that he return home as soon as possible, lest his Samantha lose interest in him. If only he had known she was already here, he might have avoided a bit of trouble."

"That sounds so romantic," swooned Fiona.

Heidi clutched her chest where her heart was when Henry repeated the last story segment to her, but this time instead of gasping in fright, she let out an embarrassing *awww* sound.

Sam rolled her eyes. It was kind of sweet, in a weird way. She smiled, and allowed some honesty into her thoughts. Luke wouldn't have wanted their roles reversed. He would have been furious had Cosmo bit her instead of him, and likely both of them would have gotten killed in that scenario. She was the magic one, apparently. Their savior. *The Unicorn Whisperer.* They would make quite the pair, he and her. The Unicorn Whisperer and the Master of Morningwood.

She burst out laughing, raising the curious eyebrows of the others around her.

"Sorry," she said, blushing, and waggled the wine bottle. Perhaps she should slow down.

Chapter Thirty

T he room was dark, save for the tiny flame next to the bed,
struggling to stay alive above a puddle of melted wax.
Luke knuckled the sleep dust from his eyes with his free hand.

His other arm was imprisoned beneath Sam's warm shoulder. One of her arms was slung across his stomach, her head on his chest. Her hair cushioned his chin and teased his senses. Her scent mixed with the wine in the air. She'd been drinking. Hopefully in celebration, not in mourning.

He smiled. The rhythm of her breathing was soothing, almost too soothing, but he fought to keep his eyes open. He wasn't about to let himself slip from consciousness again.

He moved his head slowly, as not to disturb her.

Another sight reloaded his smile. Henry was curled up between his feet, wrapped up in his own bushy tail.

A woman he did not know, another brunette, younger than Sam, in old fashioned clothing like so many in this strange world, was snoring softly on her back next to the fireplace, atop a pile of clothes.

His eyes bulged and then squinted when they fell on another furry creature, much larger than Henry, much bigger than Sam even. The creature was sleeping in the corner of the room atop a traveler's bedroll. His heart beat faster at the sight of it, for it was a creature of nightmares, with devil's horns and long sharp claws. Yet it had been in the room before he woke up, and Sam and the others were able to sleep in its presence. If it wanted to kill them, they'd already be dead. His heart relaxed, slightly.

He wanted to get up, to eat something and to stretch the stiffness out of his legs. But he did not, *absolutely* did not, want to disturb the sleeping beauty on his chest.

So he lay there and starved and suffered in bliss, until sometime after the candle flame drowned and floated away in a gray wisp, when sleep took him back.

Chapter Thirty-One

S am's mouth was dry and pasty when she woke. Her head was throbbing.

Stupid wine, she thought as she drug herself out of bed. She kept her eyes narrowed, not yet ready to embrace even the filtered power of the morning sun as it shone through the curtained windows. Nor did her ears appreciate the happy chirping of the chickadees outside. It may as well have been *Metallica* rehearsing in the garden. Her thirst urged her towards the closest water source, the pail next to the bed, blessed with unicorn slobber. At that moment, she didn't care how disgusting the idea of it was. She grabbed the pail and tipped it back, careful not to spill any as she drank.

It didn't taste like slobber. Just boring old room temperature water. But it didn't *feel* like water. From the second it touched her lips, the familiar tingling sensation she had come to associate with magic rippled through her. It tickled down her neck and into her stomach where it swirled around and around, before spreading down her legs to the tips of her toes, washing away the muscle aches and the soreness in her feet. It traveled outward, through her arms and fingers, and finally exploded inside her head as if it had found the place that troubled her the most, and her headache was gone. Vanished. She felt brand new.

That water really does work.

With renewed hope in the process, she looked to Luke. He was still out, but something was different about his face. There was a smile there, and Sam found it to be an infectious one. Then she saw something else that was different about him, and her smile broke into a chuckle. The Master of Morningwood was proving himself worthy of the title.

She took this as indisputable evidence that he was alive and well, but she wanted him to wake on his own. As quietly as possible, she crept away from the bed.

Fiona was snoring peacefully by the fireplace, but Heidi's sleeping mat was empty, and Henry was nowhere to be seen either. The Percht's backpack was by her mat, so she likely hadn't gone far.

Now what trouble is that pair getting into?

She received her answer after working up the fortitude to pull back the curtains by the front door. Heidi, with the chattering squirrel perched on her shoulder, was coming up the stone path to the doorway with a tray of steaming coffee mugs in her clawed hands. Sam opened the door to meet them on the path.

"Oh my goodness," she said. "You're a dream. Thank you so much. But... but how??"

"It was a team effort," beamed Henry.

"Nobody at the coffee shop was bothered this time?"

"Well, there was a *bit* of screaming," he admitted. "But it all worked out in the end. I must confess, our success can largely be attributed to the innocence of children."

"Oh?"

"Indeed. It was a little girl, whom you may well remember, that stilled the hearts of the cowardly old waitresses. She was not at all frightened of Heidi. In fact, she gave our Percht a fright by approaching so quickly, only to marvel over the braids in her hair."

Sam smiled. "Lia. So they've made it?"

Henry nodded. "They have. Though we did not make the acquaintance of Sophie or Gerald this morning. They arrived late last night in poor condition, the girl claimed. She will try to rouse them for a breakfast meeting a little later. I hope I was not being too presumptuous when I accepted her offer?"

"Not at all, Henry. I'm up and about, and I'm sure once Fiona gets a whiff of this coffee she'll be up too. Um, Danke, Heidi."

Heidi smiled her toothy smile and offered Sam one of the precious mugs on her tray. The more Sam interacted with the Percht, the less frightening she became. Her smile always seemed to touch her big blue eyes.

"There's an extra here for Luke, should he awaken," said Henry. "I noticed, at least, that parts of him were already awake this morning."

Sam laughed, "Yes. I noticed that too. I think he's going to be fine."

"I hope so," came a dry voice from behind.

Sam turned to see Luke leaning against the door frame. It was not a "cool guy leaning against the record player" kind of pose, like he might have hoped, but more of a "There's no way I can stand up without this wall" kind of pose. His body was twisted awkwardly in a poor attempt to hide the fact that at least part of him was having no difficulty in staying upright.

She bowed theatrically, "Welcome back to the land of the living, oh great Master of Morningwood."

This added some color to Luke's pale cheeks. "You've heard that, have you?" he rasped.

"You really must start taking better care of yourself, my boy," said Henry.

She saw him look not at Henry on Heidi's shoulder, but directly at Heidi, and she watched for an expression of terror to chase the smile from his face. But instead his features brightened.

"Yes please," he said, nodding to Heidi and her coffee tray.

Heidi handed him a coffee, and the two of them exchanged friendly nods.

"She doesn't bother you?" Sam asked.

"Should she?"

Sam chuckled. "Well. No, she shouldn't actually, but you haven't met before, and she's not exactly *human*. You missed quite the show yesterday when the villagers saw her."

Luke shrugged. "*She* hasn't tried to kill me yet, *and* she brought coffee. Unless this wonderful smelling cup is full of steaming motor oil or poison, I think we're good." He took a sip. "Mmm. Yep. We're good."

She took a sip of her own. "A fair point. Heidi is very sweet. She speaks German, actually. Or Grimmish, as they call it here."

"Ah, right on then." He bowed his head to Heidi, "Danke."

"Gern geschehen!" said the Percht, happily.

"Eh, you lost me there," said Luke.

Henry repeated his response in Grimmish, and Heidi laughed and waved a dismissive claw.

"Alles gut!" said the Percht.

Luke looked thoughtful, "All good?" He gave a thumbs up.

Heidi bobbed her head and returned his thumbs up. "Alles gut."

"Ahh," said Luke, "See? Learning already. But if you don't mind, can we sit down for a bit? I'm gonna flop here pretty quick."

"Yes, of course!" said Sam, "But first..." She took him by the back of his neck and kissed him for as long as she could before his breath chased her away.

Her face soured. "I'm gonna need you to brush your teeth after that coffee," she insisted.

"But I haven't got a toothbrush." He blushed. "Or toothpaste."

"I have a spare brush," she smirked, and hooked her free arm in his to guide him back inside to the dinner table.

The promise and smell of coffee failed to revive Fiona completely, but it did bring her to a state in which she was capable of incoherent mumbling. Fiona's idea of celebrating the return of her human body had apparently been to destroy it. Heidi left a coffee on the floor next to her to allow the aroma time to work its magic. "Thank you," was the interpretation of her grunts.

"So how do *you* feel," Sam asked Luke, "besides excited."

His face turned another shade redder. He took a long sip of his coffee and paused to savor it before answering, "To be honest, I feel like shit, but thanks for asking. Where are we? This doesn't look like the city."

"Correct," said Henry. "This is a lovely little village called Three Goats. Much quieter, isn't it? The birds here *sing*. They don't screech."

To spite the squirrel, the cheery melody of the chickadees was split by the jarring cry of a blue jay. Henry scoffed and shook his head in disgust as one of the blue birds flew by the kitchen window. "I stand corrected."

"Be nice, Henry," said Luke. "How did we get here? And why? Sightseeing?"

"Not exactly," said Sam. "I mean, we did see some unicorns. That was kinda cool I guess."

Luke's eyebrows disappeared into his hairline. "Really?"

"Kinda *epic* actually. You missed out."

Luke tilted his head quizzically.

Sam laughed and explained to him the aftermath of the library incident, the wild wagon ride, and the deal with the unicorn cure.

He frowned, "I'm really sorry, Sam. It must have been a pain in the ass lugging me around. You should have just left me."

Sam shook her head, "Don't be foolish. Jasper did most of the lugging anyways."

"Jasper?"

"He's a mule we rented in Jasmine, I think that's what the village was called anyways, to get us the rest of the way here. He's- Oh no! Be right back."

"Where are you going?" Luke called to her as she rushed out the door.

She didn't remember hitching Jasper to anything the previous evening. He could be anywhere, and rental car companies could be ruthless. It was probably the same with mules.

Luckily, Jasper was not much of a wanderer. She found him behind the house next to a garden bench, happily destroying some ornamental shrubbery. She hugged his furry neck, thanked him for being awesome, and fastened his lead to the bench, leaving him ample freedom to carry on as he was. There was, after all, little more he could do to ruin the bush.

"Sorry about that," she said when she returned to the dinner table. "Had to tie up my mule, you know. Things I'm always saying back in Halifax, right?"

Luke grinned. "Yes. Well you were spending a fair bit of time with a jackass. Never tied him up though."

Sam shot him a look that flattened his smile with worry. "Not yet."

Sam's gaze fell to Heidi, crouched down beside her backpack, organizing her things. It was an enormous pack by human standards. If full, even Gerald or Luke would struggle with it, if they could lift it at all. The Percht finished by fastening her bedroll to the bottom, and placed a pair of books in a front compartment for easy access. When she noticed Sam watching her, she smiled.

"Er, I don't mean to be rude to our coffee delivery lady," said Luke, "but what exactly *is* Heidi? She looks a bit like that Christmas creature. Krampus?"

Heidi gasped.

"Oh! I'm sorry," he said, "I didn't mean to offend you."

Heidi said something in Grimmish.

"Oh dear," said Sam, then explained, "She had a boyfriend named Krampus once. He was a jerk. I'm not sure if the Krampus you're thinking of is technically a Percht or not, but you have the right idea anyway. In our world, there's a pagan tradition where people dress up as these creatures to chase away evil winter spirits."

"I see. Fighting fire with fire, eh?"

"Something like that, I suppose. At any rate, she's not going to stuff you in her backpack and haul you off to eat you like Krampus might."

"Still, she must have had a hard time getting around, not speaking any English. It'd be hard enough to explain yourself to someone who's running and screaming even if you *did* speak their language."

"You're right."

Luke really *was* right. How *did* Heidi get this far without speaking any English? From what she had heard, it was a long way to any German speaking settlements. She must have stopped in other villages before this one, and anyone who didn't know what she was would certainly be asking questions, or running. Otherwise, she should have found someone to teach her the language. Maybe she took some crazy route through the mountains? *Or...*

She asked Heidi how she had gotten to Three Goats.

Heidi's eyes lit up as if she were happy to be asked. She took the books back out of her pack, and brought them to the kitchen table. The book on top was the guidebook she had showed them yesterday. The Percht was grinning when she said that she *cheated,* though Sam needed Henry's help with the translation.

"Cheated?" Luke asked.

Heidi set the guidebook aside, revealing the book beneath. It was bound in leather and had no title. Luke's face mirrored the look Sam gave him, a look that suggested they both suspected the answer even before Heidi's explanation was translated by Henry. It was, in fact, a travel tome. Heidi inherited it from her great grandmother.

Sam squeezed Luke's hand. It was all coming together at once. *What luck!*

The Percht seemed just as thrilled by their reaction to the magical book as they were hearing about it. She pushed the book towards them, but before she removed her clawed hand, she relayed another complicated message to Henry, though once it was in English, the message was simply, "Don't look for too long at any of the pages or you'll disappear." Something that they already knew far too well.

Sam explained to Heidi exactly how they had arrived, tickling a chuckle out of her. Through Henry, Heidi said, "If the book is in any way helpful in finding your way home, you are welcome to use it."

Sam flipped open the book, again invoking the wonderful tingling sensation in her fingers. As with Luke's book, there was a page of Latin gibberish at the beginning. After that began the landscape portraits. She gave Luke another giddy smile.

The first page showed a mountain town with Bavarian style houses, their slate roofs capped with snow. The picture focused on a water fountain. The water within was frosted over with ice, and the cobbles around it looked slippery as well. Sam got chills just looking at it. In the center of the fountain was a statue of a large and hairy creature. A hairy, *horned* creature. A Percht. This alone might have suggested it was where Heidi had come from, or at least near to it, but the picture was also labeled, confirming it was Heidi's hometown, Nefrew. The Percht could open the book and go back home whenever she wanted.

Sam asked how she was able to keep the book in her possession when she traveled. Heidi poked at a black feather sticking out near the back of the book. She explained that the feather served as a bookmark, and so long as the bookmark was in the book, the book would travel with her. Otherwise, she would be in for a long walk.

"Yes," said Luke. "She can say that again."

Every page was labeled, definitely more user friendly than Luke's version. Unfortunately, there was nothing Sam or Luke recognized as existing in their world. Whenever they weren't sure of something, they asked Henry, and he invariably told them he knew of it, which meant no, it would not get them home.

"Damn," Luke cursed, after they had went through the whole book. "I guess we'll need a different one."

Sam sighed, "I guess so."

He put his hand on hers. "But hey, we found each other. That's something. We'll figure it out."

Sam smiled, and kissed him on the cheek even though he tilted his head to accept one on the lips. He gave an exaggerated look of betrayal, to which she responded by pulling her spare tooth brush, still in the package, out of her tote bag and waving it in his face. She was rather amazed that she found it so quickly. The feeling sadly dissolved when it took her much longer to find the toothpaste.

"After you've done that," she said, "Do you want to go for breakfast? Sophie and the others are waiting for us at the café."

"Of course," Luke replied. "I'm starving."

"Always hungry, this one," said the squirrel.

"It's been almost two days, Henry. I *should* be starving."

Fiona groaned. All eyes fell to the young sorceress laying by the fireplace. She had rolled onto her side, facing the dinner table. She offered a lazy wave to Luke.

"Nice to meet you, Luke," she said.

"Likewise. How ya doin'?"

"Fantastic," came the obvious lie. "But I'd be better with a bagel. Two Goats bakes the best bagels."

"Everything's better with bagels," Luke agreed.

"What are we all waiting for?" said Fiona.

Everyone blinked at her.

"Oh right," she said, "Somebody help me up?"

An elderly waitress, wearing her hair short and her pale green skirt long, moaned in a voice that was hushed, but not hushed enough, "Oh Goddess no, not again," and then in a louder, clearly disingenuous voice, said, "Welcome, welcome! Any table you like... dears."

And they really could choose any table they liked. The moment Sam's party entered, everyone in the Two Goats Café decided they would take their meals and coffees to go. Many of them left out the back door and through the garden gate. One customer left behind an untouched bagel, generously buttered, which Luke shamelessly snatched and ate.

"What?" he asked.

Sam shook her head.

"Don't mind them," said Fiona to Heidi, who was the only thing keeping her on her feet. She patted the Percht on the back to make her point understood. The young sorceress had stubbornly refused Sam's offer of unicorn water before they left, though by the time they reached the café, she admitted she had made a mistake.

Luke was less reluctant. In fact, he was eager to try the unicorn water, and was now walking easily on his own, and grunting less since the kinks were out of his legs.

Their timing was perfect. Lia bounded down the stairs, with Sophie and Gerald shambling along like zombies behind her.

Sam applauded, "You did it Lia! You kept them safe."

Lia, with her chin high, shook her green braid proudly and added, "And I got them out of bed!"

Sophie sighed, "Yes, congratulations child. Don't do it again."

Gerald yawned and gave a salute.

Both of them were surprised to see Heidi, but not at all bothered by her appearance. Gerald saluted her as well, and Sophie spoke, in Grimmish, to her. Heidi was pumped.

"That makes me happy," smiled Sam. "She has another person to talk to."

"Sophie can speak several languages," said Gerald. "I've been to a few of the Percht villages with her as well, but my Grimmish is... *nicht so gut.*"

It would have been nice to take an outdoor table in the beautiful garden, or at least a window seat, but the majority was in favor of breaking their fast away from the oppressive morning sunlight. She took a table in the center of the room with Gerald, Luke and Lia, and of course Henry, who sat on Luke's shoulder. Fiona was slumped over the table next to them, having made a pillow out of a pile of napkins. Heidi and Sophie chatted over top of her.

"So," said Gerald, "You got him to the unicorns." He nodded to Luke. "Good. I'm sorry we couldn't get here sooner. We left Jasmine in the middle of the afternoon but..."

"They took *so* many bathroom breaks!" groaned Lia.

Gerald sighed. "Yes."

Luke laughed. "Survived a zombie witch thing, only to be taken out by an evil roast beef sandwich."

"Mm... Yeah. I don't know which I would have preferred. I'll never look at waystation sandwiches the same again. Thought I might need some of that unicorn water myself, but I'm not feeling quite so terrible this morning."

"Well there's still some left in the bucket at Fiona's if you'd like some." Sam offered.

"Not necessary, but thank you."

The waitress was noticeably trembling when she brought them a round of coffees and took their breakfast orders, paying special attention to the large black Percht, lest she provoke its monstrous wrath. She wrote down Henry's request for a tray of whatever nuts they had without sparing the talking squirrel a second glance. Heidi merely chuckled at this, and, through Sophie's translation, ordered pancakes.

"What's your next move?" Gerald asked. "Any ideas yet?"

"I'm not sure," Sam admitted. "Heidi has a travel tome, but it doesn't have any destinations from home in it. So we can't use that one. Which makes me think that probably most of the tomes we *might* be able to find would be the same. I mean, somebody would have to have been to our world to create a portrait of it, right?"

Henry nodded. "It would seem likely."

Luke scratched his beard, which was starting to get rather scruffy. "Hmm. If someone has to be in our world in order to create one of these pages, there must be some way to get there *without* a travel tome. Maybe we don't need to look for a person or a thing, but a place."

"Perhaps," said Henry, "but you'll need a person or a thing that can tell you where this place is, my boy."

Luke looked thoughtful, then curled the side of his mouth into a grin. "True enough. But that person or thing will be in a *place*, Henry."

Sam rolled her eyes. "Very helpful, smart asses."

"Hey now," said Luke. "That's the only part of me that's smart before breakfast."

"You had a bagel," she argued.

"Not enough. Let's talk again later."

When the food was ready, it was a different waitress who brought it. Another older woman, more hunched than the first, but a thousand times braver. Her green eyes sparkled with kindness. The first waitress was cowering behind the front desk, pretending to be busy. The second waitress asked as she served each one of them, whether or not they needed anything else, even Heidi, before waddling away.

Sam had a multi-grain bagel with egg and cheese. She watched with amusement as Luke tried to take a proper bite of his enormous breakfast bagel variation, three eggs, cheese, and two sausage rounds. He couldn't stretch his mouth around it. He resorted to nibbling the edges to wear it down first. She laughed when he mumbled a curse for spilling sausage grease on his suit. He looked at her, his head low and face red.

It was good to have him back, but the matter of returning home still remained. There would be hell to pay if she wasn't home by Christmas. Her family would be worried. Her grandmother in Europe would be expecting a call. If they took even longer, the things in her apartment would have to be hauled away somewhere, and probably there would be a fine or a fee.

She shook the thoughts away as she watched Luke desperately dabbing at the sausage grease with a napkin. She smiled. He was alive and well. The other stuff could wait another day, couldn't it?

After breakfast, Sam didn't wrack her brain or press the others for a solution to her problem. Instead, she stole Luke away to the beach, where they spent the rest of the morning kissing in the sand, hardly conscious of the judging quacks of the ducks around them. She made him tell her his secrets and she told him hers, though he was less inquisitive. He insisted he knew nothing of the travel tome beforehand, that he assumed his house was cursed, but not magical. She believed him. They laid on the beach until their hunger could no longer be satisfied by the lips of the other.

They had supper at Two Goats. There were no other eating establishments in the little village. The meal was sponsored by Melody, the wife of the red haired man Luke vanished with at the fountain. His description of her brought to mind the woman she saw breaking the penis off of a Poseidon statue near the Wooden Hearth Inn. Luke was certain it was the same woman, so they toasted their meal to Melody and the "dickless

Poseidon." The cowardly waitress shook her head, and muttered to the braver one, "Kids these days." Sam was happy not to be a drain on Sophie's coin purse for once.

Later, they borrowed blankets from Fiona and followed the path to the unicorns, but before they reached the clearing, Sam pulled Luke off the path into the woods to find a more private place to lay down the blankets. The unicorns would be awhile yet anyways, she told him with a mischievous grin. His eyes narrowed in suspicion.

They walked until the trees and shrubs shrouded them from view of the trail, and chose a bed of moss on which to place their blankets.

She thought to say, "It's no couch, but it will do," but she didn't have time to put her thoughts to voice. Luke's lips found hers, and then the rough bark of a pine tree was scratching against her back. She closed her eyes and let the scent of pine, of Luke, and of peppermint toothpaste wash over her. His lips and scruff tickled her neck. She didn't need to tell him her thoughts. He had already read her mind. Like magic, their coats disappeared from their bodies. She found them when she opened her eyes, carelessly strewn atop nearby bushes.

Chills fluttered through her as his lips teased lower. When he reached the bottom her neck, her shirt had to go. It sailed into a granite boulder and slid to the ground. Her skin bristled with goosebumps despite the warmth of the air.

His kisses resumed their journey downward while she struggled with the buttons on his shirt. Stupid buttons. She bit back the urge to just tear the thing off, his soft lips reminded her that they had time. Soon it was off and hanging over the top of a young spruce tree, hiding its eyes from what was to come next. More clothing littered the earth around them as their lips and fingers sought new territory to explore, until they fell naked into the scratchy wool blankets and forgot entirely about the strange world around them.

Later, they lay on their backs, sweaty and breathless, staring up at the pale sky through gaps between the leaves on the trees. Chickadees twittered and fluttered from branch to branch. Sam brushed an ant from her arm, and smiled as Luke exhaled happily. They were quiet, relatively, for a time, until Luke broke the silence.

"Sam."

She rolled over and slung her arm across his chest. He was looking in her direction, but beyond her, into the trees.

"Yes, Luke?" she asked, and kissed his chest.

He spoke calmly, but with a hint of concern. "There's a unicorn watching us."

Her eyes bulged. She turned her head to follow his gaze and immediately grabbed an edge of the blanket to fold over herself.

About twenty feet or so away, in the direction from which they had came, there was indeed a unicorn. Most of its body was concealed by the density of the forest, but its gleaming white head stood out like a portrait wreathed in green foliage. Unicorns weren't exactly well equipped for forest espionage. Its purple eyes casually blinking. It was looking right at them.

It had arrived silently, or perhaps, she shuddered, earlier, when they were making too much noise to hear the branches snap or the dry leaves rustle beneath its hooves. Now she wished it had been true that they only appeared before virgins. It was one thing to be watched by the birds and the bees, but another thing entirely to be watched by a unicorn.

A soothing voice entered her mind.

"*Don't mind me,*" it said.

The unicorn bowed its horn to them, and turned and trotted off, snapping twigs and rustling leaves, making a ridiculous amount of noise with every step.

Sam groaned.

"Better a unicorn, than a rat," Luke said.

She punched him in the arm.

Chapter Thirty-Two

Luke snapped a low hanging branch from a birch tree and stripped it of all its offshoots, effectively creating a switch, or a natural whip.

"So, they chase people with these?" he asked, brandishing the weapon for Sam to see.

They were back on the beaten forest path, blankets slung over their shoulders, heading towards the village. Although Sam had spoken earlier of the absolute necessity that he witness the gathering of unicorns at the brook, they did not attend it. Sam had lost her desire to take him, and he had no desire to argue about it. He had seen *one*, after all. That was enough. A horse with a horn. She appreciated his understanding. She did not, however, appreciate his "If you've seen one horny horse, you've seen them all," comment. She was also unimpressed when he couldn't find the condom after he had taken it off. He could have sworn he'd set it on that rock. Probably it was lost in the leaves and nobody would stumble across it, but it still sucked to litter. *Always leave nature as you found it*, as the saying went.

"Yes," said Sam of the birch switch. She was explaining the role of Perchten in Austrian tradition. "They chase people and they hit them. But I was quite young when I saw them. As a rule they're usually pretty friendly towards small children. My dad wasn't so lucky though." She laughed. "I remember mom laughing while one chased dad around a fountain, whipping him mercilessly. They don't *really* hurt anyone. They just make a show of it. Still, I was terrified."

"I can imagine," said Luke. "A parade of people dressed up like Heidi, growling and stomping around. Can you imagine if one of them turned out to be the real deal? Like, you go to unmask one and it's not a mask at all. Just an actual Percht, out enjoying the festivities."

"Luke!" Sam shouted. She grabbed his shoulder, stopping him in his tracks.

"What is it?" he asked, tightening his grip on the switch.

She spun him around and yanked him in for a kiss. Not at all what he was expecting, but he wasn't about to complain.

"You're brilliant," she cried. Her smile lit up her face.

"I am?"

"Well. Maybe. We'll have to see."

"What does that mean?"

She laughed. "It means we'll see how brilliant you are. I don't want our hopes to get too high just yet though. Come on. Throw that stick away."

Luke tossed the switch aside and allowed her to take the lead back to the village.

They met Sophie and the others at the mouth of the forest path. They were heading to see the unicorns. Lia was sitting on Heidi's shoulders, peeking out from behind her horns. Her heavily bedazzled arm jangled noisily when she waved. Henry appeared atop the little girl's head, his bushy tail raised in salute.

"Are the unicorns out yet?" Lia asked excitedly.

Luke opened his mouth, but Sophie spoke first.

"No point in asking them," the old woman said. "They wouldn't know."

Sam's cheeks started to flush. "What do you mean, Sophie? We just came from the trail."

"I don't remember getting so full of pine needles when last I was here. The trail's not so narrow as that. Look at you. It's all down your jacket, in your hair. Fiona, I'd wash those blankets before I used them again if I was you."

Fiona only laughed and shrugged. Luke was surprised to see her carrying a bottle of wine, but given her young age, he supposed it wasn't *that* surprising.

"Well, we *did* see a unicorn, actually," said Sam in a small voice. Her face was fully red now.

Luke stepped forward and hung an arm over Sam's shoulder. "Yes we did. Purple eyes. White fur. Pink horns. Lovely creatures. I'm glad I had the chance to see them."

Sophie laughed. "I bet you are. I'm happy you enjoyed your honeymoon. Lia wants to see the unicorns while we're here as well. Will you be joining us, or are you going to look for unicorns in Fiona's bed while she's away?"

"Eh, no. I think we're good for unicorns today," he said. "Don't want to oversaturate my eyes with too much beauty all at once, you know."

Sam elbowed him in the ribs. "He's right," she said, "but wait. Before you go, I want to ask Heidi something. I think I'll need some words though, if you don't mind. Sophie, or Henry. My *Grimmish* is so rusty."

Henry stepped up immediately, "It would be a pleasure to be of service, m'lady."

Lia giggled, and reached up to scratch him.

Sam actually did quite well in asking the Percht her question, which meant that Luke had almost no idea what was being said. The Percht spoke slowly for her benefit, but for him it was impossible to tell where one word ended and another began. It must be the same for someone listening to English if they didn't know how to speak it. He was forced to rely more on facial cues to at least get the tone. Sam grew more excited each time Heidi responded, and once she glanced at him with a broad smile on her face. When it was over, she yanked him in for another kiss.

"You *are* brilliant."

"Thanks, but uh, what's up? I feel a little left behind."

"Ah, well you won't be left behind tomorrow. We're going to Nefrew."

Luke raised his eyebrows. "To Heidi's village?"

"Yep."

"Okay. Sure. Whatever. But why? Ah, hold on. Give me a second. You said that *I'm* brilliant." He took a second. "You think there *are* real Heidi's in Europe on these Perchten Runs, eh?"

Sam smiled and nodded vigorously. "I thought there was a chance when you mentioned it, but now I'm sure of it. Heidi says that some people from her village head to this Sky Castle place once a year, and someone named Hymir takes them somewhere *far away,* and they're only gone for a week or two. She doesn't know the details, but she hopes to make the journey herself someday. Only older Perchten are allowed on these trips."

"Well, maybe they go down south," Luke reasoned. "They live in the cold mountains. Maybe they just take a trip somewhere warm."

Sam narrowed her eyes. "Well, let's hope it's Cancun, then. I think it's worth a shot, don't you?"

"I'll go anywhere with you, baby."

The palm of her hand swung and stopped just shy of his cheek. She wagged a finger at him threateningly.

"Sorry," he laughed. "What I meant to say was *Let's do it. Why not?*"

"That's better," said Sam.

"Does that mean you'll be leaving us?" Lia asked, her voice sad, her face sadder.

Luke saw the feeling reflected in the pout of Sam's lips. She would miss the little girl. "Oh Lia," she said. "I'm afraid it does."

Lia tapped Heidi's shoulder, and the Percht lowered to one knee, allowing her passenger to disembark safely. Lia threw her jingling arms around Sam's waist, and even Luke, who did not know the girl, felt sad to be leaving her behind.

"I don't want you to go, princess. You can stay with us. Sophie wouldn't mind. We have a big house in Summerfall. It's really pretty there. You'd love it."

Heidi, large and frightening as she appeared, put a clawed hand to her chest and sniffled.

"You know, Sam," Luke said, "Maybe we *should* join them at the unicorns."

Sam looked at him, the earlier embarrassment washed from her eyes by welling tears. She nodded. He wrapped his arms around them both and kissed Sam on the forehead.

Clouds crept in quickly, swallowing the remains of the setting sun and blanketing the clearing below in dark shadows. It wasn't raining, but a gentle mist planted cool kisses on Luke's cheeks and hands. Maybe the damp weather would keep the unicorns away. For Sam's sake, he hoped it might, though he was more amused than embarrassed by the earlier voyeurism.

Luke sat a few feet away from the others, listening to Henry chatter away on his shoulder. The squirrel was expressing his regrets, and explaining to him his part in the attack Luke suffered in the library.

He raised an eyebrow. "So when I asked you if I had released a demon into the world by freeing you, I was right."

"Well, in a roundabout way, perhaps," the squirrel chuckled nervously. "But not directly. I, myself, am not a demon."

"I know, Henry. I'm only teasing. I appreciate everything you've done for me and Sam. Really."

"Think nothing of it, my boy. Your shoulder is a fine one to perch upon. I've enjoyed our short time together."

"Too short, maybe. Hey, you could come with us."

Henry shook his head. "An enticing offer. But I dare say little Lia over there is going to miss her princess quite dearly when you two leave. I might just stay behind and help her through the grieving process. Perhaps I can even help her to control her magic."

Luke smiled. "That's very noble of you. She'll forget all about Sam with you around."

His smile upgraded to a grin when the unicorns made their appearance. Not because of the unicorns themselves, but because of Sam pulling his hat down even lower over her face. She stayed behind when the others went down to greet the not-so-mythical creatures. He slid over towards her and said, "You know, they probably won't even recognize us with our clothes on."

He sent a hand to his waist to block the expected strike. He caught her fist and gently handed it back to her. She leaned her head on his shoulder. "They're going to come with us tomorrow," she said. "Sophie, Gerald, and Lia. And Heidi. There is a page in Heidi's book that can take them home after we're gone from Nefrew."

"Well, that'll be nice, won't it?"

She nodded unconvincingly. "I suppose. But the goodbyes will be prolonged. Dragged out. I'm always terrible with good-byes. I'm glad to spend more time with them, sure, but the pending goodbye will be looming over me now until it happens. Every time I look at them, I'll be thinking about the goodbye to come. I almost want to steal away in the night, you know? But that would be shitty. They've been so good to me through all this. A complete stranger."

"Ah, I know. I feel the same about Henry. He saved me from a gruesome death more than once now."

"Yeah," Sam smiled. "And I mean, a talking squirrel is pretty awesome."

"Oh you two are going to make me cry!" whimpered Henry, startling them both.

"Henry? I thought you went down with the others."

"No, Luke, I've been right here on your shoulder. How quickly you forget the world around you when your attentions are on prettier things."

"Oh," Sam groaned. "So you heard when he—"

"I heard nothing at all of your reasons for not taking a closer look at the unicorns," the squirrel was quick to say.

"Your dishonesty is appreciated, Henry," said Sam.

"Think nothing of it, my dear."

It was after breakfast at Two Goats the next day when the companions bid farewell to Fiona. She promised them all room and board anytime should they ever return to the village, and she promised Henry she would be far more careful with her grandfather's spell book in the future. A final promise was made to Heidi, that she would educate her fellow villagers about Perchten, to improve their hospitality towards horned guests in the future. She left them each with a hug.

Luke and the others remained in the café, huddled around a table where Heidi's travel tome sat closed.

"Can it send us all at once?" Luke asked.

Sam relayed the question to Heidi, who shrugged and said something in her language.

"She's never tried it with a group before," Sam explained. "She's only used it once actually, to come here. To be safe, she's just going to take out the bookmark, and let us all go through one by one. She'll come through last."

Luke and the others nodded their understanding. Heidi spoke again, drawing laughter from Sam, Sophie, and Henry. Luke was happy to have someone to share the lack of understanding with in Gerald.

Henry translated, "It will be her people's turn to scream and run, she says, when people start popping up in front of the fountain."

Luke smiled. "Yes, well, if it's anything like last time, I'll be too busy vomiting to enjoy it. Maybe we should have saved breakfast for *after* we traveled."

"We're going to need these," said Sophie, who seemingly pulled from nowhere a thick brown wool coat and handed it to Gerald. She reached into her robes again and produced a matching coat of a smaller size, and passed it off to Lia. Then, with widening eyes, Luke watched her pull out a third coat, a gray one, for herself, as well as a bundle of colorful scarves and several pairs of gloves.

Sam laughed when she noticed his gaping. "It's bigger on the inside," she explained.

"I see..." Luke replied.

"Heidi doesn't look like she needs one," Sophie remarked, "but I'm sorry that I don't have any coats for the two of you. It's going to be cold in the mountains. I do have some extra warm gloves though. And scarves. Here you are. And, oh. Hats. I should have extra hats as well."

"Ah so there's that grandmotherly side of you," Sam teased. "Coming out at last. I bet you knitted these yourself, too."

"She did," said Lia. "Well, everything but the coats."

Sophie scowled. "That's enough out of you, ladies. I can take them back."

Luke added a gray scarf and brown toque to his stylish green suit, and stuffed his fingers into a pair of hot pink mittens. He laughed, and gave Sam a grin, and a thumbs up.

"You look great," she said.

"I know."

When they were all bundled up for the wintry weather to come, Sophie paid for their meal, and told the waitresses not to be alarmed when their group started disappearing. They said it was fine, so long as they weren't turned into chickens again.

"Alright then," said Luke. "I went first last time. So I guess I may as well go first again."

He opened the book.

CHAPTER THIRTY-THREE

High atop a snowy spruce, a golden eagle was perched, surveying his domain as the rabbit he ate for dinner digested in his stomach. He was mostly brown, really, save for a small patch of golden brown feathers on the back of his neck, but he wasn't about to sneeze at the prestigious title.

An enormous nest of furry black beasts with horns and sharp claws lay below him. They constructed square dwellings with pointy tops on them that were nice for perching. Fearsome as the creatures were, they posed no threat to the eagle. They could never catch him even if they wanted to. They couldn't fly.

A river of cold, sparkling water ran through their nest, and dropped off the mountain in a noisy rush. Sometimes he would find rabbits by the river, like he had today. During warmer times, the small pool beneath him provided an excellent source of songbirds for him to eat. They'd flutter about on the white rock in the center of it, and bathe in the pool when it wasn't frozen. The white rock was shaped into a remarkable likeness of the horned creatures who lived in the nest. The songbirds were merely a delicacy though, a tasty treat, not really worth the effort, but sometimes it's just nice to remind others who's king. Typically, he fed on rabbits and foxes. They were usually plentiful.

When fresh meat was scarce, however, he could always visit the nest of ice and stone, just a few wing beats further up the mountain. He didn't often do this, as the furry faced earth bound creature who resided there was moody, and had a much longer reach than the horned beasts below. He did, however, seem to have an endless supply of fish to eat.

Life was good in his frosty corner of the world. He lived there for many years. It held few surprises for him. So it was, that when a green earth bound creature appeared suddenly in front of the frozen pool, he couldn't help but release his bowels onto the branches beneath his perch. He cocked his head to train his eagle eye on the creature, and blinked in further surprise when another similar creature appeared beside the first one. It quickly fell beside the other, and the two of them regurgitated their last meals onto the stones.

A few of the natives were passing by, and dropped what they were carrying in shock. Some cries of alarm reached the eagle's ears, and more of the horned creatures came out of their dwellings to see what the fuss was about. Another creature appeared, and another, and soon six creatures in all had appeared in front of the frozen pool. One of them looked the same as the natives, black furred and horned.

No, thought the eagle. *There's seven!*

The smallest one, a pesky squirrel, was the only one that didn't immediately lose its lunch. It scampered up the white rock in the center of the pool, and looked directly up at the eagle. The eagle's eyes widened. He gripped his branch tighter. He didn't know what to expect.

The squirrel *waved* a paw at him. It was not at all afraid of him, and that made *him* afraid. After a moment, the squirrel returned to the other newcomers and didn't spare him another glance.

The golden eagle flapped its great wings and was off to tell his mate about what he had seen. She wouldn't believe him. She'd think him nutty.

Sam was helped to her feet by a Percht who wasn't Heidi. Black fur covered his body, but his gnarled, woody looking face was bright red, and his sunken eyes were a dark brown, almost black. His horns were pointier, sharper looking than Heidi's, and he had a pair of tusks. He looked very much like a demon, but his words were kind and his toothy smile was somehow not sinister. He was also quite careful not to scratch her with his deadly claws as he pulled her up by the arm pit.

While their initial arrival had sparked some shock amongst the residents of Nefrew, their reaction was rather tame, and their welcome was considerably more friendly than the one Heidi received from the people of Three Goats. Perhaps a dozen Perchten had shown up to greet them and see if they were alright. The vomiting was not as bad as Sam expected, but it must have looked pretty wild to anyone who witnessed it out of nowhere.

One of the Perchten turned out to be Heidi's grandmother, Agnes. They looked as related as a pair of Perchten possibly could, except where Heidi's hair was red, her grandmother's hung to her waist in wispy white strands. The pair exchanged hugs, and Heidi quickly explained her reason for returning earlier than expected.

Becoming braver with her language skills, Sam was eager to ask where they might find the castle. When she received her answer, and turned to follow the old Percht's pointing finger, all she could say was, "Oh."

It was right behind her.

"Oh wow," Luke added. "Fancy."

As castles go, it wasn't really very fancy. It was more of a fortress, with a long and high wall of stone with crenellations encircling an enormous crenelated pillar at its center. There were no towers on the walls, no flapping banners. There wasn't even a gate between the opening in the front wall. Everything was gray, with a tint of icy blue. The *fancy* part of the image, was that the entire thing rested atop a floating pillow of clouds.

"An air castle!" squealed Lia.

"How are we supposed to get up there?" Luke asked Heidi. "I don't suppose they do helicopter tours here?"

Heidi, of course, didn't understand him.

"Maybe there's a magic elevator," Sam suggested. "Or some kind of teleportation portal thing. Or— Ooo!"

She shivered as a chilly breeze whipped through the village, kicking snow up into little swirling tornadoes. She buttoned her coat, and took the scarf that hung loose over her shoulders and wrapped it around her face. Luke did the same with his scarf, but he had no proper coat to button, just his thin blazer. He waved dismissively with his pink gloved hand when he noticed her concern, though he was shivering violently.

"I believe air travel or magical means of transportation won't be necessary," chuckled Henry.

The breeze pushed the pillow out from underneath the castle, rolling the clouds out like the tide, but the castle stayed in place. It was merely built at a higher altitude on the mountain, just above the clouds. It looked as if someone had punched off the mountain top and plunked a castle there. A switchback path was the obvious way to reach it.

Sam frowned. "Well, that's not quite so exciting."

"But a lot simpler," Gerald reasoned.

Agnes warned them that the path had not been cleared since the last snowfall, and that travel up to Hymir's Castle would be treacherous for humans without claws on their feet, but still possible if they were careful. Luke's chattering teeth suggested that the treacherous path was the least of his worries, even before he urged them to begin their ascent sooner rather than later. Nobody argued, though Heidi's grandmother might have chatted for hours had Heidi not promised to visit her for tea and tell her all about the unicorns when she came back down.

They began to walk away from the village and toward the castle when a clap of thunder startled them.

"W-what luck," Luke grumbled. "For us to land here at the same time a storm is brewing..."

"That's no storm, Luke," Henry corrected him as a longer series of thunderclaps boomed around them. "That's probably Hymir."

"No way," said Sam. "What is he? Some kind of giant?" *Wait a minute.* There *was* a giant called Hymir in Norse mythology. "He *is* a giant, isn't he?"

"Indeed he is," said Henry.

"Really?" Luke asked. "Is he one of the oil giants?"

Sam sputtered a laugh. "Very funny, Luke. Oil giants. Hymir is some sort of king, I think. Well. I mean. He does have a castle."

"Well he could have paid for it all with oil money? Henry?"

The squirrel shook his head. "No. Hymir was never one of the oil giants. He's what you might call, *old money.* Last I heard he wasn't much of a king anymore either. Someone killed all of his men after some ridiculous contest, and giants are very slow breeders."

In the legends, that *someone* was Thor. Thor broke Hymir's unbreakable cup in a test of strength by smashing it on something that was harder than the cup itself. Hymir's head.

"I've never met him," Henry continued, "but I've heard he has a bit of a temper."

"Well t-that's comforting," said Luke as another bout of giant thunder rumbled across the mountain.

"That sounds so much like thunder," said Sam. "He must be a real nuisance to any aspiring meteorologists in the area."

She was pleased to see the corners of Luke's frozen lips perk up at that.

Lia was more excited for the giant than anyone. Likely she was the only one who didn't consider the possibility of being squished or eaten. She held Sam's hand as they walked, and told her more about the bedroom she could have in Summerfall if she would just come live them. Sam stopped herself from mentioning to the girl that technically she actually would be homeless at the end of the month.

The road was wide and cobbled up to the point where the mountain rose steeper in a hurry. There, Sam had to let go of Lia's hand. They would each need both of their arms for balance and to grip the side of the mountain when possible as they climbed the narrow switchback. Frequently, the group was forced to trudge through knee deep piles of snow where it had fallen from above in heavy clumps. At one point, they were forced to stop and wait rather than risk progressing blindly when a passing cloud bank rolled in. Where the snow was not as deep, it was icy. More than once, Sam found herself slipping and falling towards the dangerous edge, and her heart would leap to her throat, but each time Luke was there to pull her back with his hot pink mittens.

Heidi had the easiest time of it. Her clawed feet gripped the ice like snow chains. Sam was especially glad for Heidi's presence then, specifically for the travel tome she carried with her. If things didn't work out at the castle, she didn't want to chance the switchback again. Using the tome would be worth the vomiting to avoid teasing fate.

Maybe only an hour had gone by in reality, but it felt like an entire day was spent getting to the next landing. Frosty white clouds floated from her lips in quick bursts as her breathing grew heavier. Her feet were freezing from wading through snow drifts and her fingers were beginning to sting at the tips.

Finally, she stepped with wobbly legs onto the castle's plateau.

The view from the village had not done justice to the sheer enormity of the castle walls. She felt like a mouse, or a squirrel, as their feet crunched slowly toward the giant's castle. There was no path, just a wide open field of snow between them and the opening in the wall.

Thunder rolled and rumbled again. Much louder now, its echo seemed to come from every direction. The ground shook beneath them. The group exchanged concerned looks.

"I'm not feeling so brilliant now, Sam," said Luke. "Maybe this is a bad idea."

"If you've got a better one, I'd love to hear it," she said.

"We l-leave this m-mountain and forget about home. We find a nice w-warm place somewhere in this world, and I'll build us a house."

She smiled. That didn't sound too bad actually, but they had come too far to turn back now. The group pushed on and passed through the opening in the wall into a vast and mostly empty courtyard.

Mostly empty, aside from an enormous man fishing from a large hole cut in a frozen pond. At first glance the furry man could have been labeled as a Percht, but only the curly white forest of hair on his head belonged originally to him, that and the beard that flowed like a frozen waterfall from his cheeks to the top of his broad chest. The rest of him was wrapped in a patchwork of harvested furs that had once belonged to animals of various shades of browns and blacks and whites. From a football stadium away, it was probably a fair guess that the giant was at least as tall as a four story building.

The giant gave no indication that he noticed their approach. He was sitting on a giant wooden stool, with the castle keep towering behind him, utterly intent on his fishing. Occasionally, he would tap his feet. That was where the thunder was coming from.

Sam swallowed. They weren't yet within squishing distance. They could still turn back, though the giant could probably throw something pretty big pretty far if he wanted to.

Suddenly, the giant roared with triumphant laughter. His thunderous joy echoed over and over, and soon was accompanied by the rumble of snow breaking loose from the mountain and crashing down in a raging torrent. Hopefully not in the direction of any villages, though it was impossible to see anything over the high stone walls. The giant's fishing rod bent low, and he twisted his body to fight its pull. He had something, and it must have been something big because it yanked the giant off his stool. He nearly fell over, had he not planted his feet so hard that Sam stumbled forward from the resulting shock wave.

They continued their approach, but at a considerably slower, more cautious pace. Lia, however, wanted to run ahead and see what the giant was catching.

"Oh I think you'll see it easily enough, Lia," said Gerald, holding her back.

The giant was solid now, his body twisted, his feet planted like a mighty oak. He reeled and reeled on the ridiculously bent rod, until, with a snap of his wrists and back, he tore his catch up and out of the hole. Accompanying the catch was a geyser of water, exploding into the air as if the giant had been fishing in a whale's blow hole. The blast easily crested the castle keep and showered down around the laughing giant. In the center of the watery explosion, hooked to the fishing line was, appropriately, if not impossibly, a *whale*.

It slammed into the earth next to the giant, and this time Sam fell to her knees when the shock wave hit. Everyone but Heidi stumbled and fell in some way. Henry fell from Luke's shoulder, but Luke caught him. The wave even reached the peak of an adjacent mountain, causing it to throw off the entirety of its snowy blanket, exposing naked stone to the world.

Luke shook his head in astonishment. "W-what the hell is a whale d-doing on a mountain?"

Sam laughed. "What's a giant doing *existing?*"

"F-fair enough," he conceded.

Heidi pointed at the fishing hole and spoke excitedly.

"That must be the what?" said Sam, not understanding the whole thing. "The world...*something?*"

"I believe she called Hymir's fishing hole the *world pool*," explained Henry.

Sophie nodded. "It's probably *bigger on the inside,* as you might say, princess."

Heidi went on to say that the world pool was how the Perchten traveled for the winter pilgrimage.

"B-but it's filled with water," said Luke.

Sam shrugged. "And our travel tome was filled with paper, yet here we are."

Everyone froze when the giant turned towards them. His blue eyes, bigger than Sam's head, bulged wider when he saw them. An iron crown sat low over his forehead, but not low enough to hide the huge dent beneath it. It looked as if someone had shot a cannon ball into his face. Or a *cup*. There could be no doubt that the giant before them was the one from Norse legend.

Sam smiled weakly. "No turning back now, hey?"

"N-n-nope," said Luke. "Er, t-that's the cold chat-chattering m-my teeth. I'm n-not, you know, p-p-pissing myself. Not y-yet anyways."

Lia, too full of blissful, childish ignorance to be at all concerned, was the first to answer the giant fisherman. Her bedazzled arm waved melodically. "Hi, Mister Giant! I'm Lia, and these are my friends. That's a big fish!"

The giant blinked. The fact that Sam could see the small movement meant that they were well within squishing distance, but the giant *smiled*. Not one of those creepy *The Shining* murder smiles, nor one that alluded to thoughts of eating them. A happy smile. He had just caught a *big fish* after all. Any fishermen would be smiling at that. Perhaps he was a friendlier giant than the stories portrayed him.

"Greetings," boomed the giant. "You startled me. I was not expecting guests, especially not humans."

"Er, sorry," Sam offered, her voice small. Every bit of her felt small in the presence of the enormous being.

The giant's hearing was exceptional. He flapped a hand at them. "Nonsense. It's no matter. You are more than welcome here in my humble abode. It gets rather lonely here by times. Come closer so I can get a good look at you."

Before Gerald could grab her, Lia ran to grant the giant's request, jingling all the way.

Sophie sighed. "There really are limits to what one can do to keep a child from getting themselves killed. At a certain point you really have to just let them get on with it."

Sam laughed. "Well, he really doesn't seem *that* bad. Not at all what I was expecting."

Lia reached the giant and stood just a few feet away from his leather wrapped toes. She looked up at him with wonder, and said, "You're huge!" before turning back to the others, eyes wide. "He's *huge!*"

The giant chuckled. "I wish I could get my wife to say that. Just once."

"Are you Hymir?" Lia asked.

"That I am, little one. What brings a human to my castle? The only visitors I ever get these days are the Perchten, and suddenly come five of you, a Percht, and a... a squirrel."

The squirrel bowed theatrically from Luke's shoulder.

The giant's brow knit together. "Is that you, Ratatoskr?" His tone darkened. "I'll not be drawn into any foolish conflict by your deceitful tongue. I'm too old for such games."

Everyone looked to Henry, who shook his head. "You have the wrong squirrel, Hymir. Never met the fellow."

Hymir eyed him suspiciously, but nodded. "As you say. But you heard where I stand."

"His name is Henry, not Rata- rat... whatever." said Lia. She introduced herself, and everyone else in turn.

"A pleasure to meet you all."

Sam stepped forward, acutely aware of how quickly the giant could step on and crush her. "Uh, hi. We've come to see about using your world pool thing to send Luke and I home."

"Sam and Luke want to go where the Perchten go," Lia added, and then whispered loudly, "but you should tell them no. I don't want the princess to go. She can live with me. Luke too. Sophie won't mind."

Sophie scoffed, but smiled.

"A princess, you say?" the giant asked.

Sam groaned.

But the giant continued, "I'd be hard pressed to go against the wishes of a princess."

Maybe being a princess wasn't so bad. She could be a princess if it meant that she could go home and not be eaten by a giant. Why not?

She glanced into the hole from which the giant had pulled the whale. No normal ice fisherman would cut a hole that big. It was really more of a small pond. The water was alive, a gentle whirlpool swirled in its center. Would going home be as simple as jumping in? There was a long list of things she'd rather do then jump into a pond on a freezing cold mountain, and what about the whale laying limp and defeated nearby? Surely it hadn't come from dry land. There weren't any whales in Austria. The country was land locked. The Perchten would have a bit of a swim to get to any Perchten Runs. Oh, but of course, they had Perchten Runs in Germany too. Maybe it was a German whale, and the portal went to Germany. They would come out further from her grandmother's then, but they could manage.

"It's too late to send any Perchten through," said Hymir to Heidi. "You have to blend in with the locals over there. The otherworlders get stirred up over anything that doesn't look like them. But I don't see any reason why we couldn't ship a human through."

"T-thanks m-man," Luke chattered.

"Yeah," said Sam. "Thank you so much!"

Lia tucked her gloved hands into her arm pits and gave the giant a sour look.

The giant coughed "Ah but please, since you've come all this way, why don't you stay and visit for awhile? It's a beautiful day for a picnic in the courtyard."

"Is it?" said Sophie, frowning as another chilly breeze whipped through.

Luke was on the verge of shivering to death, but Sam didn't want to risk upsetting the giant. What if he decided not to let them through?

Hymir merely smiled at the obviously hesitant faces looking back at him, and clapped his hands with glee. "I'll make us some sandwiches. It'll only take a moment."

It might only take a moment for Luke to become an icicle.

With a grunt, Hymir hoisted the whale up over his head and onto his shoulders. Sam and her group stepped back in case he lost balance, but the giant was built like an ancient tree. The raising of the whale revealed an enormous black cauldron hidden behind it. It sat atop a pile of loose branches and logs. They'd have to wait while the giant got a fire going. How long was it going to take to cook a whale? It was going to take a lot longer than *a moment* to cook a whale.

Sam frowned. At least the fire would be warm.

Hymir steadied the whale on his shoulders with one arm, and gave the cauldron three sharp raps. In a blink, the wood beneath the cauldron caught fire, and water began to bubble within. Then the giant dropped the whale on top of the cauldron. Of course, being way bigger than the cauldron, it wouldn't fit inside. Not until the giant squished it down with a series of powerful shoves, deeper and deeper, until the entire whale disappeared inside the cauldron. Lia clapped her hands at the magic trick.

As Sam stood awestruck, the giant reached inside only seconds later and produced two sandwiches. Whale meat with vegetables stuffed between two slices of bread. He handed one to Lia first, and the next to Gerald.

"Uh, w-where did the b-bread come from?" Luke asked as the giant reached in again.

"I'm not sure if any of this is supposed to make any sense," said Sam, accepting her own sandwich. The bread was dry, not sopping wet from being in a cauldron of boiling water.

Heidi, who didn't eat meat of any kind despite her carnivorous appearance, shook her head at the offered whale sandwich. Hymir nodded and held up a finger, then dipped the sandwich back in the cauldron. When his hand came back up, the whale meat was gone, and only vegetables occupied the buns.

Henry accepted broken off pieces handed to him by Luke.

"I'd offer you some mead, but..." the giant shook a thought from his head. "That's not important."

Apparently, Thor had once came to Hymir's castle in search of Hymir's cauldron. The cauldron could produce unlimited amounts of mead, so naturally the alcohol fueled Norse pantheon would want such a thing, and after breaking Hymir's cup on Hymir's face, Thor acquired the cauldron. The cauldron Hymir was using now must be a replacement.

The sandwich was excellent, and the heat from the fire was enough to make Sam unbutton her coat. Luke's teeth stopped chattering. The giant was thrilled to have company, and he and the group chatted and laughed for a good while, until Luke had a thought.

"Hey now," he said, laughing. "This is amazing. I just realized something."

Hymir smiled, "And what is it you've realized, friend?"

"I just remembered a book of stories I read once. You're *Hymir. The* Hymir. The one from like, the Norse legends. There was one where Thor, this god of thunder guy, came up here and took your cauldron. Obviously, it wasn't entirely accurate, because there's your cauldron. Magic and all. Right there. So he never took it, or maybe he did, and you eventually got it back?"

From the second Luke mentioned Thor's name, the smile on Hymir's face began to deflate, and his bushy eyebrows slumped downward. By the time Luke finished talking, the giant was snarling. His knuckles cracked as his fists overtightened.

Henry leaned into Luke's ear and quietly said, "Probably should have warned you not to mention the T word in the giant's presence. Hymir's original cauldron is long gone. Your stories were correct."

"Oh," said Luke. "Shit." He shook his head, and started to chuckle.

Sam nudged him. "Luke!" There was nothing funny about the fuming giant.

He threw his arms akimbo in a helpless gesture and addressed Hymir. "Hey, look. I didn't mean to upset you. Really really. Please don't mind me. I'm just a dumbass. I'm not sure how," he chuckled again, shaking his head, "but I seem to have developed this *ridiculously* inconvenient habit of pissing off *really* big people. I shouldn't have-"

His next words were lost, drowned beneath a thunderous roar. "HOW DARE YOU!?"

"I d-didn't dare anything," Luke stammered. "J-just a d-d-dumbass." The blazing forest fire beneath the cauldron had thawed him. There was no blaming the return of his stutter on the cold.

"Yes!" shouted Henry. "The boy is as he says. *Just a dumbass.* Nothing to ruffle your feathers over. Surely a great and noble, and might I add, incredibly handsome, giant such as yourself is far too wise to see the boy's words as anything but harmless."

Hymir snorted, like a bull about to charge.

"Come now," the squirrel continued. "There isn't any need for hostility. We are in no way associated with the aforementioned troublemaker. And there is little chance of him returning here. Last I heard, thanks to the enabling powers of a cauldron that produces unlimited mead, all he does is sit around drinking himself foolish. A shadow of his former self."

Hymir exploded. His roar shook more snow from nearby peaks. Sam's heart skipped a beat as the giant heaved the enormous replacement cauldron across the courtyard. Nearly too fast to follow, the cauldron smashed into the perimeter wall and leveled a considerable chunk of it before disappearing into a pile of dusty rubble.

"So... many... years," Hymir growled.

"Excuse me?" said Sophie. Both her and Gerald moved in front of Lia.

The giant shook his head and looked away from them. His massive shoulders began to rise and fall.

"So many years..." he said again. His voice broke. *Was he crying?* "So many years of therapy. Undone with a single name. Am I so weak?"

The group exchanged looks. Each with the same wide eyed, confused expression.

When Hymir turned back to them, his eyes were indeed shiny with tears.

"I am sorry," he said, and he sat down on his stool with his head in his hands.

Henry was the first to find words in the face of the pitiful scene. "Now Hymir. Surely you are better off without that old cauldron."

"But that should be *me* sitting around drinking myself stupid!" Hymir sobbed.

Henry sighed. "But alcoholism is a tragedy. Look how healthy you are. Rosy cheeks. Full, thick head of hair. I suggest you keep with the fishing. Fishing is a noble pastime."

Hymir sniffed. "The whale would hardly agree."

"Er, well, yes that's probably true. A very fair point, actually. And one that I don't believe you'd be capable of making were you drunk."

"Exactly. I always drank when I fished. Always. Never had a care what the whales thought back then..."

"There's nothing wrong with a little empathy," said Sam. "It's a good thing. And what about the hangovers? Hangovers suck. How many day after's have you spent on your knees in front of the toilet since you lost the cauldron?"

"None," said the giant, scratching his beard.

"Do you miss them? The hangovers?"

"I would say not."

"And this wife of yours," said Sophie. "How many fights have you had since you quit drinking? Fewer, I'd imagine?"

Hymir nodded.

"Happy wife, happy life, right?" added Gerald.

Hymir nodded again, and smiled a little.

"And what about erections?" asked Luke. "Any trouble keeping it up?"

Sam shot him a horrified look.

He shrugged. "What? Just trying to add to the positives here."

Hymir laughed heartily. His laughter rolled like thunder, sending another wave of snow crashing down the mountains. "Solid as an oak, my friend."

"Okay," said Sam, shaking her head. "This is not going anywhere good."

"Oh but it is!" said Hymir. His mouth stretched into a broad smile. "I feel less inclined to kill you all already. You lot should really consider becoming traveling therapists. Or perhaps you already are."

Sam shook her head. "No. We're not. But we'll take it, happily, if it means not being killed."

"I second that," said Luke.

Not wanting to risk experiencing another one of the giant's mood swings, Sam quickly continued, "So how about that trip to *wherever the Perchten go* for our commission?"

The giant started to nod, but then smacked his forehead. "I would gladly grant your request, young princess, but I'm afraid that this old memory of mine has betrayed me. That ship has sailed, actually. The portal to Midgard is open only for a short period. You'll have to come back in a year's time."

"A year!" Sam cried.

Lia's face lit up. Her jewelry jingled. "A year! That's so great! Thank you Mr. Giant, sir. We can do so much in a year, princess! You'll love it so much in Summerfall, you won't want to leave!"

"We can't stay here a year," said Luke, placing a hand on the girl's shoulder. "We have things to take care of in our world."

If looks could kill, Lia would be a murderer, and Luke would be dead. "Luke's right," said Sam. "But! But maybe, maybe we could come back." She looked at Luke. "Once we settle things, we can visit?"

Luke's experience had been far less pleasant than hers in the strange world. She wouldn't blame him if the conflicted look on his face led to a "No way," but a thoughtful expression replaced it, and he nodded. "Well, yes. Probably. I mean, we can always come back with the book. We just... might not be able to get back again without Hymir here. Although, now that I think about it, when I cleaned out that room where you found the book, there were plenty of bird feathers strewn about. Heidi's magical bookmark is a feather. I just assumed, naturally, that all of the feathers in the room were from birds that had got in when there were still holes in the roof. But maybe one of them was meant to be in that book."

"Maybe," said Sam. "But they're gone now. You gutted the whole room. I saw it."

Luke smiled. "Yeah, but the waste is all still in a pile beside the barn. It'll be a pain in the ass, but I can dig through it. You know, for the sake of a magical feather. It's worth a try."

"It's absolutely worth a try. And I'll help. I won't let you dumpster dive alone, Luke."

"That's so sweet of you, Sam."

Sophie cleared her throat. "That's all well and good, princess, and very romantic, but there's still the matter of the portal not going where you want it to take you." She nodded towards the pile of destroyed wall that concealed the cauldron. "Clearly it's pointed somewhere in an ocean right now. I hope you're good swimmers."

"Can't you tell it where to go?" Sam asked Hymir.

The giant shook his head. "I cannot. I'm no sorcerer. The pool has changed on its own for as long as I can remember. Sometimes it catches me by surprise. One time when I cast my line, I reeled in a camel. The creature was none too pleased. I was forever scrubbing the spit from my beard."

"Ah," said Henry. "We just happen to have two magic users among our party. Perhaps we could shift the portal, if you'll allow it."

"Of course," said the giant. "But how?"

Sam frowned. "Yes, Henry. How?"

The squirrel chuckled. "You saved Luke and restored humanity to an entire village of chickens. What makes you think you couldn't open a door?"

Sam's frown deepened. "It's not just... opening a door. I don't have any idea how to do that. Maybe Fiona would lend us her spell book?"

"There's no need for a spell book, my dear. Magic is more about feelings than words."

"Right. So I just have to *believe*, is that it? Simple as that?"

"Essentially, yes. You have it."

Sam laughed. She walked over to the edge of the pool. The water was still swirling in a clockwise circle. She tossed a smirk towards Henry, and waved her hands dramatically over the water. *I think I can. I think I can.* Of course, nothing happened.

"Do you think it worked?" Her voice dripped sarcasm.

"You didn't even *try*," Henry accused.

"I did. I waved my hands and I believed."

Henry sighed, and swapped Luke's shoulder for hers. "You waved your hands, yes, but you certainly didn't believe. You have to make the portal feel your desire to change its trajectory. Command it like you commanded Luke to stay alive back at the library."

Sophie shrugged. Gerald nodded. Heidi offered an encouraging fist pump. Lia wouldn't even look at her.

Luke took her hand. "Send us home, Sam."

She took a deep breath. It was ridiculous. Completely ridiculous, but Luke squeezed her hand tighter, and his house entered her mind's eye. She felt the crunch of his gravel driveway beneath her feet. The book that started all this was sitting in his cozy chair next to the fireplace. Then she was at the bus stop at the bottom of her street. Sitting in her apartment. Her parent's living room, whose walls were decorated with years of her paintings.

"There's no place like home," she said, and Luke laughed.

"There's no place like home," she said again. She focused her thoughts on her parents house. The Christmas tree twinkling in the corner. Her mother's smile as she rolled back the wrapping paper and freed her squirrel painting, which was now gray and looked more like Henry than the red squirrel at the park who inspired it. "Open Sesame?" A rat scurried away from Luke's couch, making off with her favorite underwear. She groaned.

The swirling stopped abruptly. Seconds passed, and the water began to swirl in the opposite direction. Rapidly. Water splashed up over the edge of the ice, soaking Sam's pant leg, but the water was surprisingly warm, not cold.

"It's uh, it's doing something," said Luke.

"I see that," she said.

And then it stopped again, and seconds later renewed its original clockwise current.

Sam and Luke looked to Hymir.

"I believe you've done it, young princess. This is how the world pool acts when it changes course."

"Great," said Sam. "So the pool will take us to where the Perchten go now? Midgard?"

The giant turned up his palms. "I wouldn't know. It responded to you."

"Er, okay. Is there any way of knowing where it's gonna go?"

The giant shrugged. "You'll have to jump in and find out. I only know that at a certain time every year, the portal goes to Midgard. I've never gone through. I only fish."

"Maybe we can just stick our heads in?" Luke suggested.

"You could try it," said Hymir. "But most who do get pulled through, and landing head first is not recommended."

Luke looked at Sam. "So I guess we should just jump in."

"Really?" she said. "That's crazy. What if we land right in the middle of your living room? You've been gone for days. The rats are probably having a party."

He grinned. "They'll scatter."

Lia ran and tugged on Sam's coat. "Please don't go, princess."

Sam wrapped her arms around her, and squeezed. "I have to, Lia. But you heard Luke. We'll come back. Summerfall, right?"

Lia sniffed, but nodded.

"Summerfall," Sam said again. "We'll find you there."

Lia jumped when Henry landed on her jacket and scurried onto her shoulder.

"And I'll do my best to fill the hole she leaves behind, my dear," said the squirrel.

Lia's face lit up. "You— you're going to stay with *me?*"

"If you'll have me, yes."

Lia nodded enthusiastically.

Sophie sighed. "Just don't let me catch him scratching up my carpets."

Henry scowled at her.

"How will we find you?" Sam asked.

"If you can find your way to Summerfall, you can ask anyone," said Gerald. "Everybody knows Sophie."

Sam smiled. "I believe it."

"We'll look forward to your visit," said Gerald.

Heidi stepped forward and wrapped Sam in a literal bear hug, lifting her off the ground and scratching her back affectionately with her claws. "Auf wiedersehen, Sam," was her farewell.

"Auf wiedersehen, Heidi."

She hugged Luke as well, and Luke butchered an attempt at repeating the German goodbye.

Henry bowed to them both. "I'm not too fond of goodbyes myself. So I will say instead, see you again, my friends. Now begone with you, before I tear up." He turned away.

"This is all very touching," interrupted the giant, a tear froze on his cheek. "Oh! Before you go, you'll want these. The Perchten always request them for the journey."

Hymir handed her and Luke each an old fashioned wick lantern and a packet of matches.

"What are these for?" Luke asked.

Hymir shrugged. "I guess it's dark on the other side?"

"That's comforting," said Sam.

"Well, if you're going, go," said Sophie, pulling her hood tighter around her face. "We'll catch colds hanging around here all day."

Sam laughed and startled the old woman with a hug. "Thank you for everything, Sophie. I'll find a way to pay you back. I promise."

Sophie protested, but squeezed her tight.

"Okay," said Sam, looking at Luke. "You really wanna do this? Jump into a swirling pool of water on a chance that I've somehow coaxed it to magically send us home?"

"Sure," he said. "Why not? I can't swim, so if it doesn't work I'll just drown and be none the wiser."

"That is an *awful* way to look at it, Luke."

He grinned, and his free hand found hers. "I'm sure it will be fine, Sam."

"What if we don't end up home? What if we end up somewhere else?"

"Anywhere with you is great, bay-"

She held up a finger.

He coughed. "Anywhere is great. Yep."

She squeezed his hand. He nodded, and she nodded back. "Let's do this," she said.

"Together, *baby*."

She wanted to slap him, but instead she took as deep a breath as she had ever taken, and held it.

They jumped at the same time, still holding hands, still clutching their lanterns, and plunged into the swirling world pool.

Chapter Thirty-Four

The ice fishing hole was nothing like it should have been. A warm and tingly rush of magic washed over her, and her clothes and hair remained dry. The water wasn't cold. It wasn't even wet. When she finally dared to draw breath, only cool air entered her lungs.

They were in a cave of sorts, the area around them illuminated by a bright golden aura. There was no water at all, at least none in liquid form. Her feet slid beneath her, forcing her to struggle for a foothold on pale blue ice. If she reached up, she could touch a solid ice ceiling. More ice rose to her left and to her right, walling them into a slippery alcove.

"If this is my house," said Luke, "I think it's safe to say the pipes are frozen." His words echoed off the cavern walls.

Sam laughed. "It actually worked! We went *somewhere*. And we're not underwater."

Luke hummed. "Well it kinda looks like we are. A little bit. If the ocean were frozen, and had tunnels carved through it."

She shook her head. "That would be ridiculous."

"What about the last few days hasn't been ridiculous?"

She smiled. "True. But look."

Beyond the alcove, the ceiling was higher. The walls out there were mostly ice as well, but patches of rough stone were visible here and there along the icy ceiling.

"We're in a cavern," she said. "An ice cavern, apparently."

And then it was all gone. Swallowed by darkness as the magic that brought them there blinked out.

Sam shivered, but not as violently as the poorly dressed Luke. The magic had kept the worst of the cold away as well.

"This explains the lanterns," he said.

His hand fell away from hers.

"Luke??"

He didn't respond.

"Luke?" she called again, feeling the empty air around her. Did he slip? Did the portal take him back?

"I'm fine, Sam," he said, as a match, and then his lantern, sparked to life.

It produced a dull amber light that barely illuminated a few feet around them, but it did well at lighting up his grin. He traded his lantern for hers and lit that as well. He raised his lantern, and cursed when he bumped it on the ceiling.

"No hole here to fall through. So I guess we didn't just drop beneath Hymir's castle."

Sam took a step, and promptly slipped, fell, landed on her ass and slid out of the alcove. Luke moved quickly to help her up and suffered the same fate. Miraculously, they both managed to hold onto their lanterns.

Finding traction to stand was much easier than expected. They had slid from the ice onto bare stone. Sweet, abrasive stone. Sam nearly stood *too* fast, stopping just shy of smacking her head on a metal railing. Luke spat curses. He was not so lucky.

The alcove they were in turned out to be the mouth of an ice formation. It looked like the head of some enormous blue-white serpent had gotten itself wedged and frozen in the middle of the cavern. It rose from the floor to the ceiling, and had a huge mouth, bristling with sharp icicles, like teeth. Hymir's portal had dropped them right into that mouth. Good thing it was just an ice formation.

To the side of that mouth was a cluster of icy stalagmites, stabbing upwards, mushroomed at the tips. They looked a little bit like...

"Dicks," said Luke, stifling a laugh.

Sam shook her head, smiling, and sighed. "Yes. That's one way of looking at them. Mushrooms might be a more mature description."

The ice monster was fenced in by waist high metal railings, as if it were some sort of display. It was certainly worth displaying.

Sam walked around the cavern, her lantern held aloft. They were in a tunnel, it seemed, and they could go either up and away from the ice formation, or down and around it. The immediate path upwards appeared to be nothing but white ice. It was impossible to tell if the ice ended anywhere close. They'd never get traction. Not without Percht claws. The thought of being piggybacked through the caves by Heidi was amusing, but since Heidi wasn't with them, hopefully it wasn't necessary. As she surveyed the upper direction, she bumped her shin on a low wall of wooden planks. It stretched along the width of the cavern, as if to corral travelers to go back down along the left or right of the ice formation. Down it was.

"Left or right?" she asked.

Luke hummed thoughtfully as he wandered around the right side of the snake head, past the dicks, while she started around the left. He called to her just as she rounded the formation. "Hey! There are steps over here. And more railings. There's like a walkway or something built above the ice."

"I know. I can see you."

"Oh. Hi!"

Two catwalks ran parallel along the sides of the tunnel, each heading downward.

"It looks like we're at the top of a loop trail," he added.

Sam agreed. "Maybe it's a tourist thing."

Luke backtracked and followed her down the left side. The lanterns weren't the brightest things, but the flickering light was amplified slightly by reflecting off of all the glittering ice. No doubt they would have slid right to the bottom if not for the catwalk. The catwalk made their descent as breezy as the cool wind that gusted up occasionally from below. The moans that accompanied the wind might have been creepy, had they not held promise. It meant there was an exit. Somewhere.

They walked in awed silence, taking in the hauntingly beautiful surroundings. It was like a wave had rushed through the tunnel, splashing up the walls on either side, and here and there straight up the middle, and just froze instantly. All of it, at once, creating beautiful pale blue shapes. Some sharp, some smooth. Sometimes the catwalk would end and the path continued on firm stone through narrow corridors of ice until the tunnel widened again, and another catwalk took them further down.

Before they knew it, a rectangular beam of light greeted them. A wooden wall was constructed to fit tight to the mouth of the cavern, with a doorway framed in its center. The door was either gone, or propped open outside.

The cavern breathed deeper with every step as they neared the doorway, causing their lanterns to flicker violently, until a sudden gust snuffed them out completely. There was no point in relighting them.

"The moment of truth," said Luke.

Through the doorway, the mouth of the cavern yawned open in a huge arch, and they found themselves standing in a rounded dent in the side of a mountain.

Just beyond the dent was the beginning of a partially roofed trail with a wooden railing that snaked down the mountain. Another switchback, though far safer looking than the one outside Nefrew. It was shorter in height, but wider so it wasn't as steep. After a handful of switches, the path leveled off and stretched over to a forested peak where it disappeared into the trees. Beyond, was a sea of mountains and fields and clear blue sky.

"This is definitely not Nova Scotia," Luke said.

"Nope," said Sam, but she was grinning. She'd seen images of this view on the Internet and in travel guides, though she'd never been there in person. "Hymir's castle..." She shook her head and laughed.

Luke looked at her like she was crazy.

She smiled. "We're not in Nova Scotia. A Percht would have a hard time blending in in Canada, don't you think? But we *are* in our world."

"Great. But where?"

"Austria! It makes so much sense now."

"Does it?"

"It *does!* This cave. This is the *Eisriesenwelt*. Any idea what that means in English, Luke?"

"Um. *Nein?* Ice something? Ice caves?"

"Good effort. World of *Ice Giants.*"

"Ah. Well that does make some sense then."

"Doesn't it though? Even better, there is an ice formation in there called Hymir's Castle. I bet it's the one we landed in."

Luke nodded. "Probably, yeah. Looked more like a snake's head to me, though."

Sam continued, "And once we get to the other side of that forest ridge, I'm sure we'll be able to see a castle up on one of the hills down below, overlooking the town of Werfen."

"Great. Well, that's a start. But how are we going to get back to Canada? I don't have any money, or any ID. No passport."

Sam wiggled her tote bag. "I happen to have all of that."

"Of course you do," he laughed. "Well, at least I won't have to give hand jobs at the bus stops to get us across Europe."

"You just keep your hands in your pockets, Luke. I'll be your sugar mama. I'll take care of the bus stuff."

When he raised his eyebrows, she quickly added, "With my *credit card*, dummy. We can go visit my grandmother, and stay there until someone can send you your passport."

"Um, well, that might be a long wait, since I don't have one."

Her eyes widened. "What? Really? Have you ever been out of the country?"

"Nope. Unless you want to count our recent trip to Atlantis. That's gotta count for something."

Sam smiled. "I'd say so, but you've been missing out! It's a big world out there, Luke. Two of them, apparently. Come on, *baby*." She smacked his butt. "Before we freeze up here. Let's go get a coffee. We'll figure the rest out from there."

EPILOGUE

Perhaps she had been too rash, too impatient. What she sought with demand and violence had been given freely to another.

And simply tossed onto a rock.

Foolish mortals.

Entwined in the aftermath of procreation, they didn't have a clue. Casmolochasba Pantazis was weak, but not so weak that she couldn't will the prize into her possession from a distance, completely undetected.

Their acknowledgment of her victory was not necessary. She left them in their clearing, and found a quiet place of her own to finish the deed.

In a similar clearing amongst the tall pines and thick firs, she let slip her robe slip from her shoulders. A gentle breeze kissed her bare skin as she released the seed from its convenient rubber vessel and onto her fingers. It was still warm.

She closed her eyes and thought nothing of planting the seed in such a way, standing naked in the middle of a forest with her back against a tree, until she discovered a witness, *several* witnesses, when she opened her eyes again.

Her face flushed. She scowled and snatched up her robe to cover herself. As she did so, two more unicorns arrived at the edge of the clearing to join the other three, poorly concealed behind some low shrubbery. Their jaws hung open, their purple eyes wide. Judging.

How very odd, came a thought, unbidden into her mind.

Indeed, came another.

"Perverts," Casmolochasba accused.

Thanks for reading! I hope you enjoyed the first installment in the Ashes and Acorns trilogy. If you are interested in subscribing to my newsletter to hear about upcoming releases, please visit:

subscribepage.io/A4NRRy